Chapter 1

WHILE THEY WEREN'T IDEAL, THE TOWERING BLUFFS lining the Missouri River an hour outside St. Louis were the best climb Ben Thomas could get today. For the last three weeks, he'd been craving the escape of the mountains like never before. His successful ascent of Everest this year had taken its toll, so much so that Ben was surprised to feel the mountains' call again so soon. But in light of what had happened, he yearned for their rigorous challenge and solitude.

If he were able to get away, he'd head to the nearest Class 4 mountain that was climbable in mid-December. Not only was climbing his biggest passion, but it was the only activity that would successfully quiet his thoughts, the only time he could shut out the world. And right now, he needed to do both.

He'd lost his oldest friend. And in losing him, Mia Chambers, the only woman Ben had ever loved, had become available.

To keep from going stir-crazy, he craved more of a challenge than the hundred-foot-tall section of bluffs along the Missouri River offered him. But he had obligations to his company, the small architecture firm he'd started six years ago, and to Mia and her son—his godson—Ollie. Maybe being there for them had become small-scale torture the last several weeks, riddled with guilt as he was, but he wasn't going to let them down now.

Ben was scaling the most technical route on this strip of the craggy bluffs, and had only been semisuccessful in getting the image out of his head of Mia crumbling in front of him when he'd told her the news of Brad's death. He was nearing the top and had reached a sharp overhang. He paused to test a tucked-away grip that had presented itself. His lats and quads were burning from exertion, and the knuckles on his right hand had been scraped raw from having to refasten a cam deep into a crevice, though he wouldn't feel it until later.

Down below, Taye, the thirteen-year-old who'd been his Little Brother for nearly two and a half years, was hanging around the base of the bluff, tossing tennis balls into the air for Cassie, a senior golden retriever who belonged to Taye's aunt. Taye was hollering up encouragement more enthusiastically the higher Ben climbed. Taye had seen Ben climb bluffs before, but he hadn't grown tired of it. Especially when Ben had to maneuver up rock overhangs like he was doing now that he was close to the top.

Last month, Ben had convinced Taye's mom to allow him to give Taye climbing lessons. Taye was the oldest of four kids, and his mom worked two jobs to make ends meet. Taye had a bigger-than-average set of responsibilities at home, and on top of that, his neighborhood wasn't the easiest place to grow up. Taye had agreed to attend a magnet school for students gifted in math, and that hadn't earned him any popularity with his neighborhood friends either. "If he learns he can climb, he'll learn he can overcome," Ben had insisted, swearing to keep the boy safe.

Taye was a natural athlete and, as Ben had suspected,

had taken to climbing the way birds took to flying. This afternoon's lesson had been Taye's second time out of the climbing gyms and on a bluff. And even though Taye's route up was one Ben had scaled dozens of times, he'd stopped Taye a good twenty feet lower than the spry kid probably could've scaled. When Taye had threatened not to rappel down unless Ben, who would climb next, agreed to scale the most challenging path up, Ben had easily agreed. He welcomed the distraction, welcomed the ability to exhaust his muscles in hope that would help quiet his unsettled thoughts.

But he shouldn't expect to feel any differently. Tumultuous as his and Brad's relationship had become, there was still a giant hole in Ben's heart from the loss of his oldest friend. On top of that, he needed to be there to support Mia as she navigated the impossible waters of losing the husband with whom she'd been on the brink of divorce.

Eight years ago, Ben had fallen wildly in love with Mia, and a few months afterward, in a cruel twist of fate, she'd married Brad. It wasn't something she could be blamed for; at the time, she and Ben hadn't even been introduced.

He'd fallen in love with her words, with her bravery, with her depth of character over the course of a five-minute speech she'd given, a speech he hadn't been supposed to hear. And since then, she'd proven those qualities tenfold.

That first afternoon, she'd revealed things that had resonated deeper with Ben than anything ever had, creating a one-sided kinship he'd never felt with anyone else. Some of the details she'd shared about her childhood

mirrored his. She'd grown up without one of her parents, and the other had abandoned her for a different life. While his self-absorbed father had been in Ben's life through adulthood, his mother had left when he was hardly more than a toddler. Abandonment, with its pain and loss, was a familiar glove.

Ben wasn't good with words, and he didn't let people in easily. But Mia had snuck into his heart during the course of that speech. He'd never told her. All these years later, she didn't even know he'd heard it. It wasn't his class, or his college even. He'd stopped by to see Brad. Later, when he'd asked Brad to introduce them, things had gotten complicated. Really complicated.

Over the years, it had morphed into one giant secret. As much as he'd like to tell Mia the whole story, Ben didn't know how to do it without revealing how much her words had meant to him. And he couldn't do that without causing her to question a lot of things about her life with Brad.

So it was a secret he kept to himself.

The only time he could successfully leave it behind was when he climbed—most of the time, that was.

He'd been introduced to the sport when he was twelve by his father, who'd been a hobbyist climber for years. That first time Ben climbed real rock, out in Moab, he knew he'd never stop climbing. Even if doing so meant he had something in common with the father he resented more than anyone in his life. He'd been sixty feet up a near-vertical stretch of red rock, and his muscles were on fire. He was harnessed in and desperately wanting to quit. He was weighed down by his gear and utterly spent. He couldn't scale another foot.

But he hung onto the rock face and caught his breath, trying to rub away the sweat that was stinging his eyes.

All he'd had to do was unhook and start his descent. Even if he was afraid the rope wouldn't hold him, he knew it would. He'd just watched his father rappel down. And Ben had scaled much higher than expected on a first try. He had nothing to prove.

But a gentle wind picked up, cooling him and breathing life back into his arms, hands, and shoulders. He looked around and realized he was doing something that would be impossible without ropes and carabiners and cams. He studied the stark and brilliant southern Utah desert and fell in love with the form of the sheer rock face rising from the earth as much as he fell in love with the sport itself.

He made it up another fifteen feet before his muscles absolutely wouldn't allow him to go higher, and from that afternoon on, climbing was in his blood. He climbed on vacations with his father several times a year and hung out at the climbing gym every chance he got, even got a job there when he turned sixteen.

He stuck to technical climbs and Class 3 mountains till his father put the bug in his head that they try high-altitude climbing. It was a different beast entirely, but they did it together a few times. Those were among the few good memories Ben had of his father. When Ben was twenty-one and his father was sixty-six, they attempted Everest with a top-rated guide. His father wanted to set some kind of father-son ascent record, considering the difference in their ages, but their climb was cut short by a series of storms, and they never made it past Camp 2.

Then, when he was twenty-two and Brad and Mia eloped, Ben had thrown himself into climbing like never before. It helped that he got his best ideas for work when he was climbing. Nature's architecture had been inspiring his designs since his earliest climbs, and his small architectural firm was thriving. He worked and climbed and resigned himself to being introduced to Mia as Brad's lifelong best friend. Later, a bit ironically, he even became Ollie's godparent.

It was hard for Ben to believe he'd made it through eight years of walking a tightrope of friendship with his best friend. It was also hard to believe that somehow, in spite of all the promises he'd made to himself, he'd not done a better job of falling out of love with Mia. Instead, without admitting it to anyone, he'd only managed to tumble in deeper.

Three months ago, he'd been bowled over when Mia left Brad and they were suddenly on the brink of divorce. Ben had done his best to keep his head down and stay busy. Not to think he might actually have a chance someday. Then three weeks ago, he'd gotten a call he'd never in his life expected. Brad was dead. An aneurysm had ended his life in seconds, stunning everyone who knew him.

Ben reached the top of the bluff after an exhausting near-vertical climb underneath an eight-foot overhang. The overhang had minimal grips and crevices at its top lip, but he was able to secure his cams at the crest of it. Afterward, he locked in his rope, grabbed on, and released his foot grips. He allowed his arms to extend straight, and his body hung free in the air a hundred feet above the trail.

"That's *so* dope, Spidey," Taye yelled up. "*Sweet!* That's me next time. If you hadn't stopped me, I could've done it today." Next to him, Cassie barked, enlivened by Taye's excitement, the sharp sound piercing the quiet afternoon.

Ben relished the relief that flooded into the spent muscles in his forearms and calves. Finally, he swung a leg up to shoulder level and hauled himself over the ridge. He collapsed on the dried grass and leaves on top of the bluff, his spare gear jamming into his back. A forest of bare trees rose above him, framed by the pale-blue winter sky.

"That was so dope." Taye's voice floated up from down below. "Only the reception here sucks, so I can't post it."

Ben swiped an arm over his face, brushing away fresh beads of sweat as his breathing slowed. "Dope," he mouthed, thinking how fast Taye was tumbling into the precarious teen world. He rolled over and rose, leaning over just enough to spot Taye's tennis ball rocketing high into the air and topping out not far below the crest of the bluff. Down below, Cassie was strategically placing herself to catch it, which she did, her jaws clamping around it securely, proving an adeptness she'd carried into her senior years.

Taye whooped at her success and pumped his fist.

"Nice one!" Ben called down, then swung his foot over the edge and began his descent. "See if you can throw one up here, and I'll toss it to her before I come down."

Eight years ago, if Ben had been told his window of opportunity to be with Mia would be handed to him alongside the crushing blow of losing his oldest friend,

he'd likely have packed his things and moved to Europe. He'd have built his architecture firm in a city where he'd be revamping homes made of stone and stucco instead of red brick. But he'd stayed here and become a godparent to Ollie and a Big Brother to Taye, and he'd steered clear of relationships and, for the most part, women in general. Waiting. Always waiting. Until three weeks ago, at least. Since then, it felt as if things were about to slip into hyperdrive.

Chapter 2

THE HIGH GROVE ANIMAL SHELTER'S SECOND HOLIDAY event this December was in full swing by the time Mia Chambers arrived for her shift. After circling the crowded streets, she found a parking spot on a side street two blocks away.

Following a string of warm late-fall days, gray clouds covered the sky and the temperature was dropping. Mia drew her coat closed but didn't bother with her gloves for the short walk.

She'd been volunteering at the shelter since she was a teenager and couldn't recall ever before having the sort of reservation about walking in that she did today. It was unfounded, she knew. The shelter's small staff and other longtime volunteers had become like her extended family over the years, and for the last three trying weeks, they'd more than had her back. They'd been sending cards, dropping off delicious meals for her and her son, Ollie, and offering to run errands.

And even though she was walking into a traditionally judgment-free zone, Mia couldn't shake the feeling that her new status would define her forever. She was a thirty-year-old widow and mother of one. And she wasn't even a typical grieving widow because she was a widow who'd been in the process of divorcing her husband when he died.

This brought to mind images of wicked witches and

poisoned apples and flying monkeys. Maybe flying monkeys were a touch over the top, but Mia couldn't suppress a wave of insecurity over how her shelter friends might now see her.

In late August, shortly after Ollie started first grade, Mia made a life-changing decision. The bad in her marriage had outweighed the good by too much for too long. She'd left Brad and brought Ollie with her. She'd tucked tail and moved back into her late-grandparents' empty house, knowing she had neither the income nor the savings to warrant a second rent or mortgage right now. The final straw had been one that had ended stronger marriages than hers. Brad had owned up to being unfaithful in a moment of weakness.

Their marriage had been anything but strong, and when Brad admitted that he'd cheated, Mia was ready to face the next step. She'd known for a while she was going to leave him. Eventually. The idea of how divorce might affect her son was what had kept her hot-gluing their marriage together.

Mia had dug in and attempted to be the best spouse she could after a giant blowup at work had finally sent Brad into treatment and he'd been diagnosed as bipolar. That was nearly four years ago. Ever since, Mia had felt more like a single mother of two than a married mother of one.

After giving Ollie a few months to adjust to their separation, Mia had made an appointment with a lawyer and begun the process of filing for divorce. A week later, more than a touch ironically, Brad had had an aneurysm rupture and had died while biking.

In one unexpected swoop, Mia had gone from feeling

as if she was finally getting her life together to being less grounded than ever.

Ben had been the one to tell her about the aneurysm that had taken Brad's life. He was Brad's oldest friend, and over the course of her and Brad's marriage, he'd also become someone Mia trusted immensely. And even that tragic moment had been a chaotic mess. She'd opened the door of her grandparents' house to find Ben on the other side of the stoop with an impossibly pained look in his dark-brown eyes.

She and Ollie had been fostering one of the shelter dogs, an Irish setter who'd since been adopted and who'd likely never be trustworthy off leash. Having caught the look on Ben's face, Mia had forgotten everything and left the door open wide enough that the frisky dog had escaped.

Rather than collapse on the couch upon hearing the news, Mia had needed to help Ben chase the overzealous dog through the neighborhood. After a vigorous several-minute run, the setter had been distracted by a family a few blocks away. They'd been out front in their yard setting up a lighted Christmas display of a large plastic Santa in a sled and a team of bright reindeer.

Mia had still been in such shock after they'd caught him that Ben had guided her back to the house the same as he had the dog. She'd hardly been able to focus, especially as the adrenaline from the run wore off, but she'd put one foot in front of the other, letting the solid feel of Ben's hand on her back guide her home.

Seeing she was in no shape to be a thoughtful caregiver, Ben had stayed and made Ollie his favorite dinner of noodles and given him a bath while she got herself

together. Hours later, as she'd curled into Ollie's bed alongside him, Ben had stepped back into Ollie's room, carrying a mug of steaming tea. He set the mug on the nightstand, then pressed a light kiss onto Ollie's forehead and hers too. After he left, Mia had held Ollie and watched the steam rising from the mug in the dim light from the night-light.

Strangely, of everything that happened that night, her memory of watching the dancing steam rise from the mug was the most clear.

The days since had been tumbling together. All twenty-two of them. Important decisions needed to be made, but most of the time, all Mia could manage was to stick to the most basic of routines.

More than anything, this was why she'd decided to start back at the shelter today. Life outside her grandparents' quiet and dated bungalow had started to feel like a stream passing her by. Ollie had gone back to school last week, but Mia had hardly ventured out except to drive him there. She needed to jump back into that swiftly moving stream too. And the shelter was the safest place she could think to do it.

As Mia headed around the firepits in the crowded shelter parking lot where s'mores were being roasted, a happy glow began to warm her from the inside, and she knew she'd made the right decision.

Just outside the front door, Patrick, one of the shelter's full-time staff members, and Tiny, a massive Great Dane, were stationed as greeters. Patrick, always a stickler for routine, was dressed in his usual cargo pants and a polo. Mia figured the fact that he was wearing a red one was his declaration of being festive.

"Hey, Patrick. How's everything going so far?"

His uneasy smile turned into a hint of a frown. "It's crowded inside. And full of children. Since that was the goal, it's going well."

Mia laughed and sank onto her heels. She gave Tiny a thorough scratch just above the collar of his red-and-white sweater but turned her face to avoid a full-frontal lick. Despite his size, Tiny was one of the most laid-back dogs at the shelter, and he seemed to really be owning the reindeer costume he was wearing for today's event. Tiny's brightly colored getup included the holiday sweater, a slip-on crocheted cap with antlers, and several brass jingle bells tied to his collar. The antler cap had slipped a bit, giving him even more of a comical look.

"That's good. I read in this morning's email that yesterday's event beat goal, and I'm crossing my fingers today's does too." Mia had known Patrick long enough to know he was here for the animals, and not to interact with the shelter's many supporters. Patrick would probably choose to do without the shelter's celebrations if he could, but he understood they were an important part of its success, and he was always a great help. And while he didn't have the best knack for conversation, he was amazing with the dogs and cats.

As Mia headed inside, she was greeted with the sound of "A Holly Jolly Christmas" playing over a set of speakers and a front room that had been rearranged and filled with several craft tables for today's event.

"Hey there, lovely." Mia glanced over to see Megan, the shelter director, headed toward her. Megan pulled her into a hug, her heavily pregnant body pressing into

Mia's stomach, reminding her how the solid-soft feel of a late-term pregnant belly was unlike anything else. "It's really good to see you, girl," Megan added.

"Thanks. It's good to be back." As soon as she said it, Mia realized she meant it. It *was* good to be back. She'd only just walked in, but somehow she already felt as if she'd shed a heavy weight. "Really good, actually."

"Hot chocolate while you get started? I'm heading outside to work that station for a bit."

A second wave of relief washed over Mia as she realized she wasn't going to be drilled with a thousand questions about her personal life. "Um, maybe later. It's so busy. Where would you like me?"

Megan made a "that's easy" face. "You've been away three weeks. I think you're more than overdue for some puppy time." She craned her head across the craft tables and pointed to a spot not far from the gift shop. "How about babysitting John Ronald's puppies so Tess can have a break? They're up front having some playtime in the pen."

"Are you kidding? That's a solid yes." Mia gave her friend a second hug and headed through the crowded shelter toward the playpen on the far side of the room where Tess was monitoring the puppy mania from a chair inside the pen. The playpen was surrounded by a swarm of people, which wasn't a surprise considering inside it were seven roly-poly husky-mix puppies. Just a glimpse of their stout, furry bodies tumbling over one another made Mia laugh.

She paused at the single open gap in the circle of puppy admirers to wait for Tess to finish telling the story of the puppies' rescue to a fresh group of visitors.

John Ronald, a stray dog who'd since been adopted by Tess's boyfriend, had been behind the abandoned puppies' rescue. And while the little guys had had a rough start, all seven were now plump, bright-eyed, and full of energy.

She couldn't believe how much they'd grown since she'd last seen them. Unable to resist, Mia knelt and flattened her hand against the wire mesh of the pen. One of the largest pups in the litter dashed toward her. The furry black-and-white pup thumped the floor with its front paws, and came to an abrupt stop.

"Hey, Mia! I didn't know you were coming today," Tess said as a few people left and there was a break in the questions.

"Hey, Tess. Yeah, I know. I wasn't sure myself, but I figured I just needed to do it."

"Well, I for one am glad you're here. Are you coming to relieve me?"

"Sure am."

"Cool." Tess stood up. "Just push that panel open to get in. You enter; I'll block. They've definitely figured out it's a way out of here, and they're craving room to run. My advice to you is to keep a chew toy in hand at all times. They're a gnawy bunch."

As soon as Mia was in, Tess draped her in a warm hug while three different puppies tackled Mia's boots. "It's so good to see you, lady. How you holding up?"

In Mia's opinion, Tess's petite frame and Italian-American looks were a perfect match for her peppy personality. "Good. Better now. I've missed you guys. And the place looks great. I love the tree. And those ornaments... I assume those are our current pets?"

Near the front window, an impressive short-needled pine was adorned with animal head-shot cutouts glued to pipe-cleaner bodies. Mia thought she'd recognized several dog and cat faces as she passed by.

"Yep. Patrick spent the last few weeks photographing every animal in the place. And you know how he is. Somehow, he found a way to get great pictures of over a hundred animals. The last couple days, the Events Committee made them into ornaments. They're all on the tree. And every time one of our guys is adopted between now and New Year's, their ornament will go home with them."

Mia clicked her tongue. "I swear, this place finds a way to outdo itself year after year."

"This is my first year, but with the twelve-day string of festivities that's under way, I can't imagine coming up with something better next year."

After they'd spent another few minutes catching up, Mia played linebacker to keep the puppies at bay, and Tess stepped out. Chew toy in hand, Mia sank into the plastic chair and was soon assaulted by one of the puppies. She buried her fingers in its silky fur as the little guy gnawed her sleeve with sharp milk teeth. Each one was adorable. Mia couldn't imagine picking a favorite. She'd heard big plans were underway for their eventual adoption and couldn't wait for the big reveal. She also couldn't wait to show them to Ollie when he got here. There'd be no leaving here this afternoon until they'd both had a sufficient puppy fix.

Mia had joined the shelter's dog-walking program when she was fifteen and pining for a dog but living in her "No pets ever" grandparents' home. That house, the

one she'd gone back to when she'd left Brad, was just a little over a mile from here.

Growing up, Mia had dreamed of getting both a dog and a cat as soon as she had a place of her own. Then, her last year of college, she'd eloped with Brad after getting pregnant with Ollie. When Brad had turned out to be allergic to both cats and dogs, it had put a damper on those dreams.

She'd appeased her animal love by continuing to volunteer here as she raised Ollie in a petless home. As a volunteer, she worked with both the cats and dogs, cleaning cages, brushing and playing with them, and taking the dogs for walks. After graduating with an art degree, she'd even become the shelter's unofficial go-to artist.

While her primary focus had been on raising Ollie rather than building a career, Mia ran an online business as a pet portrait artist. Thanks to the support and encouragement of the shelter's now-retired founder, Wesley Hines, she'd also been encouraged to advertise her business at the shelter. Over the last few years, the shelter had even held portrait sittings on the fourth Sunday afternoon of every month, the profits of which were split between her and the shelter.

As she babysat the puppies and answered questions, it occurred to her that even with the chaos of late, owning a dog was a real possibility for the first time in her life. Her grandparents had passed away, and Mia's mom had given her free rein to live in the house as she pleased. In Mia's mind, that definitely included the addition of a forever pet.

Before she knew it, forty-five minutes had passed.

Her phone buzzed from her back pocket. She pulled it out, checking to see if it was Victor or Irene who'd texted. When Brad's parents had picked Ollie up this morning for the holiday matinee at the symphony, they'd promised to have him at the shelter by three so he could enjoy some of the festivities. As she'd guessed, the new text was from Irene. They'd just parked a few blocks away and were walking over.

She slipped her phone back into her pocket and looked up to find Tess and Megan headed her way. "So the puppies have been out an hour and a half," Megan said as they reached the playpen. "I can't believe they're still going strong, but I'm guessing they've about used up their adrenaline reserves. How about we take them to the back room where it's quieter, and they can calm down? Want to help get them set up?"

"Sure," Mia agreed. She spent the next several minutes helping to haul the wriggly puppies to the back.

Once they were snuggled into a fuzzy blanket in their quiet kennel, Mia excused herself to find Ollie. Since he hadn't come in through the front door, she was betting he'd gotten sidetracked by the festivities outside.

She headed out front to the parking lot and spotted Ollie at the s'more-making station around one of the firepits. Twenty feet away, a few talented volunteers dressed up as elves were telling holiday stories to a small crowd seated on straw bales gathered around a second firepit. Some of the attendees had brought dogs of their own.

Victor had purchased a few s'more-fixing packets, and he and Ollie were spearing fat marshmallows with long sticks. Irene stood off to the side, looking thin and deflated, stirring up Mia's sympathy.

"Hey, buddy," Mia said, running her hand through her son's soft, thick hair as she joined them.

Mia suspected Ollie would grow up resembling her side of the family more than Brad's. He had his father's hair—golden blond—rather than Mia's thick and wavy chestnut-brown hair. But he had Mia's blue-gray eyes and heart-shaped face. Ollie tended to be quiet and introspective like her too. His dad, on the other hand, had been neither quiet nor someone who looked within.

Strangers had taken notice of Brad the same way people noticed a striking sunset. What Mia knew that others didn't was that while Brad had been beautiful, it was as if he were built on a shoddy foundation. It had taken constant work—his own, and hers too—to keep that foundation intact. She'd had help along the way, mostly from Ben, and from a few of Brad's other friends as well.

Ollie, who'd been so intent on spearing his marshmallow that his tongue had seemed stuck to his bottom lip, gave her a giant grin after he was victorious. "Mom!" Nearly spearing Mia next, Ollie locked his arms around her waist.

Ducking to avoid an imminent s'more-stick stabbing, Mia hugged him with one hand while securing the stick with the other. "Did you guys have a good morning?"

Ollie rolled his eyes and let his shoulders drop dramatically. "The symphony was *so* boring. But we ate at the Old Spaghetti Factory."

Mia ignored Victor's obvious disapproval of Ollie's lack of excitement over the symphony. He was a seven-year-old boy and allowed to have his opinions. "Let me guess. You had spaghetti and meatballs."

Ollie made a show of extending his stomach as he rubbed it. "I ate my entire plate."

"Your entire plate? I bet that was crunchy," Mia teased, ruffling his hair. It took him a second, but he got her joke and stamped one foot as he laughed.

While Victor assisted Ollie with his s'more roasting, Mia did her best to make conversation with Irene. However, Irene seemed less interested than ever in making conversation with her.

Mia wasn't sure of the rules, but it seemed that without the divorce officially happening, Irene and Victor would forever be her mother- and father-in-law—her disapproving mother- and father-in-law, that was. Mia hadn't been enough for their son in the eight years she'd been married to him. She had no doubt she wouldn't be in his death either.

But she wasn't going to let that get to her. They'd lost their only son, and Mia was willing to give them some leeway. For now, at least.

What really mattered was that they work together to create a new reality in which Ollie would continue to thrive. And hopefully, Mia would also get herself back in the process.

She had a feeling one of the easiest ways to do this would be by expanding their little family of two with something four-legged that had a tail.

Chapter 3

THE DIGITAL CLOCK ON THE DASHBOARD OF BEN'S Jeep placed him a solid forty-five minutes ahead of schedule for a client meeting. This morning, he'd be presenting a series of designs to a family who was converting a hundred-year-old church into a home. He'd poured hours into the designs, manipulating ways to enable the family to modernize and add warmth while keeping the majority of the stained glass, archways, coffers, and even the belfry.

Showing up this early at a client's home wasn't ideal. Ben told himself this was the reason his foot seemed instinctively to ease off the gas pedal as he neared the exit leading to the house in Webster Groves where Mia had been living since August. He'd resisted shooting off a text to check in with her before leaving this morning. Most likely, if he asked if she needed anything, she'd thank him but say no, just as she'd been doing the last few months. She wasn't one to ask for help. Or even accept it when it was offered.

But he remembered the way she'd leaned against him in a rare moment of surrender at Brad's funeral. It was over before he'd been able to react or even savor the soft smell of her perfume or her toned but ample figure pressing into him. Too soon, she'd stood straight and locked her shoulders, the Atlas of her small world.

What if he just showed up? If he knocked on the door

instead of texting. He'd done that dozens of times without a thought when she'd been married. Just because she was on her own now didn't mean he wasn't still Ollie's godfather. And more than any time in his young life, Ollie needed him.

She's probably in a rush to get Ollie to school. Ben tapped his thumb in indecision on the steering wheel but took the exit anyway. Two blocks in, he passed Ollie's favorite bakery. Seeing that the parking lot wasn't crowded this morning, he pulled up and ran in for a couple of their favorite mini-quiches—ham and cheese for Ollie and spinach and fontina for Mia—and an assortment of scones and muffins. Mia had mentioned they froze well the last time he sent Ollie home with a bag of them after an outing with him and Taye.

Ben pulled into an open spot in front of the home where Mia had grown up. It was a quaint brick bungalow. The dark streaks on the roof and some erosion on the chimney pots showed it was in need of some TLC. Seeing it reminded him of just one more way he'd like to help her if she'd let him. *If*.

As he headed up the path, he spotted her through the bay window. She was at the counter in the kitchen, grabbing something from a cabinet. Through the darkened window, it wasn't easy to make out much, but his insides twisted all the same. She was the only woman he'd ever met who caused his chest to tighten and his gut to burn hot at the same time.

And that was before she answered the door in fleece pj's that were only half successful in hiding her lack of bra, no makeup, and hair still mussed from sleep. He locked his gaze on her face to keep it from straying south.

"Hey. Morning. I, uh… Did you call? My phone's in the bedroom." A blush lit her cheeks, and she clamped one arm over her chest as she pulled the door open wide.

"Morning. I was about to, but I figured if I did, you'd shoot me down," he said with a smile.

Ben heard a flush and splash of water from the opposite end of the small house; then a familiar golden-haired head popped around the corner. "Ben!" Clad only in a long-sleeved pajama top and Spider-Man underwear, Ollie charged down the length of the living room and locked Ben in a bear hug around the waist. A dog, a hefty-set Lab that Mia must have been fostering for the night, trotted over and sniffed his shoes and pants with hesitant curiosity, a slow pump to its tail.

"Hey, buddy!" Mia reached for the bakery bag that Ben held out. After she relieved him of it and both hands were free, he scooped Ollie into the air and held him high overhead, sending Ollie into a familiar fit of laughter. Ben knew Ollie's emotions ran the gamut since losing his father, and it was good to see him in a moment of easy bliss again. "How's it going, little man? You're getting so big, pretty soon I'm going to be wearing you when I do this."

His godson had Mia's face shape and her smile, but the rest of him was all seven-year-old boy.

"I don't care if you wear me." Ollie locked his arms around Ben's head and laughed some more. "I'll be a hat, and you can wear me all day."

"Something tells me you'd be the squirmiest hat I've ever worn."

Mia joined in, tickling Ollie's exposed belly. "I think

Ben would need the world's best chiropractor if he wore your wiggly body all day, Ol."

"So who's this?" Ben asked when he set Ollie down.

"Clara Bee. She's been at the shelter for a couple months. She's pending adoption, and this is a bit of a home-living test before she goes out at the end of the week. She was featured in the last newsletter. She's got quite the story."

Ben held out his hand, and Clara Bee gave him a tentative lick. He sank to the balls of his feet and, when she didn't shy away, gave her a thorough scratch under the chin, burying his fingers in her soft, golden fur. "Clara Bee, huh? After Clara Barton, right? Yeah, I remember reading about her."

She was a middle-aged dog who'd been living in subpar conditions and had had litter after litter before being taken from her home and brought into the shelter. She'd needed hip surgery but had come through it fine.

As if in thanks for the scratch, Clara Bee pressed in and swiped her tongue over Ben's ear. He'd never have guessed she'd had very limited human interaction for the majority of her life. Dogs, Ben figured, were simply hardwired to be good companions. He'd seen that in places like Nepal where most dogs were either free-roaming or strays. Even with minimal care and food, their bond with humans was inspiring.

"Thank goodness for the shelter, huh?"

As Mia agreed, Ollie lifted the brown paper bag from her hands and peeked inside. "*Yes!*" With his free hand, he rubbed his stomach vigorously, sending his pajama shirt up and exposing his trim belly and bony ribs.

Ben chuckled and stood up. "Did you eat yet?"

"I was just trying to get him to the table," Mia said. She gave Ben a hopeful glance. "But this certainly is more enticing than a soggy bowl of cereal. Can you stay?"

"For a little while. What time do you head out with him?"

She turned to check the kitchen clock. "Twenty minutes or so." A hint of her flush returned when she met Ben's gaze again. "I'm glad you came by. And I'm good if we're a few minutes late. It's not like they'll stick him in lockdown."

"Oh, can we be late? Please can we be late?" Ollie looked from his mom to Ben. "I *hate* journal time."

"How about instead you make quick work of this breakfast, and I drive you to school but try to get you there on time?" Ben said.

Ollie's eyes opened wide, and he dashed to the window. "You're in the Jeep. Sweet! Mom, please can he drive me? *Please?*"

Mia laughed and shook her head. "That's fine by me." She took a step toward the kitchen, then stopped and glanced downward, drawing Ben's attention toward the body he'd been doing his best not to notice. "You guys start without me. I'll throw on some clothes."

The flannel gown she was wearing was unbuttoned just to the point that it accented the rise of her breasts, and her fuzzy socks highlighted her toned, smooth calves.

"Ol, show him where the plates are, 'kay?"

"Come on, Ben," Ollie said, heading for the kitchen. "Do you like coffee or orange juice? My mom likes coffee, and I like orange juice. But I only get to have it if I also drink a glass of water."

Clara Bee followed Ollie into the kitchen, sniffing the bag of bakery items in his hand. Ben trailed along behind them, very glad he'd listened to his instincts and stopped by. It felt a bit like old times, when everything was easy between them, only it was different too. It was a new road, a new path they were blazing, one that was somehow as familiar as it was foreign.

And Ben was more than ready to head farther down it.

Mia stepped out of the shower and was sliding the glass door closed when her phone beeped from the bedroom. After knotting her hair in a towel and tying a second towel around her torso, she headed over to the dresser to check the new text.

Clara Bee hopped off Mia's bed and trailed behind her, tentatively licking the back of one still-wet calf.

Ollie had been begging for a puppy for Christmas, but Mia was secretly hoping he'd fall in love with one of the adult foster dogs they'd been bringing home each weekend. She had a feeling he might've with this sweet girl, had there not already been a family ready to bring her home sometime this weekend.

Having reached the dresser, Mia swiped her hands across the front of her towel and lifted her phone. *Ben*. She'd hoped the text was from him.

Made it with 2 minutes to spare.

Her hands froze over the digital keypad. A handful of unworthy replies swam through her head. Why was coming up with a response so difficult?

Great. Thanks!

She groaned. He'd dropped off a delicious breakfast and driven his godson to school, not delivered the mail.

Thanks for the food and for coming by.

Still too generic, and you know it. Unsure what else to say, she shot off the text anyway.

Before this summer, it had been easy to talk to Ben, easy to be in the same room with him without blushing. He was Ollie's godfather, and he'd helped her keep Brad together during the harder times in her marriage. She'd counted on him in a hundred different ways.

And he'd never let her down.

Anytime. It was good to see Ollie. Good to see you too.

It was good to see her. Mia's heart thumped in her chest. Did he remember that night on his balcony? She'd hardly seen him since then, and whenever she did—like this morning—she could feel her cheeks burning hot.

As if Mia's indecision was palpable, Clara Bee paused her licking to glance up at her. Mia scratched the top of Bee's head, then turned back at her phone.

Good to see you as well.

She was about to say "thanks again" when another text arrived.

That's good. Because I've decided to take a more proactive approach to overcome your resistance to help. ☺

Mia bit her lip as a smile spread across her face.

Hmm, if this proactive approach comes with spinach-and-fontina mini-quiche, I'm good with that.

She debated adding a wink back but turned it into a regular smiley face instead.

So I had you at quiche, huh? Well, I'm good with that.

"I think this is Ben fixing things," she said aloud, laughing. Clara Bee pricked her ears and cocked her head. "Thank goodness, because I didn't know how to do it."

Mia thanked him again for driving Ollie to school and set her phone down to get dressed. Ben wasn't to blame for the awkwardness that had been between them the last four months. *She was.*

The team at his firm had held a surprise party at Ben's downtown loft on his return from Everest. It had been a remarkable night and a late one. Ben didn't crave being the center of attention, but when he'd realized there was no way around it—he'd summited Everest and his friends wanted more than the single picture and snippet of information he'd posted on Instagram each day—he regaled his guests with some of the wilder things that

had happened up there. One story, about Ben's ladder slipping from under him and him hanging over an impossibly deep crevasse until he could be pulled up by his team, had shaken Mia to the core.

She'd stepped out onto the balcony after getting Ollie to sleep on Ben's bed and sucked in a deep breath of summer night air. The party had continued in the main loft, but out there she could no longer hear Brad's voice booming across the room, and she willed the silence to soak into her pores. She'd stared out at the night skyline, contemplating the impending end of her marriage.

She hadn't been in love with Brad for a long time. It was just so much more obvious to her when she was around Ben. She wanted a chance to love someone who was whole and complete and wouldn't drain the energy out of her. And even though she'd never seen him in a committed relationship, it was obvious Ben could be that for someone.

And a part of her she'd done her best to ignore had wanted that someone to be her.

The first time she'd met Ben, she'd been pregnant with Ollie. She and Brad had recently eloped, and Mia had already been questioning the impromptu decision. Her internal reaction at meeting Ben had been something akin to "Holy crap," and she'd attempted to quell it. Most of the time, it worked. He was a friend and Ollie's godparent.

But the night of the party, hearing his stories and spying the windburn still noticeable on his cheeks, her feelings had been impossible to ignore. When she'd noticed the light frostbite scars on his fingers, she'd wanted to close her hand around his and not let go.

She'd been thinking all these things on the balcony of his loft as she stared out into the night at the beautiful silhouette of the city. And then Ben had joined her, and it had just been the two of them for the first time in forever, and Mia could feel the wildness of the mountain still seeping off him.

They'd been talking, their voices low and intimate. And Mia had ruined it. She could tell herself a hundred times that her actions had been innocent. All she'd done was brush her fingertips over his lips—and maybe lean in a fraction of an inch—but she couldn't block the truth from her awareness. It had been a lover's touch. Intimate and telling, and Ben had understood.

After a wild second in which Mia's breath had caught in her throat in anticipation of a kiss, he'd cleared his throat and stepped back. Mia had done her best to avoid him after that. It wasn't hard because a little over a month later, she'd walked out on her marriage.

Ever since then, her cheeks had flushed hot almost every time she found herself in the same room with him.

But it was time to let that go. However mixed up her feelings were for Ben, he was still Ollie's godfather, and Ollie needed him. Especially now. The truth was, she needed him too. There was no sense refusing the friendship he was so ready to offer just to avoid a bit of embarrassment on her part.

Mia had tugged on a pair of jeans and was fastening her bra when Clara Bee leaned in against Mia's leg. Bee was a leaner, and whenever Mia was the recipient of the loyal dog's leaning, it made her smile. Dogs only leaned against people they trusted. Bee had only been at the house for two nights, but Mia was going to miss her.

After she finished dressing, Mia headed into the kitchen and jotted down a short but imperative list of to-dos, stroking the smooth, silky fur at the top of Bee's forehead as she did. She tapped the eraser on the table, attempting to recall all the things she'd remembered in the middle of the night that needed her attention. The first item to make the list was to get back to her and Brad's house on Maryland Avenue in the Central West End. Among other things, Mia needed to go through the bills.

For the last few weeks, her thoughts had been too foggy to think about money. Mia had put her career on hold to raise Ollie—and to help keep Brad on track— though she'd contributed to their income some with sales from her pet portraits. Their joint savings were slim, and for the most part, they'd lived on a tight budget.

Mia next jotted down half-a-dozen other items she'd left behind when she moved out four months ago. Back then, she hadn't bothered to go through the tubs of winter clothes, but it was more than time to do so. She hoped Ollie's snowsuit still fit. He'd been swimming in it last winter, but with the way he was growing, there was no telling until he tried it on.

The final item to make the Post-it note to-do list was a single word, but also the biggest and most important of all.

Decide

It stared up at her, giant and daunting.

Clara Bee seemed to sense the hesitation sweeping over Mia and leaned against her leg more heavily. After giving the Lab a reassuring pat, Mia broke a piece from

the last mini-quiche, popped a chunk into her mouth, and let out a small moan of appreciation. The rich and creamy quiche was probably one of Mia's favorite foods ever. She savored the last of it, determined not to think about the big decision awaiting her or about how the delicious quiche made her mouth water a bit like it had this summer on Ben's balcony when every part of her had craved to know the taste of his lips.

Finally, she stood up and shook her shoulders, trying to shake away her thoughts. "Want to go for a ride, Bee?"

Clara Bee wagged her tail and followed Mia around as she got ready to leave. After they were loaded into the car, autopilot kicked in as Mia headed to the ninety-year-old home she'd shared with Brad and Ollie since the week before Ollie's first birthday. She'd been back only a couple of times since she'd left, and they'd been quick trips like this one to pick up a few things.

She parked directly out front and looked up and down the block, bracing herself. She wasn't ready for the neighbors' questions or awkward silences or sympathy. When the street proved empty and quiet, she released a breath of relief. Bee shoved the front half of her body between the bucket seats and brushed her warm tongue over the side of Mia's neck.

Mia shut off the car but didn't move. The bare, gently swaying branches of the stately sycamore reflected in the lower-floor windows, resembling a thick pair of eye-lashes, blinking a hello in the gray December morning.

"We won't be in there long, sweet girl." *Who are you consoling? Bee won't be greeting any old ghosts when she walks inside.*

Mia's attention was drawn to the ivy on the east

corner. It was starting to grow up the side again. Like a hundred other chores, keeping the ivy from climbing the brick had been Mia's responsibility. She'd tried to remove it several times, but it had grown back fast and thick. Mia had finally decided the ivy had a stronger will to live than she did to kill it. She'd hacked away at it every few months, and in her recent absence, the mighty dark-green leaves had made steady progress up the side and front of the house.

Mia closed her eyes and tried to envision the next few months playing out. Should she keep the house, move her and Ollie back in, and convince her mother to put her parents' house up for sale? For the last three weeks, her thoughts had circled with no resolution. But it was time to decide.

For certain, Ollie's best memories of his dad were here, and to be fair, Ollie probably had a lot of them. He'd been too young to have been exposed to the darker things: irrationality and wild impulsivity; credit cards that had been maxed out before she'd even known they'd been applied for; Brad's anger at himself. Anger at her. Anger at the world.

And now his dad was gone.

Mia sucked in a breath and tumbled out of the car and into the brisk December morning. She zipped her coat all the way to her chin as if it were a shield.

Bee didn't need any coaxing to hop down from the back. Once out, the sweet dog pumped her tail hard enough that her hips waggled, and she stared up at Mia if asking "What now?"

"I'm so glad you're with me, girl. It would suck to do this alone."

She headed up the concrete path to the covered porch where Ollie had cuddled on her lap and watched the storms roll in when he was little.

Victor and Irene had offered to work something out that would enable her to stay here, insisting it would be best for Ollie. A generous gift from Brad's parents had enabled them to put a sizable payment down when they bought this place.

But Mia couldn't help but think that if she took this level of help from them, she'd lose a piece of herself. She'd left this place and had had no intention of coming back.

She unlocked the bolt on the front door and let herself in, then kicked off her shoes. She kept the coat on, but the chill from the hardwood floors seeped up through her socks. Someone had turned the thermostat quite low, and there was a pile of mail nicely stacked on the kitchen table.

Clara Bee didn't seem to notice the chill. Once Mia unclipped her leash, she trotted around, exploring the rooms on the lower floor, the sound of her nails echoing in Mia's ears.

Who'd come here after getting the news, Mia wondered. Something told her it was probably Ben and not Victor or Irene. Whenever they went out of their way to do something, they made sure she knew about it. Her heart went out to think of Ben and all the things he'd silently been doing to help out even when she'd been putting him off.

She made quick work of grabbing the tub of winter wear from the basement, then headed up the stairs to her and Brad's bedroom. Bee followed her, trailing just behind Mia's heels.

As she crested the top step and headed down the hall, Mia realized she was an interloper here now. Every room greeted her with a collection of memories of a life she'd wanted to leave behind.

Even if Mia was set on moving herself and Ollie back in, even if the good memories here outweighed the bad, she didn't want to be indebted to Victor and Irene. She needed to sell the house and hope the leftover money minus real estate commissions would pay off both the first and second mortgage.

If not... No. She locked down her thoughts. She didn't have the energy to think about that today.

She hesitated before entering the bedroom and bee-lined for the closet, determined not to let memories press in and oppress her. In and out. She was going to grab her stuff and leave, that's all.

Mia grabbed a couple more sweaters and pairs of heavier pants from her side of the closet. Bee hopped from the bench at the foot of the bed to the mattress. The sweet dog made for the mess of pillows and wadded-up comforter and circled and scratched at them, readying herself for a second morning nap.

"Sweet Bee, we aren't staying long enough to get comfortable."

Undeterred, Bee kicked up something small and shiny and blue, and it caught Mia's attention. She crossed the room with her arms full of clothes and stared at the bed next to the dog. There, in plain sight, was a condom wrapper.

You haven't seen one of these since just after Ollie was conceived.

After a troubled delivery, she'd had an emergency

partial hysterectomy. There'd been no need to worry about birth control during the entire course of her marriage.

She stared, frozen in place, thoughts rolling over her in waves.

Brad had been begging her to come back and give their marriage another chance. *And all the while screwing someone on our bed.*

Was it the same woman he'd cheated on Mia with, the one he'd promised had been a mistake and had meant nothing to him? Or someone else?

She noted the anger inside her. It was there, rising to the surface, making her want to yell and stamp her feet. But something else, a sharper and stronger emotion, fought it and won.

For the first time in a long time, Mia felt free.

And one thing was brilliantly clear. She was never, *ever* coming back to live in this house.

Chapter 4

ALTHOUGH THE LIGHTENED-UP VERSION OF *A Christmas Carol* that Taye's middle school was performing tonight was packed with comic relief, Ben hoped he didn't end up second-guessing his decision to bring Ollie along. He'd promised to bring him back in September when Taye had been awarded the part of Jacob Marley, but a lot had changed in Ollie's life since then. Even filled with jokes and modern slang, the play still carried its share of heavy messages, which Ben wasn't sure Ollie needed so soon after losing his dad.

Ben had mentioned his hesitation to Mia, and they'd come to the decision that Ollie should still attend. Ollie idolized Taye. He had helped Taye practice his lines half a dozen times over the last few months and was excited to see his performance.

But as the audience quieted and the second act started, Ollie leaned against Ben and resumed rolling one of his Hot Wheels atop both their laps and along the side of Ben's chair.

Ben wished Mia had come along, and not just because of the opportunity to spend a few hours with her. He wanted to see if she really was holding herself together, and since no one could read Ollie as well, she'd know if a quiet, introspective moment was becoming something more challenging.

But she'd been off tonight. A headache, she'd

claimed, though Ben suspected something else was boiling under the surface, and he intended to ask her when they were alone. When he'd suggested she stay behind to have a few rare hours to herself, and Ollie had seemed excited for the one-on-one time with him, she'd taken him up on the offer.

Ollie shifted, nestling deeper into the crook of Ben's arm as up on the cafeteria stage, Ebenezer watched his family's merriment from outside a makeshift window.

Ben couldn't remember a time that Ollie hadn't been comfortable snuggling up next to him or clambering for a ride atop his shoulders. Somehow, he'd managed to navigate the rocky waters of loving Ollie unconditionally despite the fact that he was secretly in love with his best friend's wife. Ben's love for Ollie was pure and clean, and nothing could touch it.

He'd been at the hospital the night Ollie was born four weeks early after Mia and Brad's car accident. The wreck had been a bad one. Brad had been distracted and had driven into a concrete divider, injuring himself and sending Mia into early labor.

Afraid his feelings might show, Ben had done his best to avoid her before then. In fact, before that night, he couldn't remember having exchanged more than a few minutes of conversation with her. He'd even convinced himself that he'd been doing a good job of burying his love for her.

But then he'd seen her in the hospital bed, in pain and vulnerable and afraid, and he knew the love he had for her wasn't the kind that could just be gotten past.

In the hospital that night, he'd been the one to pass Ollie to his father, and he'd held Mia's hand sometime

later when they couldn't stop the bleeding and she was told she'd need an emergency hysterectomy. Out of that crazy mess of a night, he'd been named Ollie's godfather, and he'd been a regular part of Ollie's life ever since.

Aside from when he was away on a climb, Ben had spent an evening every week with Ollie since the boy was three and a half or four. Tonight was a Friday, but their usual night together was Wednesday and one of Ben's favorite nights of the week.

Enthralled by Ben's climbing stories, Ollie had wanted to learn to climb. Their Wednesday nights most often involved a trip to the climbing gym, followed by dinner and hot chocolate or ice cream. As the seasons went by and Brad became less and less interested in sticking to routine, it had usually just been Mia in the house when Ben brought Ollie home.

He'd lost count of how many times he'd stayed to help get Ollie to bed. The boy was a cuddler and most so right before sleep. Ben loved reading with him or lying next to him and listening to the creative kid make up stories that became more outlandish the sleepier he got. After Ollie fell asleep, Ben would sit in the kitchen with Mia, reminiscing over the highlights of Ollie's day and anything else the conversation led to. These quiet hours sharpened his longing for a life that might have been his if fate hadn't intervened.

Most of those years, all that stuff had been easy enough to do. He was in Mia's life as a friend, and he was Ollie's godfather. That was it, nothing more. He got pretty good at blocking out the other stuff, like how beautiful she was and how he could imagine the way their bodies would fit together, or the way he appreciated

the easy curl of her mouth when it turned up in a soft smile or the impossible deep gray-blue of her eyes.

But things had gotten complicated this summer after he returned from his second attempt at Everest.

He hadn't meant to, but he'd carried his love for Mia onto the mountain with him. He'd only done three climbs at altitudes higher than seventeen thousand feet. He'd hoped the first two climbs had prepared him for the way the lack of oxygen messed with a person's thoughts. But the higher he got on his ascent, the harder it was to think, to reason, to be anything but present, and the harder it was to separate himself from that love.

Ben had always looked forward to climbing because it took one hundred percent focus, one hundred percent presence. But this time, even as exhausting and dangerous and rewarding as the ascent had been, he'd not been able to leave his love for Mia behind. Even during the hardest, most technical parts of his climb, she'd never been far from his mind. He'd seen her face on the mountain, and as he'd fallen asleep in his tent at night, doing his best to doze in the severe cold and ignore the shallowness of his breathing and the way, that high up, it was hard to tell when he was asleep and when he was awake. Everything up there was a dream. A magnificent, waking nightmare. And Mia had been with him through all of it.

He'd come down that mother of all mountains laid bare. He was weaker than he'd ever been in his life, and the experience had been transcendent in a way he'd not expected. He'd also come down committed to telling Mia the truth. No matter how complicated it might make things, he'd lived with his secret long enough.

Ben had lingered in Nepal at Kathmandu for an extra week, trying to recover his strength and put back on some of the weight he'd lost as he worked through the enormity of what declaring the truth might mean. For all of them.

And then he'd come home to St. Louis and walked into a surprise party that his staff had thrown for him, and two very different things had kept the words from rising to his lips. The first had been the look on Mia's face out on the balcony the night of the party, and the tender hesitance in the way she'd reach out to brush her fingertips over his bottom lip. She'd met his gaze, and he'd seen it in her eyes for the first time. She loved him; he just wasn't sure in what way. Maybe she wasn't either. It occurred to him that no matter how much he might want to persuade her, he needed to let her work through her feelings and whatever came of them.

Then, a week later, the second thing had happened. This one was a phone call from Brad.

"I messed up." It was the first thing Ben heard due to a skip in reception. "It didn't mean anything," he'd added. "It was one night, eight months ago. I was drunk off my ass, and it didn't mean jack. It was ten minutes in a car."

Fury had flashed through Ben's veins as his friend's words sank in. "You cheated on her! If this isn't some sad joke, you know I'm going to kick your ass!"

"You're too late to preach. This girl... She's practically a kid, and she's pregnant."

"Shit, Brad. Shit. Define 'practically.'"

"She's legal, if that's what you're asking. Twenty maybe. I haven't seen her in months, but she tracked

me down and says it's mine. She wants to give the kid
to some couple she found online. Only first she wanted
to see if I wanted dibs."

"On the baby?"

"Yeah, on the baby."

Dibs. On a human life. A wave of nausea had rolled
over Ben. "Have you told Mia?"

"Not yet. I don't even know if the kid's mine."

"Does she know you cheated on her?"

"You know things haven't been good. If I tell her I
cheated, it's over. I'm sure of it."

Ben's silence had likely made as strong a point as the
words that followed. "Maybe it needs to be over."

When Brad spoke again, the tension in his voice was
sharper than Ben had heard in years. "You'd like that,
wouldn't you? Thanks for the help, buddy." After that,
the line went dead.

From that point on, their already-strained friendship
had been pushed to the brink.

Brad told Mia about his infidelity in August, just after
the kid was born but before the DNA test results were
in. Most likely Brad had taken one look at the baby and
known he didn't need to wait for test results. Somehow,
even wrinkled and helpless, the kid bore an uncanny
resemblance to his father.

And now Brad was dead, and Mia didn't know any of
this. But Ben knew way more than he wanted to know.
The girl had fallen in love with the baby and kept him.
Brad had been funneling her money he didn't have to
help her keep afloat. Mia had no idea of the baby's exis-
tence or the bad financial shape Brad had gotten into
during the last few months. And Ollie had a half brother

living twenty minutes away in a two-bedroom apartment shared by four punky twenty-year-olds.

Ben was at an impasse. How could he tell Mia any of this when he'd been keeping so much from her for so long?

He couldn't. This was the sort of news that wasn't his place to share. Besides, when he thought of telling her, it was hard to decide if it would be in her best interest... or in his.

Though he did his best to focus on the play and the middle schoolers who got their lines right more times than they didn't, Ben was only successful when Taye was onstage. When it was over, he and Ollie wove through the crowd and met up with Taye's extended family.

Ben offered to take them all to dinner, but the group was headed to Taye's aunt's house. Ben and Ollie hung out with them until the parking lot cleared, and Ben snapped a dozen pictures, promising to make plans with Taye tomorrow.

A half hour later, Ben found himself across a booth from Ollie in the Pancake Hut, cutting the most perfectly round of Ollie's pancakes into zigzag slices. He was doing his best to visualize the weight of all the secrets swimming inside him sliding off his shoulders and settling on the tile floor, but it wasn't working.

Ollie crunched a slice of bacon and watched the pancake cutting, his slight, bony shoulders hunched forward uncharacteristically. Ben wondered if he were processing some of what he'd been exposed to tonight, but decided not to lead the conversation into anything heavy. Once the first pancake was cut into zigzags, Ben reassembled it into the nearly perfect circle it had been

and started cutting small, deliberate pieces from the second pancake.

Ollie leaned way out over the table and twisted around to see the shapes from Ben's perspective. He'd been making shapes out of Ollie's pancakes since he was two.

"I like the zigzags." Ollie's nose was a little stuffed, and he was close enough that Ben could smell the bacon and orange juice on his breath. "What's round and zigzagged?"

Ben cocked an eyebrow and added a few small circles on two of the zigzagged lines, a topper, and a hook, and scooted the rest of the second pancake to the side, then twisted the plate so that Ollie could see it upright.

"Oh! An ornament! Cool. You never did an ornament before. Mom has one just like that on the tree."

"Yep. I noticed it when I picked you up. I think it's an antique."

"It was my great-nanna and pawpaw's. All the ornaments are. We aren't using ours this year."

"That makes sense." Ben waited to see if Ollie would offer more. He suspected it would be best to let Ollie lead the conversation tonight.

Ollie slid the plate across the table and started to sink back onto his bench, but changed his mind and slid in next to Ben, ducking underneath the table and squirming up onto the seat next to him.

"It's cold," he said by way of explanation.

Ben draped an arm across the boy's back and pulled him closer. Ollie leaned against him as he decorated his pancake ornament with drops and squirts of syrup. At first it looked good, but as was typical, he kept going

until it was a syrupy mess. Then he looked up and grinned mischievously, making Ben laugh. "With all that sugar in you, you aren't going to be able to fall asleep tonight."

"I can stay up late. There's no school tomorrow."

"Why?"

"Tomorrow's Saturday." Ollie stabbed a long zig-zagged slice of pancake and dangled it overhead, then munched from the end up.

"That's right. I knew that. Only since we're hanging out, it feels more like a Wednesday."

"You'll keep coming on Wednesdays, won't you?" Ollie's eyes grew wide in anticipation.

"Yeah, of course, Ol. And not just on Wednesdays either."

Ollie released a sigh, and his shoulders dropped as he abandoned his fork and lifted a wedge of pancake with his fingers. He dipped it into a puddle of syrup before popping it into his mouth.

"Do you think Jacob Marley was buried in a yern?"

Ben had just taken a bite of his own pancake, bacon and pecan, and it stuck in his throat at the question. He washed it down with a gulp of coffee. Most likely, there was much more to that question than had been spoken. "Well, first off, Jacob Marley is a fictional character, Ol, just like the ones from the stories your mom reads you. He isn't—wasn't—real. So he never actually died."

"But would he have been?"

"I don't know, honestly." He suspected the answer was no, but didn't want to go into the fact that cremation was more popular now than it had been back in Charles Dickens's time.

"I thought my dad's yern would be bigger," Ollie added, washing down his pancake bite with a gulp of milk.

Ben blinked. This was the first time Ollie had said anything about his dad's funeral.

"It's called an urn, and I can see why you'd think that."

"They knew for sure, didn't they? Before…" Ollie dropped the remaining half slice of bacon he'd just picked up and focused his attention on the table, making sticky marks with the tips of his syrupy fingers. He curled forward as if preparing for a blow, breaking their connection. "They for sure knew he was dead?"

It came out in a whisper so quiet Ben had to piece it together. "Yeah, Ol, they knew for sure."

As he sat with Ben's answer, Ollie drew a sticky line connecting the syrupy fingerprint smudges. Finally, he settled back against Ben. "Mom says spirits don't have bodies, but in my dreams, he looks the same."

Figuring the topic was best pursued by Mia, Ben started on a safer subject. "Did I tell you that your dad and I were seven like you when we met? He drew pictures in syrup too."

Ollie smiled. "Did you?"

"Maybe, but I think I had more fun making pancake towers."

"Did you always like to draw buildings? Even when you were my age?"

"No, not always. Though when I was your age, I had a pretty sizable Lincoln Log collection. I didn't start drawing buildings until after I started climbing. It was the landscapes and rock formations out in the southwest that first made me think about architecture."

"What're Lincoln Logs?"

Ben paused with his ceramic coffee mug halfway to his mouth. "You've never played with Lincoln Logs?" When Ollie shook his head earnestly, Ben added, "We'll have to fix that. They're like LEGOs, only they don't lock in the same, and they're small wooden logs instead of plastic blocks."

"What do you build with them?"

"Buildings mostly. Towers, cabins, fire lookouts, fences, that sort of thing."

"I've seen 'em. If my mom gets me some, could you come over and play them with me?"

"Yeah. Sure. I'd like that."

"Are you going away again? To climb another mountain?" Ollie had been using his napkin to wipe up the smears of syrup on the table near his plate but stopped to look up at Ben.

Ben could hear the worry lining Ollie's tone and guessed it had more than one layer. He chose his answer carefully. "Well, Ol, climbing's in my blood. There'll always be a mountain calling somewhere, but I don't plan to climb anything for a long time that will take me away from St. Louis—from you—the way Everest did."

"Because Everest is in Nepal? Mom and I watched a lot of stuff about it on YouTube."

"It's more than just how far away it is. Mountains like Everest are really high in altitude, which means the air is thinner. A big part of your trip is getting your body used to operating with a lot less oxygen than it normally gets. It's called high-altitude climbing, and right now, the only climbing I want to do is climbing that won't require that kind of preparation."

"Did you save any animals on Everest? Like you did in the Rockies?"

Ben speared a link of sausage. "I gave a couple stray dogs my dinner once, when I was trekking up to base camp. And if you're thinking of the deer, it was at Mount Rainier, which is further west than the Rockies. It's in the Cascades."

Ollie twisted on the bench, pulling his knees up into his chest and twisting to face Ben. "Will you tell me the story again?"

"I'm pretty sure you've heard it enough to tell it to me, haven't you?"

"I like it better when you tell it."

Ben chuckled, but since it was a story Ollie never tired of hearing, he said, "Well, my buddy and I were hiking up Mount Rainier, and we came across a distressed mama deer. We looked down into the ravine and saw a fawn who couldn't climb up to her mom."

"Poor baby deer." Ben suppressed a smile over the way Ollie's eyes grew round like saucers even though he knew the ending by heart.

"Yup," Ben said. "She was too tired to climb up, even when the mom went all the way down and up again to show her the way."

Ollie dipped a bit of pancake into syrup, then licked it before popping it into his mouth. "What did you do?"

"I rappelled down the ravine…"

"Was it steep?"

Ben lifted his forearm until it was nearly vertical. "Like this."

"That's steep!"

"It was. So, I went down there with some blankets

and rope. I was planning to catch the frightened thing in the blanket and tie the rope around it and pull it up with me. You know it was probably only three or four months old, and even not weighing much more than you, it could still do one heck of a job defending itself with those strong legs and hard hooves. Baby deer look defenseless, but they're pretty courageous when they feel the need to defend themselves."

"That deer could've beat you up."

"Quite possibly. And as you know, once I got down there, I could see it was intent on knocking me over if I didn't catch it first. But as it turned out, a human showing up gave it the adrenaline boost it needed. I was trying to corner it, and we were facing off…"

"Like this?" Ollie asked, raising his arms like a goalie.

"Exactly like that." Ben nodded. "Well, it ran right around me and scampered up the ravine to its mom, and they both dashed into the trees without looking back."

"Mom says they didn't stop to thank you because they were too afraid." Ollie shook his head sagaciously. "Do you think animals remember like we do? 'Cuz if they do, I bet that mom reminds her baby about the day you saved her." He held up a sticky finger. "Or almost clobbered her!"

After their laughter died down, Ollie spent the rest of the meal asking Ben to retell some of the more fantastical climbing stories that he hadn't grown tired of hearing. Ben didn't mind. Since he'd climbed mountains and rock faces on five continents so far, he'd accumulated his fair share. And when he had a genuine-hearted audience like Ollie, retelling many of these tales was nothing but a pleasure.

Chapter 5

WHEN MIA AGREED TO PAINT THE MURAL THAT WOULD complete the renovations that had been under way at the High Grove Animal Shelter for the last seven months, she'd been a touch intimidated. Not only would she be using a different medium—acrylics instead of pastels—but she did her best work when it was quiet and the world seemed to fall away. At home, this was much easier to do than it would be in the main room of a busy animal shelter.

Thankfully, Mia had been a shelter volunteer long enough that she had Megan's trust. Megan had given her a key several weeks ago so she could come and go whenever she pleased.

Tonight, after Ben and Ollie had taken off for Taye's school play, Mia had expected to stay home and bury herself under the covers and catch up on the sleep that had evaded her last night. When that hadn't worked, she'd come here instead. Pastel work had long been something Mia found cathartic. And on the heels of the condom-wrapper find, she'd needed the release that would accompany sketching more than she'd needed to crawl under a blanket. And on top of that, the dogs and cats here were always the best medicine.

The mural wall had been prepped with high-grade primer and was ready for her to begin painting. Not ready to dive into anything permanent tonight, she'd

hung several sheets of oversize paper on the left corner of the wall and was using the set of charcoal pencils she kept in her car for impromptu sketching. Before she began painting for real, she'd need to get the dimensions worked out and acclimate to working on a vertical surface rather than an easel or a desk.

A month ago, she'd completed half-a-dozen small-scale sketches. The one that had been a favorite of staff and volunteers was a dynamic scene highlighting some of the shelter's most famous rescues. One of them was Trina, the shelter's only resident cat. She had been found as a kitten floating on debris in the flooded aftermath of Hurricane Katrina. Tonight, Trina was dozing curled up on the counter nearest the cat kennels. While it was generally accepted that her hanging out there was Trina's way of taunting the caged cats with her freedom, her calm demeanor also seemed to help newly surrendered cats relax as they adjusted to unfamiliar surroundings.

The shelter's only other resident for life was a senior dog named Chance, who'd been blinded by a bout of parvo when he was young. Tonight, Mia was sketching Chance. With the help of some strategically offered treats, he was hanging nearby while she drew him in several different poses.

He was a cream-colored cairn terrier who'd become a shelter legend due to his knack for reading people. It had become unofficial shelter policy to test Chance's response to potential adopters. It didn't matter that he was blind; he could sense people who had good animal karma and those who didn't. Mia was going to paint him eagerly greeting a young child.

In between sketches, Mia sank to her heels and gave

him a generous scratch on his belly. "You know, boy, I'm pretty sure every side is your best side." She offered him another treat, and after munching it up, he flopped back onto his side, hoping for another tummy rub. Mia laughed, unable to resist offering a scratch that sent one back leg into a flurry of motion.

She'd stood up and was attempting to discern which of the three sketches best portrayed his perpetually upbeat attitude when the front door jangled open. She jerked as it occurred to her that since she'd been working alone and it was after hours, she should've locked the door behind her when she'd come in. In the chaotic aftermath of late, she'd been forgetting things like that, little things like when to take the garbage out, things she'd never given much thought to before.

Fortunately, it was just Ollie, rushing in from the night-darkened parking lot, and Ben, trailing behind him.

"Hi, Mom!" Ollie zoomed over to greet Chance, who was rising to his feet to greet him. Ollie dropped to his knees. "Miss me, buddy?"

Chance knew most of the staff and volunteers by smell, and Ollie had been coming with her often enough that the terrier knew him too. As Ollie plopped to the floor and stuck his nose against Chance's, Mia turned to Ben.

Her cheeks seemed to warm just as much as they had yesterday when he'd come to the house. He was a friend, she reminded herself. He had been for years. This didn't need to be any different than slipping back into a comfortable pair of shoes she'd not worn for a few months. There was no need for her blood to race at the sight of him.

Only it did.

Tonight he was wearing black jeans and a light-gray sweater that was just snug enough to highlight his remarkable build, and his hands were tucked noncommittally in his back pockets. With his dark hair and eyes and classic good looks, he reminded Mia of a stunning night sky. She attributed that to his eyes more than anything. They were an impossibly dark brown, almost black, complementing the reserved air he had about him. He had the understated confidence of someone who'd made it to the top of Mount Everest and back down safely but didn't go out of his way to tell anyone about it.

"Hey. We spotted your CR-V in the lot as we passed by."

"I meant to text you. I guess time got away from me. How'd Taye do?"

"Good. Great, actually. Nailed his lines."

"Did he? Great! I'm sorry I missed it." She released a breath. "I honestly thought I was going to crash, but I couldn't sleep."

It occurred to her that if anyone knew who Brad had been sleeping with, it could very well be Ben. He and Brad had grown apart a bit over the years, but at one point there'd been no secrets between them.

Mia wasn't entirely sure why a part of her cared as much as she did, and if Ben did know something, he wasn't showing it.

He joined her in front of the mural wall and silently appraised the sketches. Ben's architectural talent made her squirm under his inspection of her fresh sketches. She reminded herself that he'd praised her work before.

He'd even chosen to support the shelter because Ollie loved it so much.

"They're all Chance, right?"

"Yep." Mia hadn't realized he knew the shelter animals well enough to identify Chance in a rough sketch, but then again, the terrier was a legend around here. "I was trying to find the best way to show his upbeat attitude."

Ben turned his attention to Chance. The happy dog had rolled onto his back, and Ollie was scratching away at his belly. One of Chance's back legs was thumping hard enough it could still be heard over Ollie's adorations. After a smile lit Ben's face, he motioned toward one of the sketches. "They're all good, but this is my favorite. The way his ears are forward while he's sniffing the girl's sandal takes years off but still shows his age. That isn't easy to do in a 2-D sketch."

"Thanks."

When she'd met Ben for the first time, he'd had a dog, a Lab mix who'd died a few years ago. Before he left for Nepal in April, he'd mentioned wanting to get another dog when he got back, but he hadn't yet.

"It'll be different," she said, "not working in pastels. I'm a bit worried it'll look flat. It's so easy to show light and dimension in pastel work. I'll be using acrylics, so the project will have more of a cartoonish look than I'm used to." Drawing portraits of dogs and cats had become her specialty, Mia reminded herself, and she was determined to rock this mural.

After pausing just long enough to give his words importance, Ben said, "You showed both in these sketches, and you were only using charcoal. You'll be able to do it."

She was about to thank him again when he reached out and brushed his thumb above her left brow, smoothing away what she guessed was a smudge of charcoal from not being mindful of the mess on her fingertips.

Mia stilled at his gesture. She could pretty much recall the number of times Ben had initiated any form of physical contact between them, and it wasn't many. His touch sent an unexpected jolt of electricity down her limbs.

She swallowed as she realized a part of her was trying to memorize the feel of it. It had been a long time since she'd savored a man's touch.

"You look tired, Mia." He dropped his hand and returned it to his back pocket. "And before you tell me you're fine and you've got everything under control, just try to remember you don't have to do this alone."

Her shoulders dropped. "I know that. I do. And thank you. It's just so complicated." She stole a glance at Ollie to make sure he was still one hundred percent absorbed in Chance. He was. "There is something I was, uh, hoping to ask you." She did her best to keep her tone light, but emotion crept in at the end, and it was clear by the way his brows furrowed that he'd picked up on it.

"Did he…did he tell you what it was that he told me before I left?"

She'd wanted to ask so many times before. After today, she was done holding back.

Ben's look was sharp and direct. "Yes."

Mia exhaled a breath she hadn't known she was holding. To keep the anger pressing in at bay, she busied herself by gathering up her charcoal pencils. "I don't know if it was her or someone new, but there was someone

after I left too." She stole a look at Ollie. He was giggling as the eager dog licked his palm. "The funny part is that when he broke it to me about the first time, he said it was ten minutes in a car. That it meant nothing."

"Mia, he—"

She held up her hand. Her insides might as well have been a shaken soda bottle. She struggled to keep her voice low and calm so as not to draw her son's attention. "And up until the end, he was begging me to come back." She nodded toward Ollie. "For Ollie's sake, he kept saying."

Before continuing, she pressed her thumb and forefinger against her temple and forehead. The headache from earlier was returning. "I went back to the house yesterday to get some things." She stepped close and dropped her voice. Ben was at the hospital the night she delivered Ollie four weeks prematurely. He was there when she was taken in for a hysterectomy. *He knew*. "I know you'll understand the significance when I tell you I found a condom wrapper on the bed."

Surprise flashed across Ben's face, and it was obvious he understood. His mouth fell open as if he were about to speak, then closed again. From the tightness that suddenly lined his jaw and the way his lips pressed together, she could tell he was more than surprised. He was angry.

His shoulders tensed, and he crossed over to the Cat-a-Climb, the now-empty cat play area that was part of his renovation designs. Mia followed him.

Across the room, Chance had switched from licking Ollie on the hand to the neck, which was the next available patch of bare skin, and her son's laughter had

escalated. This made a part of her wish to be seven again and to have the world full of small, surmountable problems. *Like losing a father?*

No, journeys weren't necessarily easy at any age.

"I'm sorry, Mia. I don't know what to say."

She straightened. "Do you know who it was?"

He shook his head abruptly. "No. Not even a clue. Those last few months, we barely spoke at all."

She wanted to unleash a tirade of all the things she'd been holding in, but she heard a quiet voice reminding her that all she was doing was airing her soiled laundry in front of Ben.

Shaking her head, she stepped back a foot. "I should get Ollie home."

She'd turned and started to cross the room when Ben caught her hand. His dark-brown eyes were fierce with intensity. "Mia, it wasn't you. It was *never* you. You and Ollie brought out the best in him; it just wasn't enough. But that was his failing, not yours."

Mia nodded and blinked back a flood of tears she'd not expected to press in behind the anger. He stepped in before she could brace herself. It hardly seemed real. She was in his arms, tucked against him, hot tears spilling onto his sweater.

And it was comforting in a way nothing else had been in a long time. Knowing it couldn't last long, she wrapped her arms around his hips, soaking up a bit of the strength that carried him up rock faces that seemed impossible to scale. After a few, practiced breaths, she found her voice. "It was hard for so long."

His arms locked around her tighter, one around her back, the other hand locked tight over her hair, cradling

the back of her head. "It's over now. You can heal. No one wanted it to happen like this, but it's over all the same."

Mia pressed back a sob. There was so much there, slamming against the surface even harder because of Ben's words. She wanted to give in and sob into his shoulder like a child, but across the room Ollie was still giggling at Chance. The last thing he needed right now was to see her fall apart.

With a strength she didn't feel, she shoved the tears down and stepped back. She dragged the cuffs of her sleeves over her eyes and sucked in a shaky breath. "I just… I can't." Her throat locked up, preventing her from saying anything else. It was too big a truth to admit that if she held on to Ben now, she'd never want to let go.

And even if a part of her didn't want to admit it, that wasn't what any of them needed right now.

Chapter 6

MIA LOVED HER SATURDAY MORNINGS VOLUNTEERING at the shelter more than any other morning of the week. The happy place had been a part of her weekly routine for half her life for a reason. The animals and the success stories were more healing than therapy to her. And the staff and volunteers had become like her extended family.

She'd been bringing Ollie with her since he was still a toddler. Back then, he was content to pet Chance and Trina or watch the cats in the Cat-a-Climb. Now that he was older, to keep him busy for a three- or four-hour stretch, she'd bring along a tote bag full of fresh books. He'd sit for hours in front of the cat cages and dog kennels and "read" to the animals. For the most part, Ollie's version of reading was to look at the pictures and make up his own stories.

Some of the staff and volunteers had noticed that while Ollie was plopped in front of cages, flipping picture-book pages, and telling stories, he often held the interest and attention of the dogs and cats he was reading to. So much so that Megan was checking with the shelter's lawyer about starting an official kid-oriented reading program, and Mia was crossing her fingers it would happen.

This morning, Ollie was plopped in front of a row of seven dogs that ranged in size from wiener short to

Great Dane tall. He made up story after story from the two illustrated Harry Potter books included in today's reading bag. As she cleaned kennels, Mia heard him saying endearing things like "Since you're dogs and not birds, it'll be hard to imagine flying in a car almost as high as the clouds. You probably don't even notice the clouds, but they help make the sun not so hot in summer, and they bring snow sometimes in winter."

His fantastical stories warmed her heart as she cleaned kennels and rotated the dogs in and out of the play yard. As she worked, she changed out their dishes and offered fresh toys for the day.

She was bringing in Clara Bee from the play yard when Tess asked her, Patrick, and Adrianne, a volunteer, to join her and Megan in the front room for an impromptu meeting.

Mia got Clara Bee settled in her kennel, exchanged yesterday's chew toy for a new rope, and gave the sweet dog a pat on the head. "Sweet girl, one more day and you're headed to your new home. I may cry when you leave, but I promise they'll be happy tears."

Finished with Clara Bee, she asked Ollie to relocate his reading stool to the Cat-a-Climb in the front room. The timing was perfect since he was in the process of switching out books.

Ollie trailed after her without complaint, and Patrick, who'd been hosing out a newly empty kennel, followed, eyeing Ollie a bit dubiously. Patrick was great with animals—spectacular, actually—and a bit awkward around adults, but he looked at kids and babies as if they were alien life-forms. Mia was well versed in Patrick's eccentricities, having known him

for the six or seven years he'd worked there, so she'd never taken offense. Thankfully, Ollie hadn't seemed to notice.

Up front, everyone was gathering around Megan, who was on a stool behind the main counter. A bit uncharacteristically for a Saturday morning, especially one less than two weeks before Christmas, the only customers were a man and woman speaking in Russian over by the cat kennels and a woman heading out the door with two bags of gift-shop purchases.

As soon as everyone was together, Megan gave them an apologetic grimace. "So I know it's our busy season, but I've just canceled the Saturday walk, and I'm hoping to divert as many of us as we can get by without over to Forest Park. My friend Bernie from animal control called. A jogger spotted some lady freeing several dogs from the back of a van near Steinberg Skating Rink. From what Bernie said, the dogs are loose and running everywhere in the park."

"By freeing, do you mean dumping?" Fidel's mouth turned down in a frown.

Megan gave a helpless shrug. "It sounds like it. Animal control has two people on it, Bernie and another guy who's having a hard time on the uneven ground after a knee replacement. There are way too many dogs running around for them to handle. And you know as well as I do, the longer it goes, the more likely these dogs are to end up strays. If we go now, we could help catch them while they're still safe in the park."

She paused and looked around at the group. "Insurance-wise, I can't send anyone out to work on an active dumped-animal roundup...*but* anyone who'd

like to take a break for a walk around the park won't be asked to make up their hours. Hint, hint."

"I'm *so* in." Tess raised a hand high, sending her long, dark hair tumbling over her shoulder. "I'll call Mason too. I bet he's up for it. Now that he's so bonded with John Ronald, he's a total sucker when he hears anything about a stray dog."

"Great, Tess. The more, the merrier. We shouldn't go as far as bringing catchpoles, but we could load up with the best treats and bring slipknot leashes. We have six open kennels. Any dogs we're lucky enough to catch could be brought here or fostered into homes while animal control figures out what their owner was doing."

Fidel offered to go as well.

Patrick, on the other hand, was less fond of abrupt routine changes and looked at his watch with a furrowed brow. "I'll stay and cover the front. You'll need a skeleton crew here. Unless you want to lock the doors. But as today is the second-to-last Saturday before Christmas, that wouldn't be in the best interest of the current stock. Five or six animals could get adopted this afternoon."

"I was hoping you'd offer to stay, Patrick. I know you'll have everything handled."

Mia raced through her options. She desperately wanted to go, but bringing a seven-year-old along on an attempt to catch unknown dogs wasn't the smartest thing to do.

"I'm almost done in back and would love to help," she said. "Let me see about getting someone to watch Ollie." She stepped off to the side to call Irene and wasn't that surprised when Irene didn't answer. Her mother-in-law hadn't been quick to answer many of Mia's calls in the

last few months. Even if she returned the call later, it would likely be too late for Mia to join the group.

Mia sucked in her lower lip. Her mom was in Kenya where she'd spent the last fifteen years teaching. A few friends who had kids Ollie's age came to mind as possibilities, but Mia decided to try Ben instead. Over breakfast this morning, Ollie mentioned that he'd been invited to join Ben and Taye on whatever outing they had planned later this afternoon. And an outing with Ben and Taye would be one of the few things Ollie would be happy to leave here early to do.

Ben answered on the third ring. "Hey, Mia." He was breathing hard enough to catch her attention, and his voice was strained.

"Uh, is this a bad time?"

"No. I'm at the climbing gym with Taye."

She did a double take as she put the obvious together. "Are you on a wall right now?"

"Ahh, maybe."

"How high? Do you want to call me back?"

"I'm good. Taye's belaying me. And he's doing a great job."

Mia laughed. "How is it you don't drop your phone?"

"It was zipped in a pocket. And I wouldn't answer it right now for just anyone."

A swell of happiness radiated out from her chest. "Well, if you're sure you don't want to call me back, remember yesterday morning when you said I never ask for help? I'm calling with a favor, and I don't even require a mini-quiche to ask first."

Ben chuckled and agreed even before Mia dove into the reason for her call.

"You can't say yes before you know why I'm calling. I could be asking you to hop on a raft and float down the Mississippi with me. Wait, what am I saying? You climb mountains high enough to enter the death zone. You probably wouldn't blink an eye at that."

"You're right. Anytime you want me to float the Mississippi with you, I'm game. Even if Huck Finn and Jim did it first."

Ben would float the Mississippi with me. Not that she actually had any desire to do that. It was just the way he'd agreed. The ease in his tone. Her peculiar sense of delight was seeping down into her fingers and toes, but with a bit of effort, she forced her thoughts back on the reason she'd called in the first place. Once she'd finished filling him in on what was going on in Forest Park, Ben easily agreed. "Yeah, sure, but do you have any idea what kind of dogs they are, or why they were dumped?"

"I don't, actually. Megan got a call from her friend in animal control. All she knows is that a dozen or more dogs were let loose in the park this morning. We're hoping to catch some and bring them back here."

After a pause of a second or two, Ben said, "Tell you what, Taye's been up a couple times, but before we leave, he wants another shot at the top. I'll meet you at the park in forty-five minutes and hang out with the boys until you're finished. If you'll agree to join us when you're done, we'll figure out how much time the boys have and where they'd like to go."

Something about the way he said it caused Mia's cheeks to flush. They'd hung out together before, loads of times, she reminded herself, but that didn't calm her rush of nerves.

She agreed, and they committed to meeting in the parking lot by the Steinberg Rink, a spot where they'd be able to find one another in the sprawling park.

Then, with a rush of excitement swelling inside her, she headed over to tell Ollie the news.

—∞—

Right after pulling onto Jefferson Drive, less than a quarter mile from where he was meeting Mia, Ben had to slam on his brakes. A dog—he was guessing a border collie, judging by the color, shape, and size—dashed in front of his car. It jumped sideways as the Jeep jerked to a halt.

The striking black-and-white dog looked up at them and woofed. He woofed again and ran in a circle around the Jeep before dashing off, bound for the sprawling lake to the west.

"That dog is *sweet*," Taye murmured.

As the dog sprinted toward the lake's eastern shore, Ben spotted a small flock of ducks congregating on the water's edge. Clearly, the dog had spotted them as well. As Ben watched, the dog skidded to a halt at the edge of the lake and began rushing back and forth and barking as the ducks flapped their wings and rushed closer toward the middle.

A fisherman standing on the bank nearby attempted to shoo him off.

Ben often jogged the trails in the park and couldn't recall having spied a stray dog within the park boundaries before. In addition to its miles of trails and typical park amenities, Forest Park also held the city's zoo, art and history museums, and planetarium. The thirteen-hundred-acre park was too busy for strays to take up residence in it.

But at least one of these recently dumped dogs was having a heyday.

If the rest of the dumped animals were as energetic as this one, it wouldn't be easy to catch them. In an open, flowing park such as this, the dogs weren't going to be cornered. They'd have to be cajoled with treats and encouragement, but they'd have to tire out before being enticed by such things.

Although Mia had only asked him to watch Ollie, Ben intended to lend a hand, and he was glad to have Taye with him. Ben pulled into the parking lot in front of the rink. Seeing a small crowd of ice skaters out on the ice, he raised an eyebrow at Taye. "You ever skated before?"

"Me? Nah. But I bet I could cut some grooves into that ice."

"It's harder than you might think. But you're a natural athlete, so maybe you're right. We could give it a try later, if we can talk Ollie and Mia into it after we round up some of these dogs. What do you say?"

Taye studied the skaters. "Yeah, that's dope."

Ben humphed at Taye's expression as he stepped out of the Jeep. The temperature was hovering just under forty degrees, but the sun was out and it was shaping up to be a pleasant mid-December afternoon. "What does your mom say when you say that?"

"You met her. 'Dope' ain't mother language."

He chuckled. "Yeah, well, it's not seven-year-old boy language either, if you can help it." Taye had turned thirteen in November, and Ben had noticed more changes in him the last few months than in all the time he'd known him. He figured it was a combination of puberty and

middle school. He was a good kid, though, and he was great with Ollie. Ben figured he'd gotten practice helping to raise his three younger siblings.

As he shut his door, he saw that Mia and Ollie had already arrived. They were standing by the edge of the rink, watching the skaters. As always, Ben's chest tightened at the sight of Mia. Seeing her was a blend of torture and pleasure. He could scarcely imagine one day giving in to his desire and, instead of offering her a simple nod as he and Taye approached, pulling her into his arms and pressing a kiss to her cheek or, better yet, against those remarkable lips.

Mia's cheeks were flushed an enticing light pink, and Ben wanted to lose his hands in the chestnut hair that framed her heart-shaped face, showed off her gray-blue eyes, and drew his attention straight to her mouth.

"Morning, guys. So, we passed one on the way in," he said instead.

"Did you?" Her eyebrows lifted in surprise. "Ollie and I pulled in five minutes ago. We didn't see anything."

"It's just over the hill, running along the edge of the lake. Judging by the excess energy it seemed to have, I'm guessing it won't be there long." After Ollie stepped in with a bear of a hug, Ben ruffled his hair. "How you doing, squirt?"

"I wanna help Mom catch the dogs, but she says it may not be safe."

"Let me figure it out with your mom. We'll come up with something."

Ollie mumbled in agreement and turned to Taye to ask about the dog they'd seen, and Ben refocused on Mia. "Still no idea who dumped them and why?"

She shook her head. "Nope. I think the police are looking for the dumper. All Megan was told was that a woman was seen freeing them from the back of an old conversion van. That was nearly two hours ago now. You'd think they'd have run off that energy by now."

"Yeah, no kidding. So where's the rest of your group?"

"Driving around, searching for signs of them." Mia pulled a walkie-talkie from one jacket pocket. She had a drawstring bag slung over the other shoulder, and a leash handle was poking over the top. "If you're good with the boys, I'll head up that way and radio them if the dog is still in sight."

"If you don't mind, I'd like us to stick together. I could drive you around in the Jeep. The boys can help look out."

Mia dropped his gaze for a second, then met it again. "Yeah, sure, if you want."

"I do want," he replied, causing her blush to reappear. "And Taye and I were talking about doing some ice skating when we're finished. How's that sound, Ollie? Assuming we can talk your mom into it."

Mia looked from Ben to Taye as Ollie gave an enthusiastic yes. "You're good with all this, Taye?"

"Yeah, it's cool," Taye said. "But if we catch that dog we just saw, Ben, you gotta keep him until I can convince my mom to let me have him."

Ben laughed and shook his head. Taye wasn't going to quit until he had a dog of his own. The kid took his aunt's dog out whenever he could, but she'd would never part with Callie for good. "Sorry, kid. I'm not making any promises there. Your mom is going to have to make that decision when it's right for her."

"Come on, man. You know I've wanted a dog forever. And that one's the one. I know it."

As the group headed back to Ben's Jeep, Ollie chimed in with a similar request of his own, and Mia laughed as well. It was good to see her laugh.

In minutes, they'd transferred the two kennels Mia had brought to his Jeep, the boys were loaded in back, and he was driving back up Jefferson Drive. As they crested the hill, Ben was disappointed but not surprised to find the dog seemed to have moved on. He scanned the roads and surrounding hillside but didn't find so much as a trace.

"Hey, wait," Taye said as Ben pressed the gas pedal to continue on. "I think I just saw him. He ran that way. Into those trees." Ben followed the direction Taye was pointing. It was a small clump of trees on the northeast side of Jefferson Lake.

"Was it black and white?" Ben asked.

"Yeah, I think. Mostly it was just white, I guess. I don't know. Maybe it was one of his friends."

Ben looked to Mia. "I can drive around, but we'd have to leave the car along Faulkner Drive. I jog the trails there sometimes. There are smaller ponds and wetlands that way that I bet the dogs would be drawn to."

Mia shrugged. "Sure. It's worth a shot."

Chapter 7

MIA WAS GLAD IT WAS SUNNY AND THE WINTER WINDS were light. It was the perfect day to be outside. Ollie was usually good for a mile or so of walking, unless it was summer and the sun was scorching. Then his shoulders would slump like they were made of hot wax, and he'd complain every step of the way. She was hoping the excitement of looking for dogs would help keep him going for a while.

The rest of the staff and volunteers had dispersed in pairs throughout the park and were maintaining contact through the walkie-talkies. Fidel and Sarah, one of the volunteers, seemed to be the closest at the moment, perhaps a few hundred yards west. Half a mile away, Megan and Adrianne had come close to catching a dog on the golf course, but the skittish animal ran away before they could get the slip leash over it. Tess and her boyfriend, Mason, were scoping out the woods across from the Jewel Box after a jogger pointed them to where one of the dogs had been sighted. From what everyone could gather, none of the dogs seemed to have a collar, and so far, almost every one of them seemed to fit the description of a border collie.

Mia shook her head that a dozen or so wound-up border collies had been let loose in the park. At the shelter, the crew was always saying that just when you thought you'd seen everything, hang around a bit longer.

Mia was certain this unofficial rescue effort would be talked about for a while to come.

As they'd headed up Faulkner Drive to the spot where Ben parked the Jeep, she'd spotted two different news vans on the park roads. Mia wouldn't be surprised if it turned out they were here to cover this story.

For nearly half an hour, she and Ben and the boys scoured the quiet waterway, a restored section of River des Peres that flowed through this section of the park, but didn't spot a single dog. Along the waterway's banks, they turned up several water birds, dozens of squirrels, and one groundhog, but there were no signs of the escaped canines.

The first few minutes around Ben this morning had been both awkward and exciting, and Mia had had to force herself not to think about the wink he'd added to the text or the way he'd said he wouldn't answer for just anyone. Somehow, he was both the Ben that she knew well and yet he wasn't. After taking a few minutes to process it, she'd realized she was okay with that.

And it made her want to know what he was thinking.

Mia was about to suggest they look elsewhere when Ben called her attention to the large prairie wetland south of her. Mia was standing on the Victorian Bridge that had been in the park prior to the 1904 World's Fair, and Ben was fifty feet ahead on the wetland walking trail. Taye and Ollie were at the water's edge, poking sticks into the mud after not having any luck with their search.

"I must have scanned past it a couple of times, but look over there in the cattails," Ben called. "On the other side of the wetland. Its coat is reddish brown and white, so it blends in, especially in the sunlight."

Mia scanned the thick cattails but didn't see what he was talking about until she picked up on a slight movement in the brush. A dog was sprawled at the edge of the wetland, collapsed on its side and nearly camouflaged by the tall wintry-brown grass surrounding it. Even from here, she could make out the folded forward, triangular ears that were a common characteristic of border collies. Its mouth was hanging open in an easy pant, as if the animal was exhausted but content. *Well, at least one of them has gotten worn out.*

Since Mia was farther back than the rest, it made sense for her to circle back first. She cupped her hands and called to Ben. "Want to stay there where you can see her?" When he gave her a thumbs up, she added, "Yell if she takes off. I'll circle back and come up behind her. Once I'm south of her, you can come back around and flank her on the north side." She couldn't say why, but she had a suspicion the dog was female.

Ben agreed with her plan, so she asked Ollie and Taye to stay put, then walk with Ben. Soon, all four of them were in place on the west side of the wetland, the boys flanking the middle, and she and Ben on opposite ends. The prairie grass was so thick, it was impossible to see if the dog was still in her spot, though Mia hoped to spy an area of rustling grass if the dog took off.

"Ollie and Taye, remember not to grab at her if she runs your way," she reminded them. "Since we don't know how she is around people, you shouldn't do anything more than toss some treats to her. Ben and I'll decide whether or not to try to catch her, depending on how she's acting." Then to Ben, who was now about a hundred feet away, Mia called out, "I'll go in."

Ben's lips seemed to press into a frown before he nodded, but from here that was possibly just her imagination.

Mia headed into the dried prairie grasses, most of which were chest high. She did her best to meander through the least dense pathway possible in hopes of not scaring the dog away with a noisy approach. The further in she got, the more loaded with burrs and fluffy seed pods her furry fleece jacket became. She raised an arm and blew at some of the fluffy pods. "I'm a walking dandelion."

Closer to the water, the grasses were even taller. Eventually she was meandering through cattails that were over her head, and the spongy ground under her feet soaked through her shoes and moisture-wicking socks.

Although she could hardly see more than a few feet in front of her, she hadn't heard Ben call out that he'd seen the spooked dog running off, and she hadn't heard her jump into the water either. When she reached the edge of the wetland, Mia headed what she hoped was north based on the angle of the sun. She was doing her best to orient herself in the tall grass when she heard a startled yip directly in front of her.

Mia stopped in her tracks. The dog was just feet away. As frightened as the poor thing appeared, Mia was surprised she hadn't run off. Instead, the startled animal jumped to her feet and faced Mia, letting out a single growl that rolled into a startlingly loud warning bark. Then, almost immediately, the beautiful animal sat back on her haunches and cocked her head cautiously up at her.

"Easy, girl. I'm not going hurt you." Moving slowly

but confidently, Mia pulled a couple of moist treats from her jacket pocket and held them out. She was by no means an expert, but knew now that she had the dog's attention, it was important to maintain nonthreatening eye contact and not make any sudden movements. She wanted to keep the dog's attention without scaring her off. "Something tells me you're hungry after all that running."

Mia held her hand steady, not tossing the treats or overextending her reach. With the border collie's keen nose, she'd be able to smell them.

"How'd you wind up in here by yourself, girl? Did you get lost, or are you a loner by nature?" The dog was strikingly beautiful up close. And Megan had been right; she was collarless.

From the dog's distinctive coat pattern, Mia knew she was a red merle. The remarkable-looking animal had soft brownish-red patches of fur that blended into creamy white along her belly and legs. The top of her head was mostly dark brown, and she had light-brown, almost golden eyes. She looked grungy and her coat was matted in places, but that might've happened this morning while running loose in the park. Otherwise, the remarkable animal showed no obvious evidence of being mistreated.

Rather than backing away when Mia clicked her tongue, the dog barked again, causing Mia to jump in surprise. It was quite the ear-piercing bark for a dog her size. Perhaps the tall grass surrounding them was channeling it in her direction. Hoping to entice the dog closer, Mia sank to the balls of her feet and extended her hand with several treats on her fingers.

The border collie cocked her head and wagged her tail, watching Mia intently. When the curious animal neither moved closer nor backed away, Mia tossed a few treats in her direction. The pretty girl bent to sniff them, her eyes still on Mia, then swept them up with a few quick flicks of the tongue.

Still offering a soft stream of praise, Mia fished into her pocket for a new round of treats. She was extending her hand when the dog burst forward and began inundating Mia's chin with eager licks.

"Good girl!" Mia exclaimed before it occurred to her to make fast work of sliding the slipknot leash over the dog's head and pulling it snug with one hand while drawing the dog's attention to the treats with the other. "Well done, Mia Chambers," she murmured to herself.

When the dog didn't mind being petted, Mia gave her a thorough scratching of her shoulders and hoped it would take the dog's attention off the fact that she'd been caught.

Keeping the treats extended but just out of reach, Mia stood up and started to coax her in the direction of the car. At first the sweet-tempered dog followed along willingly, intermittently jumping up in attempt to reach the treats.

By the time they were out of the cattails and making their way through the shorter prairie grasses, the dog seemed to notice the leash around her neck for the first time. She stopped following Mia and shook her head, then sat on her haunches to scratch it with her back foot. When that didn't work, she started tugging backward and barking. Mia held tight, terrified she was going to lose her grip.

The dog's panic escalated the way many shelter puppies did the first time they felt the tug of a leash, making Mia suspect this dog had never been walked on a leash before. She held tight while the dog tugged and lurched and squirmed. Even though the four-legged creature was only thirty-five or forty pounds, it was all muscle. The jerks and jars raced along Mia's arms, settling in the joints of her elbow, shoulders, and neck.

She was debating how long she could hang on when Ben reached her. "I don't…think she's…ever been leashed," Mia managed to get out.

Ben slipped off his jacket and circled behind the panicking dog. Mia was impossibly close to losing her grip when he lunged forward and clamped his jacket over the top of her, draping it over her face and the upper half of her body. To Mia's surprise, it was as if a switch had been flipped. The dog went from intensely struggling to frozen in half a second.

"I thought I was going to lose her." Mia exhaled. "Thanks, Ben."

"Yeah, well it looked like she was going to tug your arms out of their sockets." Hands clamped over the jacketed dog, Ben raised an eyebrow Mia's way. "You okay?"

Mia rolled her shoulders and shook out her hands. A sharply stinging case of rope burn was setting in. "Yeah, I'm good."

Ben lifted the dog into his arms. "How about we save the leash lesson for later?"

"I won't argue that."

Not wanting the extra leash to trip Ben up, she draped it over the dog's covered back and Ben's shoulder and

got a strong whiff of wet dog in the process. "Whoa! I'm pretty sure that's wet dog at its worst."

"Yeah, no kidding. She must've gone for a dip in the wetlands earlier."

"How are you not gagging?" Mia fanned her nose.

"Spend seven weeks acclimating and climbing Everest, and you'll never think the same about how things smell."

She laughed and squinched her nose. "While you were climbing, I think I read a lifetime's worth of blogs about life at base camp and higher. I don't even want to try to imagine."

"When you get high enough, the saving grace is that it gets too cold to smell anything."

"I don't know how you made it through any of it, honestly." Mia suppressed a shudder and pulled the walkie-talkie from her pocket, mindful of her stinging palms. She turned up the volume after having muted it as she'd headed into the grass. She'd not wanted the crackly sound to scare the pretty girl off. Fidel was talking; he and Sarah had caught a dog as well.

"We just caught one too," Mia offered when he finished. "We're in the wetlands north of Steinberg Rink. She was deep in the cattails. She's friendly and she's had treats before, but it doesn't seem like she's ever been on a leash. She was freaking out. Now Ben's carrying her in his jacket. Her face is covered, so she's calm."

"Awesome, Mia! And Ben!" Megan piped up on her walkie-talkie. "Adrianne and I just got one who was chasing a jogger through the park. He ran into our arms when we finally got his attention. I wouldn't put him at more than eight or nine months, and I doubt he's ever

been leashed. After a few complete flips trying to free himself, he surrendered. But like you said, he's friendly as can be. I wouldn't guess he's ever been mistreated."

"Same here. And as far as anyone's seen, they're all border collies?" Border collies were a popular, sought-after breed. Mia couldn't imagine someone dumping a dozen of them in the park for no reason.

"So far," Megan replied, her voice crackling over the radio. "Crazy, I know."

Mia slipped the walkie-talkie into her pocket and stumbled on a mound of uneven ground. She caught Ben's arm, her hand automatically locking around his rock-solid triceps. She let go fast. The heat radiating up her arm from her hand wasn't from the rope burn.

"Thanks for helping," she said to fill the silence. "Sorry you're getting all full of burrs. With them and the wet-dog smell, I owe your jacket a dry cleaning."

Ben gave an almost imperceptible shrug of one shoulder. "I'm happy to be here. And I wouldn't have left you to do this alone."

His answer made her breath catch in her throat. For the second time in one day.

They took a few steps in silence, the only sound the rhythm of their feet and legs as they pushed through the dried grass. When the silence felt more intimate than his words, she felt a need to fill it. "How old do you think she is? I'm guessing two or three, though border collies always look young to me."

"Your guess is better than mine."

Mia ducked to inspect the portion of the dog's belly that wasn't covered by Ben's jacket. Several distended teats were visible, and the encircling hair was patchy,

LOVE AT FIRST BARK

thin, and short. "She's had some pups, that's for sure, but it doesn't look as if she has active milk now."

She glanced over her shoulder and scanned the tall grass behind them for any sign of movement. "I think I would've seen if she'd had pups nearby, don't you?" She stopped walking and closed a hand over Ben's arm, intentionally this time. "Ben, I won't sleep tonight if I don't go back and check. There probably aren't any, but I have to make sure."

He'd stopped alongside her, and his brown eyes held her locked in place for a solid second before he nodded. "Go. I'll get her in the crate and come back and help. She'll be safe inside it. What about the boys? Let them hang out in the mowed grass, or do you want their help searching?"

Mia glanced over at Ollie, who seemed happy enough to be hanging out with Taye. "They can decide. I'm sure they'll want to help you get her situated first. Tell Taye if he wants to help search, I can deburr his clothes before you take him home."

When Ben nodded, Mia wasted no time turning back into the deeper brush near the wetlands. She doubted she'd notice any paw prints unless they'd made a significant impression in the spongy ground, something a lightweight border collie puppy wouldn't easily do. She did, however, notice plenty of areas at the base of the grass where small animals seemed to have been moving between the water and drier earth. Without prints, she had no idea if the trails were carved by rabbits, muskrats, or newly lost puppies.

Doing her best to move through the grass in a steady pattern, Mia searched the area as the sun fell behind a

cloud and a slight wind picked up. Her hands were stinging from rope burn. She kept her fingers splayed open to
keep the cool air flowing over them.

Before long, she'd acquired hundreds more burrs and
clingy seeds, enough that she could feel them poking
through her jeans and stiffening her jacket. She made
kissing sounds every so often as she walked, hoping that
if there were any puppies, they'd been socialized enough
to have a positive association with people and to respond
with a whine or bark.

Five or ten minutes into her search, Ben joined her.
"We'll separate to cover more ground," he said, surprising her by reaching for one of her hands. He turned it
over and inspected her palm. "I brought a burn cream
sample from the first aid kit. How bad are they hurting?"

"Just stinging some," she admitted.

Ben tore open the packet and squeezed some of the
creamy, white ointment onto her palm. He cupped her
hand and gently brushed a dollup across her sores. "Tell
me if it hurts."

Tell me if it hurts. So much had hurt for so long… What
could she possibly say to him? His grip was strong and
confident. Mia's insides were in a twist again, the same
as when they were standing on his balcony this summer.

"That helps. Thanks." She swallowed and pulled her
hands away when he was finished applying the cream.
From the corner of her eye, she noticed the boys meandering the wide berth of prairie grass on the west side of
the wetland. Would they notice if she stepped close and
wrapped her arms around him? If she buried her face in
his chest and soaked up the feel of him like she wanted
to? If she told him all the things that hurt?

Before she could summon herself into action, Ben headed into the deep grass in the opposite direction.

Mia was left to calm her racing heart and refocus on the search, with her hands stinging in a different way.

Another five or ten minutes passed, and Mia began to feel it was fruitless. She was going to feel bad if the extra search was for nothing, considering the burrs they were all accumulating.

Over at the edge of the road, Ben had left one window of his Jeep down. Even this far over, Mia could hear the border collie's wildly irregular bark. If Mia could hear it, so could any puppies that had been accidentally left behind. Surely if there were puppies in this mess of grass, they'd be crying for their mother.

After a while, Fidel radioed in that two more dogs had been caught on the far side of the park. Both were fully grown border collies. Mia wasn't sure if the person responsible for this would turn out to be a breeder who'd reached their wit's end in terms of care, or if this was the work of a border collie hoarder.

She was close to giving up the search when she and Ben met up in the middle of the grassland a second time. Ollie and Taye were thirty feet away, and Mia could hear Ollie starting to whine that he was tired. Probably because Taye was taller and better at creating a path in the grass, Ollie had been following him around the prairie while carrying a tall, bent cattail like a wand.

Instead of meeting Ben's gaze, Mia studied the burrs on his jacket. It was a sleeker material and had accumulated far fewer than her furry fleece, but it still struck her how the seeds and burrs in the creases of his elbows and along his sides gave him a certain vulnerability

she'd never spotted before. He was so athletic and lithe that *vulnerable* wasn't a word she'd ever associated with him.

"I think you were right to insist on this, Mia. When I put her in the crate," he said, oblivious to her thoughts, "she wanted something in this direction, and badly. If it comes to that, we can try walking her around here on the leash again. Maybe she'd get over her dislike of it enough to lead us to whatever it is she wants."

Mia was about to reply when a soft sound not far behind her caught her attention. "Did you hear that? It sounded like a sneeze. A tiny one."

"Yeah, I heard it. It came from that way." Ben pointed toward the dense patch of grass behind her.

Mia backtracked and pressed carefully into the dense, dry grass. She scanned the ground but found nothing except a thick crown of fibrous sandy-colored roots that rose above the soil.

"I don't see anything, do you?" Ben was a few feet back, searching too.

"No, but the grass is so thick in here. Do rabbits sneeze? I'm guessing they do."

Then, rather than carefully parting the grass the way she was doing, he noisily shook a section.

To Mia's surprise, a high-pitched yip erupted from the ground near Ben's feet. Mostly hidden in a mess of dried grass, a furry puppy had been startled and was attempting to back deeper into the grass. It just wasn't having much luck. It was sandy-brown, cream, and white with long fur that looked as if it'd be as soft as down if it wasn't full of mud and burrs.

Ben was quick to react a second time, snatching up

the puppy between his hands before it could get away. He tucked the writhing animal against his chest, and the puppy squirmed and growled a comically nonmenacing growl until it realized it was good and captured, then gave up and yawn-whined for several seconds before vigorously licking Ben's sleeve, making Mia suspect it had been dozing.

"Oh my gosh! Nice work! Really nice work."

Ben laughed. "I didn't expect to find one like that."

"What a cutie." Mia lifted the pup's exposed back leg and checked. "This one's a boy."

"What do you want to do now? Do you think there are more?"

Mia scanned the grass in hopes of a glimpse of another puppy. "Since there's one, you'd think there'd be more. Except for the fact that in a strange environment like this, little guys his age should want stick together. What would you put him at, three, maybe four months max?"

Ben lifted the wriggly pup in appraisal. "That would be my guess."

She brushed her fingers across the soft, downy fur atop the pup's forehead. Seeing that the little guy didn't object, she moved on to massage his silky ear. She laughed when, after a grunt, he leaned in to it. "Why don't I call Ollie and Taye over, and we'll make some noise and stomp down the grass around here? If there are any others, it should stir them up."

When Ben agreed, Mia yelled to the boys to come see what they'd found.

After the boys cooed over the puppy, the group spent another twenty minutes stomping down patches of grass throughout the area but didn't find evidence

of any more puppies. When they finally gave up, they reunited the puppy with its mother, and judging by their similar markings and eager greeting, there was no doubt they were mother and pup.

Next, they crated the puppy and slipped the leash back onto the mom. Mia and Ben took turns attempting to lead her back into the prairie, but she seemed to want nothing more than to head back to the car where her pup was waiting. As a last resort, they brought the puppy out and allowed him to walk freely next to his mom, but it didn't help their search. The mother had no interest in anything aside from expressing her annoyance at the leash.

Feeling as if they'd exhausted all possibilities, Mia suggested they call it quits. After all the extra searching, it seemed logical to assume he was the only pup here. And on top of it, a cold front was rolling in, the group was inundated with burrs, seeds, and scratches, and Ollie's stamina had given out.

Maybe they'd try again later, but they'd given their best this afternoon. And thanks to their efforts, two dogs wouldn't be sleeping out here in the cold tonight.

Chapter 8

As soon as he was past the front desk of the city-run animal control department and headed into the stark, astringent, foul-smelling kennels, Ben knew he was committed.

Even before laying eyes on the dog.

Yesterday afternoon, he and Taye had spent an hour or so at the shelter before heading out for dinner, then returning to Forest Park to skate. Including the mom and pup, the group of High Grove Animal Shelter staff and volunteers had managed to capture seven dogs. A second group from a different shelter had been working the park as well and had caught five others, and Bernie and his coworker had gone back to the pound with one lone animal, a young male dog. The animal had been caught after jumping into a young couple's paddleboat in an attempt to get closer to a group of geese he'd been chasing around Post-Dispatch Lake by the Boathouse.

Bernie had texted Megan a picture of the dog, and she'd shown it to the group as they were getting the captured dogs set up in the available kennels. The image was a bit out of focus, but it was a black-and-white border collie straddling the back seat of the paddleboat, looking just a bit sullen and guilty at the same time.

"That's him, Ben!" Taye had said excitedly. "That's my dog!"

Ben had said it was hard to tell from a blurry photograph but had admitted that Taye might be right.

After spending a half hour walking around the High Grove kennels picking at the burrs on his sleeves and quietly studying all the dogs and shaking his head, Taye had pulled Ben to the side.

"That dog we almost hit is the one, man. *My* dog. The one I've been waiting for. You gotta help me convince my mom to keep him. You have to. She'll listen to you. She always listens to you."

In front of Taye, Ben hadn't committed to anything. Instead, he'd commented that even if Taye's mom was ready, which Ben wasn't willing to bet she was, the shelter was full of great dogs that needed homes.

"This is different," Taye had insisted. "I can't explain it, but didn't you ever just know something? Like really know it? This dog is my dog. We're meant to be together. I just know it."

Ben had had to work not to let his gaze stray to Mia. Yes, he knew what Taye was talking about. Knew what it meant to have someone or something touch your soul and not be able to explain it to a single person.

He'd taken Taye home soon afterward last night. This morning, when'd he'd woken up and not been able to get Taye or the dog out of his thoughts, Ben had driven here.

And even before laying eyes on the dog, he knew he was committed to whatever it took to get the animal out of here. This was no High Grove Animal Shelter. This was a city-run pound. The animals brought here were strays, confiscations, or simply lost, and the ones who weren't claimed by their owners within seventy-two hours had dismal odds of adoption.

He followed the short, shuffle-footed worker down a long row of kennels. When they reached the third kennel from the back, and Ben spotted Taye's dog lying at attention like a sphynx, watching their approach, Ben became doubly committed.

"This the guy you were describing?" the control officer asked.

Ben took in the long-legged, black-and-white dog watching from the middle of his kennel, not barking, his head cocked at attention. The dog's eyes were bright, and he had an alert, energetic look. He suspected Taye would have his hands full with this one.

"Yeah, that's him."

Ben's first dog had been an energetic border collie that his dad had brought home after taking it off the hands of a woman he'd dated for a month or two. Like Taye, dogs had topped Ben's Christmas list for several years running. He'd been eleven and had done his best to train her but had his hands full. Too full, his dad had decided. Ben came home one day to find that his dad had given her to a colleague.

If Ben had had somewhere to go, he was so furious he'd have left too. Eventually, time had buffed the sharp edge of anger, and Ben had chalked it up to another way his father had failed him. When he was fifteen, he got a summer job busing tables, a year before he was hired at the climbing gym. As soon as he had enough saved, he biked to a facility a lot like this one and adopted a stocky-legged Lab mix that he named Winston. He showed up at home with the dog unannounced and somehow made it clear that this dog's presence in the house was nonnegotiable. His dad never spent a cent on

the dog, and Ben couldn't remember him ever laying an affectionate hand on him either. But he'd allowed Winston to stay, and that had been enough.

He was the most loyal dog Ben ever had. And while Taye's home life was starkly different from how Ben's was back then, he wanted Taye to have the bond he'd had with Winston.

Spying an alertness in the border collie's eyes, Ben suspected he'd likely need to lend a hand helping to train him. *If* he and Taye could convince his mom to take him. But none of that seemed to matter compared to Ben's wish to give both Taye and this dog the chance he hadn't had in late boyhood.

"He's one of those border collies that was dumped in Forest Park yesterday," the guy said. "Guess you heard about it on the news? Hundreds of dogs just like him move through here in a month, but a story like this airs and people get moved into action."

"I didn't hear about it on the news," Ben replied. He'd heard that Channel 3 and Channel 5 had aired stories about the bizarre dumping of so many border collies into Forest Park but hadn't watched either. "I was at the park yesterday, helping to catch some of the others."

"That right? Then I guess you heard that the police traced the plates and found the woman who dumped them. She ain't coming for him. For any of them. She's a total head case. Said she couldn't afford to care for them anymore and asked the park to care for them for her. Heck, she told the cop that the park had agreed. Not a person; 'the park.'" He made air quotes at the last two words. "One of her neighbors came forward to say the woman hardly ever left her house, and the dogs were

only heard from behind a tall privacy fence in her back-yard. The neighbors didn't seem to realize how many she had inside."

"Yeah, I heard as much yesterday."

"So, what do you want with this guy?"

"I want to get him out of here."

"Afraid that ain't possible. We've got a seventy-two-hour quarantine for every animal who comes through the door. Since he ain't gonna get claimed, when his quarantine is over, he'll get an exam. Depending on how it goes, he could make adoption row. If you're still interested, you can come back then and see."

"I'd like to take him today." Ben wasn't sure of his next steps, but he knew he wanted to get that dog out of this cold and indifferent place. There was nothing in the barren kennel except for a bowl of water.

The dog's head cocked nearly sideways as he studied the two people who'd approached his kennel.

"No can do." The guy counted out the days on pudgy fingers, mumbling as he went. "He'll be examined Wednesday morning per policy. If I broke policy for you, I'd get written up, maybe fired. This case has gotten media attention, which doesn't help him not get noticed. But as long as he's healthy and doesn't show any signs of aggression, he'll come back on the other side of the building Wednesday midmorning. We do our best to give them fourteen days after that."

Ben frowned. If it were a private institution, he wouldn't stop until he'd figured out a way to bring the dog home today, but it was city-run, and as unlikable as the guy seemed, Ben didn't want someone's reprimand on his conscience. "What time Wednesday?"

The man shrugged, and Ben noticed a crust of dried food in his unkempt beard. "Eight or nine. But there's no guarantees the dog'll pass."

"I'll be here Wednesday morning. Guarantees or not, see to it that he passes."

Ben held the man's shifty gaze long enough to make certain he'd been understood, then headed out of the unpleasant building.

Between now and Wednesday morning, he'd get a crate and some supplies ready to house Taye's dog until he could convince Taye's mom their struggling family needed another mouth to feed. Ben shook his head as it dawned on him that he hadn't imagined any of this when he'd answered Mia's call yesterday morning from the climbing gym.

It was different, letting her in. Ben still needed reminders it was okay to let the image of her remarkable face linger when it came to mind, when he was so used to pressing it down and repeating that she was another man's wife. Or letting her smoky eyes stir his soul when she met his gaze or her sultry voice waken the long-slumbering heat in his belly.

For the last eight years—and truth be told, for years before that—the only uncertainty Ben had allowed in his life had been in his climbing. And even then, to stay alive at high altitudes and on near-vertical slopes, he'd been forced to operate with rigid control.

With Mia in his world, he was going down a path that would bring a dog into his home for who knew how long. He'd not had a dog for a few years now. He'd been climbing too often in recent years, away from his loft in downtown St. Louis too long to give

in to any whims he'd had in recent years to adopt another.

The truth was, with Mia in his world, Ben figured he could be talked into anything.

Chapter 9

MIA DRUMMED HER FINGERS ON THE COUNTER MONDAY morning as she attempted to Skype her mom for the third time in a few hours. It had become their routine to check in twice a week, Wednesdays and Sundays, but her mom hadn't picked up yesterday's call and had been MIA all week aside from a single short email.

All day yesterday, Mia's thoughts had been spinning between the moving encounter with the mom and pup in Forest Park and the few hours after getting them settled in a kennel in quarantine. The few hours that were spent skating in Steinberg Rink and grabbing a quick dinner at Fitz's where, even despite the cold, Ollie and Taye sucked down root beer floats in glasses as tall as their heads and giant burgers as well.

She kept telling herself that Ben was Ollie's godfather, and she had no reason to feel guilty for spending a few fun hours with him. Though she knew perfectly well that the way her heart had been racing most of that time was causing the guilt more than anything else.

Ben had been a big part of Ollie's life for years, and him taking Ollie out for a night of fun was nothing new. Until now, though, Mia and Ben's relationship had been pretty much limited to the check-ins before and after outings like Saturday night.

As she'd adjusted to the ice, Ben had wrapped an arm around her waist and even locked his hands over her

hips once or twice. But he was skilled on the ice from years of hockey in his youth, and he'd known her hands were sore from rope burn, so maybe that was expected.

It was innocent fun, Mia kept telling herself. There was no harm in it. Who cared that his steady and reassuring voice in her ear had made her insides turn to Jell-O? Or that his hands on her hips had heated her blood? And even if she was crushing on him, that didn't make her a bad person. Her marriage had been all but over long before she'd walked away in August. Even if there had been honest-to-goodness flirting, which there hadn't been, there would've been no cause for objection.

She was itching to talk to her mom about Saturday night, even if she dished out advice Mia didn't want to hear. Lynn had a knack for getting to the heart of the matter, and she was a "take your medicine straight" kind of woman.

Mia also wanted to tell her mom about the rescue in Forest Park and the dogs they'd found. She hadn't told Ollie yet, but she'd made the decision to foster the mom and pup full time at the house, and she wanted her mom's okay to keep them here. The house had belonged to Lynn since Mia's grandma passed away six months ago. Lynn had no intention of returning to live in America in the foreseeable future. While her mom had given her permission to stay indefinitely, Mia still felt as though she should get permission to bring dogs into the house full time. And even though she'd be taking the dogs on a foster basis, she had no reason to think she wouldn't one day follow in the footsteps of dozens of other shelter volunteers and create a foster fail by adopting them.

Suspecting that her mom's rural Kenyan school was having internet problems again, Mia typed out a quick email instead, comically begging for forgiveness about the dogs rather than permission since she had no idea when Lynn would get to read it.

As she looked around her grandparents' small home and thought that starting tonight, two dogs would be pattering around these wooden floors, Mia's stomach flipped in excitement and with a bit of nervous indecision as well. Brad's life insurance policy had been paltry. Even once his car and the house were sold, she was quite possibly going to have an income shortage. But even knowing this, bringing the mom and pup home felt like the right thing to do.

It was Christmas, and Ollie still believed in Santa. He might not recover some parts of his years of easy laughter and make-believe and having both his parents at his disposal, but he could still enjoy the magic of the holiday season. And the happy noise and commotion the dogs would bring would make the quiet winter nights a lot more joyful.

Determining to keep the news a secret from him until the dogs were there, Mia's next call was to the shelter, asking if she could foster the pair after the vet examined them this afternoon. Patrick answered and took a message for Megan. True to form, he took the news matter-of-factly, adding that the new mastiff who'd come in yesterday could use the larger quarantine kennel that had been allotted to both mom and pup late Saturday afternoon.

Mia was stepping out of the shower when Megan called back, bubbling over with excitement about Mia's

decision to foster the pair full time. She also offered to loan Mia some of the costlier supplies from her personal stash. At her house, Megan had two spare kennels and a stair gate, as well as a few ceramic bowls and leashes.

Megan lived in Webster Groves too, a mile and a half away, but on a considerably more fairy-tale street than the one where Mia had grown up. Mia arranged to meet Megan there when she went home for lunch.

When Mia pulled up to where newlywed Megan lived with her husband, Craig, she parked alongside the curb, admiring the stately brick two-story house and lush flower beds lining the home. Megan was in the front yard with Sledge, the gorgeous German shepherd she'd adopted over the summer.

As Mia got out of the car, Megan met her at the curb and pulled her in for a hug. Sledge had trotted along at her heels. The remarkably trained dog even waited to get Megan's permission before stepping close to greet and smell their visitor.

"I have news," Megan said. "Bernie called. You guys were right about there being only one puppy."

"Really? Thank goodness. It seemed like that, but I'll sleep better knowing no puppies were left out in the cold. I guess the woman's talking?" Mia bent down to Sledge's level and gave him a brisk rubdown on his neck. His back leg lifted off the ground and thrummed the air to the beat of Mia's scratching.

"Yeah. She signed over custody of the dogs in lieu of charges being pressed against her. She had thirteen and described each one. Apparently, the conditions in the woman's home weren't altogether deplorable, but they weren't good either. And she said some things that

triggered doubt about her sanity, like how the park had promised to care for the dogs until she could afford their food again."

"Wow. Well, I hope she gets the help she needs. And in the meantime, all her dogs get adopted into great homes, including the one who ended up in animal control."

"Yeah, I hope so too. Her signing off like that makes everything less complicated for adopting them out. And since they're border collies and it's Christmas, I have high hopes for quick turnarounds for them. You're coming by around three to meet the new vet, right? He's doing the dogs' exams."

"Sure. Ollie gets out at three, so I'll be a bit late. I guess I'm still a bit out of the loop. I didn't know there was a new vet. What happened to Dr. Washington?"

Megan's shoulders dropped. "He's retiring. He's been talking about it for a couple of years, but I've been in denial. He's been our main vet ever since I started. It'll be weird not to be able to turn to him for advice."

"Yeah, I'm sure. Hopefully, the new vet's good."

"I don't know about good yet," Megan said, cocking an eyebrow, "but I don't think it's just my pregnancy hormones that had me doing a double take when I was introduced to him last week."

Mia laughed. "What do you mean?"

"All I'll say is that in his scrubs, he looks more like he's auditioning for a guest appearance on *Grey's Anatomy* than he does like a typical vet."

"Funny." Movement out of the corner of Mia's eye drew her attention toward the house. Patrick was walking down Megan's porch steps with an armload of supplies. "Hey, Patrick, I can help." She jogged across the

lawn and awkwardly relieved him of one of the folded crates, then headed back toward her car alongside him. "I hope you didn't come just to help carry things. I could've managed."

"I didn't. We're on our way to the Sabrina Raven estate." Patrick looked to Megan, who was joining them with Sledge still at her side. "The dogs can be adopted out now."

Although the home and land would soon be sold to one of the shelter workers and her boyfriend, the Sabrina Raven estate had been the shelter's off-site location where a large-scale rehab of rescued fighting dogs was taking place.

While Patrick's expression was matter-of-fact as usual, an ear-to-ear smile popped up on Megan's face.

"The injunction that was keeping the dogs in limbo was lifted," Megan added. "Someone who works in the system pushed hard to get the case moved through before the holidays."

"Nice!" Mia gave Megan a high five after setting her crate down next to her trunk. "That's the best news I've heard in a long time. Those dogs have been through so much, and they've come such a long way."

"You're not kidding. I was a believer from the start, but I'm still amazed by their resilience. Kurt's deciding this morning which ones are ready to come over now. There are three or four for sure, he says, plus Zeus, who's going to be adopted straight into a home down the street from the estate, and Toby, who's going back to his previous owner. The dogs who are ready but still need homes will come back with us this afternoon. That's why we're taking two cars. Pepper is one of them. And

her puppies are over eight weeks old and weaned, so they're ready to be adopted out too. Can you believe we're going to have a whole mess of Rottweiler-mix puppies at the shelter right before Christmas?"

Tears unexpectedly stung Mia's eyes. There hadn't been much to celebrate lately, and this joy warmed her like hot chocolate on a frigid day. "This makes my Christmas. I'm not even kidding. And since some of those guys are going on the mural, it'll be great to get to know them better. I'll get to do some on-site sketches of them before I start painting the wall."

Megan pulled her in for a second hug. "Girl, I know your world's in chaos, but it makes me so happy you're going forward with the mural. And just as happy that you're taking on these dogs. It'll be great for Ollie. You too, for that matter."

Mia released a breath. "Thanks, Megs. I appreciate it. I can't wait to start painting, actually. I just need to make it through Christmas first. Most likely everyone else will forgive me for not having the holiday spirit this year, but I can't let Ollie down. Knowing how dog crazy he is, just having the dogs in the house will probably be enough. But I don't want him to miss out on the cookie baking and the light displays and all that. I'm working at the shelter's gift shop tomorrow afternoon during the Ugly Sweater/Cute Mutt contest, and Ollie's coming. He's got six or seven of his favorite Christmas books piled up to read to the dogs."

"He's such a sweet kid." Megan nudged Patrick who'd spent the last minute precisely arranging the folded kennels in Mia's trunk. "Isn't he, Patrick?"

Mia knew Patrick well enough to be certain he'd

heard the conversation, even though he'd not been engaged in it, which was probably a factor of his high-functioning autism. When the shelter was busy, he frequently astounded people with his ability to process two or three simultaneous conversations. He also wasn't one to say anything but his complete truth. "I don't have enough experience with seven-year-olds to answer that accurately, but he's gentler with the dogs than most kids that age."

Mia bit her lip to keep a straight face, while Megan turned away to cover her mouth. Thankfully, Mia knew Patrick well enough not to take personally his lack of enthusiasm for anyone under twenty.

"He'd be touched to hear you say that, Patrick. He looked up to you even before learning you could recall every animal who'd moved through the shelter for further back than a year."

"The more years I'm here, the harder that gets to do. I could give him some pointers, if he'd like. Tomorrow, if he wants. This afternoon, I'll be getting the dogs settled in."

Mia thanked him for the offer—Patrick offering to spend any amount of time with a child was rare—and promised she'd let Ollie know. She shut the trunk and promised to meet them back at the shelter in a few hours.

As she headed to the store for the remaining supplies she'd need before picking up the mom and pup, it hit Mia that for the first time in nearly a month, her heart felt light, and the remaining few days before Christmas seemed to hold a brush of the sparkly promise the holiday had when she was younger.

—ᴧᴧᴧ—

Mia stepped into High Grove's new exam room after getting Ollie settled with his books in front of the cats at twenty after three. It took no more than a single glance to see what Megan was talking about when it came to the new vet. He was young, early thirties maybe, and athletic-looking. He had short, dark hair and bright, greenish-hazel eyes that stood out from across the room. Mia had a feeling there were enough single volunteers about his age here that there'd be no shortage of offers to assist him with the animal checks.

With a dog, an exam table, and three other people, the room was a touch crammed, but it was a dedicated and quiet exam space and far better than not having one. At the moment, a nearly all-black border collie was on the table. Mia was pretty sure he was one of the guys who'd been captured by Fidel and Sarah. Patrick was holding the shivering dog in place while Dr. Wentworth examined him.

"Hi, Mia," Megan said, waving her into the small room that had been converted from the backup storage closet during renovations. "This is Dr. Wentworth. He ended up getting here early, so he's checked out most of the dogs. Dr. Wentworth, this is Mia. She's our volunteer who was interested in fostering the red merle mom and pup."

After exchanging a quick hello with the vet, Mia turned to Megan. "Was?"

"Sorry. Not was." Megan released a little breath. "They're yours still, of course. And other than being treated for worms, they're healthy. All of them seem to

be. But Dr. Wentworth noticed something about the red merle mom and pup that I didn't even think of."

Megan paused and looked at the vet, but he was focused on examining the dog's ears. "They seem to be deaf," she said. "Which isn't a problem, of course. But it'll involve more extensive training on your part. Especially when it comes to the little guy. And I know you're thinking of adopting if it works out, so I wasn't sure how much you'd want to take on."

Mia's jaw fell open. "You know, that explains a lot. I accidentally snuck up on the mom and scared her yesterday, and we got really close to the puppy without him hearing us. And that bark of the mom's. It's *so* loud. I know that's common in deaf dogs."

"When he's finished up with this guy, Dr. Wentworth wants to give you some pointers."

Mia nodded. "Sure. We've had a handful of deaf dogs come through over the years, but I can't think of any puppies. Other than using hand signals, is training that different?"

"There've been two known deaf puppies since I've been here," Patrick said. He was just a little breathless from the effort he was putting out to restrain the young, nervous collie. "Sometimes deafness isn't detected before they're adopted, so it's likely there've been more."

After a quick sideways glance at Patrick, Dr. Wentworth said, "The biggest challenge for deaf puppies is their socialization." He stood straight again and gave the dog on the table an encouraging scratch on the shoulder.

He had great eyes. Not as melty as Ben's, but they were very direct. *What are you doing, thinking about his*

eyes? And really, what are you doing thinking of Ben's eyes right now?

She cleared her throat. "Like puppy playdates and things?"

"Yes. Puppies learn how hard to bite by the squeals of their littermates. Deaf dogs don't always realize that a puppy who pulls away may be doing so to escape a play bite that's too intense. This can lead to their littermates not wanting to engage in play with them."

He paused as if making certain Mia understood, then offered a sympathetic smile.

"At this point, we don't know if he had littermates. I'm guessing he's about thirteen weeks, so maybe they were sold off. Since he was clearly raised with a lot of adult dogs, he was most likely taught the lessons he needed when he tried to play with them. If they were gentle enough with him, he should be fine. He doesn't seem too timid, and that's a good sign. The mom seems considerably more so, so she may have been dealt a few traumatic lessons early on, but I didn't notice any tendency to snarl or snap."

He paused and tapped the exam table with his index finger. "Listen to me. It sounds like I'm trying to talk you out of them. I'm not. Deaf animals make stellar pets. But I do want you to understand that there will be more effort up front."

Mia nodded. "Last night, I brushed them down and fed them, and everything went fine. They were both as sweet as could be, and the mom was super attentive. The puppy seems like any other three-month-old puppy."

"So, you're still interested?" Megan asked.

"Yeah, of course. I don't mind putting in the extra training effort either."

The vet ran his hand along the black collie's back and patted a hip. "Great. Tell you what. Let me finish up with this guy, and we'll take them somewhere where I can give you some pointers."

Mia thanked him and headed out of the exam room with Megan. Megan closed the door and ran a hand over her swollen belly. "Girl, I love your heart. I would've made the same decision."

They both headed straight to quarantine without discussing it first. Inside the room packed full of dogs, Mia scrubbed her hands, then knelt in front of the large kennel where the red merle mom and pup were dozing, cuddled together in one corner. The mom must have been in a light doze because she opened one eye and lifted her head. The puppy was out like a light. His legs twitched as if he was running after something. Mia offered her hand for the mom to sniff. "I'm sure you don't like getting a whiff of our strong soap every time you smell someone, do you, girl?" As soon as she said it, Mia shook her head. "You know, deaf or not, that kind of affectionate talk would be a hard habit to break."

Megan smiled. "If Sledge were deaf, I'd coo at him just as much as I do now, that's for sure."

Mia glanced up at Megan. "So, what do you think of the vet? I was only in there a few minutes, but he seems to really care about the dogs."

"Yeah, I got that too. I guess time will tell, but he seems to know his stuff. I keep forgetting to do it, but he said we should call him Gabe because when people call him Dr. Wentworth, he thinks his father is in the

room and he can't focus. Only I'm not quite sure if he was serious about the dad thing or if he just has a dry sense of humor."

"Dry or not, a vet with a sense of humor? And Dr. Washington sold him his practice?"

"Yeah, right. Poor Dr. Washington. I'm going to miss him, but something tells me that with Gabe around, most of the group won't. At least not the young, single ones. Especially when word gets around he spent a couple years as a firefighter before vet school."

Mia stood up and pointed a finger. "That explains those broad shoulders a lot more than a set of textbooks."

It was Megan's turn to laugh as they headed out of quarantine to wait on the new vet to finish his exam. "Well said, Mia."

Chapter 10

As she scurried from the storage room to the gift shop with a full box of "I Like Big Mutts" mugs, Mia hummed a rendition of "Bells Will Be Ringing" that sounded more like "Sweaters Will Be Itching." Why she hadn't figured out that sewing five yards of holiday tinsel and a few dozen ornaments onto an old green sweater would make for the itchiest thing she'd ever worn, she didn't know.

Not only was every inch of skin itching from the waist up, but the tinsel was poking through her lined bra and into her boobs. And on top of that, she was exhausted. She was just starting to envision getting Ollie to bed early and soaking in an oatmeal bath when she remembered why she was so wiped out. Through no fault of theirs, Mia had been too wired with excitement by the mom and pup's first night in the house to sleep much.

The first order of business yesterday had been to help them feel comfortable. Potty training would be a priority, as would introducing them to sign commands. At Dr. Wentworth's instructions—Gabe's instructions—Mia was introducing the most important signs up front: sit, stay, look at me, and good job. The signs she'd decided to use to communicate these commands were commonly used in dog training: a closed fist for sit, a hand flat out for stay, the American Sign Language sign for "call me" to get attention directed on her, and thumbs up for good job.

Before bringing them home, Mia had given the dogs baths in the shelter's wash station. At first, she'd attributed their odor to a swim in the wetlands. After hearing about the house where they'd been living and seeing that they both needed work in the potty-training arena, she suspected the smell had roots much further back than that swim. As she'd bathed them, she'd wondered if perhaps it was their first experience with a bath. More than likely it was the pup's, but it wouldn't surprise her to learn it was the mom's too.

To conquer the daunting but necessary task, she'd asked Patrick to step in and help bathe the puppy. She'd managed to bathe the mom alone and had had no problem. Rather than struggle, the sweet-tempered dog froze from head to tail when she was placed in the wash station. Mia had done her best to make quick work of the bath, though she'd needed to lather and rinse the mom twice. As Mia's volunteer work had taught her, wet dog was never pleasant, but this wet mom had smelled like a sewer.

As Mia had suspected from their brief encounter, the young mother was as sweet and mild-tempered as dogs came. She'd waited, without a single attempt to struggle away, her only sign of movement a mild tremor rippling across her back and down her haunches, endearing her to Mia even more.

The puppy, on the other hand, had squirmed and struggled and whined loudly enough when his turn came that Mia had paused several times before calling Patrick in to help. She'd never heard a puppy whine that loudly and wasn't sure if it was because he was deaf—deaf dogs, especially young ones, were known to have a

whole range of vocalizations—or if she might be hurting him. She'd made sure the water was lukewarm, and the shampoo was the gentle, hypoallergenic, all-natural brand that the shelter staff used on puppies.

It wasn't until his bath was finished, and he whined just as loudly when he'd spotted the towel being draped over him, that Mia decided he must just have a flair for the dramatic.

Once the mom and pup dried out, their mottled brown-and-white merle patches were shiny and attractive, and the smell radiating off them was only mildly off-putting up close. Mia hoped another bath would rid them of it completely, but she'd give them a few days to settle in before attempting a second one.

Last night at home, Mia had focused on getting them introduced to the house and giving them lots of opportunities for potty breaks in the fenced backyard. Before Ollie went to bed, he and Mia had stood with blankets draped around their shoulders as they watched the mom and pup chase each other around in circles in the pale-yellow light from the floodlights. Once, when the mom had stopped short and the puppy tumbled into her and rolled like a roly-poly, Ollie had laughed so hard he'd dropped to his knees clutching his stomach.

Later, when she'd finally gotten Ollie tucked into bed an hour and a half after his normal bedtime, his eyes had popped open as he pulled out of an easy doze. "I was dreaming about Dad. What about calling them Sadie and Sam?" he'd asked.

While it wasn't the first time Ollie's good memory had surprised her, Mia had still been caught off guard. Three or four years ago, Brad had pitched an idea for

a cartoon series featuring a moose and a grizzly bear named Sadie and Sam. Ollie hadn't been any older than four when Brad had abandoned the idea for a different one, but she could remember how Ollie had loved sitting at the table at breakfast and asking Brad to sketch the unlikely pair. She wouldn't have guessed Ollie would remember that.

She'd answered that they were good names and suggested Ollie try them out a few days to make sure they fit. Even though she didn't say it aloud, somehow she knew right away the names were going to stick, and Sadie and Sam would become a part of this strangely fated journey of theirs. And all morning, the names had fallen easily off Mia and Ollie's tongues.

After working her way through the crowd filling the small but unique gift shop in one corner of the shelter's front room and refilling the picked-over mug table, Mia glanced at the clock. It had been twenty minutes since she'd last checked on Ollie. He was back in the kennels reading his favorite holiday stories to the dogs. Due to the popularity of this afternoon's adoption event, the Ugly Sweater/Cute Mutt contest, two volunteers were stationed in the kennels, answering questions and taking dogs out to the play yards in the back lot upon request. One of the volunteers, Sarah, had promised to keep an eye on Ollie.

And while Mia trusted Ollie not to open any kennel doors or go anywhere else in the building without asking her first, she still checked in frequently. After working her way back through the holiday shoppers, Mia found her son on a short stool in front of Tiny, the gangly-legged Great Dane. Tiny was as calm and

laid-back as dogs came, so the commotion and people and holiday music filling the shelter this afternoon weren't fazing him.

Most of this afternoon's shoppers were clad in gaudy sweaters, taking advantage of the sale. Despite the event's name, anyone who came in wearing a holiday-themed sweater—whether it was tacky, humorous, or just plain festive—received twenty percent off adoption fees, training classes, and gift-shop purchases. There were also prizes awarded every hour for funniest, most original, and tackiest sweaters.

Mia had made her ferociously itchy sweater in antici-pation of this event one quiet night in early November. And even though it was the itchiest thing she'd worn in…well, ever, she was glad to be wearing it. And even gladder Ollie was seeing her in it. Whether they were swimming against it or paddling along with it, the current of life flowed on. She and Ollie needed some fun too.

She squatted beside him, balancing on the balls of her feet and smiling over the two-sizes-too-big pug-in-a-Santa-hat sweater he was wearing that had been handed down from one of the volunteers' kids. He was reading *Snowmen at Night*, oblivious to the craziness around him and heedless of the fact that Tiny was sprawled across his kennel, dozing with one eye partially open.

Ollie also wasn't technically reading. He was looking at the pictures and making up his own fantastical version of the story. In this one, it seemed that the hot chocolate the snowmen were drinking was from a magical cave in Cairo—how he'd thought of Cairo, Mia couldn't guess—and would enable them to survive the heat and rain that melted other snowmen into puddles.

"How you doing, kiddo?"

"Can I have another cookie? I'm hungry."

Mia clicked her tongue. The home-baked cookies on the adoption counter varied in size, but she was pretty sure the one Ollie had picked the first time had been big enough to count as two.

"If you're hungry, how about you eat half the banana I brought, then you can have one more cookie. I'm picking this one out though."

After puckering his lips in indecision, Ollie shrugged, then went back to his book. "Okay."

"I'll be back." Mia squeezed his shoulder as she stood.

She exited the kennels and reentered the front room, her attention momentarily caught by a baby in a young woman's arms. Too young to walk, the little guy was wildly pumping his fists, thrusting forward, and grunting like a gorilla at the young, playful cats dashing up and down the ramps in the Cat-a-Climb as if he could will his way in there with them.

The little guy's excitement made Mia chuckle. Ollie had been much more subdued as a baby. He would've pointed and watched the cats in wonder, but he'd been more like her, a test-the-water-first kind of kid. Mia had a feeling this little guy was a dive-in-and-learn-how-to-swim-later kid.

"Cute baby," she said to the young couple as she passed by.

She didn't give any thought to the fact that they didn't respond until after she'd made it through the crowd to the drawer behind the gift store check-out counter, grabbed the banana from her purse, and was headed over to the adoption counter where the cookies

and cocoa were being served. That's when she noticed the group of three was headed her way.

The baby was dressed in a blue polar-bear onesie, and the tall, thin-as-a-rail girl holding him, who Mia wouldn't guess was a day over twenty, was wearing a snug-fitting reindeer-face sweater with glittery 3-D poms as ornaments hanging from the antlers. Two of the poms were strategically placed over the girl's boobs, drawing Mia's attention to the fact that the sweater was as tight as it was short. An inch or two of bare skin showed between it and her jeans. The guy, dressed emo in all black, was a foot shorter and had a sallow, withdrawn look about him.

The baby was craning his head behind them at the cats as he grunted.

Since it was clear they were beelining Mia's way, she swiped one of the smaller cookies from the counter and turned to face them. "Can I help you with anything?"

The girl stopped a few feet from her and gnawed her lip for a solid second. "He's not much for sitting still."

At first, Mia was confused, but then it hit her that the girl seemed to be answering her "Cute baby" comment.

Mia was about to answer when the little guy stopped craning his head back at the cats and turned to look straight at her. He had big, round cheeks and brilliant-blue eyes and silky, sparse strands of golden-blond hair. In a clear attempt at communication, he opened his mouth and let out a long, plaintive "Ooooh!"

And even though she'd always been more dog crazy than baby crazy, Mia wanted to sweep him into her arms.

"He's trying to crawl but hasn't figured it out yet," the girl added.

"Once they do, they never want to sit still," Mia replied. Something was off. She tried to place it and pay attention at the same time. "Were you, um, wanting to look at a cat? Since it's so busy right now, the more timid ones aren't being taken out of their kennels. But the younger and more playful ones are fine."

The girl shook her head, sending her long hair careening over her shoulders. "I can't have a cat. My landlord doesn't allow pets. She's not crazy about babies either, but we already had a signed lease when Brody was born."

"Oh." Mia couldn't think of any other way to reply; that was entirely too much information. The emo guy had pulled out a phone in what Mia was pretty sure was an attempt at avoidance.

"I wanted to give you something," the girl said, color rapidly darkening her cheeks. "To read. Later."

The girl practically dropped the baby into the guy's arms and shuffled through an oversize bag slung over her shoulder. After a bit of searching, she pulled out a wrinkled envelope.

"Me?" The single-word attempt had been to clarify whether the envelope was something for the shelter or for her personally, but nothing else came out. Adrenaline was dumping into her system. Something was off. *Really* off.

When the girl didn't reply, Mia switched the cookie and banana to one hand and accepted the tattered envelope with her other.

"Thanks," the girl said as soon as the envelope exchanged hands. "We have to go. But good luck with your sale."

Mia wanted to stop the girl from rushing toward the

door but couldn't find her voice. For a second or two, the baby's gaze stayed locked on her before his attention was caught by the jangling bells on the door. Mia wanted time to stand still so she could think. Something was *so* off. Her ears were buzzing.

Somehow, she made it into the kennels and gave Ollie the banana and cookie and a kiss, then forced her legs to carry her to the storage closet. She flipped on the light, stepped inside, and shut the door behind her.

The envelope was a generic return-bill envelope; she could see rounded-letter, girlish print on college-ruled paper through the clear address window. With shaky hands, she pulled out the letter and read:

Mia,

So I guess there's no good way to say this. If there was, I'd have thought of it by now. I wanted to tell you months ago, but it wasn't mine to say.

So I'm telling you even though I know he'll cut me off. But whatever. I'm sorry. That's the first thing. I didn't know you. Marriage bonds—someone else's—don't seem to matter at night in a bar when you've been drinking. At least they didn't back then. I get it now.

Brad was going to tell you, at least that's what he promised. But then you left, and the only thing he wanted was to get you back.

Funny, but now that it's on me, I see how hard it is. So, I guess I'll just say it. We had a baby. Not on purpose. I hadn't had a period in a year. I guess you don't need the details.

But Brad had another child, and it seems to me you need to know about it.

His name is William, but I call him Brody. He's hard to take care of. I feel like I'm sinking sometimes. Was it like that for you? I wasn't planning on having kids. Maybe ever. But I love him. More than I'd ever love a guy. He's just intense. I don't trust many people with him, and my mom's a pothead.

I know it's a long shot, but I could use someone in his life who I could trust. Once you think it over, maybe we can talk.

Sorry again.
Stacey
314-555-0165

Her knees had given out halfway through, and Mia had collapsed onto a box of overstock clothing that was beginning to crumple under her weight. When she finished the letter, she skimmed it again, looking for a punch line or something that might indicate this was all a dream.

No.

She'd felt the truth in the shape of that baby's face and in his eyes and his exuberant personality; she'd just not been able to understand it.

Mia folded the letter and numbly tucked it in the back pocket of her jeans. The truth, great and horrible at the same time, crushed down.

And nothing—big or small or seemingly inconsequential—would ever be the same.

Chapter 11

SOMEHOW MIA MADE IT HOME AND GOT THE DOGS out of their crates and to the backyard. After the playful mom and pup had pottied and run in a dozen circles, they followed Mia and Ollie back inside to the living room. She couldn't possibly think of signs or training or anything right now, so she was just letting them run.

She left Ollie in charge of the dogs while she went into the kitchen to make his favorite quick dinner, pasta with butter and Parmesan cheese. Her hands were shaking wildly enough that Mia didn't manage to get the spoon into the butter tub until the second try. And she was lucky when she didn't splash boiling water all over herself while draining the noodles.

It was a good thing Ollie was completely consumed with the dogs. She was in shock too deep to have much of a filter. If he noticed and asked what was wrong, she didn't have it in her to make up a story.

Mia could hear him on the floor with the puppy and knew by his stifled giggles that he was letting the little dog lick his face again. Ollie's laughter rang out like a strange, distant reality.

She had a seven-year-old son, and she was back to living in her childhood home where everything was familiar and foreign at the same time. Brad's affair had been with someone she'd be shocked to learn could legally buy alcohol, and he'd fathered a child.

A child. Ollie had a half brother.

A sibling had been the one thing she could never give Ollie, no matter how much she might've wanted to. A forever thanks to the car accident she and Brad had been in. She'd gone into labor early and ended up losing her uterus.

But not only had Brad been able to reproduce, *he'd done so.*

There was a baby—*another human being*—on this planet who shared half her son's DNA.

For the second time in an hour, Mia's knees refused to hold her upright. She sank to the floor behind the wall in the kitchen where Ollie couldn't see her. She needed to tell him his pasta was ready, but she couldn't move. It sat on the counter, steaming as it cooled.

A child. A baby. A baby. A child.

Ollie was still laughing, and the puppy was barking. Sadie walked around the corner and approached Mia timidly, sniffing her hair, then her face, arms, and hands. Mia gently pulled her into a hug, and Sadie wagged her tail.

Ollie has a half brother who's going to look more like his dad than he does.

She folded in half at the thought, pressing her forehead against the cool tile floor. She needed to throw up. It would help her focus. It just wasn't coming. Instead, her nausea rolled in slow circles around her belly, like a dryer fluffing a delicate set of clothes.

Beside her, Sadie tentatively licked the back of Mia's ear.

"Mom, are you okay?" Ollie's voice, coming from much closer than the living room, was pitched in panic.

Remembering her son had just lost a father and didn't need the stress of finding his mom in a ball on the kitchen floor, Mia found not only the strength to get up, but to make up a story as well. "Yeah, babe, I'm fine. I lost an earring, and I was playing a game with Sadie while I was looking for it. Hungry?"

"Starving."

For a second, she stared at the pasta, willing herself into action for Ollie's sake. Thankfully, it worked. Mia sprinkled Parmesan on top and handed the bowl off to him.

She realized she'd forgotten the fork when he set the bowl on the table and returned to fish through the drawer for his favorite, a plastic Spider-Man fork that had come in a kid's meal and could never go in the dishwasher.

He returned to the table and hunched over his bowl, as hungry as the puppy when presented with his dinner. "It's cold." Ollie dropped his fork and looked at her questioningly.

"You can microwave it." Mia was trying to hold the numbness at bay by staying active. She was rinsing off a few leftover plates from lunch and setting them in the dishwasher.

"I'm not allowed to use the microwave."

"That's right. Sorry." She shut the dishwasher door and crossed over for his plate on unsteady legs.

"Do you have a headache?"

Ollie's words stabbed her heart. "No, baby, it's just been a long day. And if I did, it would be okay. Big people get headaches all the time. Kids too, sometimes." She pressed a kiss on the top of his head, then lifted his bowl in two hands.

How long would it take Ollie to let go of the fear that had come with losing a parent? His pediatrician had recommended he see a therapist, and Ollie's first appointment was next week. What a hell of a lot of shit Mia would have to give the woman a heads-up about.

It occurred to her it might help for her to talk to someone too, especially now. This afternoon's news wasn't something Mia was ready to tell her friends, any of them. She'd tell her mom of course; she told her mom pretty much everything. But there was the whole living on the other side of the planet and not having much access to technology thing her mom had going on. After promising to do her best to come back and help out as Ollie adjusted to losing his father, but failing due to an expired passport, Lynn was as good as missing in action.

There was Ben. Mia was certain all she had to do was text that she needed to talk, and he'd be over in minutes. He'd put Ollie to bed, and afterward he'd sit here in the kitchen much as he'd done back in her old house.

But she wasn't entirely sure she was ready to tell him this. It was just so impossibly monumental. Somehow, speaking it aloud would make it more real. Then, too, she wondered if he knew her marriage had been all but void of sex for a long time. Ben knew most of what she'd gone through. He'd understand. But what would he think when he heard about this baby?

She must have been staring into the space, because she scorched Ollie's noodles in the microwave and had to start with a fresh bowl. When she finally gave it to him, Ollie looked a good deal less enthusiastic about his dinner.

"Sorry," she said, slipping into the seat next to him.

"Are you gonna eat?"

"Maybe later. I'm still full from that candy-cane cookie."

"Those were good."

Mia ran her fingers absentmindedly through Ollie's hair as the puppy rounded the corner with one of the couch throw pillows in his mouth. This was a total fail of puppy-watching, she realized.

"No, puppy!" Ollie noticed almost as soon as she did and jumped up. Mia was proud to see him run for the replacement teddy bear from Ollie's old stuffed animal collection they'd gifted to the puppy. "Chew this, pup."

When the puppy dropped the pillow in exchange for the bear, Ollie remembered to praise him with a thumbs-up sign, then dashed over to the couch to return the pillow. In spite of her inner turmoil, Mia felt a rush of pride. Ollie was ready for a dog of his own. And it seemed he wanted this one as much as she wanted the mama, even though this high-energy puppy would be a lot of work for a long time to come.

It had only been a little over twenty-four hours, but Mia couldn't imagine letting them go to another home. *Sadie and Sam, you're here to stay*, she thought, giving Sadie a scratch on the head. She was sitting at Mia's feet, watching Ollie eat.

No sooner had Mia thought of this than an image of Stacey in that tight reindeer-face sweater with poms covering her boobs popped into her mind. Rail-thin body, long legs, straight dishwater-blond hair.

At first, there'd only been the shock over the baby. But now something else was rising to the surface.

Ripe, overwhelming anger.

Mia was still coming to terms with how much of herself she'd sacrificed to enable her marriage to work. Brad had been the shiny, bright picture hanging on the wall that other people noticed. She'd been the nail straining to keep him from crashing to the floor. *And he hadn't even been faithful*.

Her thoughts circled back to the bright-eyed baby with his exuberance for everything, especially the cats. Maybe he was innocent and infectiously cute, but that baby had no connection to her. She could tell the girl—tell Stacey—to screw off and do her best never to think about them again. Mia had no responsibility to them.

What had Stacey thought she'd do? Hear her sad story and sign up for babysitting shifts the way she signed up to make meals for meal trains when help was needed? Mia had every right to hate her and zero reason to help her.

Only that your son has a half brother, and you know full well there's a connection here bigger and stronger than you want to admit.

Mia's mom had spent the last fifteen years in Africa dedicating herself to the causes of others. Mia knew what it meant to live selflessly. But she wasn't her mother, and she was seriously pissed.

She yanked her hands out of her hair and dropped them to the table hard enough to rattle Ollie's bowl and draw his attention from the puppy onto her. He'd gone back to sitting on the floor playing tug-of-war with the puppy and had abandoned his dinner.

Hearing the smack, he looked her way with widened eyes as though she was both delicate and explosive.

"Sorry, bud," she said, somehow managing to fake a

carefree tone. "You know those nights when you're falling apart, and I tell you to get some sleep and everything will feel better in the morning? I think tonight that's advice I need."

He nodded and headed back to the table and his noodles. "I can put myself to bed, if you want."

Dear God, Mia, get ahold of yourself. She pulled him into a hug and breathed in his little boy scent — soap and puppy and the lingering hint of metal from his Hot Wheels. A wisp of calm washed over her like the promise of rain on a scorched desert. "I wouldn't miss reading to you and tucking you in for anything."

If she was able to sleep, she'd stay in bed with him and hopefully make it through the night. Only she suspected there was no way she'd be able to drift off in this state.

Ollie stirred his noodles with the puppy chewing at the tips of his thick socks. Finally, it occurred to Mia that Sadie and Sam needed their dinners too. She prepared their food, hands still shaking, and set their dishes on the floor after miraculously getting them both to sit at attention after several tries with her closed fist, a remarkable training success considering how out of it she was.

Ollie wound noodles around his fork, then munched the loose strands from the bottom up as he watched the dogs inhale their food. Both mom and pup ate like dogs who, if they didn't make fast work of their meals, wouldn't have one. Considering the environment they'd just come from, this was to be expected. Mia didn't think they'd ever been mistreated, but they were still a touch underweight and recovering from being confined with eleven other dogs in a closed-off house with their

only access to the outdoors a small backyard sectioned off from the neighborhood behind a tall privacy fence.

After Ollie finished eating, Mia gave Sadie and Sam a second chance to potty, then forced herself to get down on the living room floor with Ollie to play with the dogs. They rolled tennis balls back and forth to one another across the expanse of the hardwood floor. Both the puppy and Sadie chased the balls, pouncing and sliding like baseball players into home base as they wagged their tails. For a while, it seemed like they'd never be able to make a dent in the puppy's energy, or Sadie's either.

Sadie tuckered out first. She picked up one of the smaller, softer balls in her mouth and carried it to a corner where she held it between her front feet and daintily chewed on it. A nearly endless number of rolls later, the puppy tired as well. He plopped down on the floor next to Ollie, his head half-lifted in the air in noncommittal interest as he watched the nearest abandoned ball roll away.

By eight thirty, after another bathroom break, it was time to get them back in their crates and get Ollie to bed. Mia read two chapters of *The Mouse and the Motorcycle* without processing a word as images of a bright-eyed baby and a pair of precisely placed poms swam through her mind. When she was finished, Ollie chose a picture book, *The Polar Express*, and flipped through the pages, making up a wild story of his own. He yawned halfway through and declared he'd finish his story tomorrow night.

He was dozing off before Mia had folded the book shut and placed it on his nightstand. She pressed a

kiss against his forehead, allowing herself to savor his soft, smooth skin. After his breathing was deep and even, she lay there forever, trying to create the same peace in herself by matching her breathing to his even, relaxed breaths.

Only it didn't work. Finally, she slipped out of the room and headed downstairs. Both mom and pup were sleeping peacefully. They were in separate crates placed alongside each other, curled on their beds. The puppy was sprawled out, his back legs splayed wide, while Sadie was curled into a ball.

Mia headed to her grandparents' ancient computer and drummed her fingers as she waited for Skype to pull up. She typed in her mom's screen name and held her breath. *Please, Mom, answer. You're the only one I can tell this to.*

When it rang and rang, Mia collapsed her forehead atop the old wooden desk. She was scraped raw and exposed and needed her mom. It shouldn't matter, Mia told herself. She should be a pro at living without her mom. She'd been managing just fine for half her life.

However, tonight there was a volcanic eruption building inside her, and she needed to let off some steam. If she didn't, she was going to start smashing things.

She could jog. She hadn't jogged in months, and the idea of the rhythmic pounding of her feet on pavement promised to be therapeutic. But it was winter and night, and she didn't want to leave Ollie alone in the house.

With no other escape, Mia thought of the wine. There were still a dozen bottles in the basement, left over on the storage shelves from her grandparents. Her mouth watered at the thought of losing herself in

a glass or two. Some scraped-raw part of her screamed *Yes* even as a more sensible part warned her to find some other way to disassociate from the wild storm of feelings inside her. She'd always been the lightest of lightweight drinkers, and no matter how much self-care she gave herself, hangovers were a constant companion after a night of drinking.

Tonight, the idea of uncorking one of those bold, spicy cabs or merlots and drowning her emotions seemed as if it might be worth the blazing hangover she'd get tomorrow. Half a glass of wine, and she'd be riding a wild buzz; a full glass, and she'd be able to numb the hurt and unspent anger raging through her.

With the dogs dozing contentedly in their kennels, Mia jogged down the steep, narrow basement stairs and over to the storage shelves. She chose a Napa Valley cabernet because she liked the label. She knew nothing about wine and suspected her grandparents hadn't had highly refined wine palates either, so it was a crapshoot anyway.

Up in the kitchen, when she realized the bottle had a screw cap, her faith in her choice waned even more. Not that it mattered much. It would do the trick. She poured the dark-red wine into one of her grandparents' handblown Italian glasses, lifted it to her lips, and let the flavor pour over her tongue. It burned her throat on the way down. She took a break and cleared her throat, bracing one hand on the counter, then drank until she could feel a buzz kicking in, racing through her veins.

"*Damn baby!*" She forced away an image of the little one, only for it to be replaced with a flash of Stacey in that damn reindeer-face sweater.

As if a glutton for punishment, Mia headed to the garage and fished the letter out of the glove box. She'd shoved it in there when she'd loaded Ollie into the car, after feeling as if it had been burning a hole through her jeans' pocket and into her skin.

Holding the letter between her thumb and forefinger as if she were carrying something infected, she came back inside, picked up the wine, and headed for the couch.

"She even writes like a fricking kid." Instead of dots, Stacey finished off her *i*'s with little circles, and her letters were big and round and girlie. Mia read the letter twice more and, on the second time through, stopped a quarter of the way down.

> So I'm telling you even though I know he'll cut
> me off. But whatever.

Mia's vision was blurring fast, but she blinked and stared at that single line, willing it to make sense. She'd read past it the first time, thinking it was a grammatical mistake. "He'll cut me off," she said aloud into the quiet room, punctuated only by the rhythmic breathing of the dogs. That didn't make any sense. Brad was dead. How could he cut her off?

Stacey couldn't mean Victor, Brad's dad, could she? Mia couldn't imagine Brad's parents knowing this and keeping it a secret from her. As imperfect as this made their son look, it also meant they had a second grandchild.

If not them, then who?

Mia chugged another few swallows of wine and gasped. *Ben!* It had to be. This new awareness ripped through her sharper than the sharpest of knives.

She slammed the glass down on the coffee table and processed this new thought. Her buzz was growing, and her thoughts were coming slower. She was flipping hot and still wearing her ugly sweater, and Ben knew this life-changing truth and hadn't told her.

Betrayal washed over her, trailing behind the buzz. How could he not have told her? They were the two people who'd orbited Brad's crazy and stayed. And she and Ben had a history. All those years. All that talk. And Ben had held her hand that night in the hospital when Ollie was born and Brad was in another room being treated for his injuries from the car accident.

Whether she wanted it to be true or not, it had to be Ben. There was no one else. His father had left him a big chunk of money, and he made a good living as an architect. He didn't even have a pet anymore, so he could certainly afford it.

She sway-walked across the room to the kitchen and fished through her purse for her phone. On the way back to the couch, she tugged off her sweater and dropped it on the floor. It was so fricking hot. She attempted to unbutton her jeans but couldn't manage to work the button free, which was all fine and dandy till she had to pee later.

Still burning up, she crossed over to the thermostat and turned off the heat. She hovered next to it when she was finished, trying to remember what she'd been about to do.

That's right. Ben. It was harder to walk, and the room was swaying. Mia sank to the floor close to the coffee table and swiped Stacey's note off the top of it. It took several tries, but finally she snapped a picture

of it. It took another few tries to attach it in a text and send it to Ben. His number was near the top of her texts. She'd texted him yesterday about the dogs being deaf and again this morning about the dogs' first night in the house.

Knowing she was too out of it to type accurately, after searching for the right words to explain the betrayal she felt, she pressed the voice-to-text button and added, "Et tu, Brute."

She squinted at the text that appeared, trying to make sense of it.

    It to brew day

Close enough. She sent the text and dropped the phone on the floor next to her. Her gaze landed on the bottle of wine. She lifted it and shook it. She'd downed a few glasses and fast. She was going to pay for it, and she was most likely going to throw up.

And she didn't feel any better about Stacey and the reindeer-face sweater or about that damn baby. "*Damn baby*."

Her phone buzzed, went silent, then buzzed again thirty seconds later. She knew without looking that it was Ben, but she'd made her point. For tonight at least.

With nothing else to do, she sank to the floor. First she sprawled out. Then when her stomach was a nauseous mess, she curled into a fetal position and closed her eyes.

Finally, sleep was beckoning her. She pushed toward it, ignoring a new round of buzzing that was both impossibly close and far away at the same time.

Chapter 12

UNDER MOST CIRCUMSTANCES, BEN CONSIDERED THE four-year-old Aston Martin V12 Vantage stored in the basement of his converted warehouse loft a wasteful extravagance. It—and a handful of other things he didn't need, including a shit-ton of money—had been willed to him when his father passed away. In spite of years of threats to cut Ben from his will, his father had been generous in death, though Ben figured it had been more his father's attempt to keep the wealth in the family than anything else.

Knowing the Aston was valued almost as high as some of the lofts in his building, Ben intended to sell it. He'd just been waiting for the estate to be settled and to feel a bit more closure. In terms of closure, he'd thought his Everest climb would do it, considering the climbing he and his father had done as a team was probably the only thing he'd enjoyed doing with him.

When he did sell it, Ben had it in his mind to give the money from the Aston to one of the organizations helping to support the Sherpas in Nepal. He'd not meant to put it off, but his father's estate had been tied up in probate for several months, and then Ben had been climbing. Since he'd gotten back, he'd been too distracted with Mia leaving Brad to deal with it.

He'd driven the car a handful of times and had gotten pulled over half of them. For the most part, cops had

seemed to want to see the car up close more than they'd wanted to issue a ticket.

Knowing he could cut the drive from his loft in downtown St. Louis to Webster Groves from twenty minutes to ten if he didn't get spotted by a cop, Ben grabbed the Aston's keys and headed out.

Fricking Stacey. The kid was lost and stressing, yes, but bringing Mia into things like this wasn't going to help her. Brad's parents, maybe. But not Mia.

Mia didn't have anything that Stacey wanted. Brad had had a paltry life-insurance policy, barely enough to cover funeral expenses. And Ben wasn't sure if Mia suspected it yet, but Brad had accumulated a considerable bit of additional debt while they were separated. Ben had rerouted some of the bills to his accountant. He'd been waiting for the dust to settle before talking to Mia about finances. He was hoping she'd let him wipe the slate clean, but he suspected she wouldn't agree to it easily.

But now she'd have to deal with this first.

It had taken him a minute to understand what she'd texted him. The picture was considerably off-center, and he'd had to zoom in before he was able to decipher some of the content of the letter.

Then there'd been the *It to brew day*. Had she meant it was a day to drink? He hoped not. He'd never seen her drink, but he knew she was a lightweight when it came to alcohol. She admitted that freely and stuck to sparkling water at social events.

He picked up his phone and dialed her number again. She didn't answer, but it wouldn't have been an easy conversation over the thrum of the engine. Besides,

he'd made incredible time on the highway and was already exiting.

In Webster Groves, he rolled through the empty streets, passing storefronts including the shelter, and then quaint houses shining under the glow of Christmas lights, emanating a peace that eluded him.

It was two minutes till ten when he pulled to a stop in front of Mia's grandparents' house. Light flowed out several windows past its cottage-like exterior into the night, but the red and white lights she and Ollie had strung on trees and bushes and the house were off. When he knocked but got no response, he jogged around back.

Panic flooded in when Ben spotted her through one of the half-closed blinds at the back of the house. She was lying on the living room floor, clad in a bra and jeans. An open bottle of wine sat on the coffee table a few feet away.

He tried the back door, but it was locked as well. After pulling in a breath, he kicked it full force. It exploded inward, the dead bolt ripping from the frame, and thwacked against the wall.

Sadie jumped up in her crate, barking and alert, having been alerted by the flying debris or the flood of fresh air. Mia didn't so much as stir. Ben crossed over, wasting only a second to assess the situation. The bottle was nearly empty. For Mia, that was a bender. Kneeling beside her, he heard her soft, even breathing as the barking died down, and he exhaled a giant breath of relief.

He grasped her shoulders and shook her gently but persistently until her eyes blinked open. "Mia. Wake up."

She looked at him from behind a tousled mess of hair. Her eyes fell closed, then opened again. She swallowed

and winced, lifting up a hand to bat him away. "Go away." Her voice was sluggish, as if she'd been in a deep sleep, and hearing it made some of his tension wane. "Go. You didn't tell me. I don't want you here. I texted you. 'Et tu, Brute.'"

Ben suppressed an unexpected chuckle. She was drunk off her ass and quoting Julius Caesar. "Wait, was that what you texted? I couldn't figure it out."

Had she meant that he was Brutus? The cut that hurt the most? He gave into the desire and brushed her hair back from her face. When the feel of it against his fingertips stirred the long-slumbering fire in his gut to life, he pulled his hand away. She was shirtless. He was already working to keep his gaze from trailing over her body.

"Mia, I'm sorry. More than you know or I can explain. When you're sober, I'll do my best." He couldn't tell her everything. At least, not yet. But he could explain some of why he hadn't told her about the baby. "For now, please accept my apology and let me help you."

"No. I just wanna sleep."

"Let's figure out how drunk you are first. Did you drink everything that's missing from that bottle?"

Moving with sloth-like slowness, she pressed the palm of her hand against her forehead. Her eyes stayed closed. "I think… Yes. Some got on my sweater." Lowering her hand, she brushed it against her chest, drawing Ben's attention to her pale-pink lace-and-satin bra and, worse, the phenomenal full breasts swelling up from it.

Focus, dumbass. She could have alcohol poisoning.

Her eyes fluttered open as her fingertips connected with skin. "Oh God. That's awkward. I think… I

guess…" She still hadn't attempted to lift her head off the floor, making it clear she was miserable.

"Your sweater's on the floor. Want me to get it for you?"

"No, it's too hot. A T-shirt or something. From my room."

She'd been sleeping in her grandparents' old room, so Ben headed in there. Ollie was in Mia's childhood room. Ben knew from the couple times he'd picked Ollie up over the last few months. She'd given both rooms a fresh coat of paint and new decorations, but Ben was still itching to offer to help her remodel some of the dated fixtures and appliances if she planned to stay here. Running his architecture firm, he'd established connections with remodelers. He could make it happen easily.

He sorted through her closet and chose a soft, light-green V-neck T-shirt.

"I owe you a new back door," he said, returning with the shirt. He knelt, balancing on the balls of his feet. "Can you sit up?"

She nodded but didn't move. Seconds ticked away. Her eyes were closed, and he suspected she was drifting off again.

He closed a hand over her bare shoulder. Even though he did his best not to notice, her skin was enticingly smooth. "Mia, can you sit up?"

When she replied that she could, but didn't make an attempt to do so, Ben slipped his hand under her arm and pulled gently, encouraging her upward.

She shook her head.

"Hey, no falling back to sleep." Dropping her arm, he switched tactics and slid his hands under her torso. He

lifted her gently, slowly, but even so, as soon as she was in a sitting position, she waved him away.

"I'm gonna puke."

He made a dash for the bathroom and the small trash can at the side of the sink. When he returned, she was on her hands and knees, shaking her head.

"This was a bad idea."

"You'll feel better if you can get it out." He sank next to her again and closed a hand over the small of her back, running his thumb in slow circles over her smooth skin. It'd be easier to focus once she was ready to pull on the shirt, but asking her to do that right now would be cruel.

On the other side of the room, Sadie whined softly. Once Mia was in a better space, he'd let them both out to use the bathroom. The puppy, whose crate was butted against his mother's, was still fast asleep, sprawled on his back, his furry legs in the air.

A minute or two passed, but Mia didn't vomit. Ben swept her hair back and struggled to keep grounded in the moment. He returned to the bathroom and grabbed a washcloth from the smallest and shallowest linen closet he'd ever seen. He ran the washcloth under cold water, then squeezed out the excess. Mia's skin had been hot, and she was sweating even though the temperature in the house had dropped dramatically—and he didn't think that was just because the side frame had been ripped loose on the back door. It was thirty degrees outside, but for some reason, the heat wasn't kicking on.

When he returned, she was sitting back on her heels, eyes still closed. He knelt beside her and wiped her face clean.

"Thanks," she murmured.

"Are you feeling good enough to get your shirt on?"

Her eyes fluttered open, and she looked down. "Oh no. It's so hot. I forgot. Yes."

As he helped her slip into it, it occurred to him that'd he'd never assisted a grown woman *into* her clothes. It was quite different from when he'd taken Ollie to play ice hockey and had had to help get him into his gear.

Mia had hips and thighs that Ben wanted to lose himself between and breasts he wanted to savor with his mouth and hands, and it was close to impossible to ignore all that when he was helping slip a shirt over her head.

"When I feel better, remind me to die of embarrassment." Her words were still slow and slurred.

"Why would I do that? You're the most beautiful woman I've ever met. And even if you weren't, there's no reason to be embarrassed."

She opened her eyes more fully and stared hard, her head cocked sideways. "Was I awake just then? Did you really say that?"

"Say what?" Ben repeated, a smile brushing his lips. He reached for her hand. "Come on. Let's get you into bed. You're coherent enough that I'm okay with letting you doze. I'll wake you in twenty minutes and have you sip some water. Even if you don't like it, I'm going to keep waking you for a while."

He tried to help her up, but halfway there, she shook her head. "I can't."

Knowing she'd be better off in her bed than on the cold floor, Ben lifted her before she could protest. He carried her to the bedroom, wishing he'd thought to pull

down the fluffy comforter first. However, as overheated as she felt, she wouldn't be keen on lying underneath it.

As soon as she was down, she curled into a pillow and mumbled her thanks. He jogged back into the living room and grabbed a throw blanket off the couch. He covered her despite her protests, knowing it was important not to let her body temperature drop. He left again, determined to figure out first what was wrong with the heat in this frigid house, then he'd take care of the dogs.

Funny, he thought as he walked away. He'd come here ready to face an onslaught of questions and anger but had gotten neither. Not yet, at least. They were certainly still coming when she sobered up, and he'd face them. Learning about Brad's infidelity had all but severed his and Brad's friendship when he'd learned about it in July. He could tell her how much he didn't approve and how angry he'd been.

But Ben couldn't explain why he'd not been able to trust that telling her this would've been in her best interest. He didn't know how to separate it from the fact that he loved her, that he'd loved her for a long, long time. And how could he trust that telling her wouldn't simply be serving his own best interest?

So he'd tabled it. After hours of tortured thought, he'd convinced himself that not learning the truth yet was better as Mia focused on helping Ollie get over losing his dad.

But for tonight, unexpectedly, he could savor being with her and not feeling as if he needed to lock a part of himself in a vault simply to keep her from noticing how much he loved her. And that was the best thing that had happened to him in a long time.

Chapter 13

FROM NOT FAR AWAY, A SINGLE SHRILL BARK JERKED Mia from the doze she'd slipped into. Her head pounded against her temples, and her stomach was a sea of nausea and sharp cramps. Her body had become an inferno, boiling her from the inside out.

It was torture to move a single inch, but she managed to roll up to a sitting position and braced herself on the edge of the bed. Moving would suck, but she stood up, moving with the care and precision of someone walking over a lake covered in thin ice, determined to at least brush her teeth, wash her face, and have a drink of water.

Halfway across the bedroom, she made a dash for the toilet. Her head threatened to explode, but after sitting next to the porcelain bowl for a few minutes, her stomach began to settle.

She was still facedown over the bowl when the sink faucet turned on, making her jump. For a second or two, she froze as she looked up to see a full-grown man a foot from her in the darkness. Then tiny flashes of memory returned. Ben had been here for the last few hours taking care of her, attentive and quiet and soothing.

She'd let go of her anger at him. She was still a reeling mess about the baby, but she'd forgiven Ben for not telling her, even though she couldn't remember his explanation for holding out on this impossibly

momentous news. Oh well. She'd revisit it with him
when she was sober.

He'd been wetting a washcloth. After squeezing out
the excess water, he swept her hair aside to drape it over
the back of her neck.

The single short strip of cool moisture was welcome
relief to the inferno still inside her. "Thanks. You've no
idea how good that feels."

Aside from the faint-yellow light from a single night-
light, it was dark in the bathroom and adjoining bedroom.
Mia was glad Ben hadn't switched on the overhead light.
She sat back on her heels and accepted a second washcloth to wipe her face. "Ollie hasn't woken up, has he?"

"No, he's out like a bear in winter."

This brought a smile to her face. "When he was a
toddler, he fought going to sleep, but not anymore." Ben
knelt beside her and refolded the washcloth at her neck
so that a fresh, cool side touched her skin. A soft moan
of pleasure escaped. "I don't remember being this hot
from the inside out before. That was the stupidest thing
I've done in years." Gathering her strength, she pushed
up onto her feet and leaned over the sink, first running
her hands, wrists, and arms under cool water. Then she
loaded her toothbrush with toothpaste and brushed away
the acrid taste in her mouth. It was weird brushing her
teeth in front of Ben. Intimate.

When she was finished, Mia felt a bit better. The world
was still spinning and her ears were buzzing, making her
suspect she was still a bit drunk. "What time is it?"

"Close to one. I heated up some chicken broth and
a cup of mint tea. I know you're hot, but both are supposed to be good for a hangover. I can bring them to you

in bed, or you can try the couch. You wanted to head there before you fell back to sleep last time."

"The couch would be nice."

A rush of surprise swept through her as his arm locked around her waist, drawing her against him and guiding her out of the room.

His body was unfamiliar and foreign and alarming in a pleasant way. He had a mountain climber's physique, lithe and strong, with muscles toned naturally rather than from a weight-lifting routine. That much was obvious just looking at him. But feeling his strength against her was disarming.

In the living room, the overhead light was off as well, but two lamps were on. It was light enough that it occurred to her she probably looked like death warmed over. As she cautiously sank against the corner of her grandparents' distressed leather couch, she realized she was wearing a pair of gym shorts and a green T-shirt she hadn't been wearing when she'd put Ollie to bed.

Her surprise must have been noticeable, because Ben said, "You, uh, had to pee about an hour ago and didn't want your jeans back on."

His words sparked a single flash of memory. She'd been standing in the bathroom and stepped uninvited against him. She'd tucked her head into the crook of his neck, feeling the wash of comfort when those strong arms finally closed around her in return.

How long had he held her? She didn't remember anything beyond that. No wonder he'd been so comfortable helping her to the couch. She'd already thrown her drunk self into his arms. And please God, say she hadn't undressed in front of him.

He headed into the kitchen and came back carrying the broth and tea on a snowman serving tray she'd had displayed on the counter. After sliding a coaster out of the way, he placed the tray at her side.

She crossed her legs and cautiously sipped the tea. It cradled her aching belly, so she took another sip. Ben took a seat in the middle of the couch, a respectful foot of leather cushion between them.

"That baby has to be six months old, and all night I kept doing the math." Her voice pitched in anger, stirring her splitting headache. "He didn't tell me he slept with her because he felt *guilty*. He told me he slept with her because he knew he'd fathered a child. He would've taken a DNA test by then. If he even had any doubt."

The muscles in Ben's jaw tightened, but he said nothing in Brad's defense.

"The other day you told me he loved me." It didn't matter that her head felt like it could explode. She needed to say this. "You were either lying, or you were wrong. He didn't love me the way you're supposed to love the person you're with. Honestly, I didn't love him that way either anymore. So maybe it shouldn't hurt so bad, but it does. Even if we were together for Ollie, that doesn't mean I didn't make sacrifices. I was the glue that helped keep him together the last couple years, and he screwed some twenty-year-old kid. And now she has a baby. A half brother to Ollie."

The tears that had been building slipped over her lids. She wanted to weep—to outright sob away the pain—but somehow she contained herself. Her head might possibly explode if she didn't. Instead, tears slipped out as if from a faucet that hadn't been shut off all the way.

"I'm sorry, Mia." Ben closed a hand over the back of her head and stroked her temple with the side of his thumb. Once again, his touch was immensely comforting.

"That damn baby." She swiped away her silent tears. "Before I knew anything tonight, before she said she had something for me to read, when I thought she was just a kid in a tacky sweater, I saw that baby. He looked at me, and I felt this crazy connection. I guess it was because he looks a bit like Ollie, but he looked right at me and smiled, and I had this feeling that I never knew existed before I had Ollie. Like it wouldn't be hard to go to the ends of the earth to protect him."

Before she became conscious she was doing it, Mia returned the mug to the tray and curled into Ben, only without her usual reserve. She pulled close and locked her arms around his torso, burying her face in his chest. Her legs even landed on top of his.

As she remembered them doing earlier, his arms closed around her more hesitantly. Mia didn't care. She savored the comfort of them more than any blanket or pillow could give her. Her tears continued to flow unabated, soaking into his shirt.

"What should I do?" she asked, her voice muffled in his chest. "Tell me what to do. It'd be so much easier if Brad were alive. I could tell them all to go to hell. Only he's not, and now Ollie has a brother and I don't know what to do."

Ben's cheek pressed against the top of her head. "What you're going to do tonight is recover. You have time. Neither Stacey nor that baby are going anywhere. And right now, you're still a little drunk. You'll be able to think about it more clearly in the morning."

She pulled back enough to look at him. She swiped the tears from her cheeks with the angled slit at the neck of her T-shirt. "Do you want to know a secret?"

Ben shook his head. "No, not tonight. Tomorrow, if you still want to tell me."

Mia wasn't deterred. "I was going to break up with him before I got pregnant with Ollie. I was in it, but I wasn't in it, you know? But the condom ripped and I was late, so I took a test and it was a yes, and later when I told my mom I was going to marry him, she said if I betrayed my heart, then surely it would betray me. She always says crap like that. Crap you can't understand, so of course you remember it. You know what I mean?"

Rather than answer, he brushed the tears from her cheeks, then let his fingertips trail along the wetness lining her jaw and down to the hollow of her neck.

Mia wanted an answer, but all she got were his somber brown eyes boring into her. In the space of his silence, it was easy, too easy, to lean in and press her lips against his. And like when she'd pulled against him, he wasn't quick to respond. It was just her, one second tumbling into another, kissing him, savoring the strength and supple-ness of his lips, the shape and feel of the ridge of his jaw in her hand, the shaved short whiskers against her palm.

Her courage came from the wine. She knew that. She was somewhere between fading drunk and hungover, and none of her usual reservations kept her from crawl-ing on top of him in search of more.

Finally, he responded as she sank atop him. His mouth opened against hers, creating an inferno of want and longing inside her.

She'd been married for a couple months the first time

she saw Ben, and her heart had slammed against her chest at the sight of him. Maybe it had been because she'd always had a thing for guys with dark hair and brown eyes, or maybe it had been because of the controlled, quiet air he had about him, but he did it for her. He always had. She'd done her best to ignore it, but she'd wanted this for a long time.

His hands closed over her hips, claiming them, and she ground against him without losing a beat in the kiss. She could feel his body pressing into hers. A few layers of unnecessary clothes were the only things that kept him from fitting perfectly into her.

She was still overheated and her head pounded, but she wanted him, wanted to feel his mouth on her skin, wanted him inside her.

And for a moment, she thought she'd be lucky enough to get it. One hand slid to the small of her back; the other got lost in her hair. His kiss strengthened, his mouth pressing hungrily against hers.

Then, almost as abruptly as he'd responded to her, he was pushing her off him and crossing the room, dragging his hands through his hair. He made it to the breakfast nook at the front of the house adjacent to the kitchen and leaned both hands against the table. "No, Mia. We can't. Tonight's not going be our first time. It isn't right. Not yet. Especially when you consider what brought me here tonight."

She was catching her breath and considering his words—all of them—when headlights pulling into the driveway shone onto his face, dulled only by the thin sheer in the front window. He let go of the table and stood up straight, watching the car pull in.

From where Mia sat, she couldn't see, but she waited silently, attempting to quell her racing heart and wondering who'd be pulling into her grandparents' driveway in the middle of the night.

And wondering what Ben had meant.

She could hear the car idling outside. It didn't make sense. No one would come here in the middle of the night. It was probably a wrong address. *Or it's Stacey. The kid looked like she was on the verge of a breakdown.*

"Are you expecting anyone?"

"No. Do you think it's Stacey?"

"It's a cab. Someone's getting out of the back." Mia heard a car door shut, and Ben's face lit with surprise. "Not just someone. It's your mother."

Mia's jaw dropped open, and the last of her boiling blood cooled on the spot. "I'd ask if you're kidding, but I can see you aren't. I guess now I know why she hasn't been answering my Skype calls."

She shook her head, at once stunned and happy and a little bit angry too. Her mom was here, and as always, her timing was impeccable.

Chapter 14

CONSIDERING HOW SHE FELT, MIA MIGHT WELL BE recovering from a wicked strain of influenza while roofers pounded on the ceiling. But her only ailment was the mother of all hangovers, and the noises were from her mom banging cabinet doors and sliding drawers, prepping for the mandazi she was making for breakfast, and Ollie, down on all fours, crawling around the floor as he pretended to be Sadie's second puppy. Sam was trailing behind him, licking the tops of his heels.

The couch would be more comfortable, but it was out of view of the kitchen. So Mia planted herself at the table in the breakfast room, her knees tucked tightly against her chest, and did her best to ignore the pain in her sitz bones against the hard chair. Rays from the mild December sun streamed in through the front window and against her back and shoulders.

"The last time I had a hangover, Faraja served me a steaming bowl of goat's head soup." Lynn's voice was unnecessarily chipper. "I was skeptical, but it works wonders. That had to be five or six years ago now."

"Oh come on, Mom, please. I can't take those visuals right now."

Lynn tsked as she shook out flour from the bag into a ceramic mixing bowl without measuring it. "It's easy to forget how sheltered Americans are with their preportioned chicken breasts and preshaped hamburgers. Oh

well, the mandazi may not work as fast as the soup, but the carbs'll be a comfort."

Mandazi were subtly sweet African doughnuts made with flour and coconut milk and spiced with cardamom. Lynn made them every time she came. They always made it onto Ollie's lists of favorite things.

Mia had spent the last few minutes analyzing what felt so off about her mom breezing back into her life as if she'd never been away. Her mom gave one hundred percent of herself when she was with her. On the other hand, when her mother was in Kenya for months and years at a time, Mia sometimes wondered if she thought much about her and Ollie and this left-behind life.

It wasn't until Mia realized Lynn knew in which drawer to find the mixer that she was able to put her finger on what felt so different about this visit as compared to the last several. Mia was living in her childhood home again. For the last eight years, Lynn had stayed here when she'd come back to the States and had visited Mia's house in the Central West End as a day guest.

Suddenly, Mia felt uncharacteristically vulnerable about the prospect of living under the same roof with the mother who'd abandoned her fifteen years ago for a greater love, a more enticing opportunity. This morning, probably heightened by her angry, sharp hangover, Mia didn't feel that far removed from the teenager who'd sat at this very table doing her homework, wondering why she was even doing it when the one person she cared to show it to wasn't going to be around to notice she'd done it.

But, as Lynn said whenever the world came crashing down, "Such is life."

When Ollie, still in puppy mode, crawled to the base of Mia's chair and sat on his haunches panting, Mia leaned forward and patted him on the head. "Good dog."

If she knew one thing, it was that wild stallions couldn't drag her from Ollie. True, she'd been a few defining years older than Lynn when she'd gotten pregnant, twenty-two versus seventeen. But the idea of abandoning her son so she could live out a dream felt about as foreign as walking on the surface of Mars.

"Good little puppy," she repeated, burrowing her forehead against the top of Ollie's hair. Sam, who was still Ollie's willing companion, jumped up and began to snap and chew at Mia's hair as it tumbled around.

"I'm the big brother," Ollie said. "I'm showing him how to be a good dog. This way he won't chew on the chairs and pillows. Did you hear me trying to teach him to bark while I was in there? I put his paw to my throat so he could feel it. His barks are so loud they hurt my ears."

"Mine too," Mia agreed. "And good thinking, Ol. I suspect it'll take a while for him to find his bark though."

"Mom, can I go pee outside? If I show him, maybe he'll get it faster."

Mia fought down her automatic "no" response. "That's an interesting idea, Ol, but I don't think it's time to start peeing outside yet. The most important thing we can do is to offer him lots of chances to go to the bathroom out there, and always right as he comes out of his crate. But I did promise you could take them out in the backyard today by yourself. If you want to try it, go ahead. Just make sure you have some treats

and remember to praise him visually as soon as he goes. Show me your signs first, please."

Ollie ran through the short gamut of signs he was using, nailing each one, then dashed for the treat bowl on the counter. He grabbed a handful, stepped over to give his grandma another giant squeeze, then dashed around the corner, grabbed his coat, and ran out the back door. The haphazard thing was opening and closing this morning, but barely.

Although Mia had no memory of it, Ben had busted it on entry last night, then patch-screwed it back together as she'd slept. She'd checked her phone this morning to find a text from him with a brief explanation of how he'd kicked it in to check on her, damaging the frame in the process, and would be replacing it. He'd ended it with a very unsatisfactory "I hope you're feeling better this morning."

And not a single word about the kiss.

Mia wasn't sure she could put it entirely to her hangover as to why this had made her want to cry. She'd thought about addressing the kiss when she texted back and had attempted a few sentences but erased them before sending the message.

Maybe she'd have more courage when she was less hungover. She wasn't in the right state of mind to address the kiss this morning. "Sorry for climbing onto your lap last night and all but sucking your face. It just happens to be a nice one... Your face, that is..." didn't seem like the best way to broach the topic.

No sooner were Ollie and the dogs outside than her mom said, "So I hope you intend to talk fast. I know you, Mia, and I know when you've got something you

need to clear. If we wait till Ollie goes to bed tonight for you to start talking, it's going to be a touch anticlimactic since we'll both be exhausted, me from jet lag, and you... Well, no need to state the obvious."

Mia straightened in her chair till the tips of her shoulder blades nearly touched. Her mom's dramatic flair often had the opposite of its desired effect and goaded her into silence. Just not today.

"It turns out Ollie's got a half brother."

Lynn paused with the cap of the coconut milk an inch above the counter. "I don't... What?"

"A baby. You know about Brad's affair. It seems he left behind a six-month-old baby."

After a few seconds of silence, her mom sat both carton and cap on the counter and walked over to the table. Before sinking into the nearest chair, she swept her long, breezy African-print skirt out of the way. She had Mia's oval face and gray-blue eyes, but her skin was aged from the sun and her hips were wide enough that they seemed to create the rhythm to which her skirts flowed.

"I thought you were going to tell me you and Ben had gotten together. The energy was in the room when I walked in last night. But a baby... I didn't see that coming."

Doing her best not to get hung up on how perceptive her mom proved to be time after time, Mia ignored the comment about her and Ben and the energy in the room and attempted to focus on thoughts of the baby. She could only clearly remember a few minutes of last night, and nearly each one of them had been while she was kissing Ben. She'd been worried that

she'd been too drunk to gauge it accurately, but judging by her mom's comment, the kiss had in fact been a magnificent one. A terribly timed magnificent kiss. "The baby's mother wants to know if I'm interested in having him in Ollie's life," she said instead.

"Oh, does she now? Well, that answer's simple enough. *No*. If you want another child in Ollie's life—in your life—you can adopt. If you don't, well, the world needs more only children. Only children are self-motivated, and let's face it, there's the population issue to consider. And the last thing you need is to clean up another one of Brad's messes."

"Mom, I really wasn't asking for your opinion. You wanted to know why I drank. So I told you."

Her mom studied her longer than necessary before answering. "I can see you're still processing this. What did Ben say?"

Mia swallowed. "I was drunk. I don't remember him sharing his opinion on the baby. Mostly he just let me talk. Or babble, more accurately."

Lynn sucked in an exaggerated breath before returning to the counter. "My advice to you is to give it time, but once a rock is carved by water, it's always carved, even after the water's diverted."

Mia groaned. "Mom, can you please skip the imagery and just say what you mean? I have a headache and everything hurts and my patience is about as thin as it's ever been."

Lynn stirred the mandazi mix, then added several dashes of cardamom, also without measuring. "My first great love was your father. You know that."

Of course Mia did. The story of her mom's gargantuan

love for the father Mia had never met was something she'd never forget. In her mother's words, it had been the type of love that "if you let it in, could swallow you whole. Only it doesn't because it's the love you're meant to have." Until she'd given birth, Mia had granted her mom a bit of exaggeration due to her natural poetic flair. But she'd felt that way about Ollie from the first second she held him in shaky-from-anesthesia arms. It was the most powerful emotion she'd ever felt.

"Loving your father the way I did was the first time I stepped out of my safe place," her mom continued. "I was sixteen when we got together and seventeen and pregnant with you when he died. You and Africa are my two other great loves, and I'm sure these are the only three I'm meant to have. Of course I love other things, like Ollie and the children at my school, and Imari, who's been joining me in bed a few nights a week for almost six years, but it isn't the same."

Mia was never sure how she felt about being one corner of her mom's triangular all-encompassing loves. Over the years, her mother's explanation had often felt like an excuse. *Sorry, Mia, I've given you fifteen years, but Africa has been calling. If your father had lived, we could've raised you there together. Without him, I've got to choose between you.*

Maybe her mom hadn't put it in those exact words, but that was how it came across all the same. Over the years, it had bothered Mia sometimes more than others. She'd even given an impromptu speech in college about it shortly before graduation. The final speech was to cover influences in art and life, and she'd been planning to give an entirely different—safer—speech on Monet.

She'd had a few dozen note cards and a well-rehearsed speech ready to go. But instead, when it had been her time to present, she'd left her note cards on her desk and gone up to deliver a short, totally unpracticed speech on how her father's absence, and her mother's life choices after losing him, had been the most important factors governing not only the art she'd created, but her life.

The words had tumbled out. She'd almost lost her courage halfway through, but had found it in a pair of kind eyes. She'd spoken from the heart and, even just minutes after delivering the speech, could hardly recall a single thing she'd said. What she remembered was the silence that had hung over the room when she finished. There'd been no questions, no applause. One girl, after wiping her eyes, tentatively raised her hand and thanked Mia for her openness.

She'd done it hoping for a bit of closure. It had helped. A little. She'd beelined out of the theater as soon as it was over.

But that was the past. Rock carved by water, as Lynn had said. What mattered now was deciding what was best for Ollie, and for her. She spent the rest of the morning shoving away alternate images of the remarkable lips she'd gotten lost in and the bright-blue eyes of an inquisitive baby who seemed to have looked into her soul.

Chapter 15

I HOPE YOU'RE FEELING BETTER THIS MORNING. OF THE million things boiling up to the surface as he'd texted Mia, that was all Ben had allowed himself to add to the impersonal message before pressing Send.

He could've done better. Far better.

Ben paced the parking lot at the side entrance of animal control, waiting for the animal health examiner to arrive. Did Mia remember kissing him? Her buzz had been waning but not gone, and the day's events had left her uncharacteristically vulnerable. He didn't trust himself to say how much it had meant when she'd climbed onto his lap in a beautiful moment of surrender. It had been raw and real, and it had come from the heart just as it had on the balcony this summer.

But he didn't know how to tell her how much it meant without telling her everything. The layers were too entwined to pull one truth apart from the rest.

All he could do was give her time. He was typically one to ascribe things to coincidence over fate, but he suspected there was a bigger reason than chance that her mom had arrived when she had. Before spotting the cab, he'd been close—too close—to crossing that room again and forgoing any sense of better judgment to heed the white-hot fire racing through him. Instead, he'd spent a half hour listening to Lynn gripe about the U.S. embassy and her general distaste for the elitism of passports as

she rummaged through the cabinets searching for ingredients to make a stomach-settling tea for Mia.

Now it was a few minutes before eight on Wednesday morning, and temps had dipped into the twenties last night. Ben rubbed his hands together to fight off the cold. The animal control building didn't open to the public until ten, but when he'd called yesterday, he'd gotten hold of Bernie, the shelter director's kind-hearted connection there. Bernie had shared that the animal health examiner—in Ben's mind the judge, jury, and executioner—arrived at this time to evaluate the dogs before the doors opened.

Bernie suggested that an early-morning reminder of Ben's interest in the wily border collie wouldn't hurt matters.

A few minutes past eight, a middle-aged guy with pasty-gray skin and a faded, alligator tattoo extending up his neck headed toward the employee entrance, a thick set of keys dangling from one hand. He looked equal parts hard and depressed, and Ben hoped Bernie knew what he was talking about by suggesting Ben meet him like this.

"Which one is it?" the man asked with a sigh before Ben uttered a single word. His tone carried the resignation of someone with disdain for the responsibilities of his job but who also wasn't interested in making the changes necessary to free himself from them.

Ben took the man's lead and responded just as frankly. "He's a young border collie, black and white, less than a year old."

"The one captured in Forest Park? I noticed him yesterday. Doesn't care much for confinement."

"Yeah, well, I wouldn't either. I'm not sure if you've heard, but over half of the dogs he lived with are under the care of the High Grove Animal Shelter. They're healthy and acclimating great. And I'm committed to whatever it takes to care for and acclimate him as well."

"That can be easier said than done, or we wouldn't have so many dogs moving though here like we do." He jangled his keys, sorting through them until he reached the one he was after. "Building opens at ten. Come back then. I know who you want. I'll do my best to clear him as available for adoption. So long as he isn't aggressive, I can hold him for you until a quarter after even if we don't have the space for him."

Ben considered his options. He wanted to know what traits defined aggression in these trying circumstances, but he didn't want the words to come across as a challenge. Pissing the guy off might only give him a reason he didn't have now to find something wrong with the dog.

It took reminding himself of his belief that people mostly did their best and were true to their word to be able to let go of his indecision. "Thank you, sir. I have faith that your best will be good enough to make that happen. And I'll be here waiting at ten."

Ben left, feeling the man's eyes on his back for several seconds, and headed back in the direction of his loft, which was two miles away. Coming here, he'd seized the opportunity for movement after being awake and restless since well before dawn and had chosen to walk rather than drive.

He had a mound of work waiting for him that included wrapping up the designs for a green home remodel far

out in the county. It was one of the projects he'd been most passionate about lately, and he hoped to wrap the designs up today. After last night, he'd not been in the space in the early-morning hours to focus the attention the project warranted. The property owners wanted to remodel an older ranch in dubious condition into something both modern and sustainable. Ben's designs featured recycled and reclaimed construction materials, solar panels, sustainable landscaping, and water efficiency, among other elements.

The problem was, even hours later, his blood was still simmering hot and he knew he wasn't in the space to focus on the project this morning. As he walked, the freezing air finally began to cool the inferno inside him. The North Face coat he was wearing was warm enough, though he'd have done his hands a service to have grabbed a pair of gloves before heading out. Three fingers on his left hand stung sharply. They'd been affected by frostbite on his descent, and the nerves were still sensitive to the cold. By the time he neared his building, they were hot and stinging. He'd never needed gloves in St. Louis, but he would this winter if he was outside for any duration, due to mild but lingering nerve damage.

But having to wear gloves was a small price to pay for his successful summit of Everest. Several fellow climbers this year had paid steeper prices, a few far steeper. Two climbers he'd met at base camp later lost their lives on the descent, and a Sherpa had come down with high-altitude cerebral edema and would never be able to climb above base camp again.

Once in his loft, Ben checked in via phone with the six-person staff who'd helped him take his small firm

from an underdog to a serious player on the St. Louis scene, then showered, ate a quick breakfast, and assembled the crate he'd bought yesterday.

He'd not had a dog in several years, but the reality of dog ownership was sliding back in. Ben would either have to kennel the animal almost as soon as he was picked up, or he'd need to take him to work and into a client meeting this afternoon. Neither scenario was ideal. He'd decide based on how the dog was acting when he picked him up. If it seemed like the dog could handle an office environment, Ben could send his assistant out for a bed and some chew toys.

He wasn't leaving himself open to the thought that there was any way the animal wouldn't be waiting and ready at ten when he went back. He was confident that this mode of thinking was how he'd made it up—and down—a few of the world's trickiest peaks: not leaving himself open to any possibility other than returning safely to base camp, whether it meant abandoning an attempt at a peak when storm clouds began to build on the horizon or forcing himself to trudge along, one step after another, when his strength was diminished and countless pains were nearly unbearable.

Keeping his head down and focusing on the end goal was the one lesson he was proud to have learned from his father; they'd just had very different goals.

On the surface, his father had had everything, from a luxury car, a condo in Vail, and a beachside duplex in the Keys. He'd also had a string of four wives over his lifetime and had been a man of insatiable wants and needs.

He'd met Ben's mom, his third wife, in Cairo, where

she'd been performing as a belly dancer on a cruise ship. His father had been wrapping up a divorce from his second wife when he'd traveled there on business and had been captivated by her dancing and her exotic Lebanese beauty. He courted her long distance for nearly a year before he won her over and she agreed to marry him and come to America.

Ben only had one memory of her that he could recall with any clarity. He'd been young, less than three, and she'd been rocking him in a chair as she sang. He could remember his fingers tangling in her long silky hair, and he couldn't recall the song, but her voice had been sweet and thick like honey.

Whether it was Ben's self-absorbed father or America or motherhood, the life she'd entered wasn't right for her. She left his father—left *him*—and returned to her childhood home in Lebanon shortly after Ben turned three, taking nothing aside from the clothes on her back, even though the prenup she'd signed entitled her to far more.

He never saw her again, and when he was sixteen, he got word that she'd passed away unexpectedly.

If it hadn't been for Brad's friendship back then, Ben probably would've ended up in serious trouble. Brad's dad was almost as much of an asshole as his had been, and Brad had related to being the child of a father who always wanted more but who could never connect. At sixteen, he and Brad had hung out, drinking and smoking pot when they could get their hands on it, watching movies, and listening to music.

Ben finally led them out of the funk they'd fallen into by convincing Brad to join him on a hockey team,

which put an end to most of their drinking and smoking, and was an entirely better outlet for Ben's anger. In his late teens, when he wasn't climbing, which was sporadic then, the only things that kept him from sliding into a dark place were hockey and the stupid shit he did with Brad.

Finally, in college, the anger finally began to recede and Ben stopped allowing his parents' actions to define him. He found an outlet in architecture, an enticing mix of design and method, and he remembered that there were things he loved about the world.

Then a week or so before graduation, he got out of class early and headed to Brad's campus in Webster Groves for no reason other than wanting to get the weekend started early. He'd sat in the sprawling lecture hall, identifying the kids who'd be giving speeches by their level of fidgetiness. He'd noticed Mia right off. She'd been sorting through her cards way too fast to read them, and her brows had been knotted in a look of intense ferocity.

Then she got up and talked—unscripted—about how her life had been defined by the father she'd never known and the mother who'd left for something better, and how there were moments in every day where she was both a person and a shell of a person, and Ben had felt as if she was talking right to him. There'd been a moment when he was pretty sure she was. She'd paused as if struggling for words for the first time since the speech started, and her eyes had locked on his. He was pretty sure he'd nodded in encouragement, even though he'd been transfixed by her gaze.

He'd wanted to connect with her more than he'd ever

wanted to connect with anyone. He'd been frozen with indecision when the class ended. Her speech had been raw and real, and he could probably live his lifetime again and not be as moved by someone as he'd been by her in the five minutes of her speech.

After a speech like that one, he'd suspected she'd want to retreat, but he hadn't counted on her ducking out a side door and vanishing down one of the corridors before he could reach her.

He couldn't blame anyone but himself for enlisting Brad's help a few days later to find her but not being honest as to how much meeting her would mean to him. How could Brad have known when he'd been the king of indifference for so long? That fact seemed to have been cemented when Ben hadn't shown up at the coffeehouse to "accidentally" run in to them. His father had had a heart attack that morning, and when Ben had finally gotten to a phone, he'd learned that Brad had hooked up with Mia himself, assuming Ben had lost interest in her.

He couldn't hate Brad for fate having stepped in—at least not until learning he'd cheated on her last year. And so soon after Brad and Mia started dating, Ollie had come into the world, and Ben had loved him with a protective, white-hot heat that had surprised him.

After Ollie was born, there'd been nothing to do but wait. Ben couldn't quell his feelings for Mia, and he couldn't find the strength to walk away completely. So he'd waited, climbing when he could, and pouring every other ounce of energy into his firm.

But it was different now. Last night, Mia had climbed onto his lap. He'd felt her desire in her kiss, and nothing was ever going to be the same.

———∿∿∿———

Taye was glowing, so much so that Ben kept chuckling every time he looked his way. The grin Taye had pasted from ear to ear hadn't faltered in half an hour. The same could be said for Turbo's energy. The dog had been chasing a tennis ball—and the occasional pigeon— nonstop across the wide expanse of roof above Ben's loft, and he'd hardly stopped to pant. Ben didn't want him wearing the pads of his feet raw, but he'd not yet been able to call him in with treats.

After he'd gotten a good glimpse of the dog's speed and nimbleness, Taye had come up with the name, and Ben suspected it would stick. Although he hoped some of the young dog's inexhaustible energy level was due to his confinement over the last three days, Ben was willing to bet it'd be years before this guy was as calm as Sadie. Even her pup had more controlled energy than him.

Ben had arrived at animal control at quarter to ten and had breathed a sigh of relief when the doors were unlocked soon after by Bernie, who'd given him a wink and told him that Turbo was up for adoption. After the fees were paid and the paperwork was finished, Ben hadn't had the heart to lock the nervous guy in a crate for the next several hours.

As he'd suspected, it'd been close to impossible to get much accomplished at the office. He made it through two meetings, apologizing to clients even though they didn't seem to mind. He spent another hour wrapping up the designs on the green home and emailed over the preliminary drawings. He'd kept the leash on Turbo, who refused to lie down or do much else aside from sit

on his haunches and stare Ben down and whine when Ben looked in his direction.

He'd cut out as soon as he could, then called Taye's mom and gotten permission to pick him up after school. The look on Taye's face when Ben picked him up in the Jeep with Turbo in the back was one Ben wouldn't forget.

And while Ben didn't want to dampen Taye's mood, it was also important he keep the young teen grounded in their current reality. Not only was Taye's mom working two jobs, she had four kids to raise and money was tight. And Ben had known her long enough to be certain she wouldn't accept handouts. He intended to be respectful of this, but he also knew how much Taye needed a dog. It had been the only thing the hopeful kid had put on his Christmas list for the last three years running.

"Look, Taye, when you go home tonight, you need to remember your mom is going to need some time to think this over. Any dog with this amount of energy is going to be a huge responsibility, and your mom already has her share of that."

"Yeah, man, I know."

"In the meantime, I'll hire a trainer, and we can figure out what makes him tick. I could also use a dog walker a couple days a week. I won't be able to get home at lunch every day, and I suspect it'll be awhile before I can trust him out of a crate. Next week, I'll try taking him in with me again, but if it's anything like this afternoon, it'll be next to impossible to get anything done. Your little brother's helping to babysit your younger sisters after school now too, right?"

"Yeah, when I have practice or if my mom lets me hang with friends."

"Let's see how she feels about you taking an Uber here a couple times a week after school. That way you can still get your time with him."

"That'd be dope, man, but can you ask her when you take me home?"

Ben agreed and, when he couldn't draw Turbo's attention to the bag of treats, tossed him another ball. Unlike a retriever, Turbo had no natural interest in returning the balls. Instead, he dashed after them and herded them around, nudging them with his nose until he lost interest. Then he'd run the length of the roof again just for the joy of running.

Taye's school was three miles from Ben's loft. While the streets surrounding the loft weren't an ideal place for a teen to hang out alone late in the evening or at night, Ben was comfortable letting Taye come and go alone after school and get Turbo outside for some exercise even in winter when it was dark early.

The five-story building had been the first warehouse-conversion project Ben had taken on not long out of college. Seven years ago, the then-dilapidated building had been in a run-down few blocks of mostly abandoned warehouses, but it had also been in the right trajectory with the city's growth and restoration, and by the time the lofts were rentable, the city reclamation efforts had reached it.

Ben had kept his favorite of the sixteen lofts that had been completed in the building. It was on the fifth floor, just below them. He'd since overseen the design and restoration of three other downtown buildings, most of which were more upscale and had fewer imperfections than this one, but he hadn't had the inclination to move.

His loft was airy and unassuming and had a decent view of the Arch and the Old Courthouse. It had also been a dream realized. He'd been told by his career-prejudiced father that he needed to go into law since before kindergarten. Growing up, his father's at-times ferocious intensity and drive had felt inescapable. This place had proven he'd gotten out from under his father's thumb.

Ironically, despite his father's displeasure over Ben's choice of major, he'd also been the biggest player in enabling Ben to get this building's initial loan and make his dreams of building restoration a reality. After recovering from a heart attack and triple bypass, he'd gifted Ben with a hundred-thousand-dollar line of credit for graduation that Ben had paid back and then refinanced under his own name. His father's brush with mortality had softened but not transformed him for the last six years of his life.

Ben suspected he'd also received the unfair lion's portion of his father's estate over his half sister and half brother from his father's first marriage because Ben had needed and wanted it the least of the three of them. Even though he'd been told emphatically that his career choice would leave him deprived of his father's estate, Ben suspected his dad's change of mind was his final attempt to assert control over his domain.

Having given up hope that Turbo would start to fetch, Taye jogged around the roof, collecting the abandoned balls. Ben watched as the teen tried a different approach to connect with the dog. Taye plopped down cross-legged onto the concrete roof and picked a ball to bounce in front of himself.

It worked. Soon Turbo was captivated. He circled around Taye, his tail wagging and his high-pitched bark adding enthusiasm to the air. Taye laughed and bounced the ball just out of Turbo's reach. Rather than being deterred, the excitable dog lunged close and inundated Taye with slobbery licks.

Taye laughed harder, a deep, rolling belly laugh Ben couldn't remember hearing from him before. Smiling, he pulled out his phone and snapped a few pictures. He texted them to Mia and asked her to share them with Ollie.

Two minutes later, she sent a picture of Ollie. He was on the couch sandwiched between Sadie and Sam, his thumbs raised in a double thumbs-up. A few seconds later, the picture was followed by a text.

> Woo-hoo! What an awesome thing you're doing. Tell Taye we're super happy for him. And Ollie's asking if dogs can have playdates.

Chuckling, Ben did a quick internet search. He came up with a picture of a motley crew of dogs wearing bandannas for bibs and seated at a picnic table with giant dog treats in front of them. He took a screen shot, sent it, and added:

> Tell him heck yeah.

> Great. It's a date then…er…playdate. You, me, Taye, Ollie, the dogs. And I'll leave the wine at home.

Her reply had relief sweeping over him. So she definitely remembered. Ben tapped the side of his thumb on his screen a second, deciding how to respond.

> Perfect. And sans wine is good with me. Then if you want to pick up where we left off, I'll know it's not the alcohol talking.

He sent it and waited, the beat of his pulse tapping out the seconds. Close to a minute passed, and she hadn't responded. Taye was standing up and dragging his sleeve over his cheek to wipe off Turbo's slobber. Ben was slipping his phone back into his pocket when it vibrated again.

> Um...okay.

Um...okay. It wasn't exactly a yes, but it wasn't a no either. With a shrug, Ben put his phone away. That was good enough. For now.

Chapter 16

MIA STARED FROM THE IMPERFECTLY ORGANIZED LIST in her hand to the items in the bags she'd just loaded into the car, doing her best to give everything one final thorough check. Showing up at Ollie's school to lead the craft-making for his class holiday party without essential supplies wouldn't be the win she was hoping for today.

She'd signed on as craft lead at the start of the year, without any hint of how complicated her life had been about to get, proving she had absolutely none of her mom's ESP. She counted everything a third time, after getting lost partway through each of the first two.

There was no getting past it. Her thoughts were elsewhere.

It wasn't the easiest thing, tabling action until she'd had a few days to process everything that had happened the night of Ugly Sweater/Cute Mutt contest. But somehow she was managing it. Mostly.

The whirlwind of indecision inside her wasn't making it any easier. But the fact that she wanted to give Ollie the best Christmas possible was the kick in the butt she needed. It was the final push before the holidays and Ollie's last day of school, and she needed to focus on making it a successful one.

For the most part, all this was easier said than done in the once-almost-too-quiet home that had turned into a bit of a zoo overnight. Lynn, as usual, brought with

her color and light and delicious smells from the exotic dishes she cooked. Adding to that were Sadie and Sam and their wildly loud barks and occasional messes and constant desire to be in the thick of things. Not that Mia minded. They were a happy and welcome distraction. Their continuous antics spread laughter along with the chaos.

All in all, considering the less-than-ideal environment they'd come from, they were surprisingly well behaved. The biggest areas in which they needed focused training were house-breaking—something even Sadie hadn't mastered—and constant vigilance to prevent Sam from gnawing through Mia and Ollie's things, from toys to furniture to pillows.

But even with these distractions, two things were always in the back of Mia's mind. The first was Ben and the bring-me-to-my-knees kiss they'd shared. And those texts. Dear God, she'd probably faint when she had to face him in person again.

It didn't help that she distinctly remembered grinding her hips against him. *A copious amount of wine can't make you grind your hips, can it?* No, whatever she might wish to think, that was all her.

And there was no kidding herself. Ben knew it too.

Embarrassing as it might be, every time she thought of those few minutes, she was no better than an insatiably hungry little bird who'd been given a minuscule bite of dinner from its mom. *More, please. Lots and lots more.*

The second thing she couldn't stop thinking about was the fact that somewhere in the city, there was a baby who shared half of Ollie's DNA. This awareness was wrapped up inside the memory of that baby's

remarkable blue eyes and the full-body grunting he'd done as he reached for the cats. And even if she decided the positives of welcoming that baby into her and Ollie's lives outweighed the negatives, it would mean publicly acknowledging Brad's infidelity, and that wasn't something she was eager to do.

Thankfully, there was more than enough else to focus on while she gave these momentous events time to settle in. The most pressing, at the moment, was Ollie's class party. After that, she'd focus on the last-minute shopping and grocery lists and cleaning. All this kept her one solid step from getting swept away in indecision.

Reassured that she'd packed everything she needed, Mia shut the trunk and jogged back inside for her purse. When Christmas was over, she would need to address the kiss more directly than through a text. Even if it was a touch humiliating. As her mom was fond of saying, calling attention to the embarrassing and the ugly was the best way to shrink the elephant in the room.

She'd also place a call to Stacey. Mia had no idea yet if it would be to tell her to put her offer where the sun didn't shine, or if it would be to tell her that, for Ollie's sake, she'd bring the baby into their lives at some level. But she was going to make the most of Christmas first.

Twenty minutes later, Mia found herself loaded down with bags and headed into Ollie's classroom. She hovered on the threshold, fully appreciating what her son had faced going back to school after the funeral. Looks darted her way, and conversation faltered before she was even in the room. She'd anticipated as much. The group of regular classroom volunteers had somehow been tight-knit even at the start of kindergarten.

While most of the moms of the kids in Ollie's class were nice enough, Mia would have needed more than her twenty fingers and toes to count the times she'd heard, "You're so young, you wouldn't get it." As if by being only twenty-three when Ollie was born, she'd not been exhausted, or her boobs hadn't looked like they'd gone into shock the month after she'd stopped breast-feeding and her milk dried up, or she hadn't gotten her share of stretch marks during pregnancy or, one of her favorites, the demands of a young child somehow only hampered the sex lives of those thirty and over.

And now, not only was she younger by five or ten or even fifteen years than everyone else, but she was also a widow.

As she'd unloaded the supplies for the popcorn-filled snowman cups the first graders would be taking home, Mia realized she didn't care if she ever fit in with the other mothers. The only thing that mattered was how, in his own way, Ollie had already braved this path before her. He had come back to face his classmates and fallen back into the routine of childhood and glue sticks and recess and single-file lines. And he was healing.

This gave her the strength to make it through the party with her focus right where it needed to be—on Ollie and his friends. The clear-plastic, popcorn-filled snowman cups were a hit. The kids munched bites of popcorn as they added felt carrot noses and eyes and real buttons to the cups. Next, they glued the cups together and filled them with more popcorn. When the party was over, Mia chalked her part up as a much-needed success.

On the way home—Ollie got out early since it was the

final day before break—she asked if there was one place Ollie would like to go before school started back up.

From his spot catty-corner behind her in the back seat, he answered with zero hesitation. "Everybody says you can't go to the North Pole, but it seems like it would be easier to get there than heaven."

Mia was fumbling to find the best answer when he added that with Mimi—his name for Lynn—here, and Sadie and Sam, all he wanted was to make a snowman bigger than the ones in his books.

After she arrived home and got Ollie in the back-yard with the dogs, Mia pulled up the next ten days of weather on her phone and frowned.

"Yeah, so Mom, there aren't by chance any African snow dances you've committed to memory, are there?"

Lynn's eyebrows raised optimistically. "I sense a touch of sarcasm and am choosing to ignore it. Not snow particularly, but I know plenty of chants and mantras to call for precipitation. Why?"

"It was mostly meant to be rhetorical, but what Ollie wants more than anything is to build a snowman over the break, and it looks like we've got a ten-day stretch of warm weather and rain."

Lynn cocked her head and looked out the window of the breakfast room into the yard. "Then he shall have snow." Her tone was as confident as if she'd just had personal confirmation from the weather gods.

Mia's first inclination was to shake her head, but the older she got, the more faith she was developing in her mom's predictions. When Lynn didn't pursue it, Mia decided she wouldn't either.

After all, she decided, it was St. Louis, the city where

everyone said if you didn't like the weather, just stick around. In twenty-four hours, it might turn into something else entirely.

—◦—

The thing about Lynn, Ben had learned over the years, was how intuitive she proved to be, over and over again. The first time he'd glimpsed this, he'd spent no more than a half of cumulative day around her over the space of a couple different meetings. It was Ollie's second birthday party, and the house was crowded with people Ben had never met and others he didn't much care to know any better than he already did.

Back then, he'd had one failed attempt at Everest's peak but had made it up Denali successfully. When strangers found out he climbed mountains, the subject had a way of becoming the focus of conversation, whether or not he encouraged it. That afternoon, he'd fielded a dozen questions, from "Was it scary?" to "Did your hands get cold?" to the inevitable "Have you ever seen someone die?" when a ten-year-old kid asked him the one question he had no answer for.

"What do you think you'll find at the top?" the kid had asked, his eyes wide. For whatever reason, Ben remembered that the boy had a stuffed nose and he'd been breathing out of his mouth.

"Just the top, I guess," he'd answered after giving the question a bit of consideration.

"But what's at the top?" the kid had pressed. "Does it look different?"

"I suspect that it's more about what he hopes to leave behind than what he's trying to reach." Lynn had

answered for him, even though she'd only recently come in from the kitchen and Ben hadn't thought she'd overheard the conversation.

It had been a striking-enough answer that the kid was stumped, and when someone called out from the other room that it was time to open presents, no one had brought it up again. Certainly not Ben, who'd looked Lynn in the eye long enough to decide he was better off not confronting her to see what had prompted her comment.

She'd shown her insight more than a few other times over the years, so he probably shouldn't have been as surprised as he was when she was outside his building midmorning on Christmas Eve, ringing to be let up.

"I didn't think you knew where I lived," he said after he'd buzzed her up and let her in.

Turbo circled her a few times before tentatively stepping forward to sniff her. He'd been pacing Ben's loft with untouched energy despite the four-mile jog Ben had taken him on in Forest Park that morning. After a thorough sniff of Lynn's flowing orange-and-purple dress and the bare toes showing through her open-toe sandals, he trotted back to the wall of windows that faced out to the street five stories below. Licking his jowls, the watchful dog sank hesitantly to his haunches as if he were taking up guard duty and would be ready to dash after something at the slightest notice.

"I didn't, but just because I've been living in Kenya the last fifteen years doesn't mean I haven't learned how to use the internet to find people when I've got the mind to. And Mia has you in her contacts. Her privacy code is disappointingly simple."

Lynn didn't seem fazed by the fact that it was thirty-eight degrees outside and she wasn't wearing a coat. Her chestnut hair was long and loose except one strand that was dyed with a blond-purple tint and braided. Aside from the fact that she was nearly two decades older and the African sun had worn groves into the laugh lines around her mouth and eyes, she and Mia shared a keen resemblance.

Ben chuckled. "Fair enough." He motioned toward the couch and chairs in the center of his loft that faced the windows overlooking the Arch and downtown St. Louis. "Have a seat. Can I get you a cup of coffee or tea?"

"I'd take a cup of rooibos tea, if you have it."

Ben shook his head. "I don't, but I've got a Himalayan blend you'd probably like."

Lynn raised one eyebrow appreciatively, drawing his attention to a deep-set wrinkle along her forehead. "I could be talked into that."

Rather than heading for the couches, she followed him into the kitchen. He was filling his cast-iron kettle when she asked what he was doing for Christmas.

"Uh, heading to my sister's tomorrow. Why?"

"What about tonight? It's Christmas Eve."

Ben shut off the tap. "Working, most likely."

"Working? When you could be spending one of the best nights of the year with your godson?"

He lit the stove and set the kettle onto the blue flame. "What's this about?" She had Mia's gray-blue eyes, and when she looked right at him, he had a feeling she could read all the things he wasn't voicing.

"I suspect you aren't going to believe me when I tell

you I've had some very clear messages from my spirit guide. It's why I'm here."

He huffed. "Lynn, you're gonna have a hard sell if you expect me to believe that not only is there conscious life after death, but there are spirits out there interested enough in us to send us messages."

"But you believe in intuition, if I remember correctly."

"Yes, and I believe listening to it kept me alive in a couple of the most dangerous places on the planet."

She waved a hand dismissively. "You and I have two names for the same thing. What you call intuition, I call a message from something greater than our individual selves."

"And what does this have to do with Christmas Eve? If you're about to tell me I'm going to have a string of ghostly visitors tonight, I'll give you fair warning that I've had my fill of that plot for the year."

A smile brushed her face before she breezed through the galley kitchen and over to the windows where Turbo had his nose pressed to the glass. "I always liked you. Much more than that dimwit she married. Though you're nearly as stubborn as she is." She paused to sweep her hair into one hand as she looked out at the Arch. "Put it to intuition if it comforts you, but the other night when I first came in, I walked into something. When Mia told me about the baby the next morning, I assumed I'd been confused. But I'm damn good at reading energy, and the energy seeping off both your pores that night was primal. Carnal even."

Hot anger surged through Ben's veins. He crossed to the edge of the kitchen. "If you've come here to accuse me of something, go ahead and say it."

"I didn't fly halfway across the world to spend my Christmas Eve making accusations when I could be baking cookies with my grandson. I'm here because I want my daughter to reach for something she may be too afraid to reach for on her own. I'm sure you knew as well as me that she and Brad weren't exactly peanut butter and jelly. But that thing I caught wind of the other night between you wasn't new or fresh. It was just declared. And it wasn't only coming from you this time."

He'd grown used to the quirky and direct way Lynn went about things, but this cut him to the quick.

"I'm right, aren't I?" she continued. "You do love her. You've loved her longer than you'd like anyone to know."

Ben headed to one of his leather chairs and took a seat, balancing on the edge, resting his elbows on his knees. "Yeah, I love her," he said once he'd taken a minute to collect himself. "You're right. I've loved her for a long time." His voice was foreign in his ears, but stronger than he'd have expected. He spent the next ten minutes confessing the sleeping dragon of a lie that he'd kept bundled inside for so many years. The words toppled out, the weight of them falling from his chest like bricks tumbling to the ground.

He explained how he'd been the one who'd been moved by Mia's speech eight years ago, not Brad—not enough that Brad would've sought her out, at least—and how after not being able to find her on campus on his own, he'd asked Brad to connect them.

Then he went on to explain how his father's first in a string of heart attacks had prevented him from meeting

up with them as planned, and how Mia and Brad had gotten together as a result.

"In retrospect, that makes so much more sense," Lynn said when he finished. She'd joined him after turning off the whistling kettle halfway through and was seated at the edge of the couch perpendicular to him. "But time is as precarious as love, and I suspect it just wasn't yours yet. Not then."

Not sure how to respond to that, Ben stood up and headed for the kitchen to fix her tea. "Even loving her like I do, the way things turned out… I'd never have wanted this. Not this way."

"I know. And that must be some guilt you've been carrying, but as we say in Kenya, 'A rope parts where it's thinnest.'"

When Ben didn't reply, she said, "What I'm saying is that Brad's undoing was his undoing alone." Ben was nodding in confirmation when she added, "We also say that a baboon laughs at the buttocks of another baboon."

He huffed. "Yeah, I'm not sure I get that last one."

She joined him in the kitchen, shrugging. "I can't really say it fits our current situation, but I've always been fond of it. And it never fails to make the children laugh."

He chuckled and pulled down two mugs from the cabinet. "So what now?"

Lynn leaned against the counter, her sun-lightened hair spilling over one shoulder. "I was just about to get to that. Am I correct in assuming you're still quite far from destitute?"

"Comfortably far, yes."

"Good. Because I came here today to ask if you'd be interested in taking us on a vacation—Mia, Ollie,

and me. And the dogs, I guess. Between now and New Year's while Ollie's off school. Assuming you can get away for a few days."

Ben was intrigued. "Where to?"

"North. Minnesota, hopefully. I used to vacation there with my parents when I was young. Ollie's biggest Christmas wish is to build a snowman, and up there, there'll be plenty of snow. And you and Mia under one roof for a few days certainly wouldn't hurt anything."

His stomach flipped stronger at the thought than when he'd crossed the Khumbu Icefall. "Have you said anything to her about it?"

A hint of a smile brushed her lips. "I've found these sorts of things go over best when you tell the child at the same time as you tell the adult who's most likely to object."

Ben laughed, the last lingering tension vacating his limbs. "Lynn, you're something else. Don't ever let anyone say you aren't."

She drummed her fingers on the counter. "That's a yes, isn't it?"

He could picture it perfectly. A cabin in snowy Minnesota with the four of them and a handful of dogs in need of some training and TLC. It certainly wasn't how he expected to spend the holidays.

It was a thousand times better.

"It's a yes, loud and clear." And the one thing he was most committed to was no longer looking back.

~~~

Mia's hands were beginning to sweat inside a pair of rubber gloves as she knelt to scoop out the last of the

litter pans on the bottom row of the cat kennels. It was Christmas Eve, and the shelter had closed at noon. It was operating with a minimal staff to cover animal care for the next day and a half.

Traditionally, she and Ollie spent this afternoon making cookies, but with Lynn here not knowing what to do with herself and baking up a storm as a result, the kitchen counters were spilling over with breads and cookies. When Mia had asked Ollie if he was interested in switching things up this year, he'd been happy to come with her while she worked an open shift instead. He'd brought along a backpack full of books and had been entertaining himself for the last hour and a half.

Mia was locking shut the lower litter door of the last kennel when she noticed Patrick had come in from the dog kennels in back of the building and was behind her.

"Don't tell me you're finished before me?" Typically feeding the dogs took about twice as long as the cats. Depending on the needs of the individual dogs, it could take even longer at times. And Patrick was good, but not that good.

"I won't, because I haven't."

Mia twisted, craning her head upward and resting her elbows on her knees. Rather than ask for clarification, she pressed her tongue against the roof of her mouth and counted out a few seconds as she waited for him to say more. He'd dressed for the occasion in a green polo today, and his flyaway brown hair was disheveled the way it got when he bent over a lot.

And as usual, he didn't pay it any notice. "What is your social media policy for Ollie?"

I sure didn't see that coming. "Um, are you asking if he has his own accounts? He doesn't. He's too young."

"No. In regards to him appearing on Facebook and Instagram."

Mia stood up and tugged off the gloves, glancing toward the glass doors separating off the back half of the shelter. Ollie was planted on the floor seemingly without a care in the world, with his pile of books outside the kennel of a Bernese mountain dog who'd just come in and didn't have the best vision. "I don't really have a set policy. Can you tell me why you're asking?"

"Yes. The way he reads to the dogs would make a good post. Posts with both dogs and children have a fifty percent higher-than-average click-through rate. It would take fifteen minutes to set up and film. It will make a good one- to two-minute post."

"That's sweet, Patrick. Really sweet. Do you have a particular dog in mind?"

"The two of Pepper's puppies that haven't been adopted."

Mia nodded. "That makes sense. What're you thinking?"

"I would set up the playpen two feet in front of the tree. Ollie would sit inside with them. If we put in three fresh chew toys, they would leave his clothes and book alone."

"A Rottweiler-mix puppy video on Christmas Eve. Patrick, you're a genius! And as long as Ollie's name isn't listed and I'm not tagged, I'm fine with it. Great, actually." Mia dropped her gloves over the top of the spray bottle. Patrick had developed quite the knack for knowing what the shelter's eighty thousand social media

followers liked to see and share, and she could imagine this post being a big success. "I'm done here after I put stuff away and wash my hands. Want me to help you set up, or can I help in the back?"

He gave a determined shake of his head, as if she'd just offered him a cracker with soft goat cheese, one of his particular dislikes. "No, I'll set up. I'm finished feeding and watering the dogs. You could start taking out the over-seventies. Then when I finish, we'll take out the twosies."

Mia packed up the cleaning supplies and trash bag and nodded. The over-seventies were the dogs that weighed seventy pounds and over. When the shelter was closed, the outside runs were shut off, and the bigger guys needed a quick walk or some time in the play area to stretch their legs. The twosies were dogs who for one reason or another required two people's attention when being taken out. "I'd love to take some dogs out. And would you like to tell Ollie, or should I?"

Patrick had turned and was headed toward the Christmas tree by the front window but paused to give her a short but dubious look. "You," was all he offered before turning his attention back to setting up for the shoot.

Mia suppressed a giggle. Patrick thinking up this post was as much of a compliment as he'd ever offered Ollie. And even if he had no real intention of bonding with her son, Mia was happy to take what she could get.

"Hey, Ol," she said as she headed into the back. "Follow me to the supply room for a minute, will you?"

Ollie raised his head high as he looked at her. His floppy Santa hat had fallen over his eyebrows and was limiting his view. "Why?"

"Because I have some fun news."

He shrugged, shutting his book and setting it on the stool. He trailed after her in a zigzag fashion, walking from one side of the kennels to the other, and piquing the attention of several dogs.

Mia gave him the lowdown of Patrick's idea as she shelved the cleaning supplies and scrubbed up in the utility sink. "What do you think of that?" she asked as she shut off the water.

Ollie was chewing on his lower lip. He didn't look nervous, just thoughtful. "Will people care that I make up the words?"

"No, hon, not at all. In fact, I'm sure they'll love it. And Patrick's clips are usually less than a minute, so you won't have to make up an entire story."

"Cool. Pepper's puppies are almost as cute as Sam. Sam's just fluffier." He pinched the fuzzy white ball on the end of his hat. "Which story do you think the puppies would like most?"

Finished drying her hands, Mia swept him up in a tight hug. "Whichever one you want to read them, little man. As mouthy as they are, I suspect they'll mostly be chewing on the toys Patrick puts in there." She gave his belly a little tickle as she pulled away. "But you know that since you've played with them before."

"Yeah. They're slobbery and their teeth are sharp and they look more like baby bears than puppies."

Mia laughed. "Yeah, that pretty much sums them up at this point."

Ollie got resettled in front of the Bernese mountain dog, and Mia headed out the back door with Tiny. Outside was gray and overcast, but the light wind

carried a warm humidity that reminded her of early spring instead of winter. She zipped up her hoodie, but it was warm enough not to need a coat at the moment, which was a touch disappointing for Christmas Eve.

After letting Tiny trudge along and scent mark on every rock that sparked his interest in the Island of Many Smells, a rock island at the back of the lot that had become most dogs' favorite scent-marking stop, she took him for a short walk on the new path at the side of the building between the shelter and the jewelry store next door. It wove around a narrow strip of cedars and oak trees, and the shelter team had enhanced the short path with several stop-and-sniff points to keep the dogs' interest. It certainly worked for Tiny. He lumbered along, sniffing everything in sight including a few ropes and woven bird nests filled with scented pinecones, and somehow came up with a bit more urine to leave his scent along the way.

At close to a hundred and seventy pounds, Tiny was anything but small. The tops of his shoulders were higher than Mia's hips, but he walked on the leash like a gentle giant. Due to his age and large size, he was showing signs of hip dysplasia. To combat its negative effects, he was now on a few medicines and a prescription diet, and was being taken on slow, easy walks several times a day.

By the time he'd had a good stretch of the legs and she'd gotten him kenneled, Mia figured it was time to check in with Patrick. Ollie was no longer in back either. When she reached sight of the glass doors, she froze midstep. Ben was here.

Ben was *here*. Not on the other side of a phone a

safe distance away. Her stomach flipped, and adrenaline raced through her limbs. The last time she'd seen him, she'd climbed uninvited onto his lap and kissed the crap out of him until he'd kissed her back. If she could melt into a puddle, she would.

He was laughing and kneeling outside the playpen just behind Ollie. Ollie was inside, seated but doubled over as the puppies tackled him. She could hear her son's giggly laughter even before pushing past the double doors.

Patrick was catty-corner behind them, setting up the GoPro on a tripod.

"Hey, guys!" She pushed through the doors, willing her voice to sound excited and not nervous-squeaky, without much success.

Ben was the first to turn. As he rose to his feet, he offered a little nod that seemed more intimate than courteous, making her face heat even more.

This was Ben. She'd known him for nearly eight years. And she'd already sort of addressed the kiss over a text. Seeing him now didn't have to be awkward. *Yeah, right, there's no getting past this without a bit of awkward.*

"Did you call? My phone's in my purse."

"Ah, no. Your mom invited me over tonight. I was on my way and saw the car out front."

"Cool," she managed along with a nod. She swallowed and motioned toward Patrick and the camera. "I guess they filled you in on Patrick's idea?"

"We told him," Ollie said as Patrick agreed. Still laughing, Ollie pushed the excited puppies back from their onslaught and twisted to face her, rising up to his

knees. "Mom, can you guys not watch? So it's a surprise when Patrick posts it?" His cheek and sections of his hair were damp from puppy licks.

Mia glanced at Ben. "Yeah, sure, as long as you agree to take a bath before dinner tonight to get some of those kisses off."

"Patrick isn't putting the chew toys in until they've acclimated," Ben said. "That way the pups will settle down when Ollie reads to them."

"Makes sense. Well, it sounds like you two have it covered." She stepped forward and planted a kiss on a dry spot of Ollie's forehead. "Good luck, sweets. You're going to rock this."

Ben gave him a high five, then looked her way. "So what can I help you with?"

She looked to Patrick. His face was buried in the camera as he found the best placement for the tripod. "He can help with the twosies since both of the dogs we have right now are green-lighted," he said, proving for the hundredth time his ability to multitask.

Mia swallowed. Just her and Ben and short walks with one twosie at a time. That wouldn't be intimate or awkward at all. Nope, not at all.

"Uh, sure. Ollie, come find us when you're finished," she said as she headed toward the kennels with Ben following. When the double doors swung shut behind them, her stomach did a cartwheel.

A corgi-beagle mix near the doors stood up and stretched, then headed to the front of her kennel for a sniff. Mia paused to scratch what she could reach of the dog's forehead through the wire.

"So, should I guess what a twosie is?" Ben stopped in

front of a German shepherd who'd just been moved out of quarantine yesterday.

A bit of Mia's hesitation slipped away at the opportunity to focus on the shelter. "It's shelter slang for dogs who require two people's attention when they're out of their kennels. Sometimes it's because they're really stressed and need some help adjusting to shelter life. But there are other reasons too, like both the twosies here now. One dog, an Old English sheepdog, has recently come out of hip surgery and sometimes needs a boost when she's being walked. The other one, a Bernese mountain dog, is half blind and really stubborn. Sometimes he needs a boost to get moving too."

Mia grabbed a leash and a fresh handful of treats, and Ben joined her in front of Kit, the sheepdog, who was sprawled across her kennel. Kit had long, shaggy hair and was wearing a red bow on top of her head to keep it out of her eyes. "She's an owner surrender," Mia said. "Her owners couldn't afford to give her the care she needed, so they dropped her off here about a month ago. Her back left hip was bad, and she needed surgery. She seemed to be one of those medium-cared-for dogs, not abused, but not superloved either. I think she spent most of her life outside, but she was fed and her basic needs were met. They called her Cousin It because of the hair in her eyes. No one here was fond of that, so we renamed her Kit. She's sweet as can be, and she's walking better all the time."

Ben shook his head. "When I hear these things, it makes me want to adopt them all."

"I've volunteered here half my life, and for most of us, that never goes away." She shrugged. "So I just love

the crap out of them while they're here and celebrate when they go to good homes."

"Makes sense." He laughed softly.

Mia lifted Kit's support harness off the hook and held it and the leash out toward Ben. "Front or back?"

"Ah, you can drive. I'll head up the rear," he said, reaching for the harness. He stretched it out, lifting it by the handles. "Just slip it under her stomach and hold on to the straps?"

"Yep. She'll let you know how much support she needs. Usually it's mostly in the beginning, then less as she warms up." Mia opened the kennel door wide and knelt down to give Kit a good scratch behind the ears. "She's been standing up on her own. I'll give her a minute to see if she does."

As Mia hoped, not long after, Kit got her front legs under her, then heaved into a three-legged stance, holding her back left leg off the ground before tentatively placing it down.

"Good girl," Mia praised, offering her a few treats. Kit shoved her nose into Mia's palm and nuzzled around before swiping them up with her tongue.

Once Kit was hooked up and supported by the harness, they took off at a snail's pace and headed out the back door. Mia had helped walk countless twosies over the years, but she couldn't remember being so acutely aware of another walker's presence so close to her. The fact that Ben was behind rather than in front didn't help as much as she might've thought. Even before they'd stepped outside and away from the familiar smell of the kennels, she was savoring the cedary scent of his cologne. He was in jeans and an outdoorsy olive-green

wool sweater with its three buttons open at the collar, accenting the perfectly formed trapezius underneath and reminding her how much she wouldn't mind losing herself in that sculpted neck or the shadow of stubble along the ridge of his jaw.

As Kit warmed up, it no longer felt as if a snail could outpace them. They started down the strip of woods, and Kit came to a complete stop next to one of the seasonally decorated cedars. She seemed entranced with watching the erratic flight of a nearby bird. As usual, her strength was picking up as they walked. Her gait was steady and even, and Ben seemed to be holding on to the straps now as a precaution rather than to help lift her.

"So, as you may be guessing," Mia said to fill the silence, "walking most of the twosies isn't that exciting."

"I don't know what you're talking about. I could do this all day."

Mia glanced behind her to catch him raising an eyebrow at her. "What, life at a slower pace?"

"That would be a should do, not a could do."

Mia had just started to ask what the "could do" meant when something about the way he was looking at her told her she might not be ready for his answer. She stopped midsentence and pressed her lips together. She swallowed and did her best to refocus on Kit, whose head was raised as she watched a gray bird flutter about in a nearby tree, her ponytail of forehead hair flopping every which way.

Mia was about to attempt a change of topic and ask if he knew what type of bird it was that had caught Kit's interest when she heard Ben give a quiet "Come here."

Before she knew it, he was stepping in close, his free

hand locking over the back of her hair, and his lips were closing over hers.

Like the first time, his kiss seemed to address everything she could possibly be craving. Her blood raced through her veins, and she opened her mouth to his reflexively. She wanted to lose herself in his kiss, to press in against him and lock her hand around his jaw or over his shoulder. She wanted to savor his taste as much as she did the feel of him.

Only she was sober this time and Ollie wasn't far away and something about this was real in a way nothing had been in a long time, and it scared the hell out of her.

She took a step back, an almost involuntary one. "Ben, I…I don't know…" She shook her head. "So maybe I don't know what it is that I don't know. I just—"

"Mia, I know." He brushed his thumb across her cheek. "Trust me, I do. I just thought it might be easier to move forward if you weren't the only one who'd taken that risk."

An embarrassed laugh tumbled out of her. "Are you seriously telling me you just kissed me so things aren't as awkward tonight?"

"I didn't mean to imply that I didn't want to." He leaned down and lifted her chin, brushing his lips over hers a second time. He started to pull away but then met her gaze and came in again, making this kiss longer, slower.

Mia closed her hand over his shoulder to steady herself as it continued. She must've been holding her breath because she became a bit dizzy. When he finally moved away, he pulled her into a one-armed hug and brushed his lips against her forehead.

"Thank you." She laughed at herself for thanking him for a kiss and buried her face in his chest. "It helps. Mostly. I did climb onto your lap though. That's going to be hard to get over."

He chuckled and kissed the top of her head. "No pun intended, huh?"

She laughed harder and stepped back. "That's not funny." She bit her lip. "Okay, it's funny. A little funny. Seriously, Ben, everything's so complicated, and this doesn't make it any less so."

Ben locked his hand in hers as Kit woofed at the bird as it swooped closer, chirping loudly at Kit and flicking its long tail.

"You're right. Things are complicated, and I don't think that's going to change anytime soon. So how about just letting go and taking tonight and the next few days as they are? No questions. No heavy talk or decisions. Just making sure Ollie has a fun Christmas."

Mia drew a long breath and nodded. "That sounds like a really good plan. But can I ask one more thing first?"

"Yeah. Anything."

She gave an exaggerated bat of her eyes. "If that's the case, would you mind kissing me once more? If you do, I'm pretty sure I'll have the strength to make it through anything, even facing Victor and Irene on Christmas morning after this."

He narrowed his eyes, cocking his head sideways a bit. "That's two people, so I'm pretty sure that means I'll need to kiss you twice." Then his lips met hers again, and the fear and hesitation that had been rising inside her ebbed away until it was just him and her and a barking dog and a territorial little bird.

—∿∿—

Mia pulled up her weather app to confirm the same thing that a quick trip outside this morning had foreshadowed. The remaining ten days of Ollie's winter break weren't at all promising in regard to his wish to build a snowman, even a small one. Thankfully, in the lively spirit of the morning, Ollie didn't yet seem to mind that Christmas had dawned with warm, drizzly rain instead of snow.

Christmas morning also brought Victor and Irene to the house. They'd never been to Mia's grandparents' house before, and Mia wasn't surprised by their poorly hidden disdain for the dated thirteen-hundred-square-foot bungalow she and Ollie were living in. *Yes*, seemed to be their collective thought, *Mia chose this over life in a considerably nicer Central West End house with our son five months ago. Perhaps she had a brush of insanity*.

Mia had done her best to love and accept them while she was married, but the love they'd held for their son was so wrapped up in pride and judgment that she could go the rest of her life without seeing them and not be sad. However, Victor and Irene had been coming to watch Ollie open presents on Christmas morning ever since he was one, and no matter what her issues were, they'd just lost a son.

To make matters even less pleasant, not only were Ollie's grandparents notoriously stern and serious, they were anything but dog crazy. While Sadie and Sam figured out pretty quickly they'd get no affection from these new visitors, Mia wasn't doing anything to correct the dogs' wild excitement as the morning wore on.

And as Mia had learned during the previous time or

two her mom had been home over the holidays, Irene
and Victor and Lynn in the same confined space were
like Mentos and Diet Coke. Irene and Victor were
country clubs and galas and weekend trips to Aspen
and New York, while Lynn was a green-living mini-
malist who wasn't timid about sharing her opinions on
lavish lifestyles and saw no reason not to wear her
brightest African-print wrap skirt and Maasai sandals to
Christmas breakfast.

As the morning passed, Irene and Victor tossed
sugarcoated insults at Lynn, while Lynn's disdain for
their lifestyle became more brazen and unadorned. Mia
shot off a text to Ben, asking if he wanted to place a bet
on who ended up throwing the first punch, her mom or
Brad's parents. After a few minutes, he replied.

> Lynn, no question. And I hope she kicks
> some ass.

Mia laughed to herself and put her phone away after
wishing him a good day. He was driving out to see his
half sister and her kids who lived an hour outside the
city. It was probably a touch inappropriate to wish he
was here instead, and Mia did her best not to wish it, but
she did anyway.

He'd texted her earlier to say he'd watched Patrick's
video of Ollie and Pepper's puppies on both Facebook
and Instagram, and he'd loved it. Mia didn't think
she was just being a proud mom to agree with him. It
already had over two thousand views, and the number
was growing steadily.

Patrick's video turned out to be more touching than

Mia would've guessed. By the time Patrick had given the puppies their chew toys and started filming, they'd been tuckered out enough to plop down beside Ollie and have a good gnaw while he read. Halfway through the video, the chubbier of the two puppies planted his head on Ollie's lap and chewed lazily at his pants. Ollie had chosen to read "The Night Before Christmas," a perfect choice because he'd been read it enough that he'd nearly memorized it.

It was the perfect cap to this holiday, which after last night, Mia wouldn't have guessed could've gotten any better, with the possible exception of Victor and Irene breaking tradition and finding something else to do this morning. After an evening of games and good food and laughter and bedtime books with Ben and Lynn and Ollie and the dogs, Mia had fallen asleep thinking it was her favorite Christmas Eve ever.

And she was fairly certain her mom had gone back to suspecting there was something between her and Ben because of an odd comment she made as Mia was headed to bed. "I'd bid you sweet dreams, but I'm pretty sure you're already having them." When Mia asked her for clarification, her mom had simply shrugged and said it was the mulled wine talking.

Mia was a bit surprised when her mom didn't follow up with a better explanation. Lynn wasn't usually one to hold her tongue. Case in point, as Christmas morning went on, in the throes of present opening, the comments between Lynn and Victor and Irene were escalating rather than ceasing. Thanks to the antics and distraction of the dogs, coupled with Ollie's unfettered Christmas joy, her son remained oblivious to his grandparents'

dislike for one another. Mia was pretty sure a hurricane could whirl behind him and he wouldn't notice.

And even had the dogs not been deaf, Mia suspected they wouldn't have noticed the tension either. They seemed more than content in the chaos of wrapping paper and package stuffing being tossed into the air and boxes being broken down and crumpled. Sadie continuously dove under the pile of recycling, acting for the first time since Mia had brought her home like the two-and-a-half-year-old dog Dr. Wentworth had predicted she was. Sam chased her under the mound, yipping and biting at her tail and her back feet.

Ollie, who was cross-legged on the floor, belly laughed over their antics until he collapsed back against the hardwood, hands clutching his stomach. This drew the dogs' attention, and soon they flanked his sides, licking his ears until he laughed and farted at the same time. He was still laughing when he pushed up and dashed off to the bathroom, yelling at everyone to hold their noses.

When the bathroom door smacked closed, Mia caught all three of the adults' attention with a lingering "So." When she had all eyes on her, she dove ahead. "This seems like a good time to remind you guys it's Christmas, and today's about Ollie. And if you think it'll help, there's a dartboard downstairs. My guess is that physical competition would serve you guys better. But right now, I'd appreciate it if you'd please be on your best behavior."

In the sharp silence that followed from Irene and Victor and the sincere but short apology breathed out of Lynn, Mia found herself unexpectedly thinking of Brody. Had anyone come together to celebrate his first

Christmas? And holy hell, what would Irene and Victor do when she told them, whenever that was.

Hoping her words would make a difference as they settled in, Mia used the break in present opening to get Sam and Sadie outside. The dogs were going on twenty-four hours of being accident-free, and she didn't want to break this new record. Sadie didn't mind the drizzly rain and trotted out to sniff her new territory, but Sam had to be coaxed out from underneath the covered deck onto the grass. When he squatted and peed immediately, Mia inundated him with visual and physical praise and treats.

By the time she got Sadie's attention and herded them back inside, Ollie was tearing into the giant snowman-wrapped present from Lynn. It was light enough that after he had the paper off, he lifted the closed box over his head and shook it, drawing Sam's attention. The damp, furry puppy dashed around him in circles and jumped on Ollie's legs, dousing his neck and ears with fresh licks.

"I love him so much," Ollie said through his laughter. "He reminds me of Dad."

Irene was looking out the window with her arms folded over her chest, placed a hand on the back of the armchair. She pulled a Kleenex from the box on the side table and dabbed at her nose, and watching her, Mia let go of her anger.

When she turned back to Ollie, he'd pulled the top of the box open, and fake snow was pouring out onto his lap and all over the floor. Sam dove face-first into it and was yipping and wagging his fluffy tail, while Sadie backed timidly away.

"What's this about?" Ollie said, cocking his head and shaking the last of the snow everywhere.

"There's a brochure in here somewhere," Lynn said, kneeling on the floor and fishing through the mound of glistening snow. "Aha!" She waved it with typical fanfare overhead, then sank to the floor next to Ollie, tucking her long, brightly colored skirt around her. "Your mom may have mentioned you have a hankering for snow this holiday. Well, guess what? So do I, and I figured we should do something about that."

"Do what?" Ollie's eyes were big and wide.

"We can't make it snow here, but we *can* go where we know there'll be snow." She dropped the brochure—the color was flat, and it look self-printed—into Ollie's hands. "It's a cabin in the woods. Up north. There'll be enough snow that you can build an army of snow-men. And we'll make hot chocolate and have snowball fights and build a snow fort, you name it." Her gaze flitted to Irene and Victor. "The only skiing in this part of Minnesota is cross-country, but there are extra rooms in the cabin. You're welcome to join us for a few days if you'd like. We were able to get it for five nights. We leave in two days, and we'll have it through New Year's."

Mia wasn't sure what to think. Aside from the money involved, a cabin retreat sounded perfect. It would give Ollie his wish for snow, and Mia could step back a bit and hopefully make sense of all that had been rolling around her head the last few days.

And aside from the mural work that she was largely holding off on until after the holidays anyway, there was no reason they couldn't get away. However, Lynn hardly had a spare dime to her name. She'd been given

some money in her parents' will, but Mia didn't want her depleting that on a vacation.

She was about to comment as much when Ollie spoke. "What about Sadie and Sam?" Concern was evident in his voice.

"We'll bring them, of course. It's a pet-friendly cabin. Ben's coming. And he's bringing Taye's dog too. He's not sure about Taye yet. Taye's grandparents are coming into town."

Irene inhaled audibly. "*Ben* is coming? With you?" Her tone was sharp and accusatory. Hearing it didn't ease the rush of guilt that was racing just behind the unexpected delight flowing through Mia's veins.

"Of course." Lynn gave a one-shoulder shrug. "He's Ollie's godfather. I'd expect him to."

Mia's voice was locked in her throat. She could understand Irene's shock. Ben had never gone on vacation with Ollie before, and it made about as much sense as it didn't that he'd start now.

But Ollie was screaming with delight and throwing handfuls of glittery snow into the air. It cascaded down across the room, exciting Sam and sending Sadie in reverse until she was safely out of range. And no one seemed to notice that Mia's cheeks were flaming hot as it occurred to her that she was about to have five nights under the same roof with Ben, so she'd better start attempting to untangle her crazy mess of feelings, ready or not.

Chapter 17

THERE WERE NEVER GOOD TIMES TO RUN OUT OF coffee, but scraping the bottom of the tin and barely managing to come up with a measly half scoop this morning didn't help dissipate the thick fog clouding Mia's brain. She'd woken up at four thirty and hadn't been able to fall back to sleep, especially knowing Ben would be here around six in order to get an early start on a twelve-plus-hour drive.

The cabin was north of Duluth, and Mia suspected they'd be driving on snow-packed roads for the later portion of the trip. She intended to doze in the back with Ollie, then take over for Ben before the roads grew too messy. While Lynn was doing a bit of driving around town, she was out of practice enough that no one, not even Lynn herself, wanted to count on her as a driver.

Once they reached snow-packed roads, Ben would be on his own. It was funny, but even though Ben had never claimed to be confident driving on snow, something about having summited Everest seemed to make this a given. And Mia had dangerously fishtailed after hitting an ice patch a couple years back and hadn't been comfortable driving on snow since.

Her heart still pounded every time it hit her that she was about to spend five nights and six days under the same roof with Ben. She hoped they'd have time to themselves to talk, but she wasn't entirely sure what she

wanted to talk about. Or at least she wasn't sure she was ready to admit it aloud.

Lynn and Ollie were still asleep, and Mia was sorting through the bags of groceries she'd bought for the trip when her phone began to buzz. She crossed to the table and did a double take after spotting Irene's name and number on the screen. Whatever was she doing, calling at so early an hour?

"The last few days, I've been thinking how much he'd want to be a part of this trip," Irene said as soon as Mia answered.

Mia had thought the same thing, but the trip had also been Lynn's idea, and if Brad were alive, they'd be wrapping up a divorce, not going on a trip together. However, pointing that out to his grieving mom didn't seem like the kind thing to do. "He would very much have enjoyed a winter trip to Minnesota," was the best answer Mia could come up with on the spot.

"I have the urn. With his ashes. I wasn't planning on dispersing them yet, but when I couldn't sleep last night, it occurred to me that perhaps the best way to honor him is to leave a part of him up there. Not only there. Other places too. Places we know that he loved."

Mia tended to disagree with Irene more often than not. But it occurred to her this could be good for Ollie, help him get a bit more closure. All in all, he'd been holding up well, especially since the dogs had come home with them, and for the last week or so, his laughter filled the house as often as ever. But he also got angry or broke down over simple things, like when the scissors weren't under his usual command or when he found a hole in the pocket of his favorite sweatshirt or

when he couldn't find the match to the sock he'd picked
to wear.

"I think that's a good idea, Irene."

"When I first thought of it last night, I wanted to send
the urn with you, but I can't help but feel as if I need to
be there for this. I haven't been able to talk Victor into
it, but if you have room, I'd like to ride along. I'd stay
a few days and fly out of Duluth, then meet Victor in
New York. We're going to Italy for a few weeks. To
get away. I'll pack light for Minnesota, and Victor will
have the rest of my things with him. I won't take up
much room."

It was a plea, or at least as much of a plea as Mia
had ever heard from Irene. And although she couldn't
imagine Lynn and Irene under the same roof for any
stretch of days, much less in the same car a full day,
Mia's heart told her this wasn't something she should
discourage. She felt a swell of disappointment, knowing how it would change the dynamic—whatever that
dynamic might've looked like.

And though it was a quiet whisper of a feeling, some
part of her realized Irene might be the goalkeeper her
heart needed while she figured out what all those kisses
had meant…on Ben's part and hers.

"Yeah, of course. Do you, uh, want us to pick you up,
or are you coming here?"

"Thank you, Mia. Thank you. And Victor will drop
me off."

After clarifying a few things, like the time Ben was
due to arrive, Mia hung up and shook her head in disbelief. Irene and Lynn and three dogs and a little over seven
hundred miles. It was going to be a really long ride.

Chapter 18

EVEN THOUGH SHE USUALLY HAD A HARD TIME sleeping in cars, Mia somehow managed to doze most of the way through Illinois. She wasn't sure how Ben had managed to swing such a nice rental, but the metallic-silver Escalade ESV transporting them to snowman land was decidedly upscale. Using her fluffy coat as a blanket and propping her pillow against the window, Mia decided her middle-row bucket seat was as comfortable as any seat she'd ever ridden in. And even though the floor space in the middle and rear of the SUV was taken up by overflow luggage, Mia propped her legs on top of a duffel bag that was crammed in near her. To get everything to fit in addition to the dogs' kennels, they'd needed to be creative with space.

When Ollie had found out that with Irene riding along, one person would need to sit in the third row while the other half of the row would be folded down to make room for one of the dog kennels, he begged for dibs to sit back there. With the dogs in eyesight, a pile of books, and his imagination, he made it a hundred miles farther than Mia would've guessed without asking for a potty break.

When he finally declared he had to pee, he'd held it so long that he'd not been able to wait for a gas station. Ben pulled over near a stretch of empty fields, and Ollie did his business with the car shielding him from the highway.

Just north of Rockford, Illinois, close to the Wisconsin border, they stopped at a state park so that everyone, including the dogs, could stretch their legs. To Ollie's delight, there was ample snow on the ground, particularly in compacted mounds on the sides of the sidewalk, but judging by its slight discoloration, it wasn't even close to fresh. Mia had to remind him several times as they walked to the restrooms that it wasn't safe to eat.

"It's coming," she promised. "Bowls and bowls of it. I even packed the sprinkles."

Whenever it snowed heavily enough, they'd set out a bowl to collect snow, and Ollie would get to add sprinkles like it was ice cream.

After the group had gone to the bathroom and it was time to walk the dogs, neither Lynn nor Irene were interested in doing anything more than stretching their legs on the short, cleared path that led to the lake, so that left Mia and Ollie and Ben to walk the dogs. Since Sam was young and clingy enough, he could be trusted off leash to follow Sadie, and only Sadie and Turbo needed to be leashed.

The dogs had dozed in their crates for the most part, lulled into sleep by the drone of the highway, but now they were wide awake and more than ready to get out. After a dozen steps down the wooded trail, Ollie tugged Mia's sleeve. "Hey, Mom, this is Sam's first snow, isn't it?"

"I hadn't thought of that, but yeah it is." Although the puppy didn't seem too fazed by the experience, it did seem as if Sam was lifting his furry feet a bit higher than typical. The snow on the walking trail was packed, and he wasn't sinking in. Mia figured he'd have a different

experience all together once they got to the cabin and he experienced fresh, untouched snow.

Ollie frowned as Sam trotted alongside his mother, who was tentatively sniffing every mound and twig, her tail tucked tight against her bottom.

"I don't think he gets how fun it is. Sadie either."

Seeing Sadie's hesitation, Mia wondered if she'd ever gotten outside the house where she'd lived before. All the new experiences she was getting had to be daunting for a sheltered dog, especially one who'd been raised by a hoarder.

On the other hand, Turbo was pressing against his leash, pushing forward hard enough to prance sideways like a racehorse as he gazed into the trees at something Mia couldn't see. If he even noticed the packed snow under his feet, it wasn't apparent.

Mia had a hard time imagining Turbo handling the housebound life they'd led without going completely stir-crazy. Perhaps what they were seeing now were the residual effects of all that.

"They'll get used to it," Ben offered, ruffling Ollie's hair.

Ben didn't seem bothered by Turbo's intensity. Mia had heard him comment in the car about how energetic the dog consistently proved to be. This, added to what she'd heard from Megan and Tess about the rest of the group, had her suspecting she'd brought home the easiest two of the bunch.

When Mia's gaze settled on the strip of dark-blue leash wrapped around Ben's hand, her pulse burst into a sprint. Like the rest of him, his hands were strong, masculine, and lean, nothing wasted, nothing extra. She

could perfectly imagine splaying those fingers apart and pressing her lips against his palm. And then letting them trail up his wrist until they were impeded by the cuff of his coat sleeve.

To keep her thoughts from slipping down an unexpected rabbit hole of desire, she locked her attention back on Ollie, whose coat was hanging open and who'd accumulated more than his fair share of crumbs on the button-down collar of his pullover shirt from all the car snacks he'd devoured. She gave the collar a quick shake and sent most of the crumbs flying to the ground.

This wasn't the first time Mia had attempted to fight off an attraction to Ben. Or even close to it. She'd allowed herself an extended look at the photographs of him at Everest base camp in the feature *St. Louis Magazine* did of his second attempt to summit Everest. She'd taken such a careful look that she could perfectly recall how well snow and sunlight and fresh air favored him. And made her lose her breath just a little.

Suddenly, it occurred to her that addressing what those kisses had meant might be harder in the magical snow-globe land where they were headed. And it didn't help that it wasn't only her imagination any longer. She'd felt those hands sliding up the bare skin of her back, and she'd lost herself in those fabulous lips, even if it had only been for a short while.

Now it was if there were an electrical field drawing her body toward his.

Realizing she'd totally been derailed from Ollie and Ben's conversation, Mia struggled to curtail her thoughts. Ollie must have asked how come the dogs' feet didn't sting from touching the snow because Ben

was explaining how dogs and wolves had specialized blood vessels close to the pads of their feet that kept them just above freezing temperatures when walking on snow.

"Were there dogs on Mount Everest?" Ollie asked.

"There were a few stray ones hanging around base camp. I heard that sometimes they follow climbers up the mountain some, but they didn't on my ascent."

"There's snow there all year round and it's always cold, my dad said. I'd live there if I could. I'd always want it to be winter. Would you?"

Ben gave a light but quick shake of his head, reminding Mia that she'd not heard him say much about his trip to the summit. A fellow climber died from acute altitude sickness when he was at base camp, and another had died later in the season. She'd read that in the article. She'd wanted to ask about it, but she'd never had the opportunity.

"You know, Ol, there's cold, and there's Everest cold," Ben was saying. "Even at base camp, it's really high up and the air's thin. It gives you a headache almost all the time. And it's hard on your lungs. I'm glad I went back and climbed it again. But no, I wouldn't live there. There are plenty of places where you can get to a snow-capped mountain all year though. Places that are a lot more forgiving than Everest."

Ollie's mouth puckered into a sideways frown as he locked his hand in Ben's free one. "That sounds even colder than the North Pole."

As Ben and Ollie fell into a conversation about altitude and direct sunlight, Mia felt a sharp rush of gratitude for Ben. Regardless of what was happening

between her and him, God willing, for the rest of Ollie's life, or at least until he was grown, Ben would be there for him. And if she was being totally honest with herself, maybe, just maybe, he'd be there for her too.

―――

As Ben drove through the dark night, he realized it was probably a good thing Irene had come along. After the make-out session outside the shelter, Ben was having a hard time keeping his continually burning desire for Mia in check. Irene being here had kept his hand from closing over Mia's back or hips a half-dozen times today.

As Ben drove through the dark night, he was growing more and more confident that there would be a time for him and Mia, and all he needed to do was be patient.

Hearing Irene talk of how much Ollie was like his father reminded Ben of the other child Brad had fathered. Just as he hadn't found a way to tell Mia about the baby before Stacey approached her, he hadn't come close to figuring out a way to tell Irene or Victor. Not only was Ben not convinced it was his place, but he had no idea how he'd find the words. "By the way, the martyr of a son you're mourning, not only did he cheat, but there's an illegitimate grandson you might want to meet" wasn't going to cut it.

Sooner or later, he was going to have find a way. Perhaps it would come out here over the next few days. Maybe Mia would want to do it. Ben needed to talk to her, to bring light to some of this stuff. And this trip would be the best opportunity he'd get for some time alone to do so.

If he could first promise himself he'd keep from

kissing her again, that was. At least until she was good and ready to be kissed.

She'd driven for four hours this afternoon, and by that time, Ollie had been ready for a break from the far back, so Ben sat in the middle row with him, playing checkers on a magnetic travel board that had been balanced on the armrest of Ollie's seat. Lynn sat in front, regaling them with her Kenyan schoolhouse tales, and Irene dozed in back.

Ben had sat diagonally behind Mia, admiring the perfect line of her chin and the delicate shape of her nose. Her hair was growing out again, fast too. The sexy, short haircut she'd gotten this summer had drawn his attention to her smooth neck like a beacon. Now it had reached shoulder length again and was full and flowy, inviting him to lose his hands in it and find the smooth skin of her neck with his mouth.

To draw his wandering mind back to the monotonous task of driving long distance and away from all the things he wanted to do with Mia, Ben shifted in his seat and readjusted his hands on the steering wheel. It had started snowing an hour or so after dark. By that time, patches of packed snow were becoming more frequent on the roads, and a light snowfall was beginning. When Ben had noticed the strain in Mia's knuckles as she'd gripped the wheel, he'd offered to take over again, and when he'd promised he wasn't tired, she'd not argued.

The last eighty or so miles, the roads had become completely snow-packed. He'd dropped down to a steady sixty miles an hour, and the Escalade handled fine. In the darkness, the headlights and gentle snowfall were mesmerizing, and for the first time all day, the

entire group was quiet, captivated by the dance of the snowflakes in the headlights.

Finally, after managing a pace of just twenty miles an hour on tight, windy roads nestled in thick woods for the last several miles, Ben navigated down the long, private drive that led to the cabin. He held his breath, hoping that, after a lengthy online search with Lynn breathing down his neck before they'd chosen it, the photos, virtual tour, and reviews held true, and the cabin would be an inviting place to spend the next five days.

With Ollie craning in his seat to look out the front windshield, they rounded a bend in the road, and finally the cabin was in view. A short laugh escaped Ben as he took it in: a wide single-story ranch, peaked at the center, built with traditionally notched white-pine logs and accented with the rounded stone of the Great Lakes and a wraparound porch supported by thick pine columns. Snow-covered landscaping lights were on, sending a cascade of soft yellow out across the flat, snowy yard, and porch lights and a few interior lights glowed into the night, welcoming them after a long journey.

Ben parked in the plowed circular drive as a chorus of approval filled the car. Turbo rose in his crate and shook himself off as if anticipating the end of the long drive. Then Ollie exclaimed that Santa should move his shop here, and Ben agreed, laughing aloud for the pure joy of it.

Chapter 19

MIA COULD TELL THE SUN WAS SHINING BRIGHTLY even while she was cuddled deep into the cozy mattress and fluffy pillow of the double bed, her eyes still closed. Early-morning sunlight reflected off the snow-covered cedars and pines and streamed into her southeast-facing room, warming her face and body. It was a five-bedroom cabin, and Mia had chosen one of the two standard bedrooms that were joined in the middle by a long but narrow Jack-and-Jill bathroom. Ollie had the adjoining bedroom. The walls were notched pine, and the furniture was mostly pine too, decorated with Northwoods quilts and pillows and knickknacks and cedarwood-scented wax warmers.

She'd left it up to the other members of their party to sort out the remaining three rooms, two of which had private bathrooms and were considerably nicer than the third. As she'd helped Ollie drag his bags into his room last night, she'd listened to their conversation, curious to see how it played out. At the onset of the discussion, Lynn had insisted that since Ben had footed the entire bill—something she'd not made known until that moment—he have the master suite on the end. Irene had agreed, just a bit less enthusiastically. That left Irene and Lynn to sort out who had the room with en suite bathroom, king-size bed, and plush furniture, and who had the no-frills standard bedroom with a double bed and no TV.

Knowing her mom, Mia was certain Lynn could care less about a private bathroom or a bed that was larger or more comfortable than the hard double she slept on in the small house she shared with three other staff a half mile from the school where she taught in Kenya. However, her mom was as strong-willed as they came and clearly enjoyed goading Irene into disagreements, so Mia had suspected a contest for the better bedroom. Irene was accustomed to both upscale living and self-promotion. When Lynn instead offered right at the start to take the smaller bedroom, it seemed as if Irene was a touch disappointed in her anticlimactic victory.

Surprised by how well she'd slept, Mia tossed off the cozy down comforter and stretched. Usually her first night in a new place was mostly a wash as far as sleep was concerned, but not here. A glance at her phone showed it was a couple minutes after eight. She'd forgotten how the sun came up later this far north in winter, and earlier in summer. She'd slept almost nine hours, only stirring once when the puppy had whined and needed to pee.

She headed over to the wide window, the wooden floors cool but not freezing against her bare feet. Looking outside, she covered her mouth, smiling wide. Who needed TVs or smartphones in the face of all this beauty? Just outside the door was a winter wonderland: towering, snow-covered pines and cedars, and a blanket of white, powdery snow on the ground. Even the foot-steps they'd made last night as they'd checked out the yard had been covered by fresh snow.

A movement in her far-left field of view caught her eye, and Mia gasped in surprise. Something big was out

there, fifty or so feet away, walking among the pines. Not just big. Really big.

From her viewpoint, she was only able to see its body, a muscular, brown one, long legs, and no obvious tail. She tried to match the body she was seeing with her knowledge of horses and cows, the only animals that large she'd seen in person, but something didn't fit.

To her disappointment, the animal disappeared behind a thick pine. Mia craned her neck, hoping for another glimpse, and waited. Thirty seconds, then a minute passed, and nothing. Then she saw movement again, but it didn't make sense.

Suddenly, she gasped as she realized what she was seeing suspended in midair was actually a massive antler. The rest of the animal was still hidden behind the tree.

She dashed across her room, through the bathroom, and through the open, adjoining door. "Ollie! Ol, wake up! You have to see this!" She felt a bit bad waking him, but he'd dozed a lot in the car yesterday and had gone to bed much later than usual. Waking up now would help get him back on a normal routine.

With the zero-to-sixty sleep-to-wake cycle that Mia suspected was a childhood superpower, Ollie popped up from the mound of covers he'd been buried in.

"Is it Sasquatch?" Ollie's eyes grew big, and Mia wasn't sure if that was from fear or excitement, or both. In the car yesterday, Lynn had filled him with Sasquatch stories from her youth when she'd come up here on trips with her parents in summer and had gone on night Sasquatch search walks with a cousin led by a group of local Sasquatch hunters.

"No, sweets, it's better."

She jogged to Ollie's same-side window and gasped. Not only did she have the perfect view from here, but the animal was now walking straight toward the house. She held a finger to her lips as Ollie joined her.

Ollie's mouth gaped open. "Is it a reindeer?"

"No, that's a moose. A big one. A boy."

It was walking straight toward the cabin. His antlers had to reach four or five feet from tip to tip. He was big and powerful and completely awe-inspiring. Tears filled Mia's eyes. "He's majestic, isn't he?"

"How do you know he's a boy?"

"Because he has antlers, and moose are in the deer family. In the deer family, only males have antlers. This is the first moose I've ever seen in real life."

Mia and Ollie hardly breathed as the big bull moose continued straight toward the house, stopping once he reached the edge of the wraparound porch. He sniffed the bannister, sending a shower of snow cascading off the top. Mia wished she'd grabbed her phone, but she was afraid if she went for it now, he'd catch the movement through the glass and run off. Instead, she left her arms draped over Ollie's shoulders and watched. She could feel the excited walloping of Ollie's heartbeat as she held him against her.

The moose was close enough that she could see moisture on the light-brown, thick, coarse fur on his neck and back. She also noticed the softer, shorter velvety-brown hair around his mouth and nose, and the almost odd way his antlers projected out from the crown of his head underneath his big ears.

"Magnificent."

"Mom, can I go get Mimi?" His voice was barely a whisper.

"Okay, but tiptoe out of here until you're out of sight."

The moose was walking slowly along the side of the porch, smelling the top railing. Mia wondered if the cabin owner or one of the regular renters left out food on occasion. She also wondered what kind of food they'd leave out for a moose.

The floor creaked when Ollie was halfway out of the room. The sharp sound must have been audible outside because the moose stopped his casual stroll and cocked his head their way, one of his massive antlers bumping against the closest porch column. Mia stood frozen in place, certain he was looking right at her for the first time.

She was just barely aware of Ollie coming back into the room, whispering in the louder-than-regular-talk way that he did. Then a dog jumped onto Ollie's bed, and a series of sharp, high barks erupted through the room.

After letting out a startlingly loud snort, the giant bull moose trotted away from the house into the woods in the same direction he'd come. Once he'd made it a good distance, he turned to look at the house and snorted again.

"Wow."

Mia turned to find Ben standing behind her. When he met her gaze, she was fairly certain her cheeks flushed tomato-red. He was wearing a pair of dark-gray running pants and a white long-sleeved T-shirt and looked fresh and awake as if he'd been up awhile. Through the doorway, she spotted his open laptop on the living-room coffee table.

And you're in your pajamas. With the excitement over their woodland visitor, when she'd let Ollie go

after Lynn, Mia hadn't given a single thought to the fact that she was wearing only the button-down red flannel nightshirt that had been a Christmas gift last year or that she most definitely had bedhead.

"Can you believe it?" Ollie asked, drawing Ben's attention away from her as Turbo continued to bark from atop Ollie's bed.

Ben ruffled Ollie's sleep-messy hair. "Hardly. A bull moose like that is something to see, all right. I was outside walking Turbo a half hour ago, and I spotted a female on the other side of the lake. I didn't think we'd get any this close to the house."

Mia finger combed through her hair as Sadie let out a single bark from Mia's room where she and Sam were crated. Irene appeared in the doorway to Ollie's room, her mouth pursing sharply. She didn't shy away from looking Mia up and down, Mia bet disapproving of her bare-from-midthigh-down legs. Hopefully, her lack of a bra wasn't obvious.

It wasn't as though she'd planned this. She had to force her arms not to lock over her chest. "I'll, uh, get dressed and take the dogs out. I didn't think I'd sleep this late."

"I'll take them out if you'd like," Ben offered. "Turbo won't mind going out again, I'm sure."

Mia shrugged. "Sure. Thanks."

"With moose this close to the house, I think we should keep Sadie and Turbo on leashes. Sam'll be fine unless he starts to show some inclination of being ready to leave Sadie's side out here." Ben looked at Ollie, lifting one eyebrow in invitation. "Want to come? You can put on your boots and throw your coat over your pajamas."

"Heck, yeah," Ollie said, sounding like Taye. He raced into the Jack-and-Jill bathroom and, leaving the door wide open, started to pee a loud morning pee. The sound reverberated through the room and sent Irene away with a frown.

Turbo hopped off the bed and trotted in after him, eyeing Ollie's pee stream from a distance and cocking his head quizzically at the toilet.

"Like I said," Ben said, chuckling, "he's not one to pass up the opportunity to scent mark on something. Thankfully, he's figuring out pretty quickly he can only do it outside." Calling Turbo to his side, he passed through the bathroom to the crates in Mia's room when Ollie finished.

Mia followed, reminding Ollie to wash his hands and wondering if Ben had any idea that even though the room had only been hers for one night, his presence in it made her heart race and her palms sweat. "Sam will have an accident between here and the front door if someone doesn't hold him," she said to fill the quiet that seemed more pronounced by the combination of being in a nightshirt and having Ben so near her bed. "He still thinks anything outside his crate is free range. Sadie's doing better though. I'll hold him till you get your boots on and get Sadie and Turbo leashed."

Ben agreed, and Mia made quick work of snatching up Sam from his crate, even though he did his best to lunge free as soon as it was unlatched. Once he was snug in her arms and straining to lick her chin, she followed Ben and Sadie into the main cabin. The kitchen, dining room, and living room were part of an open floor plan under a high, airy vault.

Irene had worked her way into the kitchen and was filling the coffeepot with tap water.

"I'll help make breakfast while the guys take out the dogs," Mia offered in Irene's direction as she and Ben reached the front door. "We'll have to go to the store today, but I packed the cooler and shopping bag with enough for a breakfast of pancakes and chicken sausage and eggs."

Ollie joined them and was mumbling, "Pancakes, pancakes, pancakes," in his monster voice as he shoved his bare feet into his snow boots.

Irene shut off the water and made a show of sweeping a stray lock of silver-gray hair from her forehead. "Once you're dressed."

They were three simple, benign words, but they were delivered with such clear implication that even Ollie stopped his pancake chant to glance at Mia's nightgown. She was certain Ben picked up on it too, but Mia was unable to look his way in confirmation.

"Mom always makes pancakes in her pajamas," Ollie said with just a touch of *Duh, didn't you know?* to his tone, and Mia felt a tad vindicated.

Once Ollie's coat was on, Mia passed Sam into his arms and reminded him not to set the puppy down until he was on actual ground.

"How can I tell what's ground and what's driveway?" Ollie asked.

Ben had the front door wide open, and Mia saw he had a valid point. There was only snow and more snow out there. "Maybe it doesn't matter that much when the snow's this deep. Just remember to give him the good-job sign wherever he does his business out there."

After watching them trudge down the steps, Turbo pressing ahead as far as the leash would allow and Sadie walking hesitantly beside Ben and Ollie, Mia shut the door and headed for the kitchen. Still a touch dehydrated from the long drive, she opened the overhead cabinet doors until she found the coffee mugs. She pulled one down and filled it with water.

She was debating whether there was any real benefit in addressing the nightgown comment when Irene spoke.

"On the way here, I kept thinking how it's almost convenient, this family vacation of yours. Ben can be here to step into Brad's role. It's almost like your little family is still intact."

Mia choked on the water she was swallowing. She set the mug onto the counter. It smacked hard, and water splashed onto the granite. "Excuse me? Are you actually going there with this?"

Irene said nothing but stood straighter, squaring her shoulders.

"It's almost like you forgot a few things," Mia continued, incensed. "Like how Ben is Ollie's godfather. He's here for Ollie."

Irene raised one eyebrow high enough that it disappeared underneath her bangs. "I was just saying that it's convenient, Mia."

"It's what you seem to be implying that's troubling me."

"If the shoe fits," Irene mumbled, turning away.

Mia's blood was racing. "Irene, I *left* Brad. And all day yesterday you kept implying I was going back. Well I *wasn't*. We were getting a divorce. I'd visited a lawyer, and I'd signed papers. And I would've chosen that a

million times over what happened to him, but it doesn't change the fact that I was leaving him."

Irene smacked the flat of her hand on the counter. "My son was a *good* man. I don't need you dishonoring his memory to my grandson!"

Irene's counter smack might well have been a smack against Mia's face. "I wouldn't do that, Irene. Brad was a good father, and I wouldn't do that to my son. But none of that made him a good husband. He wasn't even a *faithful* husband to me."

"That's ridiculous!" Angry red splotches pocked Irene's face. "You're making that up. He'd have told me!"

Mia was seeing red. Flaming, angry, wartime red. And blood was pulsing hot through her veins. She could feel the heat racing down into her legs, warming her bare feet the same as if she were standing on heated tile. "Like he told you about the baby?" It was out before she could stop it. Mia could see the weight of it sinking in as Irene flushed, blinking in confusion.

"Mia…" It was Ben in the doorway. She'd not heard the door open, but he was standing there with Turbo. How long had he been there? Had he heard everything Irene had implied? "Can we save this for later? When I'm inside." His tone was soft, softer than she'd have expected.

Mia's entire body was shaking. She'd never had a confrontation with Irene that had gotten even close to this heated. Even though she'd seen Irene goad Victor a dozen times, Mia hadn't not been prepared for the crazy, wild anger that had mounted inside her in response to Irene's accusations. And after the nightgown comment, she'd not been centered enough to keep the anger at bay.

"Ollie wants his gloves," Ben added, his voice calm, nonaccusing. And he was looking at her, not Irene. "He's got Sadie and Sam, and I don't want to leave him for long. Can you get them for me?"

"You're...you're going to have a baby?" Irene's voice had dropped into a whisper.

Mia stood frozen, unable to answer her, unable to move toward Ben.

There was a shuffling on the other side of the cabin, and then a door closed. Lynn had come out of her room. "Mia can't have more children, if you remember, Irene." She, too, was considerably calmer than Mia might have expected if she'd overheard half of what had just played out in the kitchen.

Lynn walked into the kitchen, dressed in a thin, worn pair of linen pj's and not seeming to care that her tatas showed through like headlights on a foggy night, and somehow this was the only thing in the entire moment that Mia was able to hold on to. Lynn, her forty-seven-year-old mother who never seemed dressed correctly for the occasion and never seemed to care, and even though she was exasperating and self-indulgent and embarrassing at times, Mia loved her wildly.

"Mia, I'll get Ollie's gloves. Do you know where they are?" Lynn was beside her, sweeping a lock of hair back from Mia's face. Her mom's fingers were like ice against her skin.

Mia blinked, doing her best to focus and slow her racing heart. "They should be in Ollie's inside coat pockets. I put them in there last night when I was hanging up his coat."

The words were just out when she heard Ollie's high,

thin "Here they are" trailing in through the open door from out in the yard.

Ben looked at Lynn. "I'll be back in a few minutes if you've got this."

Lynn waved him off. "I'll put on a kettle of tea. I've never been much for coffee." She patted Mia on the arm. "Why don't you take a few minutes to yourself to have a shower, Mia? I have a feeling it's going to be a long day."

Chapter 20

ALL IN ALL, BEN SHOULDN'T FEEL AS ENERGIZED AS he did. He'd overheard Mia telling Irene with one hundred percent clarity that her marriage had been over, and then their argument had escalated, and Mia had burst out that bit about the baby.

While Mia was in the shower and Ollie was helping Lynn make pancakes, he'd done his best to help Irene adjust to this potentially life-changing news. He could only imagine how it was rocking her world. And this was before meeting Stacey. Stacey had just turned twenty and, with her visits to her shaman and her everyday talk of past-life experiences, couldn't be more different from Irene and Victor. Ben couldn't fathom how Stacey and that baby would fit into their life.

After a mostly silent breakfast during which Mia offered an apology that Irene accepted but didn't reciprocate, Irene retreated to her room to call her husband.

Mia looked at her mom after the rest of them had worked as a group to clean up. "We should probably go to the store to get groceries now rather than later."

Even though she'd directed the words to Lynn, Ben interjected. "I think you should come build a snowman, and we'll get groceries later." Mia's eyes widened, and when she didn't respond immediately, he pressed on. "The sun's out and it's beautiful and you need this more than you need a trip to the store."

"Yeah, Mom, come help us build a snowman." Ollie had been down on his knees following Sam around at the end of the counter, pretending to be a dog himself. He jumped up and ran to the fridge and pulled out the gallon-size Ziploc that he'd brought from home filled with carrots, cranberries, and a handful of buttons as well.

Mia's gaze drifted to Irene's closed door for a second or two, and then she seemed to straighten her spine. "I guess you can eat leftover car snacks if you get hungry later, Ol. Ben's right. Helping you build your first snowman in Minnesota is too important to pass up."

"Good choice, Mia," Lynn said. "I was wondering if I was going to have to beat you over the head with a fun stick before this vacation was over."

Ollie laughed and Mia shook her head at her mom's comment, but an easy smile lingered on her face as they headed off to get dressed.

Ten minutes later, Ben was dressed in snow gear but hanging back in his room after answering a client call when he heard Ollie yell "Oops!" He hung up and headed out to find Ollie standing in front of a wide-open front door.

"All of them?" Ben asked, hearing the barking outside.

"It was an accident. I opened the door and Turbo pushed out, and when I was trying to get him, Sam and Sadie followed me."

Ben squeezed Ollie on the shoulder when he reached the door. "It happens."

To his surprise, Turbo was still in sight. Rather than dashing off into the woods at high speed, he was thirty or so feet away, trotting around and scent marking on anything with any height to it. Suspecting it would be

next to impossible to catch him right off the bat, Ben figured the best thing to do was go with it. Turbo was a bright dog, and Ben had seen a difference in his socialization in a week. The young dog seemed to want to understand his commands, even when Ben didn't have a treat in hand.

Hopefully it would help that Turbo had been raised in a house with Sadie and Sam, and neither of them were going anywhere. Earlier it had become apparent that Sam didn't like the deep snow and did nothing more than jump between the imprints of their footsteps, and Sadie, who was currently looking up at Ben and Ollie from the bottom of the porch and barking, was the kind of dog who liked to stay in the vicinity of her people.

"Turbo could probably use some time off leash that isn't on a roof," Ben said. "Let's let him do his stuff while we build the snowman."

"What if the moose comes back?"

"He's a smart dog. Hopefully, he'll know when he's met his match. And remind me to snap some pictures for Taye, will you?"

Ollie agreed as they got into their boots. "Are you good at building snowmen?"

"I used to know how to build a pretty serious snowman. I've been in the snow my fair share of times, but I haven't built any since I was a kid," Ben admitted. "But hopefully it's like riding a bike and it'll come back."

Ollie gave him a big smile. "How can you be in the snow so much and not build a snowman? Maybe Mimi needs to beat you over the head with a fun stick."

"I guess if I'm going to get beat over the head with something, it might as well be a fun stick."

By the time the snowman building ceased, the sprawling, wooded yard no longer resembled the pristine, snow-covered wonderland that had greeted them on arrival last night. The snow had been trampled and shoveled down to a thin layer. Six snowmen of all shapes and sizes stood guard at various places: three lining the walkway to the house, two nestled into quiet coves of trees, and the last one in back overlooking the lake.

"This one is Dad," Ollie said.

Irene had been watching them from the window intermittently for a few hours and stepped outside to join them in time to hear Ollie's remark. Speaking softly, almost to herself, she said, "Maybe that would be a good place to leave a part of him." When no one disagreed, she nodded to herself and headed back inside.

After she left, Ollie declared he wasn't ready to go in, and Lynn asked, "Is anyone in the mood for a snowball war?"

Ollie whooped. "Ben, I'm on your team!" Ben laughingly agreed, and Mia watched her son wrap his hands around Ben's arm. As he'd done when Ollie was smaller, Ben raised his arm with just the slightest strain, lifting Ollie into the air. Ben pretended to struggle, saying, "Ollie, you weigh a ton!" When he finally set him down, the two of them ran off laughing to stockpile snowballs.

Mia headed off with Lynn to a cove of trees at the side yard, a wave of appreciation for Ben's upper-body strength rolling over her.

Ben and Ollie set up camp fifty or sixty feet away. The dogs trotted back and forth between the two

groups, sniffing under the bases of the trees and digging up snow piles of their own. Even Turbo was finally slowing down. Rather than circling the yard at an almost continuous sprint, he was content to hang near Sadie and Sam.

Within twenty minutes, each team had rolled an impressive supply of snowballs, and the war commenced. Mia laughed so hard it made her belly hurt.

By the time they shuffled up the porch steps, exhausted and soaked, everyone was famished. Ollie collapsed on the floor like a wet noodle, declaring, "I can't move another decimeter."

Mia applauded. "Good use of the metric system, buddy." She stepped over him, planting one foot on each side of him, facing his feet. "Let me help you take off your boots." She proceeded to tug them off, freeing several chunks of packed snow. The dogs shook, sending their own frozen clumps of snow all over the entryway, then sank to the floor. Their mouths hung open in big grins as they panted. Sam plopped on his side, looking as exhausted as Ollie, and Mia felt like laughing as she contemplated the pileup of dogs and little boy, coats, boots, hats, mittens, and frozen snow.

Ben took off his boots, pulled a broom from the closet, and gave Mia a wink as he swept the still-frozen chunks out the door. Mia's heart warmed at the simple display of domesticity. *What would it be like to have a partner who thought of such things on his own?* A new experience, she determined, and one she could happily get used to.

By the time everyone had changed into dry clothes, it was apparent the group was too famished to wait for Mia

to complete a grocery run, and the food she'd packed was nearly gone.

Before she voiced her thoughts, Ben showed he was thinking the same thing too. "Hey, what do you say we go into town to that cozy-looking restaurant we passed on the way in. I think it was called the Blue Goose."

Everyone applauded this idea. Once there, the inside proved just as cute and quaint as the outside. Ollie inhaled two bowls of macaroni and cheese, and Mia finished every bite of her white chicken chili in a bread bowl, glancing under her lashes across the table at Ben her share of times. She was sure it wasn't just her; he looked exceptionally sexy and vibrant after the romp in the snow.

On their way home, they swung by the store and tossed enough food into two carts to cook at the cabin the next several days and then some. By the time they got back to the cabin, it was nearly four o'clock and the sun was sinking on the horizon. When the groceries were put away and Mia was folding the last bag, Irene cleared her throat a touch dramatically and announced, "I'd like to scatter some of Brad's ashes near the snowman by the lake. Would anyone like to go with me?" She seemed both surprised and gratified when everyone agreed.

With Irene's help, Ollie poured some of the ashes, which fell in a disappointing clump at the base of the snowman. But then the wind picked up, scattering them onto the snow and partway across the lake.

When no one seemed quite sure what to do next, Ben stepped forward with a suggestion. "Ollie, how would you like it if we all shared a favorite memory of your dad?"

When Ollie nodded enthusiastically, Mia smiled. "Brad built Ollie the best blanket forts. They were so big you couldn't even step foot in the living room."

"And sometimes he'd lift up the tape and peek at the presents Mom put under the tree," Ollie added.

When the gentle laughter died down, Ben added, "We did a comedy skit in a third-grade talent show, and when I froze up and couldn't remember my lines, Brad did a running jump off the stage to distract everyone. It got him a trip to the principal's office."

Everyone laughed again, this time harder. "I always thought he was just being a ham," Irene added, wiping tears from her eyes.

After Brad was honored, they headed back inside. Ben made a roaring fire, and Ollie dragged a mound of pillows and his box of Hot Wheels over near it. He curled on top of the pillows and pushed the Hot Wheels around the floor next to him until bath time.

After a bath and a dessert of s'mores roasted in the living room fireplace, Ollie proved too tired for more than a single book. He drifted off to sleep with a smile on his face, and Mia's heart swam in contentment. It had ended up being a good day. A *really* good day.

Listening to his soft, even breathing, she considered giving in and drifting off beside him, but fought against it. At the very least, the dogs needed to go out again. She pushed up and scooped Sam, who'd been dozing curled against Ollie's neck and shoulders, into one arm. After pulling the covers back over her son, she headed for the door. Sadie hopped down from the foot of Ollie's bed and trailed at Mia's heels.

Training Sam was fun and exhausting and a bit

like going through parenting again, only the decisions seemed to hit faster. Mia hadn't been sure if she'd wanted to allow Sadie and Sam on the furniture since doing so had both plusses (irreplaceable cuddling time) and minuses (unwanted dog hair).

The scale had been tipped for good by the way Ollie glowed with happiness when Sam was curled up next to him in bed, and Mia figured she'd invest in a good vacuum. For a little while longer, though, both dogs would be crated at bedtime. She couldn't see how they'd ever successfully potty train Sam unless they did.

Mia stepped out from Ollie's room to find that the main cabin was empty. A single lamp was on, and the dwindling fire still glowed in the fireplace. Lynn and Irene had retired to their rooms when Mia had gone in with Ollie to help him get ready for bed. Neither Ben nor Turbo were anywhere in sight, and Mia wondered if Ben was done for the night too. He'd driven the bulk of the way yesterday and had been up well before her this morning. And he'd given the snowman building his all.

A rush of disappointment swept over her at the thought of not getting to say good night to Ben. Swallowing it down, she headed resolutely to the door with Sam. Surely she wouldn't be out long enough to need more than her coat and boots. Her snowsuit was most likely still damp, and even if it wasn't, she wouldn't be able to get into it while holding on to Sam. And if she put him down, he'd probably wake up enough to realize he had to pee and do it on the floor.

Sadie's accident-free streak was continuing another full day, and Mia was holding her breath that now that

she wasn't living in subpar conditions, Sadie had figured out going potty was for outside only.

The snow boots were all lined up beside the door on two long, thick rugs that were wet from the clumps of ice and snow that had been clinging to the boots when they'd come inside. The cold, wet patches stung Mia's bare feet as she slipped into hers. She grabbed her coat from the closet and snaked it up one arm, transferred the puppy, then snaked it up the other.

When Mia moved to open the door and realized it was unlocked, she looked closer at the row of boots. Ben's were missing. *So he's not in bed.* Her heart skittered in her chest. She opened the door with bated breath, but he was nowhere in sight.

Feeling the rush of cold air, Sam gave a determined shake of his head. His muscles tensed against her as if he was getting ready to leap. Sadie trotted backward several feet from the door as if to say "No thanks."

Holding it open wider, Mia signed to her in encouragement. "Come on, girl. It'll be a quick one, promise."

Sadie whined but reluctantly followed Mia outside to the porch. Mia shut the door behind them and figured if Sadie didn't leave the porch, then she didn't need to pee.

Bright blue-white moonlight poured over the yard, bright enough to create shadows from the trees on the snow, and thousands of stars dotted the sky. With skies this clear, it promised to be a very cold night, making Mia feel thankful for the down comforter waiting inside.

The puppy squirmed in her arms as she stepped out deeper into the yard, crunching snow under her boots, until she set him down and zipped her coat. It was

considerably colder than it had been earlier when the sun was shining, and even then the temps had only been in the high twenties.

Ben and Turbo were nowhere to be seen, and Mia wondered how far he'd walk alone at night. She headed out into the yard, unable to entice Sadie off the snow-cleared porch. After the time he'd spent outside today, Sam was accustomed to the snow. He no longer followed behind, jumping from footprint to footprint. Instead, he trotted through, creating his own path, diving underneath windswept mounds, burying himself completely, then popping up and shaking himself off.

Mia was laughing at his antics when Sadie tore off the porch at something she'd spotted, barking and racing away into the darkness at the side of the cabin. Adrenaline dumped into Mia's system, and she snatched Sam into her arms, snow and all, before he noticed and tried to follow his mom after who knew what.

She tensed, waiting, squinting to make out something in the darkness while trying to will Sadie back. It occurred to Mia that it would be safer on the porch, and she'd just taken a few steps in that direction when she heard something much bigger than Sadie walking in the direction she'd run off.

"Ben?" *Please be Ben. Please, please, please.*

She was as tense as she could remember being when Ben called out into the night, "It's me."

"Thank God," she said, heading over that way to meet him. "I was afraid the moose was back and Sadie would get kicked chasing after him." Finally Ben came into view. He had Turbo on a leash and Sadie was trailing along at his side, sniffing his pants.

"Yeah, I took Turbo for a walk but didn't want to let him off leash at night, just in case."

Mia felt a rush of hesitation as Ben neared. "I thought the dogs might need to get outside another time before I put them in their crates."

"Ollie's asleep already?"

"As soon as his head hit the pillow. It was all the fresh air, I guess."

"Yeah, it'll do that to you." Ben fell into step beside her as they wound around the trees toward the front of the house.

She swallowed. Suddenly her throat was tight, and there was no denying why. They needed to talk. For hours into the night. There was so much to discuss. The baby. This thing that was happening between them. What it might mean for Ollie.

The only problem was Mia didn't want to waste another minute of it not kissing him.

She swallowed hard. *Talk, you idiot.* "Thanks for everything. For coming and all. For being so good to him."

"I love him."

She did her best to snip through the strings of connection drawing her to him. She was at a loss for words again, and Ben wasn't helping them come any easier. She sat a squirmy and excited Sam back onto the ground. When they reached the front of the house, Sadie ran back up onto the porch and perched on the mat in front of the door.

They were both quiet as they watched Sam leap and jump in a patch of untampered snow. After a bit, he stopped abruptly to pee. When he finished, Mia bent

down to douse him with pats and scratches, then stood straight again.

"Are you ready to go in? It's freezing."

"Mia, I'm sorry I didn't tell you about the baby."

They'd each spoken at exactly the same time. Mia bit her lip. "I can see why you didn't, I guess. Would you have? Eventually."

"Yeah, definitely. I was trying to find the right time."

She nodded, conscious of her beating heart and the deep breaths she was taking. "I forgive you. Today's a day for forgiveness, it seems."

He shifted Turbo's leash from one hand to the other. "About the other night...do you remember what you meant by 'Et tu, Brute'? You texted that."

Sam trotted off from them and up to the porch, snuggling against his mom, ready to go inside and get warm. Turbo watched him for a few seconds, then looked off into the woods, not seeming to notice the cold.

Somehow, Mia knew if she told the truth, nothing was going to be the same. A tiny, nearly incoherent fear-filled voice inside her was screaming that she needed to stop this. To stop herself.

Instead, she chose to trust herself. Even if she couldn't put it into words, she knew what she was doing. Suddenly her throat loosened, and the words spilled out. "The night Ollie was born, after the accident, you were there. You held my hand because Brad couldn't. And not just that night. So many other times too. Sometimes I swear you're the only person in the world who really sees me. When I figured out it was you Stacey was talking about in the letter, it wasn't just that you knew and didn't tell me, learning that made me doubt... I don't know...everything."

She could see the pain her words caused, and that more than anything was why she let herself step in and press her lips against his. He was four or five inches taller, but on the tips of her toes, she could just reach his lips. And just like before, she liked it. She liked everything about it.

She closed her bare, cold hands over the sides of his face and opened her mouth fully to his. He had strong lips, and she could feel the stubble from one day's growth of beard against her skin.

He smelled like the Minnesota woods, cedar and pine, and he tasted like the s'mores they'd had in front of the fire. She could taste the sugar and chocolate on his lips and tongue. Her head began to swim, and she wondered if it was a flashback to drunkenly kissing him, or if she wasn't breathing. Light-headed or not, she couldn't pull away. She needed his kiss like she needed air, and he was going to have to be the one to stop it.

Only he didn't. His hands slipped into her hair, and he lowered his face to hers so that she didn't have to stand on her tiptoes. His tongue met hers, and he pulled closer as if he needed her the same way she needed him.

If he never pulled away, if he'd stand out here kissing her till they froze, Mia wouldn't complain. Kissing Ben felt more than just good. It felt right. Like she'd been traveling a long time and had finally landed exactly where she should have been all along. It was as if she could feel broken pieces of herself mending together, halves becoming whole.

And somehow, even though she couldn't explain it, she knew he felt the same way.

—∿∿—

It took Sadie's loud and determined bark piercing out across the night to bring an end to their kiss. Mia was beginning to shiver in his arms from the cold, and Ben knew they needed to get inside. His mind and body felt disconnected from each other, much like when he climbed at high altitudes. Rational thoughts were coming slowly, reaching him through a fog, this time a fog of desire. He'd waited for this for longer than he'd imagined waiting for anything, both craving it and discounting the possibility of it ever happening.

But here she was, instigating another kiss. And this time, she was sober. His blood pulsed, and he grew hot with desire. Her kiss was sprinkled with the taste of s'mores, and he could feel the wild need in her touch. Her body ground against his, an enticing combination of thighs, hips, stomach, and breasts pressing against him.

As Sadie's incessant bark filled the quiet night, they wrenched apart. Ben closed his hand against her back and drew her toward the house. "Let's get the dogs inside before Sadie wakes everyone up."

After shuffling up the steps in silence behind Turbo, they filed inside behind the dogs. Sadie made fast tracks to the couch, where she circled a few times, then curled into a tight ball, tucking her nose under her tail. Sam trotted along after her but couldn't manage the jump. He balanced on his back legs and whined up at her while Turbo stretched out on the floor in front of the dying fire.

Mia looked from him to the dogs a bit apprehensively after slipping out of her boots. Her coat was still on, and

she wasn't moving to take it off. "Do you think anyone woke up?"

"Let's give it a minute and see." After kicking out of his boots, Ben jogged over and hoisted an impatient Sam onto the couch. The little guy had made the same jump several times this morning, but he'd had a demanding and physical day in the snow and it had clearly worn him out.

Ben slipped out of his coat and headed back over to the coat closet, giving Mia space to finish hanging hers. He wondered if she was having second thoughts about what they'd been doing outside, but when she was done, she hung nearby, waiting for him to finish.

"Do you want to talk?" Her voice was soft and low and intimate.

"If you aren't tired."

She bit her lip. There was a playful light in her bright blue-gray eyes. "I'm much less tired than I was ten minutes ago."

He smiled. "Well said."

She looked from the darkened kitchen to the lamp-lit living room to his closed bedroom door. She leaned close and placed one hand on his shoulder, rising on her tiptoes to whisper in his ear. "I'd be okay *not* talking too. If you are, I mean."

He pulled back enough to look her in the eye. His blood was boiling hot, and he wasn't thinking with any tools above the waistline, and it was quite possible she wasn't either.

"You sure?"

She held his gaze but took several seconds to respond. She was breathing fast and her cheeks were flushed,

which he suspected wasn't just from the cold. Finally, she nodded. "Very."

He answered by pressing his mouth against hers and lifting her high enough that her legs locked around his waist. He locked one hand around her thigh and the other in her hair. He carried her to the bedroom, opening the door as quietly as he could, and closing it behind him before Turbo could follow him in. Hopefully, the dogs were tired enough to behave themselves for a little while.

He was close to carrying her straight to the bed when some part of him remembered that no matter how much he wanted this right this very second, he'd also waited long enough to know to savor it.

The room was big and dark and had a wall of windows on the north side. He carried her over there, still kissing her as he walked, and returned her to her feet. He pushed back her hair and kissed the smooth skin of her chin, neck, and sternum until he could tell from her breathing that she was as lost in it as he was. When he stopped kissing her and went for her sweater, she met his gaze and lifted her arms. He took his time removing her bra, sliding the straps off her shoulders and letting her breasts spill over the top, the sight of which made him ache for her even more.

After he took the bra off, he stood back, refusing to give in to his need for her until he'd memorized the way the moonlight reflected off her skin, accenting the curve of her breasts and the peak of her nipples.

Finally, too hungry to hold back, he moved in with hands and mouth at once, and she pulled him closer, locking her fingers in his hair and releasing a gasp of

desire. He was at the cusp of losing control and dragging her to the bed, but somehow he found a bit more strength and held off. With his hands on either side of her hips, he hooked his thumbs into her pants and slid them down until they were midthigh, then dropped to his knees.

She was a goddess in the moonlight, and he honored her with his hands and with his mouth until she climaxed and afterward, when it receded, begged him to enter her.

He carried her to the bed, leaving her on top of the covers where nothing would hide her from his view. He stripped off her pants the rest of the way, then followed with his. He paused just before entering her, brushing hot, wet tears from the corners of her eyes with his lips. As he kissed them away, she locked her hands above his hips and pulled him close.

"God help me, Mia. I loved you before. So much, so there's hardly anything left of me except you."

He hadn't meant to say it, didn't fully comprehend the words and partly hoped she didn't either. But then she guided him inside her until the distance between them had vanished. She pressed her lips against his ear, her tears coming harder.

"I didn't know," she answered, "and if I had, I'd never have believed it. Not before. But anything that's lost can be found."

And then words were lost to rhythm and pleasure and to the night, and Ben forgot exactly what it was that needed to be found.

Chapter 21

SLEEPING WITH BEN HADN'T BEEN IN MIA'S PLANS—
none that she'd consciously admitted—but even if it
had been, she'd never have dreamed things might play
out the way they did. She'd wanted him—needed him
in a new-to-her, whole-body way—and she'd insti-
gated it.

None of this was like her.

The night was so much more than just sex and physical connection. He'd said that beautiful bit about loving
her before, whatever it had meant, and it was the most
powerful thing she'd ever heard. After their bodies had
finally joined together, her release had been so palpable
that her climax had brought a flood of tears.

Afterward, he held her and she cried, and before her
tears had dried, their bodies had become one again. Over
the next few hours, they lost themselves in each other,
one time tumbling into another.

By 2:00 a.m., the sky had clouded over and it had
started to snow. Ben's bed overlooked a wall of windows, and the shades were pulled up and tucked under
valances. Mia curled against him, savoring the weight
of his arm around her, hypnotized by the giant flakes as
they ambled to the ground in the dim, silvery light until
her eyelids grew too heavy to hold open. Knowing she
was impossibly close to sleep and that she needed to
wake up in her own bed, she pressed her lips against his

forehead, enamored by the ability to simply touch him without hesitation, and went back to her room.

She got Sam and Sadie crated and barely had the energy to crawl into bed herself. She slipped underneath her chilly sheets knowing that even though nothing had been said about love and no promises of tomorrows had been made, their bodies had spoken a bigger truth than any ordinary collection of words. And she fell asleep feeling less alone than she had in a very long time.

Exhausted as she was, thankfully everyone, including the dogs, slept in, which probably had to do with the later sunrise this far north and an overcast morning sky. Mia woke up hungrier than she'd been in months, and after a quick trip outside with Ollie and the dogs, helped Lynn make a giant breakfast of eggs, hash browns, and mandazi.

On the car ride up, Ben had offered to teach Ollie chess. When Ollie had stepped outside to give the dogs their morning potty break, he'd noticed how much colder it was without the sun and decided he wanted to stay inside in his pajamas this morning and learn the game after breakfast.

When Ben had walked into the kitchen for the first time, Mia had expected to feel awkward with him as the reality of their separate lives set in, especially in the face of mothers and sons and dogs and never-to-be-ex-mother-in-laws. But being around him was as natural as it was undefined. She allowed herself the gift of a single benign touch while he was at the sink. She closed her hand over the back of his arm for as long as it took him to fill a glass. When he met her gaze and discreetly raised an eyebrow at her, she could've sworn

there was a lightness in his impossibly dark eyes she'd not seen before.

After breakfast, he and Ollie sprawled in front of the fireplace for Ollie's first instructional game of chess. When Mia headed out for a walk while the big flakes were still coming down, they were on their bellies with couch pillows tucked under their chests, and Ben was relaying the basic rules in a way that Ollie could understand.

As she'd stepped into her boots, she noticed that not only had Ollie aligned himself on the opposite side of the board into the same position as Ben, but he seemed to be mimicking some of Ben's movements as well. For some reason, this had made Mia's stomach flip. So she was sleeping with Ben, and Ollie was idolizing him.

Suddenly full of indecision, Mia zipped on her coat, tugged on a dry pair of gloves, and headed out into the cold and snow. And then doubt rushed in. They'd done so much last night, but they'd done no real talking. What if she was falling in deep but Ben wasn't interested in being in this for the long haul?

He told you the most romantic thing you've ever heard in your life, you idiot.

When she heard her mom's voice in her head insisting that words were easily spoken but actions created waves, Mia thought of how easily Ben had gotten aroused and how many times he'd been able to climax.

Fresh snow crunched under Mia's feet as she walked, and thick, heavy flakes fell unabated from a steel-gray blanket of clouds. The muscles in her legs had a hot, rubbery feel to them, like after the time she'd tried a hard-core Pilates class after dabbling in a few poses at

home. Some of her soreness this morning was from the hours of snow play yesterday. And some of it was from last night with Ben.

She circled around the lake, confusion muddling her thoughts and weighing her steps. The woods and lake were remarkable in the thick snowfall. She did her best to hold on to the beauty around her and let all the confusion fall away.

Somehow, even frozen and snow-covered, the big, still lake filled her with the same peace as when she lowered herself into a warm, steamy bath. Sticking to the narrow embankment, she trudged through deep snow and continued circling the lake, fascinated by how still and quiet the woods were when muffled by the falling snow. Even her footsteps seemed to be hushed.

She spotted giant tracks that could only belong to a moose, crossing the center of the lake and leading into the woods. She wondered if the big bull moose had come up to the house today and she'd missed him. On the far side of the bank, she stirred up a fluffy snowshoe hare; it crossed her path and dashed into a nearby pile of brush.

She was winding back around, closing in on the snowman where they'd spread Brad's ashes, when she spotted Irene standing next to it, looking out at the lake.

"It's beautiful in the snow, isn't it?" Mia offered as she joined her.

"It's peaceful. I'm glad to see it." Irene wrapped one gloved hand over the fingers of her other and locked them in front of her chest. "You're young, Mia. I'm not going to pretend my son was faultless. I'm not blind. But he's a part of Ollie. If you move on without him…"

She stopped and cleared her throat, and Mia saw she was near tears.

"Irene, I know that the best parts of him are in Ollie. He was a great dad. Ollie will remember. So will I."

Irene flashed her a sharp look. "I saw you outside last night. You and Ben."

A stab of surprise shot through Mia. She stood straighter, waiting for the reprimand she was certain was coming even though she'd done nothing wrong. And any attempt to justify to Irene what had been a beautiful thing would only stain her memory of it. So she said nothing in defense.

Irene had been looking out at the lake and she turned to face Mia, her piercing gaze suddenly as sharp as her tone. "You're less like your socialist mother than I thought you were. I didn't realized how ambitious you are until I saw you in Ben's arms last night. He's vulnerable right now, and he might even let you in. I shouldn't begrudge you for it, knowing how well Ollie would prosper with access to Ben's connections, to that family's money. But I do. I *do* begrudge you for it, Mia. And this affair of yours will haunt me. So know this. Brad will be between you. *Always*."

As prepared as she thought she'd been to face this, Mia wasn't. Irene's words cut, but even more than they hurt, they made her furiously angry. "*Don't* try to label my mother! You'll never get her right, just like you never got your son right. And as far as everything else…" Mia's hands clenched into fists, and her stomach was a tight ball of anger. "Screw you! Brad and I were *divorcing*, and I don't have to justify anything to you. Or take any of this either."

She turned on her heels, knowing if she stayed any longer, a torrent of accusations of her own would pour out, including many of the things she'd held back over the years.

She headed toward the cabin, but as she reached twenty feet of the back porch, she realized she was too angry to head inside. Her roiling anger didn't mesh with a cozy fire and a game of chess. And most certainly, her mom would pick up on her mood. The last thing they needed was for Lynn and Irene to get into it.

Remembering the giant moose, Mia knew it wasn't safe to charge off into the woods. Instead, she took off down the long driveway. When she reached the end and was still fuming, she trudged along the empty, snow-covered road, away from the direction they'd driven in. The snow was deep enough that walking took considerably more effort than usual, and more than anything else, this effort helped Mia distance herself from her anger.

She walked and walked, and it seemed as if the desolate road and scattered houses went on forever. Finally, the snowflakes petered out, but the winds picked up and the temperature dropped as soon as they did. A few pickup trucks and SUVs passed, the last being a lone man in a battered orange truck who slowed and looked at her hard, making Mia decide it was time to head back. She'd not brought along her phone, but it wasn't as if she had any reception up here anyway.

The walking she'd done had made her already-spent legs ache. She had no real idea how much distance she still had left to the driveway when she spotted a figure approaching in the distance. Squinting hard, she was able to make out a man with a head of dark hair and a

black-and-white dog on a leash walking her way, and she breathed a sigh of relief. Ben.

When she'd closed about half the distance to him, she heard a vehicle approaching from behind and turned to see the orange truck heading back in her direction. Chills ran down her spine. If it wasn't for the fact that Ben was in sight, she'd be in a state of panic. That single look from the driver had given her the creeps.

She was still fifty or sixty yards from Ben when the truck reached her and slowed to a crawl. Fear ricocheted through her, and adrenaline dumped into her system.

"Need a lift?"

She shook her head as assertively as possible, suppressing a shiver. It was the way he was looking at her. She imagined him browsing through a row of X-rated movies, his mouth hanging open the way it was.

"No. I'm with my friend." She pointed up ahead at Ben and Turbo.

For a couple seconds, the driver continued to roll the truck along beside her without answering. "So be it," he said finally. The truck was flipped into reverse, and the driver steered it backward at an angle until the back tires dropped off onto the shoulder, then, mercifully, he drove off in the opposite direction, his back wheels skidding.

Mia's knees went weak. Walking her anger off in the woods had felt dangerous, but she realized she'd likely been no safer out here in the middle of nowhere walking on a desolate road.

When she met up with Ben a couple minutes later, he looked as tense as she'd felt when the truck was beside her. "What'd he say?"

"He asked if I wanted a ride."

Ben pulled in a controlled breath. "Mia, I know you're your own woman, but it's too isolated here to walk alone on these roads."

"You don't have to tell me that again. I just... I needed some space. I didn't plan on walking this far."

He closed a hand over hers, their fingers entwining automatically. Her body under her thick coat was warm enough, but her hands were freezing through her thin gloves and she savored his superior warmth radiating out against her palm. Turbo jumped up, pressing his paws into her thighs and sniffing her. She paused to scratch him under the chin.

"Want to tell me about it?" Ben fell into step beside her as they headed back.

"Did Irene say anything to you?"

"No, when she came in and then a half hour passed and you hadn't come back, I asked if she knew where'd you'd gone. She said she didn't but admitted that she may have upset you. I found your footprints and tracked you here, and when I saw that truck stop beside you... All I can say is I'm glad I did."

"Me too. That guy gave me the creeps."

They walked for a while in silence until it occurred to Mia how easy and natural it was to hold Ben's hand. And it didn't feel like she was holding the hand of the guy who'd been her husband's lifelong best friend.

Brad will be between you. Always. Irene's words resounded through Mia's head as clearly as if she'd heard them aloud again.

She stopped walking and dropped Ben's hand like a hot potato. "I'm not trying to take advantage of you."

He stopped and faced her, waiting a second or two before replying as his eyes searched hers. "I know that. Is that what she said?"

"She said I'm ambitious. She saw us outside." Mia stamped one foot and clenched her fists. "And I get that I came on to you. And I know you have money, and you know that I don't. But that wasn't what last night was about."

"Are you trying to tell me or her, Mia? Because I know this already. And you know as well as I do: you could explain it to her until the end of time, and she wouldn't get it. But as I said last night, you have my heart. And I meant it."

Mia pulled in a shaky breath as they started walking again. She was getting colder by the second, and it helped to walk shoulder to shoulder with him so some of his warmth become hers. Tears stung her eyes. She wanted to bawl and scream and wrap her arms around him and never let go.

"It's just... It's really soon, Ben."

"It is. I know. And people will talk. Nothing I can do will make that any easier."

"Then what *are* you saying?"

His boots kicked up snow as he walked, and Turbo pranced ahead at the edge of the leash. "This is your path, Mia, your decision. If I could make it easier for you, I would, but I can't."

She walked beside him in silence, feeling the deep exhaustion in her legs and an ache in her bones. Her hand found its way to his again, their fingers entwining automatically.

"I don't know how to make sense of this. It's so

big. Last night…" She swallowed hard. Saying this—exposing herself this way—made her feel as vulnerable as if she was shedding layers of clothes, and it frightened the hell out of her. "If someone had told me there could be nights like last night, I'd never have believed them. And I honestly don't know what that means. I just… I have to know I can trust myself not to get swallowed up. With you. I have Ollie to think about."

The muscles in Ben's jaw were rigid with tension, yet his grip on her hand was supportive but gentle. "Last night… I hadn't planned on it happening. I should've had the strength to stop it, but I didn't." He gave her a small smile as they walked. "And that doesn't mean I have any regrets. I don't. Not one. But your life, Ollie's life, has been turned upside down. You have choices to make. And you have time. *You have time*, Mia. All that you need."

Mia chewed her lip. She could finally see the turnoff for the long driveway in the distance, and even though it would be awhile before they were in view of the house, it was disheartening to know she'd need to let go of his hand soon.

As Turbo trotted in front of them, weaving an irregular pattern in the snow as he sniffed things that couldn't be seen, Mia had a plain-as-day revelation. Eight years ago, when she'd told her mom she was pregnant and marrying Brad, Lynn had told her that if she betrayed her heart, it would betray her. Mia had asked her mom what she'd meant, and Lynn had replied that Brad would never—could never—be Mia's big love. And maybe because she'd felt the truth in her mom's words, she'd never forgotten them.

But walking beside Ben, she realized it would be easy, too easy, for him to be that for her. A big, impossibly giant love. All she had to do was let him in.

But big love required big faith. Mia felt like she was on a really high diving board, and the ladder down behind her had been taken away.

Not knowing what else to do, she pressed his gloved hand against her chest and thanked him for the only thing she could let him give her right now. Time.

Chapter 22

BEN SANK INTO THE CHAIR AT HIS DINING ROOM TABLE next to Taye, sliding the plate of cheese, sliced meat, and crackers he'd fixed to the center of the table. An unsliced apple was at the center of the plate, looking a bit mismatched with its counterparts. "I was out of bread, so it's just crackers today."

Whenever Taye came over, Ben liked to send him home with a full stomach. He remembered being thirteen and insatiably hungry. He could see this in Taye and figured it added to Taye's mom's groceries bills. Taye shrugged and loaded several pieces of cheese and meat onto one cracker. Turbo was sitting at attention at his side, his head cocked, watching the teen as if he knew exactly who to beg from.

Turbo and Taye hadn't been together in seven days, and it hadn't just been Taye who'd been excited to see Turbo. From the limited experience Ben had had with the dog so far, he'd seen that Turbo acted largely indifferent to the people he encountered at the park and on walks. But he'd barked and wagged his tail when he spotted Taye walking toward them fifteen minutes ago.

Loaded cracker in one hand, Taye twisted to face Ben and lifted his paper off the table. "So far, my resolutions are to get to fifty push-ups, to stop worrying about the refs and play my best game, not to complain when my mom makes me watch my little sisters, to visit my dad

in Memphis this summer, and the big one at the bottom
is to bring Turbo home." Taye waggled an eyebrow.
"What do ya think?"

"Those are good resolutions." Ben turned his mug
of steaming tea in a slow circle. He had never gotten in
the habit of making New Year's resolutions. He tended
to hold a few major goals or intentions at the forefront
of his thoughts, and that was it. "What about adding
something about homework? You're doing it right now,
so you're off to a good start." Taye was smart enough to
skate by without doing most of his homework, but the
older he got, the more that would cost him.

Taye frowned at his paper as he stuffed the loaded
cracker into his mouth in one giant bite. He picked up
his pencil and added "Do most of my homework" at
the bottom.

You've got to give him something for honesty.

Taye slipped the paper into his notebook and pulled
out a math packet as Turbo inhaled the crumbs that fell
to the floor.

"Aren't you going to do your resolutions?" he said
when he was mostly finished chewing.

Ben frowned at the empty sheet of paper next to his
mug that Taye had given him. He couldn't very well
write "Give Mia time" as a resolution, but this year, more
than anything else, that was at the front of his thoughts.
Those days in the cabin had been a gift. For the first
time in eight years, Ben didn't doubt she returned his
feelings. Even after asking for time, she'd found her way
into his room two of the three nights they'd had left in
the cabin, and she'd spoken her feelings with her body
plainly enough.

The night after they'd had the conversation out on the road, they'd been the last two awake again. He'd been in the living room working on his laptop when she'd come out of Ollie's room. She'd headed into the kitchen, and after her earlier declaration of needing time, he'd expected her go to bed or possibly come in and talk a few minutes if she wasn't tired. But she'd joined him on the couch looking as sexy as ever in that flannel nightshirt and no bra, and he'd been struggling to keep his blood from heating when she'd asked if it made her wicked to want a pass after asking for time.

He'd been about to clarify what she meant by "pass" when she leaned in and brushed her lips against his neck. She'd taken the lead, crawling onto his lap and instigating a wildly hot make-out session that culminated in her going down on him before he'd carried her into his room. There, they'd spent another hour or two letting their bodies speak for them.

They'd found their way to each other again on New Year's Eve, after Irene had left for New York and just the four of them had welcomed in the new year three hours early for Ollie's sake, and for Lynn's, who hadn't fallen into a regular sleeping pattern since coming back from Africa and had marked the new year as special with a sleepover in Ollie's room.

Just before midnight, it had been Ben and Mia and a bottle of champagne, and when they'd both reached for the same glass and brushed fingers, he'd ended up having her right there in the kitchen where they'd been pouring fresh glasses with the intent to step outside to ring in the new year. He couldn't help but hope that the

fact that he'd been inside her when one year passed into the next was an omen of good things to come.

But of course he couldn't tell Taye any of this, just like he couldn't write "Give Mia time" on an empty list of resolutions. So under Taye's curious gaze, Ben wrote *Learn to make pad thai, moussaka, and cacciatore*, a few of his favorite nontraditional meals, and followed it with *Restart jujitsu classes*, then *Sell the Aston Martin, Continue to focus on client satisfaction*, and ended with *Have fun with Taye and Turbo*.

Taye munched a new sandwich of meat and cheese only, no cracker, as Ben finished. "That's it?"

"If you're looking for 'Climb K2,' it won't make the list this year."

"What about hooking up with a girl? I mean, being alone is cool and all, but don't you want a family? You're like, what, twenty-eight, right? My mom was twenty-five when she had me."

Ben frowned. "I'm thirty, and yes, I want a family. I've just been waiting."

"Waiting for what?"

"It's complicated." He couldn't explain his eight-year love for Mia to a thirteen-year-old kid.

"Maybe it ain't as complicated as you're making it out to be."

"Maybe." Ben tapped the table with his thumb before abandoning the list-making to check his phone, which he'd left on the counter. "I should make sure your mom hasn't texted." When he got to the counter, he saw that she had. "She wants you home in thirty minutes. You're going to your aunt's tonight. I'll give you a ride."

By the time he finished texting, Taye was in the

kitchen sticking Ben's sad list of resolutions on the front of the fridge. The angular handwriting under his resolutions caught his attention. A closer glance confirmed that Taye had added three of his own.

Meet a girl.

Have a family.

Live happily ever after and all that crap.

Ben chuckled. "Fair enough, Taye. Fair enough."

—⁂—

Using a stiff, short-handled brush, Mia swept acrylic paint onto the painted concrete blocks of the wall in the shelter. It was good to be creative again. Before beginning the mural project, she'd been skeptical of her ability to get her unrelated sketches to come together and to do the featured animals justice. But as the disjointed images she'd sketched so many times began to merge into one dynamic scene, her confidence was growing.

Home from Minnesota and Ollie back in school, she dove into mural painting full swing. She couldn't imagine a better activity to do while attempting to sort through the chaotic jumble of decisions needing to be made, from how to handle her feelings for Ben to what to do with the baby who shared half her son's DNA.

And since January was one of the slowest months at the shelter, the main room was relatively quiet, and it was a perfect time to complete the project without much disturbance. She'd volunteered here long enough to know that after the holidays were over, the winter months could be so quiet that they could become disheartening for the staff and volunteers. In January and February, often more animals were surrendered than

adopted out. When this happened, inevitably the building filled to capacity and animals had to be turned away. And it was hard to forget that not all shelters could be as dedicated as High Grove to ensuring that each inhabitant found a forever home.

This year, Mia was crossing her fingers that the winter blues wouldn't set in along with the short days and quiet nights of January. There was so much here to look forward to this year. Megan was due to have her baby any day, and the staff and volunteers were feeling her excitement. In the back room, a poster poll was under way, with everyone weighing in on their guess as to the baby's sex, weight, and date of birth. Mia's guess was for a girl to be born on the fourteenth of January and that she'd weigh 8 pounds, 3 ounces, nearly a pound and a half more than Ollie, who'd been born four weeks early.

Another reason for Mia's hopeful attitude was that thanks to the now-complete renovations, there were ten more kennels for dogs and eight more for cats. With these extra kennels added to the record-breaking adoptions in December—a likely result of all the press and social media attention—they were entering their slowest months with more room to spare than usual.

In an effort to help keep the shelter's wave of support going, Tess, the shelter's newest staff member, had come up with a fund-raiser that was sure to get its share of media attention. The weekend before the Super Bowl, the shelter would be hosting its inaugural High Grove Puppy Bowl in the gym of a nearby high school. Although the exact dogs participating in the games were still to be chosen, the halftime show was sure to be the

highlight. During halftime, the litter of puppies that had been hash-tagged "miracle puppies" would be making their debut in the world.

By the end-of-January event, they'd be ten weeks old and ready for adoption. The litter of seven had been found in an abandoned building at the eleventh hour. They were being held a couple of weeks longer than usual because they'd been considerably undernourished when they came to the shelter. Since then, the puppies had been the talk of the town, and Channel 3 had been airing weekly updates and showing pictures and video clips. The shelter had even gotten a bit of national attention, and some of the posts featuring the seven husky-mix puppies had been the most popular in the shelter's history.

Because of the hordes of attention the puppies had gotten, hundreds of adoption offers had come in. Many of the offers had included promises of sizable donations to the shelter. A few could be considered bribes and were being rejected. For the contest, interested families had been asked to submit an essay, and candidates were now being whittled down to a manageable number, thanks to a very thorough Excel spreadsheet Patrick had created. While most interested parties lived in the St. Louis area, some were from all over the country, and a few were from overseas.

On the night of the Puppy Bowl, the chosen families would be announced, and Channel 3 would be there filming it. The media buzz the puppies had been getting was probably boosted by the fact that the stray husky involved in the puppies' rescue had been adopted by Mason Redding, Tess's boyfriend and third basemen for the St. Louis Red Birds. At Tess's request, he'd

agreed to emcee the event, and tickets had sold out in four hours.

A few years ago, Ben had designed Mason Redding's downtown loft, and they'd become friends in the process. Mia had met him once, six months ago at the party that had been thrown for Ben.

Ben never name-dropped having friends like Mason Redding. Sometimes, Mia still had a hard time believing that he—a guy who'd summited Everest and had a crap-ton of money and connections—was interested in her. Since returning home, she'd spent more time than she cared to admit convincing herself that she'd made up a connection that wasn't there. Convincing herself that his real interest was in doing right by his best friend and doing right by Ollie, and that what had happened up there had just been a matter of circumstance.

And you throwing yourself at him.

Mia stopped midstroke and rolled out her cramping right shoulder. She couldn't let her thoughts go there again, or she'd get nothing done. She'd asked for time, and Ben had promised to give her all that she needed. That was all there was to it. Nothing more. All she had to do was call, and he'd be there for her.

She was working on a ladder on a section at the top of the wall just under the ceiling, painting the yellow-red leaves of a maple tree in fall. She had another hour to paint before she needed to get home to Ollie and take him to his swim lesson tonight. The shelter was a half hour from closing, but empty aside from the staff and one other volunteer. It was already almost dark, and Mia suspected no more customers would come in before closing.

Megan and Tess had set up a large, expandable play-pen in the front room for the husky-mix puppies and were rolling balls back and forth as some of the puppies charged after them. The rest were more interested in tackling each other or gnawing on shoelaces. Megan, who was a big-but-cute pregnant ball, had gotten down on the floor with them and was relying on the edges of the enclosed pen to send back the balls she missed.

Patrick had been at one of the adoption desks for most of the day. He'd been working intently on his massive Excel spreadsheet and not interacting with anyone, aside from when he'd stopped at 10:42 and 2:42 for breaks and 12:02 for lunch.

Mia was still rolling out her aching shoulder—she was not a fan of painting with her arm over her head—when he sat back against his chair and huffed.

"I've got it narrowed down to the thirty most deserv-ing adoption applications like you wanted, Megan. But I'd prefer to limit the pool to twenty-eight. The rest will be kept in a separate sheet until after the Puppy Bowl in case we need to give them another look."

Mia wondered why twenty-eight was better than thirty since they were both even numbers, which Patrick was a stickler for, but decided not to ask. As of last night, when the application window closed, 417 appli-cations had been received. When Megan had been over-whelmed at the prospect of picking between so many moving essays and deserving applications, Patrick had volunteered and had jumped into narrowing the selec-tion process with his usual knack for practicality and thoroughness. His Excel spreadsheet expanded across thirty columns and included factors others might have

missed, like a search of discoverable social media profiles and perpetrator sites, in addition to the basics like how many animals were in the home, if there was access to a fenced yard, and if there was previous experience with training puppies.

When Megan had looked over Patrick's spreadsheet earlier, she'd asked him not to pay as much attention to a few of his columns, like the one labeled "grammatical errors in essay" and another labeled "use of nonsensical words."

For the next half hour, Mia went back to painting, and Megan and Tess continued to wear out the puppies while Patrick talked through his top picks. When he was finished, the biggest question everyone had was how they'd decide among such deserving candidates. Patrick was in favor of making a random decision through a drawing, but there were two applications that stood out above the rest, and everyone agreed they made the list no matter what.

The first and most extraordinary was submitted by the granddaughter of the man who'd once owned the abandoned warehouse where the puppies were found. Although her grandfather had lost the building to the bank in the late nineties, it had been in the man's family since the nineteen-thirties when his grandfather had built it to operate his then-thriving bottle-making factory. In her essay, the woman explained that her grandfather had passed away a few years after the company went into foreclosure, and that his family had since been saddened by the fact that the building had been empty ever since and would likely be tore down at some point in the future.

The woman, who'd been a dog groomer for ten years before earning a teaching degree, had written how pleased she was that the long-empty building had provided shelter for the puppies and that adopting any one of the seven dogs would be a tribute to her grandfather's legacy. Patrick had verified her story right down to finding images of some of the more elaborate bottles that had been made there.

The second application they felt strongly about was submitted by a family in northern Idaho. The woman had written about a team of sled dogs and driver who'd all nearly perished while training for the Iditarod several years ago. The team had survived four days of exposure while trapped and waiting out an intense early-season storm. All had suffered injuries, and the driver's injuries had been severe enough that he'd been unable to care for the dogs.

The woman and her husband had learned about the dogs' plight and, at considerable expense, had paid to have the entire dog team treated for their injuries and had gone on to adopt two of the huskies who'd suffered the most extreme frostbite. The dogs had needed lots of TLC and training as they learned to live as pets and members of a household rather than as working dogs.

Although the first several months had been hard, the woman said it was the best decision she and her husband had made for their family of five, and the two huskies had been loved dearly for their spirit and tenacity. The last of their two adopted dogs had passed away a year ago, and the woman wrote that the day her husband had declared he was ready to bring another dog into their life, they came across the puppies' story on Facebook.

Both were hopeful to be able to bring one of the puppies into their home.

Since three of the seven-dog litter looked and acted more like stubborn and rambunctious huskies than the rest, it had been decided prior to beginning the selection process that those pups would need to be adopted by people who had experience with huskies. The breed was one of several that the shelter adopted only to people who had experience with more challenging dogs. This family not only fit that bill, but everyone who read the essay was moved by the compassion and generosity the couple had shown to a team of injured dogs over two thousand miles away from their home.

With her shoulder and neck in knots from all the overhead work she'd done the last few hours, Megan decided it was time to be finished painting for the day. She climbed down from the ladder as the puppies were being carried to their kennel in the back. Setting her brushes aside, she cleaned her hands on her painting towel and scooped up one of the puppies, a bright-blue-eyed female who looked a lot like John Ronald, their beautiful husky-mix father.

Mia cuddled the sleepy girl against her neck and cheek and headed into the kennels to the private room next to quarantine where the puppies were being held until their public debut. The puppy's thick fur was disarmingly soft and carried a distinct puppy smell. Mia stroked her under the chin and pressed a kiss onto her forehead as the little girl yawned. Even after volunteering here for this long, there was a part of Mia that still wanted to lounge around doing nothing more than cuddle away the hours with little ones like this.

No surprise to her, the puppy's bright-blue eyes and strong resemblance to her father brought Mia's thoughts around for the umpteenth time to Brad and his little blue-eyed human and the phone call she needed to make. Delaying it any longer wasn't the right thing to do. It seemed like a year rather than ten days since Stacey had handed her the letter.

As she lowered the puppy into her kennel alongside her siblings, Mia forced away a memory from earlier this week of Ben hoisting her up against the fridge on New Year's Eve as he pushed back her hair and his mouth closed over the side of her neck. Her blood flooded south as her body remembered as well. Bent over as she was, she grew light-headed enough that she had to grab the kennel door as she stood straight again.

She wanted lots more of that—lots and *lots* more of that—but she couldn't think about being with Ben without thinking of the judgment that would come. From Brad's family. From friends and neighbors. From the moms at Ollie's school. This left thoughts of her personal life at an impasse. But none of this changed the fact that this baby was here. Now. And as Ben had confirmed, he was a handful for his young mom. Reaching out felt like the right thing to do.

After helping Megan and Tess get the puppies settled and cleaning up her painting supplies, Mia headed out. On the way here, the afternoon had been relatively mild and she'd been feeling indoor-bound since coming home, so she'd walked the easy mile here. Now that the sun had set and the temps had dropped below freezing again, the walk home wasn't as appealing.

While zipping up her coat and tugging on her gloves,

Mia figured now was as good a time as ever to place the call that she'd gotten as far as queuing up on her phone three or four times before. And no surprise, as soon as the ten numbers that could connect her to Stacey were lit up on the screen, her thumb froze over the call button.

Making the call felt like a no-going-back decision. She was on the cusp of swiping out of the dial screen when she stubbed her toe on an uneven slab of concrete and her thumb smacked down on the button. She could hear her phone ringing even before pressing it to her ear. *Hang up. Hang up. Hang up.*

"Hello?"

Damn. Mia opened her mouth, but nothing came out. Stacey sounded so impossibly young. *Brad, what were you thinking?*

"Um, hello?"

"This is Mia." So this was it. She was actually making this call.

"Oh! Hi." A pause. "I was afraid you wouldn't call."

Mia could hear a muffled, whiny cry in the background. The kind of cry Ollie made when he was a baby and it was the witching hour and nothing would satisfy him and it was too late for a nap and too early for bed. "Yeah, well, I wasn't sure either."

"I'm glad you did." Mia heard the muffled clearing of Stacey's throat as the baby's cry grew louder. Even though Mia had only met the young woman once, she could perfectly envision the long, straight sweep of Stacey's light-brown hair as she bent over to lift her child. "Look, there's so much I want to say. Can we meet? Brody's so fussy right now. I know I won't be

able to get half of this stuff out. And I usually come off better in person anyway."

Mia counted out a few cracks on the sidewalk as she considered the request. She'd known the question would come up. Stacey had asked as much in her letter. "Yeah, I guess. Sometime when my son's in school."

"Tomorrow's Friday. He'll be in school, right, and I'm off till four. If it works for you."

Mia had an abandoned and expensive house to get on the market, a mural to paint, and a mound of bills to wade through. She absolutely didn't need to rush this. "I could meet for a half hour maybe." Before she knew it, she'd spouted off the name of a coffeehouse in the Grove and they arranged to meet at ten thirty.

She hung up and slipped her phone into her pocket, adjusting to the silence that hung in the brisk night air without the crying baby to punctuate it. *So I guess you're doing this.*

Chapter 23

ALTHOUGH SHE'D DONE HER BEST TO HAVE IT BE otherwise, there were the lazy, unfettered mornings of weekends, and there were school mornings. Try as she might, Mia hadn't yet mastered helping Ollie manage his time on weekdays. He'd have his pants on and find something to distract himself for ten minutes before he could follow with his shirt and socks.

Sometimes it was a book. Other times it was his Hot Wheels or a set of LEGOs. This morning he'd turned on her grandparents' ancient computer with its dial-up slow connection and was using the internet to research how souls separated from bodies when Mia came inside from the backyard with the dogs. He was standing in front of the desk munching on a multigrain waffle when she glanced at the misspelled words he'd typed in the search bar.

"Ollie, you're supposed to ask before you get online, remember? And honestly, sweets, a random internet search isn't going to give you the answers you're looking for."

"*No one* has answers."

Mia could see angry tension lining Ollie's shoulders. They were drawn up almost to his ears. "Anger is a good thing," Ollie's therapist had told her on his second visit last week. "When he finally reaches it, you'll know he's gotten to another stage of processing."

She glanced at the clock. 7:42. They were going to be pushing it to make it to school on time, but Mia figured this was more important than a first-grade tardy.

"People think they have answers, Ollie. Doctors, scientists, priests, preachers. Lots of people will tell you they have the answer. And lots of them will tell you that a person with an opinion that's different from theirs is wrong."

"You don't say that. You say you don't know."

"That's true."

"You're my mom. You're supposed to know!" He clenched his fists. The waffle that had been in his left hand crumpled and fell to the floor in pieces.

Mia pulled out the rickety desk chair and took a seat and a calculated breath. She leaned forward, bracing her elbows on her knees, and looked her son in the eye. "I can see where you would think that, Ol. I'm sorry. I really am."

"Grandma Irene said Dad is up in the sky and he can see me. Only he doesn't have his body, so how does he see? And if it takes a gazillion light years to get across the Milky Way, how can Dad make it to heaven?"

Ollie's thin body was lined with so much tension he was shaking. A part of her wanted to say the right words to help him calm down. The other part figured the complete meltdown he seemed to be headed for might be exactly what he needed.

"I want Dad to still have eyes!" Ollie blurted out, stamping his foot.

Mia was considering how to respond when her son started screaming and stamping his feet repeatedly and yelling how his dad couldn't see because he was

ash in a jar and how he hated everyone for putting him there.

Mia sat still and let him scream. She'd only had a few short conversations with Ollie's therapist, but the woman had made it clear that whenever possible, Ollie should be allowed to process his feelings rather than bottle them in.

Even though the dogs couldn't hear Ollie's outburst, they'd picked up on his state of upset. Sadie dashed off into the bedroom with her tail tucked, but Sam, who'd been chomping and salivating over a nylon bone, began to dash in circles around Ollie, barking and nipping at his feet. Lynn, who'd been taking up the bathroom by showering at the most inopportune time of morning, stepped out quietly and walked to the kitchen with a towel wrapped around her hair and wearing a blue-and-orange kimono-style robe.

Within a minute or two, Ollie was collapsed in a mound on the floor, burying his face in his arms as he bawled, and Sam was pressing in and inundating him with slobbery licks. Mia had just lifted Sam up and away from her distraught son when Ollie sat up. "Don't take him. Please." He reached for Sam and pulled him onto his lap, then dragged his arm over his runny nose.

Mia sank to the floor and sat in silence as Ollie continued to cry but with much less abandon. She could hear Lynn behind the wall in the kitchen putting on a pot of tea that if they stuck with routine and headed off to school when he recovered, neither she nor Ollie would have time to drink.

Sadie, hunkered low to the floor, came back into the room and hopped to the couch, watching the commotion

from a distance. From the middle of Ollie's lap, Sam rose up, bracing his front feet against Ollie's chest, and began exuberantly licking away Ollie's tears, an act that fairly quickly turned Ollie's waning sobs into giggles.

It struck Mia how she'd spent the morning thinking of a pair of eyes that were an exact replica of Brad's, while her son had been thinking of this.

And she wanted to know what it meant. Would she be doing Ollie a service or disservice by bringing the baby into their world? She honestly didn't know. All she knew was that she was committed to treading slowly through this mess.

Bringing the dogs home had been wonderful, a way to connect and distract at the same time. But she'd been planning on fostering and eventually adopting a dog anyway. The baby was different. He was a human and, more importantly, a potential member of Ollie's tribe.

Mia couldn't help but think it wasn't a coincidence that of all the dogs at the shelter, it had been Sadie and Sam, a mom and pup, who'd made their way into her and Ollie's lives.

"Life begets life," Lynn said, coming into the room with her damp hair clinging to her neck and the wet towel balled in her hands.

Mia was suppressing a groan and shooting her mom a look when Ollie asked, "What's begets?"

Lynn sank into one of the armchairs and twisted to face Ollie. "It's an old word that no one really uses anymore, but it's a pretty word that means 'to bring or become.' Life *brings* life. Life *becomes* more life. And I can tell you, Ollie, my parents used to tell me to look to heaven for all the answers, but I remember how

frustrating that was because you can't put your finger on heaven. And I think that rather than trying to get your head wrapped around where your father's soul *is*, it may be easier to think of all the pieces of him that he left here in the world that helped make it a better place.

"There's you, of course. All those stories, all that fun, that's forever a part of you. And it's your duty to share all that as *you* beget more life. And there's your mom and his friends who are the better for having known him. There's the art he gave the world. And, yes, there are his ashes. They'll become part of the earth, and that will give life to flowers and plants, which you know feed the bees and butterflies."

Ollie sniffed and nodded. "And some birds."

"Yes, and some birds."

He fell completely quiet, processing. Finally, he sniffed and dragged his arm across his sleeve again. "Oops. I think I need a new shirt." He held out his arm and made a face, letting his sadness flow into laughter.

"I'll grab one, Ol."

"I will." He squirmed from underneath Sam and dashed off into his room with the puppy trailing at his heels.

Mia swallowed, collecting herself and swiping away a few stray tears. "I should've asked you to explain it to him sooner."

"He wasn't ready to hear it sooner." Lynn stood as the teapot started a whisper of a whistle in the kitchen, leaving her discarded towel abandoned on the chair. "It's always that way."

"Well, it was good nevertheless."

"I can't take the credit. Death comes easier in Kenya."

Mia had stood up and was collecting the wet towel from the chair when her mom reached the kitchen and turned back. "And Mia…"

"Yeah?" She knew what her mom was going to say before she said it. In that way of hers, Lynn had already said it without really saying it in her speech to Ollie.

"That baby… You're right to trust your instincts. He's meant to be in Ollie's world. I'm proud of you for being brave enough to see it."

Chapter 24

MIA'S MESSENGER PURSE SMACKED AGAINST HER thigh just underneath her coat as she neared the Fine Grind where she'd arranged to meet Stacey. She was a minute or two late, but her legs seemed to be turning to lead. She pulled her phone from her bag and typed out a text to Ben.

Is it crazy that I'm doing this?

She paced the length of a storefront with a window full of specialty cupcakes as she waited in hope of a quick response. A row of gender-reveal and new-baby cupcakes glared out at her.

No, it's perfectly sane. Admirable, even.

She was debating how to reply when he texted again.

When he's old enough, Ollie's going to thank you.

Mia suspected that just the simple fact she could text Ben and he'd text her right back was part of what helped ease the wild storm raging in her belly. Having someone unconditionally here for her wasn't something

she was used to, and she made a promise never to take it for granted.

She knew, too, that Ben would be more here than just through a text if she hadn't asked for space to work through things.

> Thanks. This helps. A lot.

She sent it off and typed out another text right after.

> Okay, I'm going in. And in case I forget to tell you later, I'm really looking forward to seeing you tomorrow.

> Same here. And Mia, you really are the strongest woman I know.

She typed out a thanks and a goodbye, rolled some of the lingering tension from her shoulders, and headed down the block to the coffee shop. Pausing out front of it, she scanned the tables through the glass and spotted Stacey—impossibly long, straight hair and all—sitting at a table with the baby planted on top, grabbing her nose in his chubby fist.

That girl slept with my husband.

It was a more than a touch surreal, walking in to face her. But the strangest part was that the jealousy and anger Mia had expected to feel just weren't there. Instead, it was almost as if she was at the zoo, walking past an enclosure, looking at a version of her life that didn't exist any longer.

Her mom had been right. No real surprise there. Lynn

was right way more often than she was wrong. Brad had never been Mia's great love.

She used to think her mom was crazy to claim that a few hours of embracing a great love was more profound than a lifetime of compatibility. Mia understood better now. She'd had glimpses of it when she'd been in Ben's arms, when their bodies were getting lost in each other.

She wasn't her mom, and she wasn't going to make a life decision based on a fleeting feeling, but she was no longer going to discount the possibility of embracing it either. Maybe Ben could be her great love. Maybe he already was.

And maybe that explained why it was so easy to open the glass door of the coffee shop and wipe her feet on the rug. To weave through the crowd of midmorning coffee connoisseurs to the wall of windows where Stacey was waiting.

Stacey had big hazel eyes that widened just enough when she spotted her, letting Mia know that even though she'd asked for this meeting, she was nervous.

"Thanks for coming." She pulled Brody's chubby fingers from what looked like a sudden death grip on her nostrils. "Ow, buddy."

Mia started to pull out the chair directly across from her but realized the baby would be blocking their view of each other, so she chose the one catty-corner from Stacey instead. Still facing his mom, his chubby legs spread wide, the baby began smacking his hands on the table as he emitted a series of short owl-like "oohs."

Mia left her coat on but slung her purse across the back of the chair before sitting down.

Stacey had her hands wrapped around Brody's hips.

She dug her top teeth into her bottom lip and looked at Mia.

She was thin as a rail, and that hair of hers went down to her waist. For a split second, Mia wondered if it had gotten in the way when she and Brad were going at it, but after pulling in a breath, she was able to send the thought away. None of that mattered. Not really.

"Is there something specific you want to start with?" Mia asked.

Stacey looked like she'd just been asked to sit in the corner. "I guess I just wanted to talk about stuff. And I wanted you to meet Brody."

Mia ran the tip of her tongue along the ridge of her teeth and shrugged. The baby had noticed she was behind him and was twisting to look at her. He grinned, showing a pair of newly emerged bottom teeth.

He reached a slobbery fist Mia's way and pumped his fingers as if perhaps he could get her to insert her nose next.

Finally, Mia flattened her hands on top of the table. "You alluded to this in your letter, but Ben shared that he's been keeping payments to you current. If you're specifically looking for child care, he's willing to fund it. And he says you knew this before reaching out to me."

Stacey nodded, sweeping her curtain of hair over her shoulder. "Mount Everest has made that clear, yes."

Mia blinked. "Mount Everest?"

"I call him that to his face too." She shrugged. "He's frigid and imposing just like the mountain."

Mia pressed her lips together to stifle a laugh. She wasn't willing to let the ice get broken yet, no follow-up pun intended.

"Look, I get you may not care, but I can't do this by myself. The whole time I was pregnant, I was back and forth about whether or not I was going to keep him or give him up. And then he was born, and it hit me that this kid is the most important thing I'll ever do." Stacey blinked until the tears in her eyes cleared. "But that doesn't mean it's easy. He cries a lot, and he's really needy. My brother's in Seattle and my mom's a pothead and I haven't seen my dad in a decade, so they're no help. And I can keep sticking him with a babysitter when I can't take it, but it doesn't really do much for Brody in the long run. And Brad said…he said you were the best mother in the world. He said somehow you put yourself aside and always find the energy to give Ollie what he needs." Stacey huffed and shook her head. "Like that was supposed to make me feel better about my lack of natural parenting skills, you know?"

Mia swallowed as the compliment echoed through her. Brad had said that. About her.

"I'm not asking you to have that kind of presence with Brody," Stacey added. "But I just kept thinking that since you love your son like that, you'd want him to have his half brother around. And they both lost someone, and so I…I just thought I should try, that's all."

Mia pulled in a slow breath. It was harder to hold onto her dislike for this girl than she'd hoped. She reminded herself that what mattered, the reason she was here, was to help make the world better for her son. "They did lose a father. You're right about that. Your son is too young to realize it right now. Ollie, on the other hand, is acutely aware of what he lost. He's seven, and he's vulnerable. *Very much so*. No one, absolutely no one, that he cares

about will be allowed to walk out of his life for a long time if I can help it. So before any connection between them forms, I'd need assurance this would be for the long haul. No matter what. Even if parenting or personality differences divide us as mothers, that wouldn't be a reason to sever a connection between them. I'd need assurance that you could agree to this."

Stacey's lips parted for a second or two before she nodded. "Yeah, I can agree to that. I probably know a bit more about you than you know about me at this point, so I'm sold. I'm from Festus originally, but I'm here on full scholarship going to SLU. My mom says I'm book smart but decision stupid, which I guess explains Brody, but oh well. For sure, I'm here another few years. After that, I don't have plans to go anywhere really. I wasn't sure I would, but I like living in the city. I'm majoring in civil engineering and thinking about switching over to Wash U's architecture program in grad school if I can get in with a scholarship. If I do, maybe Mount Everest will hire me to work at his firm. He's stuffy, but he seems fair enough."

This was a bigger promise than she'd have settled for. Mia tucked her hands under her thighs. The baby was oohing and reaching for her, but she was doing her best not to pay attention to him. She was here to make a momentous decision, not to ogle over a charismatic baby. "So…how do you see this playing out exactly?"

Stacey looked around the coffeehouse before her lips turned down in a slight frown. "I guess I'm hoping that you'll want to include him in things. I'm not big on schedules when I don't have to be, but I'm cool with it if you are. I try not to go anywhere without him when

I'm not in class and I study when he's asleep, but my grades tanked from all As to some As, two Bs, and a C last semester. I'm trying to get them back up because I want to keep my scholarship, obviously."

Mia was tempted to say she couldn't imagine the pressure of a newborn and a full load of college classes, but she checked her words at the last second. It was going to be harder than she thought not to let Stacey in. Not to let the baby in.

"We can talk schedules, if you want," Stacey added, looking around the room again. "Only I have to pee really bad, and I don't know where Micah went. You met him at the shelter the other day. I don't have a car, so he drove. Only he's like *nowhere*. Think you could watch Brody a minute? It's a bit disturbing how cool he is with strangers right now, so he won't scream or anything."

"Um, yeah, I guess." Mia swallowed.

Stacey reached into a giant bag on the chair next to her and pulled out a bright and sparkly cloth baby book. "My aunt gave me this." She had to lean to pass it far to the side to keep the baby from seizing it. "There's a fake mirror on the last page. If he fusses, show it to him. He's like his dad, I guess. He likes to look at himself."

A snort escaped before Mia could pull it back.

"He sits up fine now, but I've been keeping my hands close just in case. Sometimes he lunges for things and topples over."

Stacey took off, and Mia scooted closer to the center of the table, locking her hands on either side of the baby. He was half-turned toward her, and his bright-blue eyes lit with excitement when she touched him.

He clamped a drooly hand over the arm of her coat and burst out with a loud "Ooh!"

She blinked back a rush of the surreal, looking at him dead on for the first time.

In what seemed like a clear attempt to express himself, Brody bunched the loose material of her coat sleeve in his fist and made another loud *ooh* sound.

A smile escaped Mia, small at first, then bigger. It was impossible to contain it. He smiled back and let out another "Ooh!"

"You know what I think?" Mia asked, watching the way his bright eyes widened at the sound of her voice. "I think you're just what Ollie's been missing. And in a weird way, me too."

He lunged forward, possibly coming for her and possibly grabbing for the book resting by her elbow, but Mia caught him before he lost his balance. Then he forgot about the book and grabbed her nose, and her heart right along with it.

Chapter 25

WHEN BEN PULLED UP TO MIA'S CENTRAL WEST END house, he spotted her CR-V parked nearby. There were several open spaces on the curb directly in front of the house, but she'd parked across the street and down a bit, as if she was distancing herself from her connection to the place, and making Ben long to ask what thoughts were in her head, even before seeing her.

With the exception of a bit of texting every day, it had been six long, quiet days since they'd returned from Minnesota, days Ben had filled with work projects, a trip to the climbing gym with Taye, and long jogs with Turbo. He'd missed Ollie as much as he'd missed Mia. He missed the way the kid stuck out his tongue and breathed through his mouth whenever he was using his fine motor skills. The way he never grew tired of pasta, either doused with meatballs and sauce or drizzled with butter and Parmesan. The way his gangly seven-year-old body—poky elbows and knees and slight, long torso—fit against him when Ben was reading to him at night. Missed witnessing those still-unmasked emotions throughout the day—the whole range of them.

He missed both of them much worse than he'd ever missed them before. Only they weren't his to miss. Not yet. Maybe never.

He didn't think it was just self-preservation when a voice inside him gave a clear and distinct rebuttal to the

maybe never thought. Mia loved him back; she was just coming to terms with what it meant to bring him into her life as her lover.

He knew this from more than those couple nights when she'd been in his bed. It was from the lightness that had been in her eyes, her laughter, and the ease with which she'd smiled. That had all been directed his way so many times over their time in the cabin.

He'd parked the Jeep and was getting out when he spotted Ava turning onto the street. *Damn*. She was fifteen minutes early. Ben had been hoping to have a few minutes alone with Mia, but he resigned himself to waiting until everything was decided and the for-sale papers were signed and Ava went on her way. He reached back in for his attaché case, shut the driver's side door, and headed over to greet her.

Ava stepped out, eyeing the house the way most people eyed a fresh-baked pizza. "Gorgeous. Perfect curb appeal. Perfect location. Great street. You can send me these any day of the week, please and thank you." Finished with her once-over of the house, she stepped in to plant a kiss on his cheek. "Morning, beautiful."

"Morning, Ava." She'd been his go-to real estate agent since the first loft he refurbished five years ago. She was dedicated and knew the market well. Ava had been in his architecture classes but had dropped out in their second year to sell real estate, and he'd never heard her voice any regrets. She was a tenacious real estate agent and one of the youngest top agents in the city. This morning, dressed in a red power suit and wearing black four-inch heels, she certainly fit the part. "Is the market here still as hot as it was?"

She gave a one-shoulder shrug as they headed down the walkway toward the house. "Not as hot, but not terrible. As I said on the phone, if she lets me stage it, I'm confident I'll get her a couple contracts in the first weekend."

"Remember what I said, okay?" he said as they neared the door. "Don't mention any staging costs."

She gave him an inquisitive look, but nodded. "Yes, Daddy Warbucks."

Ben was debating rather or not to address the softly whispered comment when Mia pulled open the front door. She looked at Ben first, then focused on Ava. He made the introductions, wondering how he could slip into the conversation that Ava was married but not seeing how to do it without it being obvious. Sooner or later, Mia would notice the four-carat ring on Ava's finger. It was one of those things people noticed.

"Thanks for coming." Mia had her hair pulled back in a messy bun, highlighting her long, smooth neck. She was in jeans that hugged her hips and a snug-fitting teal cardigan that fell open to her sternum, drawing Ben's attention to the small snap buttons closing it over her breasts. God, he'd missed her. So much more than just physically, but his body ached to pull her in to him and draw in her scent and experience the pleasure of those now-familiar curves and peaks as they pressed against him.

Dropping behind on purpose as Mia led Ava upstairs to start the house tour, he headed for the dining room table and set his attaché case on top. He had a pile of paperwork to look over once more. He dreaded doing so, but he was about to bring some delicate details to Mia's attention.

One afternoon in Minnesota, they'd finally gotten around to talking about Mia's finances and some of the big-action items on her plate like this house. When Ben had asked if she'd want to stay here if money wasn't an issue, and she'd given an emphatic "No," he'd not objected. While he was deeply vested in the outcome of her decisions, he was also the executor of Brad's will and Ollie's godfather. It was a difficult line to walk. If she'd wanted to live here, he'd have helped make it happen. He was committed to helping her wade through a series of tough decisions to find what was right for her.

To further complicate things, after she'd given him permission to dive in and get an accurate picture of the bills and expenses, he'd done his best to come up with a financial plan that would pay off her accumulated debts and manage her modest lifestyle funded solely by the meager life insurance she'd be getting, the savings from their joint account, and the money she earned from her art sales.

It had been an impossible task.

So this morning, Ben faced the less-than-pleasurable job of convincing her to let him step in and help. Knowing her independence and the standards she held herself to, he suspected it wouldn't be easy.

It might help if he were able to explain everything. If he could go back a little over eight years ago to day one and tell her it had been him who'd had his world shaken by that passionate speech she'd made. Tell her that while listening to her talk that day, he'd felt as if everything in his life up to that point had been leading him to her. And how he understood that since then, their

universe had still been aligning, because how else could Ollie be explained? And he'd tell her how even if he had the power to go back and change it, he wouldn't.

But even if it meant losing her, he couldn't tell her those things. How could he when he had so much to gain by telling her something that could make her question a life she'd spent the last eight years holding together? He couldn't. All he could do was hope she'd let him in regardless, let him love her now and every day they had left. It would be enough for him.

And he hoped it would be enough for her too.

The onus was on her to talk. Mia knew that, but she couldn't make herself do it. She sat at her old dining room table twenty minutes after Ava left, staring at the spreadsheet Ben had printed out for her to review, her insides a roiling ball of anger and embarrassment and injured pride.

She'd left Ollie with Lynn this morning to get here early and get some work done. Two hours in this place, and she'd found a dozen unnecessary and expensive items that Brad had likely loaded onto his new credit card in the months after she'd left. Until this morning, she'd not realized the depth of the bender he'd been on.

Maybe some of it could be returned. That would take diving in and finding receipts and shipping the stuff back. It wouldn't be enough though. Not even close. If only she could wave a wand and all this would disappear—along with a mountain of bills she couldn't pay and this house payment too.

She was between a rock and a hard place, and Ben

was offering her money. A gracious no-interest loan to help her get back on track.

Only she didn't want it. She didn't want to need him. She *wanted* him, yes. There was no getting around that. The second she'd laid eyes on him this morning, her pulse had started racing. And that was before he'd slid out of a bomber jacket, and she'd noticed how he was dressed down for a Saturday in jeans and a snug gray T-shirt underneath an open long-sleeved cranberry-colored shirt.

It had been safer to focus her attention on the gorgeous and sharply dressed real estate agent who appeared to be much more in Ben's league than she did. After a minute or two of contained jealousy from spying Ava planting a kiss on Ben's cheek as they got out of their cars, Mia had realized that while they were familiar and easy around each other, there didn't seem to be any visible attraction between them. Ten minutes later, she'd realized Ava was married.

But none of this would help her pay the bills that were due. Or overdue. And Ben had laid out in these spreadsheets how paying only the minimum on the new high-interest credit cards was going to escalate her problem a year down the road.

"If you can get the asking price Ava suggested," Ben said into her continued silence, "which she's confident you will, you'll have eight or ten thousand left over in cash when the dust settles from paying off both the first and second mortgages and the late-payment fines that were racked up in the last few months. You can use it to pay me back, if you'd like. Or you can keep it. It'll be a nice cushion in your account," Ben said into the silence.

Mia's stomach was queasy and unsettled. She'd known it would be bad, just not this bad. She wanted to rage and to cry; she just didn't want to do either in front of Ben. Something about him having become her lover ruffled her pride about airing her dirty laundry in front of him.

She drummed her fingers and stared at the negative five-digit number in front of her. She needed money, and she needed to get it from somewhere. Or she'd have to file for bankruptcy. Aside from Victor and Irene, Ben was the only one she knew with any money to spare, and he was offering the amount she needed in a no-interest loan that she could pay back on her terms.

She thought of her mom. Lynn hardly had a spare dollar to her name, and when she did, she gave it away to people who were in greater need. There was some money in her grandparents' house. It wasn't worth much, but it was paid off. Lynn would be happy to let Mia have some of the money if it was to be sold. Only where would she live then?

"I could ask my mom to take out a home-equity loan on my grandparents' house."

Ben was silent a moment, the muscles in his jaw sharp and pronounced. "You could." It was his turn to drum his fingers. He sat back in his chair, and Mia thought she picked up on a slight shake of his head.

"People get home-equity loans all the time," she said into the silence hanging between them.

"That's true."

"But clearly you don't think it's a good idea, so can you please tell me why?" Her voice pitched, and she pushed back from her chair and started pacing the length

of the main floor, her socked feet unsatisfyingly quiet on the hardwood floors. "Since I'm asking," she added, referring to his earlier promise not to sway her in any direction she wasn't comfortable with. She pressed her thumbs into her temples as she walked, trying to ward off the headache that was pressing in.

"Since you're asking," Ben repeated, pushing back his chair and walking into the living room where she was pacing. "You're right. People get home-equity loans all the time. Only your grandparents willed the house to your mom, and she's leaving for Kenya again in a few weeks. The title would need to be transferred over to her if it hasn't been, which can take months, and then there's the condition of her credit.

"If she has any, I suspect it's not great. Interest rates are decent right now, but she'll likely pay a few points more than necessary, which will cost you more in the long run. On top of that, a refinance is simpler than a sale, but it'll take time and a lot of energy on your part. A lot of documentation and running around. And selling a house—this house—and cleaning up all the shit Brad left you with will be draining. Since you're asking me, my advice is to skip it and let me lend you the money."

Mia stopped pacing at the edge of the couch and set her hands on her hips. There was a solid eight feet of space between them, and she wanted to keep it that way. "Who's offering me this money, Ben?"

He frowned. "I don't understand."

"I'm asking in what role are you offering it to me? As executor of the will? As Ollie's dad's best friend? You've got his other family covered. Or how about as Ollie's godparent? Because our sleeping together last

week makes this a little bit messier, doesn't it? I know I started it. I get that. And I'm not sorry. Maybe I should be, but I'm not. It's just… That thing you said when we were together… It doesn't make sense. *At all*. People say stuff when they're having sex. I know that. Only I can't forget it."

It was out before she contemplated it. Mia wasn't sure what reaction she was hoping for, but it certainly wasn't to see the stricken look that passed over him. This man had climbed Everest, and her words had just taken the wind from him.

Finally, he said, "Can you just accept that I'm here for all of those reasons and more? Just because the answer isn't simple doesn't mean it isn't clean or right."

Mia folded her hands over her mouth and nose, taking a few calculated breaths. She shook her head abruptly and dropped her hands. "I don't want to need you any more than I do."

"Money isn't going to change what's already between us, Mia. I won't let it. I won't let you let it." He closed the distance between them and kissed her hard, harder than he'd kissed her yet.

Her hands found their way under his T-shirt and up the side of his ribs, savoring the feel of him the same way she savored a rainstorm after a long string of hot summer days. She was crying and shaking and kissing him all at once, and he was shaking too, she realized.

She pulled away from his kiss and tucked her head under his chin, pressing her forehead against his neck. She draped her arms over his shoulders, pulling him closer. "Then tell me it's okay to love you, because God help me, I do."

Chapter 26

"YOU'RE GOING TO NEED A BIGGER HOUSE." LYNN
had come around the corner into the kitchen. Brody was
straddled across Lynn's hip, tangling his chubby fingers
in her hair. It was their second time babysitting him in a
week. Ollie was young and accepting. Although he was
surprised, he was getting excited over the prospect of
having a baby brother, even though Brody wasn't going
to live in their house.

Mia skimmed the vegetable peeler across the surface of a russet potato for the shepherd's pie she was
making for dinner. "This house is working fine. While
I get settled."

She wouldn't have put any money down that Lynn
would warm up to Brody in the few weeks she had left
before heading back to Kenya, considering her lingering feelings about Brad. But after Lynn had spent less
than an hour with him, Mia had realized otherwise.
Lynn wasn't exactly doting on the baby—that wasn't
her way—but Mia had heard her chuckle a few times,
and her voice was starting to dip just a touch when she
talked to him.

Mia couldn't blame her. Babies were irresistible, and
Brody was certainly no exception.

"Getting settled isn't always advisable, Mia." Lynn
carefully extracted Brody's fist from a tangle of hair.
"Nor is settling. For anything. I think we should sell it.

You can take half the money and invest it in a house with a new energy to it. At least a new energy for you. I'll give the rest to the school. The eighty or so grand I would get goes a lot further over there."

Mia shot her mom a look. She wanted to change the flow of conversation, but she suspected if she made it obvious, Lynn would only press more.

Ben was in the living room with Taye and Ollie and the dogs. And Lynn was right. With the six of them and the three dogs, the house was overfull. While he wasn't exactly out of earshot, Ben was helping to supervise as Ollie and Taye practiced some of the signs with the dogs, including Turbo, even though spoken commands were becoming effective with him too.

Mia finished peeling one potato and reached for another. Her arms and shoulders were already sore from the climbing she'd done at the indoor climbing gym where they'd all spent the afternoon. Ben had only climbed once, scaling the most challenging path that Taye had laid out for him with Spider-Man-like ease. Mia could have stood there all day, silently ogling the defined muscles in his back, legs, and arms visible underneath his clothes, and thinking how supremely lucky she was to get to make love to him regularly. Taye and Ollie had done most of the climbing the few hours they'd been there, but Mia had asked Ben to hold the baby while she'd climbed a medium-difficulty two-story wall with minimal guidance. The quiet, suggestive way Ben had said "Impressive" when she'd finished still warmed her blood when she thought of it, drawing her thoughts to the quiet hours after Ollie was asleep for the night.

It was easy to let their bodies fill the night with the space of things they didn't talk about in the busyness of the day. There were so, so many things they weren't talking about. Like if it bothered him that she'd been married to his best friend for eight years. Or how she was ever going to get the courage to tell people they were together. Or if he was okay with this ensemble of Taye and Ollie and Brody in his life, or if he'd want kids of his own someday?

With all of this still unspoken, selling this house and moving somewhere wasn't a conversation Mia was ready to have with him in earshot. Everything between them was new and undefined. She loved him, and he loved her. She was still trying to get her head around why, but she knew that he did.

But being in love didn't guarantee a happily-ever-after. Especially not with Mia's world as muddled as it was right now. However, she felt with a rare clarity they'd find something pretty close.

For a while though, until it felt right, they would have to make do with things the way they were. Ben had a beautiful one-bedroom loft downtown with a remarkable view, and she was living in the smaller-than-average eighties-decorated bungalow where she'd grown up.

With all this circling through her mind, it seemed to Mia the best thing to do with her mom's line of questioning was to change the subject. "There's this thing in America called saving for retirement, Mom. Whenever we do sell this place, my vote is that we invest the money in a retirement plan for you."

Lynn headed to the cabinet next to the stove with the pots and pans. She pulled out a medium-size pot,

grabbed a long wooden spoon, and set them and Brody on the island counter. "When I leave, you'll have to scale back your cooking on nights you babysit. I suspect this one's going to be high maintenance. And pooh to retirement funds. Most everyone back home works until their bodies won't allow them to, then they're cared for by their families."

Mia paused midpeel. "You aren't ever coming back, are you? For good, I mean."

Lynn handed Brody the long spoon a second time. He was more interested in the brightly colored stones in her necklace. "No, not for good." After a pause, she added, "Though it doesn't mean I don't love you ferociously. Ollie too. And honestly, you'd send me packing if I stayed. Without African soil under my feet to ground me, I'd be a mess."

Mia turned back to the potatoes, disappointment slipping down to her toes. "Why?"

Lynn laughed a small, painful laugh. "That's an answer I can't give you, Mia. But that's the world for you. It's full of things that have no answer. Even in this age of information at our fingertips, there are still more questions than there will ever be answers. What I *do* know is over there I'm whole in a way I can't seem to be here. And as much as I hate not being a bigger part of your life than I am, you don't need me. Sometimes you think you do, but you don't. You're strong and solid."

Mia was still finding her voice when Ollie jogged around the corner, his eyes lighting when they landed on the baby atop the counter. "Ben and Taye are taking the dogs out to pee." He pressed in next to Lynn and

tugged gently at the tip of Brody's socked foot. "Are you cooking, Brody?"

Mia noted how her son's tone changed when he talked to the baby, how he formed syllables slowly and deliberately. Brody pumped his fists and grunted, as fascinated by Ollie as he'd been all afternoon, reminding her of the natural connection between babies and kids.

Ollie lifted the pot to his mouth and pretended to eat. "Yum, yum. You're a good cook, little guy."

For the first time that Mia had heard, Brody broke into a wild giggle, which made Ollie laugh just as hard. Mia joined her son at the counter as Brody pumped his fists in excitement. Ollie draped an arm over her hip and pressed his head against her side. "I'm glad we get to babysit him, Mom. When he smiles, it makes me think of Dad."

Mia scooped her son into her arms and buried her face in his neck, drawing in his familiar scent. "You know what? When he smiles, it makes *me* think of *you*."

Ollie laughed, and the sound reverberated through her chest. Maybe her mom couldn't stay, but it didn't mean Lynn wouldn't still be part of her life. And maybe Mia didn't need her so much now.

And no matter how topsy-turvy she felt at times, so much love had snuck in all around her.

Chapter 27

BEN HAD NEVER BEEN MUCH FOR CROWDS OR BEING in the spotlight, but the hopeful look in Mia's eyes when she'd asked if he wanted to be one of the Puppy Bowl referees had left him unable to turn her down. So here he was, dressed in black pants and a black-and-white vertical-striped polo, making calls over the antics of a group of playful dogs in the middle of a crowd of four hundred attendees.

Considering that this event was live and being held in a high school gymnasium, there were several modifications from the popular show on Animal Planet. Attendees watched the dogs pummel about on the sixty-foot-long artificial turf made to look like a football field, roped off in the center of the gym from the bleachers on either side. They could also wander around the various booths at the edges of the gym or head to the adjoining concession area where food was being served and a few other booths were set up.

The dogs that had been chosen to participate in the faux football game were two years and under, and the most playful and easygoing of the shelter's bunch. They were allowed on the field in two teams of two each. The four dogs on the field at any one quarter had all had several opportunities to play together in the shelter's new play yard and had done so without contention.

This event was a first, and a few kinks needed to be

worked out on the spot, but the first half hour after the
doors opened had gone smoothly. To combat the smells
of the food that was being served outside in the concession area, all participating dogs had been fed dinner
before being crated to come here, but not all had gone
to the bathroom while being walked outside the building. Every time one of the dogs relieved itself on the
artificial turf, the audience went into either an uproar of
laughter or sharply pronounced groans.

Thankfully, the Event Committee had a plan in place
for such occasions. They sent in one of three volunteers
dressed as elite cleaning-crew members and wearing
T-shirts that read "Got Pooh?" on the front and "We've
Got Your Bottom Covered" on the back.

Ben's friend Mason was emceeing the event and
had a funny line for just about everything. Ben figured
Mason was half the reason the event had sold out as
fast as it did. His St. Louis fans hadn't been able to
get enough of him this year. And even though Mason
was supposed to be commenting on the dog's antics as
football-related plays, he threw in just enough baseball
comments to keep the crowd laughing and clapping for
more. On top of that, he'd been given free rein to award
the dogs for nonsensical things like extreme cuteness
and go-getter attitudes.

Ben and Patrick, the two referees, were supposed to
have the more serious job of calling fouls as the dogs
loped around the field in supposed teams of two, tackling their teammates as often as they pounced on the
opposing team. Even worse, the dogs kept stealing footballs from their teammates and running off in the wrong
direction. To encourage the dogs to play with the balls

more than one another, the dog team coaches, Fidel and Kurt, tossed the footballs into the air every so often. The dogs were much more interested in the balls when one of the four balls was in play—in the air or in another dog's mouth—than lying abandoned on the ground.

For the most part, the dogs stayed in the roped-off Astroturf field, though a long-legged Lab mix hopped out and trotted straight to the bleachers and one of the attendees who'd snuck food inside the gym. The eager dog promptly sat on her haunches and started to beg, and the crowd went into peals of laughter and clapping until she was cajoled back onto the field, and the man headed off with his hot dog to the cafeteria.

Fortunately, everyone was having too much fun to care about the fact that the dogs weren't natural football stars. Each set of dogs was on the field for ten minutes of play before being led off for a water break, then taken to the concession hall for some time in the press zone. There, they hung out with shelter staff and volunteers like Kelsey and Mia while being petted and posing for pictures with the guests.

In between the four quarters of play, three entertainment breaks were scheduled. The first one featured a six-year-old Australian shepherd mix who was becoming quite good at agility. Tess, who'd been training him, ran him twice through a mobile agility course that had been temporarily set up on the turf around the field. He sailed through it, oblivious to the crowds and applause, and afterward was challenged to catch a series of Tess's Frisbee throws. He dashed across the turf and jumped into the air to catch them in his mouth. He'd caught three of the four. When the fifth Frisbee was thrown

and he caught it, he plopped down on the field, locked it between his front paws, and began to devour it while letting the rest of Frisbees sail past him. From the roaring applause he earned, everyone was still impressed.

Before a new group of four dogs were brought in to play the second quarter of the game, a short break was announced, and Ben headed off to find Ollie. The last he'd seen, Ollie was working the craft table with Lynn.

After not finding him there, Ben eventually spotted his godson at a table in the corner of the concession area, dipping the broken-off bend of a pretzel into a small cheese cup. Mia and Lynn were at the table with him, laughing at something Ollie was saying.

Ben froze in place a split second, debating whether to approach them. He knew Mia wasn't ready to make it public that they were together, and he didn't blame her. Their connection was a complicated one, and it had only been a little over two months since she'd become a widow who'd been on the cusp of applying for divorce. And she had Ollie to think about.

Before his feet unfroze, someone grabbed his arm. "Hey, aren't you Ben Thomas?" A guy at the table Ben had paused next to had gotten up. The group was eating and drinking beer, and from a glance, the guy holding his arm was the closest to being drunk. "The dude who climbed Everest?"

"Ah, yeah, that's me."

He extracted his arm from the man's grip politely but firmly as the man unleashed a string of self-congratulatory curses, then pointed at a guy on the opposite side of the table.

"Dude, you owe me twenty bucks. I told you it was

him!" He turned back to Ben and clapped his shoulder. "My cousin's a climber. He tried Everest in 2015 but had to stop at Camp 3 because he got sick."

It wasn't the first time he'd been recognized since coming home in late July, though it had been happening less and less lately, and Ben would be fine if it never happened again. He stood for a couple pictures and fielded half a dozen questions ranging from "Wasn't it cold?" to "Did you see anyone fall?" before stepping away.

He finally turned to find Ollie headed his way. The gangly kid had a giant grin and some nacho cheese stuck to the left corner of his mouth. "Mom says I can help you referee for the next quarter if it's okay with you."

Ben made eye contact with Mia for a moment. She offered a small smile but was quick to drop her gaze. Two or three other volunteers were at the table with her, and Ben understood. He was here as Ollie's godfather, not her lover. Someday, when enough time had passed, she'd find the confidence to let the world know he was both those things. Until then, he had no complaints.

"Yeah, but come here first." He led Ollie to the concession window and grabbed a napkin to wipe off the cheese.

"Cheeeeese," Ollie said, grinning wildly as Ben dabbed the cheese from his face. "Get it? Say cheese. Only it's on my face so I don't have to say it."

Ben chuckled and draped an arm over Ollie's shoulder. "Come on, silly. Let's call some fouls on those dogs."

Mia did her best to keep focused as she waited for the cue to head inside the roped-off area in the center of the

gymnasium. Inside it, seven husky-mix puppies were tousling about during halftime, oblivious to the crowd. She kicked herself for not getting up and going over to Ben earlier. She'd wanted to and badly. So much so, her feet had been itching inside her shoes.

But she was afraid the crazy-wild love inside her would show, so fear kept her glued to her seat. If she could do it again, she'd do it differently. He was here for her, dressed in a stiff-looking referee shirt, balancing out Patrick's very literal calls with a touch of lightheartedness that enabled Mason to keep the crowd in almost constant laughter.

The comment her mom made as Ollie headed off with him still rang in her ears. "He should be entitled to sainthood, the way he's waited for you. The way he's still waiting for you."

"Ben?" Mia had asked, confused.

Lynn had dismissed her with a wave of her hand. "No, Mia. God. Yes, Ben. Who else?"

Like a thousand other things her mom had said over the years, it made no sense. When tonight was over and she and her mom had a moment alone, Mia intended to pursue it.

Spotting her cue, Mia crossed over the rope and headed into the middle of the turf field. She'd never been to anything like tonight's event. Even by halftime, she was willing to bet it would top the list of the shelter's most successful ideas. From the constant din of the crowd, it was clear everyone was having a blast.

John Ronald, the former city-roaming stray who'd fathered the puppies and who'd been instrumental in their rescue, wasn't here. He wasn't fond of crowds, but

his story was remarkable. So the halftime show opened with a short video on the big-screen monitors flanking the corners of the field, telling his story and showing a video clip of him being introduced to the puppies when they were out of quarantine. It was a moving clip, and based on the murmurs of appreciation that spread across the audience in a wave, many eyes were no longer dry.

For this halftime event, Mia was assigned to the gangly black-and-white husky-mix male puppy that most closely resembled his father. This puppy was going to the family in Idaho who had experience with purebred huskies and acclimating working sled dogs to become household pets.

At ten weeks old, he was spunky and rambunctious, and while he didn't run from Mia, he happily pounced on her hands, growling and play biting and forcing her to make quick work of securing him in her arms. Her job was to hold him up while a highlight of his new family's essay was being read and his name, Juneo, was being announced by Mason. As playful a mood as the pup was in, it was easier said than done. He wiggled and whipped around, trying to get a grip on her hands again. After the family's photo was shown, Mia put him down so he could rejoin his siblings. He dashed off toward them, returned to attack her shoe, then dashed off again while the crowd applauded.

After all seven puppies' names and new owners had been announced, the puppies were enticed off the field by a team of volunteers dragging large stuffed animals on leashes behind them. The puppies chased after the fluffy animals, grabbing on and tugging while being led away.

After the puppies were back in their playpen in the off-limits women's locker room, Mia headed back to babysitting the dogs in the press zone. Whenever she had a minute of downtime, she kept trying to decipher her mom's comment. It didn't make sense. But it did remind her of another, much more intimate comment she'd heard. "I loved you before. So much so, there's hardly anything left of me but you."

And even more confusing was what did Lynn think she knew about anything? She lived in Africa, of all places.

Before Mia knew it, the fourth quarter was starting, and the bulk of the crowd had returned to the gym to see the finale. With two other staff and volunteers left to cover the press zone, Mia excused herself and headed over to the craft table where Lynn was helping a couple of kids make paw-print pencil rubbings on colored paper.

"What are you not telling me?"

Lynn held the paper down, her fingers splayed on opposite ends as the kid rubbed vigorously back and forth and the paw print began to take form. She didn't even look up. But Mia knew she understood her.

"Only what you haven't been ready to hear."

Mia pulled out an empty chair and sank onto it. She kept her voice low but pointed. "Who falls in love with their best friend's wife? And how would you know anyway? You were hardly ever here to see it."

Lynn gave her a sharp look. "When the world doesn't make sense, sometimes it's best to turn it on its head."

"*That* doesn't make sense."

"Neither does an honorable man falling for his best friend's wife."

Mia groaned and dropped her voice. "So then you aren't saying he was in love with me? *Before?*"

"Before what, Mia? That's the question you should be asking." The boy finished his rub, and Lynn told him to write his name on it before he ran back to the table where his parents were eating hot dogs and chips.

"Mom. Please. Things are complicated enough without you talking in riddles."

Lynn sat back in her chair and swept her long hair to one side. "I promised I wouldn't tell you. But you're on the cusp of figuring it out on your own. Tell me this. How long did you know Brad before you began dating?"

Mia shrugged. "He asked me out near the end of our senior year. We had the same major and were in a class or two together every year, so just over three and a half years, I guess."

"You were art majors and in the same classes, and you never hooked up until…what happened?"

"I gave a speech about my dad not being in my life. You too, I guess. As soon as it was over, I could barely remember what I'd said." Her shoulders lifted in a defensive shrug. "Brad was in the class. He'd been moved enough by it that he asked me out a couple days afterward."

"Was he? And here I thought the only things that ever moved that man were his reflection and maybe your son. Open yourself to the truth, Mia. It's right in front of you. Turn your world on its head."

Anger flared up along with confusion. Mia was opening her mouth to demand a clearer answer when she felt Ollie tugging on her sleeve.

"Mom, it's the last quarter, and there are only a

couple minutes left. Can you come watch? Ben let me blow the whistle twice already."

Swallowing down her frustration, Mia let Ollie take her hand and tug her into the gymnasium where the final group of dogs—two Lab mixes, one hound, and a Staffordshire terrier mix—were chasing each other around in circles, ignoring the footballs entirely, in what Mason announced was the biggest pandemonium of the night. Points and penalties were assigned as frivolously as ever, and Mia let Ollie pull her toward the center edge of the game field where Ben was refereeing.

She didn't like being in the center of so much commotion, and somehow this tension, along with her mom's words, stirred up fresh memories of the day she gave the speech that changed her life, leading the way for Ollie, even though she could never have guessed as much at the time. What had her mom meant by bringing her attention back to that day?

Whether it was the presence of so many people or her fresh anger or her mom's words, she didn't know. But suddenly Mia could recall those five minutes with more clarity than just minutes afterward as the haze of adrenaline that had led her up there waned.

She'd mostly talked about how her father not being there for any of the momentous events in her life—like prom or learning to drive or going on a first date—had defined her life more than anything else.

She was standing next to Ollie, three feet from Ben, doing her best to stir up some memory of Brad in the auditorium that day, when her breath caught in her throat. She couldn't picture Brad because she'd not been paying a single ounce of attention to him. Back then, he

was the cute guy all the girls swooned over. Except Mia. She'd mostly just ignored him.

She'd had a couple friends in the class and had done her best not to hold their sympathetic gazes during the speech because she would have cried if she did.

But for a fleeting minute, she did lock gazes with someone that day.

Someone she hadn't known. A guy with impossibly dark and compassionate eyes. And something about his gaze had given her the confidence to keep going when she'd been about to break down and had needed it most.

The gym floor seemed to be spinning underneath Mia's feet. She grabbed Ollie's shoulder and tried to keep her balance. Ben was there that afternoon. It didn't make sense, but he was. How was it possible that she'd never made the connection?

She didn't meet him for months afterward, not until she was married and pregnant with Ollie. She still remembered experiencing a sharp flash of recognition when they were introduced. It was strong enough that she'd called him out on it.

"I know you," she'd said, shaking his hand, struggling to place how. "I don't know where, but I'm sure I've met you before."

He'd shaken his head and dropped her hand. "If we'd ever met, I would remember."

It had been enough to stop her from pursuing it. *He'd not been denying it*, Mia realized. *Not really*.

There was a roar in her ears louder than Mason's baritone voice booming over the microphone, and her blood pulsed wildly. She must have been grabbing on to Ollie hard, because suddenly he was tugging on one

of Ben's belt loops and pointing at her. Ben turned and gave her a questioning glance.

"You were there." It came out as a whisper, barely audible to her own ears, so it was impossible for Ben or Ollie to hear.

Ben stepped as close as the rope barrier would allow, his forehead knitting in concern. "Hey, are you okay?" It was so loud, he'd needed to yell, and still she barely heard him.

She nodded, brushing fresh, hot tears from her cheeks, tears that were quelled by the most freeing laughter she'd ever experienced, and all her earlier fears fell away. She had a thousand questions, but she had time to get the answers. She had the rest of their lives. What mattered now was not wasting another minute with indecision or worry about things she couldn't control anyway, like what other people might think of her.

She lunged forward, knocking down the closest stanchion and forcing him to catch her.

"You were there. Ben, you were there. You were there, and you never told me."

Ollie was tugging at her, and the field-side commotion drew the attention of the Staffordshire terrier mix as the timer counted down to less than a minute left in the game. The playful young dog dashed over and pounced against Ben's hip, knocking both Mia and Ben off balance enough to take down another stanchion.

"Folks, I don't know how to call this play," Mason was saying. "It looks like a left-field love tackle to me. I got sideswiped by one of those recently myself, so I know one when I see it. And believe me, a more deserving guy couldn't get that kind of tackle tonight."

The crowd whooped and Mia laughed again, refusing to let go of her hold on him.

"And since Lilly here just made the best doggone tackle of the night," Mason continued, "what do you say we give four more points to the home team?" When the crowd went crazy with applause, Mason added, "Folks, with forty-four seconds left in the game, this should give them a solid enough lead to be safe to say these guys will be bringing home the bacon tonight. And don't tell me that Puppy Bowl trophy is filled with gluten-free, meat-free anything of the sort. These dogs deserve something hearty after this."

The crowd went wild, and no one seemed to care that there was still time left on the clock.

Ben pulled back from Mia just enough to meet her gaze. She read his lips as much as she heard him over the din of noise surrounding them. "I'm not sure what I did to deserve this, but you won't see me complaining."

She opened her mouth to answer him, but the crowd was loud and there weren't words enough to explain. So instead, she closed her hands at the sides of his face and drew him in for a kiss.

Chapter 28

DISBELIEF WASHED OVER BEN IN WAVES AFTER THE Puppy Bowl. He'd been resigned to Mia never finding out how much she'd meant to him so early on. But with Lynn's help, she'd figured it out. It was only then that he realized she needed to know. He thought it had only been him who was hampered by the truth not coming out, but it turned out Mia was set free by it too. In learning it, she let go of the guilt that had been holding her back and embraced the love between them with her whole heart.

He wondered if he'd ever get used to the ease with which their hands automatically clasped or their arms locked around each other. He'd been with a handful of women and had had his fair share of women friends, climbing buddies, and business colleagues, but he'd never shared this kind of easy physical closeness with a woman. Whether he'd done it purposefully or not, he'd kept a distance from the women he'd gone out with for any extended time. So much so that he only now realized he'd never intentionally touched a woman just for the pleasure of touching her. Before Mia, touch and sex had been entwined.

Now, he savored a gradient of pleasure he'd never known. They shared a connection, a unity, he'd never experienced. There were things that had never been spoken that somehow she already understood. He loved

her completely, and he released any fear of letting her know it.

At night, once Ollie was in bed, Mia would collapse against him, snuggling into the crook of his arm to talk about little things in her day that made her smile, from emails or texts he sent, to Ollie's schoolwork, or funny things the dogs had done. Once when he was laughing at one of her stories, she placed the flat of her hand on his chest and closed her eyes. When he asked what she was doing, she said she was memorizing the feel of his laughter. "I'm learning from Sadie and Sam. There's a whole world in vibration. And sometimes it still hits me how lucky I am to get to know you with all my senses."

For Ollie's sake, he'd continue for some time to go home to his own bed each night, but in the quiet hours after Ollie was asleep and before Ben left, they made love with abandon, then stayed awake talking about the future, present, and past with no reservations, no holding back.

Without question, it was a love that had been worth waiting for. He'd have waited far longer, had he needed to. Some people passed their whole lives and never got to love the way he and Mia loved each other.

As days melted into happy weeks and weeks into a few months, and they became more and more woven into each other's lives, Ben decided it was time to make the move that a part of him had never dreamed could happen.

—∿∿—

Mia was ten minutes late when she pulled into the parking lot of the indoor dog-training facility. Now that the

baby and dogs were in her life, she seemed to be ten minutes behind schedule for just about everything.

Ben's Jeep was here and empty, so Mia figured he was already inside with Taye and Turbo. Two months into openly dating, and it still made her smile to know her shelter friends were embracing him. They more than embraced him; they adored him. The people she was closest to, like Megan, and more recently Tess, had even picked up on how devoted he was to Taye and to Ollie, which Tess said made him the perfect blend of marshmallow and muscle. And Mia couldn't have agreed more.

"Mom, do you think Sam's ready?" Ollie asked from the back seat, mirroring her earlier thoughts. From the outside, the agility center looked massive. It was newly converted from an old gymnastics facility and, judging from the pictures she'd seen online and the size of the warehouse, it would give high-energy dogs like Turbo a course with plenty of space to run.

"I think he's ready to start agility training, Ol, but don't expect him to pick up on things as fast as some of the other dogs that'll be here today."

It was late March, and a small group from the shelter had gotten together to rent out the training facility for a Sunday afternoon.

At nearly five months old, Sam had mastered all the basic hand signals they'd been teaching him. Off leash in the backyard, he was usually quick to respond to hand-signal commands like sit, stay, lie down, watch me, and come to me. Fairly regularly, though, fresh scents and sights proved more interesting, and he'd ignore Mia and Ollie's signals until his curiosity was satisfied.

In a new environment like this, Mia suspected

they'd need to keep him leashed most of the time. If not, there'd be no holding his attention. But he was young and energetic, and there was no reason he couldn't be an amazing agility dog given time and training. Unlike his quiet and content mom, Sam was proving to be as energetic and playful as Turbo, and dog agility would be a great outlet for him.

Agility was also something Ollie seemed to be passionate about learning, and therefore something Mia wanted to foster.

She was getting Sam and Sadie out of the other side of the back seat, her body blocking the exit, when she noticed Ben coming out of the training center to meet them. Directing her attention back to the dogs, Mia held her hand out in a stop until she had both dogs' attention, then turned her hand over and curled her fingers toward her body, stepping back to make room for them to exit.

She braced for the dogs to pull on the leashes as they hopped out. Sam tugged hard, his fluffy tail raised in excitement, but Sadie stuck by Mia's side as she did in most new environments.

Ben first met up with Ollie, giving him a high five and asking how his afternoon had gone. It probably helped that he'd loved Ollie before, but Ben never forgot to take him into consideration as they began to merge lives. Mia was thankful Ben was as committed to being there for Ollie as he was to honoring the memory of Ollie's father. Brad had had his faults, but they'd not been in fatherhood, and it was equally important to Ben that Ollie have good memories of him. The stories he told Ollie about his father were often as healing for Mia as they were for her son.

She'd gone through a full range of emotions after learning the whole story—that it had been Ben who'd wanted to connect with her after her speech, and that Brad had stepped in when he'd thought his friend had had a change of heart. And gradually she'd found her way back to that place of forgiveness again.

After Ben shared the whole story, Mia had first felt cheated out of eight years she could have had with him, but then she'd thought of Ollie and had realized her life wasn't meant to happen any other way. She and Ben might have been delayed the love they were meant to have, but during that time, they'd both led lives that had enabled each of them to come into their own. And Mia was committed to not looking back. They had the rest of their lives to embrace the love they felt for each other.

"I missed you," Mia said, pressing a kiss firmly against Ben's lips as they met up on Ollie's side of the car.

"Ugh! Kissing! Yuck!" Ollie covered his eyes with one arm and extended his other arm in Mia's direction. "Can I walk Sam in?" He waggled his fingers dramatically with his eyes still covered.

"Of course," Mia answered Ollie, "but don't let him go through the door until he sits and gives you his attention. And it wouldn't hurt to have him pee first." Sam was mostly accident-free, but they were still giving him lots of opportunities for success.

Ollie locked his fingers over the leash and jogged off with Sam toward the nearest strip of grass at the side of the parking lot.

Since Sadie had a stronger bladder and had just gone to the bathroom before leaving, Mia used the opportunity to plant another kiss on Ben's lips, letting her

mouth open to savor his taste for a second or two. She wondered if she'd ever get used to the feel of him, if her heart would someday stop beating just a bit faster when he was near.

"How does it feel to no longer be a homeowner?" Ben asked, locking his hand over her hip.

Mia smiled. She'd closed on the sale of her Central West End home early in the afternoon.

"Freeing." She bit her lip, debating. She'd planned on waiting until tonight after Ollie was asleep to bring it up but decided to seize the opportunity. "However, I have a nine-thousand-dollar check burning a hole in my pocket." She reached up for another short kiss after seeing that Ollie was still focused on Sam. "I know a month ago I said I wanted to wait, but something tells me it's time. Want to invest in some real estate with me?"

"What kind of real estate?" he asked, cocking an eyebrow.

"The very personal kind. With your trained eye, I thought it might be fun to shop around and look for something in need of TLC but with lots of potential and then rehab it like Kelsey and Kurt are doing. Then when it's finished…" She glanced in Ollie's direction. He was running their way with Sam chasing his heels. "You know."

Ben stared at her a beat too long, and then blinked before turning to face Ollie.

"Cohabitate," she finished into his silence, figuring Ollie wouldn't pick up on the word.

"He peed," Ollie said, meeting up with them as they headed to the door and Sam pounced on Sadie.

Ben locked hands with Mia as they walked, their

fingers entwining automatically. He lifted her hand and pressed the back of it to his lips. "I couldn't think of anyone I'd rather do business with."

"Or cohabitate with, I hope." Mia laughed when she said it, but for the first time that she could recall, she had the distinct feeling something was off. But this was Ben, and he'd not been anything but honest with her since the night of the Puppy Bowl, so she tabled it for the evening. She had no doubt where his heart lay, and she was more than willing to give him the benefit of the doubt.

Inside, the gym was even more cavernous than Mia would've guessed. She could imagine speedy, energetic dogs like Turbo fitting right in here. The agility court was a massive Astroturf-covered floor with ramps, tunnels, ring jumps, pole jumps, two bridges, and a seesaw. In front of the course was a large waiting area with twenty or thirty plastic chairs for viewing, and tonight, the waiting area was filled with a handful of some of the people most dear to Mia.

She blinked in surprise when she spotted Megan and her husband, Craig Williams, with their now six-week-old baby swaddled in Craig's arms. Craig's teenage daughter, Sophie, was here with her eleven-month-old beagle, Tyson, even though Megan had joked the odds of him ever getting through a course without being distracted by a zillion scents seemed a thousand to one. Tyson was dragging Sophie over toward Ollie and Sam, and once they were close enough, Tyson dropped into a play bow and barked, enticing Sam into play.

"I'll watch Sadie if you want to say hello," Ben offered, reaching for the leash.

"That'd be great," Mia said. She beelined to ogle over

Evie, who was about as perfect as any little baby she'd ever seen.

"She's so beautiful, Megan." Mia hugged her friend. "And you guys look good too, considering there's a newborn in your house. Are you sleeping okay?"

Megan and Craig exchanged easy smiles before Megan answered that they were taking turns on a few shifts each night and napping when they could. "Like all babies, she's a night owl," Megan added, laughing. "Give her a little sunlight and noise, and she's out like a light."

"I remember those days," Mia said, "and I remember worrying people were wrong when they said they didn't last forever. Brody's eight months old now, and from what Stacey says, he's mostly sleeping through the night."

As a part of going public that she was dating Ben, Mia had also told a few of her closest friends the truth about the baby who'd become a regular part of her and Ollie's weeks.

An excited *whoop-whoop* out on the agility field turned everyone's attention that way. Tess and Mason were out there with John Ronald. Mason jogged alongside him, no leash in sight, and the long-legged dog trotted up and over the steepest ramp with no hesitation. After watching them for a bit, it seemed that while the dog was having no problem trotting over the bridges and ramps, he was more interested in running beside Mason than he was in doing agility for the sake of doing agility.

Tess had a goofy grin on her face as she walked over to the group. "It seems I'm not the only one who's adjusting to Mason being on the road half the time now

that the season is in full swing. He was gone for six days straight and came home this morning. John Ronald hasn't left his side since. He seems happy and content when it's just me and him. Then Mason gets home, and I could be a fly on the wall." Tess shrugged good-naturedly. "I'm good with it though."

"You need to get him another dog," Kurt interjected. "Now that you're moving in across the street, Kelsey and I will dogsit."

Tess wrinkled her nose at him. "Likewise. But that goes without saying. I love Frankie as much as I love John Ronald."

As the group continued to make small talk, Mia noticed Ben had walked over to Taye with Sadie. Taye was at the edge of the waiting area, and Turbo was hanging out by his feet. Sadie was licking Turbo's jowls while Taye was whispering in Ben's ear. Ollie was on the floor a few chairs down, playing some kind of silent game with Sam.

Mia excused herself and headed over. "Hey, buddy," she said, giving Taye a little scratch on the shoulder. "You excited to give this a try? Turbo looks surprisingly calm."

"Hey, Mia." Taye looked at Ben, who gave an almost imperceptible nod. "We got here early and were out there already. Turbo didn't want to go over the ramps while he was on a leash, so I let him off and he ran for like ten minutes without stopping. Once he calmed down, we got him to go over two ramps and that middle jump."

"That sounds like a pretty good start to me. Sorry we missed it."

"We'll try again later," Taye added.

After John Ronald was off the course, Tess suggested that Megan and Ollie bring Sam out next since puppies had shorter attention spans.

When no one else seemed to be in a hurry and Sophie mentioned that Tyson had already gone once as well, Mia agreed and glanced at Ben. "Want to come?"

"Sure." He glanced at Taye, whose eyes grew big.

"Yeah…no thanks. I'll wait a bit."

Mia grabbed the bag of salmon and sweet potato treats the dogs loved, and the flashlight from her purse, and headed out with Ollie and Sam onto the artificial grass. She couldn't put her finger on why, but Taye was acting even weirder than Ben.

"So I don't have any real idea how to do this," Mia mumbled as they headed out into the course. With just her and Ben and Ollie, this felt like heading on a trip without directions on how to get there. When she'd accepted Tess's invitation to come tonight, she'd pictured getting some kind of rundown on how to approach an agility course, but that didn't seem like it would be the case.

"The email was helpful," Ben said. "At least I thought it was. Do you have the map?"

Mia frowned and locked her opposite hand in Ollie's to keep him from falling behind with Sam. "I didn't see an email. And what map?"

"Tess sent an email with directions and a map. Don't sweat it. I've got mine." Ben pulled a folded piece of paper out of his back jeans pocket.

"Why do I feel incredibly unprepared for this?" Mia whispered. "*And* late?"

Ben gave her an easy nudge with his elbow as he

unfolded his map, leash in hand as Sadie trotted along at his side. "You weren't late. And tonight's about having fun. While following the map."

Mia leaned close to look at the map. "I don't see why it matters which ramp we try first, but I'm glad it's an easy one." She dropped Ollie's hand and pointed toward a long, low ramp in the back. "Looks like we're trying that one in the back first, Ol."

Ollie followed the direction of her finger and nodded. "Come on, Sam." In addition to the verbal call that was still habit, Ollie dipped the leash to get Sam's attention. Once he had it, he fell into a jog, and Sam, as always, was quick to follow suit.

"Since you read the email and I didn't, is there anything I missed?" Mia asked Ben.

Ben pursed his lips, and for a split second it looked as if he was trying not to smile. "Not that I can think of."

Sadie whined after Sam but didn't pull on the leash. The cautious dog looked up at Mia, and she responded with a thumbs-up.

By the time they reached it, Ollie had walked up the long ramp with Sam and was bouncing in the middle while Sam tried to eat his shoelace. It was only a few feet off the ground, and Sam didn't seem to mind one bit. "Mom, this one's got your name."

"What do you mean, Ol? And don't bounce on the ramp."

"There." Ollie pointed behind him. "John Ronald's bigger than me, and he was up here. And Sam likes it when I bounce."

Mia had just opened her mouth in rebuttal when she saw what Ollie was talking about. Centered behind the

jump was a thin, waist-high black pedestal sign with MIA hand drawn in a bold, beautiful gold font. She blinked and looked around at the other ramps and jumps and realized about half had similar signposts beside them. She looked at Ben questioningly. "Are we playing a game later or something?"

Ben furrowed his brows at the sign. It seemed a bit impossible that he'd not spotted it while practicing with Taye, but something about his expression reminded Mia of a B-rated actor who was being dramatic while trying not to laugh.

"Ben, what's up?"

He cocked an eyebrow. "No idea. I didn't notice it before. All I know is that we're supposed to follow the map."

"Where to? Where to?" Ollie said, still bouncing.

"Shouldn't we work with them here first?"

"This one's easy. Let's go to the next one." Ollie jogged down the ramp, nearly tripping as he half dragged Sam along and the playful puppy continued to attack his shoe.

What had made her think it wouldn't be as much work or more to teach a seven-year-old how to train a puppy than to train the puppy? Mia didn't know.

"It wouldn't hurt to walk the course once, then come back and start them both here," Ben offered, squeezing her shoulder affectionately.

"Okay. Where to then?" Whatever this was, Mia figured she should go with it and leaned in to look at the map again. The second practice spot was a pole jump that was set to about six inches off the ground. It also had a sign pole beside it. "That one, Ol."

Ollie got there first and went straight to the sign. "Will. This one is Will's."

WILL. Mia didn't know a Will. She looked at Ben, but he was intently watching Sadie. Mia. Will. Her heart beat a little faster. Back at the waiting area, no one seemed to be paying any attention to them as they hung in small groups talking to one another. Quietly talking, Mia realized, picking up on the tension.

Rather than jump the pole when Ollie stepped over it, Sam rested his front paws on top and wagged his tail, paused to pull in his haunches, then hopped over the rest of the way.

"Sweet! Give him a thumbs-up, Ol." Mia was a few seconds too late with the treats, but after fishing a handful from the bag, she waved to get Sam's attention. When she had it, she asked him to sit and gave him a treat when he reluctantly sank to his haunches rather than jump in an attempt to reach it. She handed a few extra treats to Ollie. "Keep these in your pocket so you can reward him on the spot, okay?"

Ollie agreed and asked Ben where to next. Before Mia could suggest they let Sadie give it a try, Ollie was jogging toward the third station. Her heart skipped a beat as she realized it was another one with a sign.

Ben took Mia's hand and gave it an affectionate squeeze as they trailed after Ollie and Sam.

"Do you know any Wills?"

Mia noticed Ben seemed to be looking anywhere but at her as he shrugged and said that he didn't.

"You!" Ollie said, turning to look at Mia in stunned surprise as he reached the station and read the sign. "Mia. Will. You. Mom, will you what?"

Ben was finally looking at her, his mouth pulled into a small, crooked smile.

"Are you going to finish that sentence?" she asked, her voice just above a whisper.

"Don't look at me. Tess sent the map." His tone was just serious enough that Mia looked across the field at the group. No one was talking anymore. Everyone was watching, and Tess had her hands clamped over her mouth in anticipation.

"Oh my God, Ben." Tears stung Mia's eyes. "Are you going to finish that sentence, or should we follow the map?"

"Follow the map!" Ollie interjected, pressing in close to look at the map himself. Ben helped him locate the fourth station and then whispered in Ollie's ear.

"I didn't know you were going to do it like this," Ollie whispered back loud enough that Mia overheard. This time, rather than running ahead, Ollie grabbed Mia's hand and tugged her along, and Ben kept their pace. Tears were filling Mia's eyes so much that she had a hard time reading the fourth sign.

It didn't matter. She knew what it said even before Ollie fell to his knees, dramatically choking himself. "Ugh! This is so much worse than kissing!"

MARRY. Mia laughed and swiped away the tears spilling down her cheeks. "Yes, absolutely yes." She reached up and pressed a kiss against Ben's lips. She laughed and shook her head. "So much yes."

Ben laughed with her. "Uh, I was a little worried about this. You weren't supposed to answer until you get to the bridge. Right now you could be marrying anyone."

"But I only want to marry you."

Ben locked her hand in his and headed toward the bridge in the center. "Ollie, check this last one out, will you?"

Ollie ran ahead and stopped at the sign. "It's an envelope."

"Want to see what's inside?"

"A million bucks I know what it is." Ollie lifted the flap of the square silver envelope that was attached to the sign. "I knew it!" His silly, playful look vanished as he pulled out a ring the sight of which caused Mia to gasp. It was an oval lavender-hued diamond on a smooth platinum band and as elegant as it was simple. It was the kind of ring Mia might have dreamed about but never imagined actually wearing. "Wow." Ollie held it with the same care he would have shown a baby bird. "This is what Mimi bought for you in Africa?"

He looked at Ben, and Ben winked, nodding in confirmation and reaching out his hand. "The stone is. Well done, Ol."

Ben took the ring before handing Ollie Sadie's leash. He turned to Mia, an easy smile on his face. "I know you answered this already, but Mia, will you marry me?"

Mia laughed and sniffed at the same time. "Oh, heck yeah. I'll marry you, Ben Thomas."

She held her breath as Ben slipped the perfectly fitting ring onto her finger. Soon afterward, she found herself lifted into Ben's arms among a chorus of cheers and whoops and hollers and Ollie falling dramatically to the turf, as if trying to prove that romance was in fact his kryptonite.

In the midst of the chaos, Sam hopped up on Ollie's back and let out a single sharp, loud bark, one that was distinct enough it caught everyone's attention.

No longer playing dead, Ollie turned his face to the side and said, "Mom, I think Sam's found his bark!"

Mia laughed. "I think he did, Ollie. You know what? I think we all did."

Acknowledgments

As I recognize the people who've helped make the Rescue Me stories stronger, I'd first like to thank my dedicated readers. The passion you have for the dynamic group of fictional characters at the High Grove Animal Shelter—human, canine, and feline—keeps the ideas flowing. I hope you've enjoyed Ben and Mia's story as much as I've enjoyed writing it. Their love story may be a complicated one, but it's dear to my heart. The idea for it blossomed into life many years ago but demanded a bit of evolution before reaching your hands.

I'm blessed to be able to help shed light on the plight of homeless animals while writing romance. Although I have rescue animals of my own, the everyday stories I've encountered while researching the lives of shelter dogs and cats have made me an even stronger proponent of the remarkable work done by shelters and foster agencies across the country.

I'd like to thank Deb Werksman, my editor at Sourcebooks Casablanca, for continuing to make this series ever stronger with her insight and guidance. I'm thankful for the myriad of support from the entire team at Sourcebooks and Sourcebooks Casablanca who've played a part in bringing Love at First Bark to life. From cover to copywriting, many hands have helped shape this book. I'd be remiss not to mention Susie Benton, Ashlyn Keil, Diane Dannenfeldt, and Kirsten

Wenum by name. Then there's Stefani Sloma, marketer extraordinaire. Stef, you're amazing. Nor can I forget to thank my agent, Jess Watterson, at Sandra Dijkstra Literary Agency. Jess, thanks for always being there when I need you.

My thanks also goes out to my family and friends for their tireless support and cheerleading throughout this journey. I want to thank Ciara Brewer and Bree Liddell for helping to keep me accountable in so many ways. Love you, ladies. Thanks to Saadia Walton for giving me the idea of the shelter reading program and to Theresa Schmidt for sharing information on deaf dogs. Lastly, I thank Ryan and Emily, my amazing kids who are growing into adults faster than I can process. Thanks for your patience and support…and for digging through the laundry basket for a pair of matching socks as often as you reheat cold pizza when I'm closing in on a deadline.

About the Author

Debbie Burns lives in St. Louis with her family, two phenomenal rescue dogs, and a somewhat tetchy Maine coon cat who everyone loves anyway. Her hobbies include hiking, gardening, and daydreaming, which, of course, always lead to new story ideas.

Debbie's writing commendations include a Starred Review from *Publishers Weekly* and a Top Pick from *RT Book Reviews* for *A New Leash on Love*, an Amazon Best Book of the Month for *My Forever Home*, as well as first-place awards for short stories, flash fiction, and longer selections.

You can find her on Twitter @_debbieburns, on Facebook at facebook.com/authordebbieburns, on Instagram at _debbieburns, and at authordebbieburns .com.

If you love sweet, sparkling romance like Debbie Burns's *Love at First Bark*, you won't want to miss this heartwarming new series from author Lucy Gilmore, featuring adorable service puppies and the people they bring together. Read on for a sneak peek at *Puppy Love*.

PUPPY *Love*

FOREVER HOME

LUCY GILMORE

Chapter 1

Now *that* WAS A DOG.

Harrison Parks stood in front of the Great Dane puppy, watching as he stumbled over his feet and struggled with the weight of his oversize head. Already, the animal's sleek gray fur was something to behold, those beautiful eyes like the sky after a rainstorm. It was easy to see what he would someday become—majestic and muscled and massive, more like a trusty steed than a canine.

"He's perfect. Where do I sign?"

A cough sounded at his back. "Um, that's a Great Dane."

Harrison turned to find the slight, well-dressed woman who'd greeted him at the door. She looked apologetic and hesitant and, well, the same way most people looked when they met him for the first time.

In other words, like this was the last place in the world she wanted to be—and he the last man she wanted there with her.

"I thought he might be." He attempted a smile. "What's his name?"

"Rock."

Yes. Rock—durable and solid, the kind of dog a man could count on. Harrison crouched and put a hand out to the animal, his fingers closed in a fist the way the woman, Sophie Vasquez, had shown him. It seemed like

overkill, this careful approach to an animal who hadn't yet reached six months of age, but what did he know? The closest he'd come to having a pet was the raccoon that lived under his back porch.

"I think he likes me."

Sophie coughed again, louder this time. "Rock is great, but he's a stability dog, I'm afraid."

Harrison turned to look up at her, struck again by how out of place she seemed among this room of scurrying puppies. It wasn't just her air of fragility, which made it seem as though a strong wind would topple her over. It wasn't her age either, although her short crop of dark brown hair and her round, sweet face made him suspect she was still in the youthful flush of her twenties.

No, it was the ruffled dress she wore, which seemed better suited for a tea party than a dog kennel.

He did his best to smile again. He was trying *not* to scare her away within the first ten minutes. It wouldn't be the first time he'd done that to a woman. Or a man. Or, if he was being honest, any living creature with a heart in its chest and eyes in its head. He wasn't saying he was a *bad*-looking man—a bit rough around the edges, maybe—but he did have a tendency to come across more forcefully than he intended. His friends blamed it on what they called his "resting brick face." *Like you're going to throw the next man who crosses you into a brick wall*, they laughed.

Which was all well and good after a long day of work, but it wasn't the least bit helpful here.

Just smile and relax, they said. *Be yourself. And for God's sake, lower your guard an inch or two to let in some air.*

Well, he'd tried. The smile—both of them—had already fallen flat, and the idea of relaxing under that woman's wide-eyed stare was impossible. No one had warned him that the puppy trainer was going to be a delicate, fragile wisp of feminine perfection. One of those things he *might* have been able to handle, but all of them?

Yeah, his guard was going to stay right where it was. It gave him someplace to hide.

"What's a stability dog?" he managed to ask.

"Well," she began, "some of our clients need dogs that can provide physical support."

When he didn't do more than nod encouragingly, she added, "As he grows up, Rock will be great at leading someone with vision issues or providing a safe landing for someone prone to seizures. You know—for stability."

"Oh." Harrison blinked. "I don't need that."

"Not really, no."

"Well, what about that one, then? He looks like he knows his way around a back alley or two."

He nodded toward the bulldog in the next slot over. Like Rock the Great Dane, this one was prancing about in one of a dozen half-walled pens built in an extension off the back of Sophie's house. Unlike other dog kennels, Puppy Promise kept none of their animals fully caged in. They had room to climb and jump and pop their heads up to say a friendly hello to their neighbors. And they did too, wet noses being pressed and kissed from one animal to another. When added to the bright-blue walls and not-unpleasant smell of organic cleaning solutions and puppy breath, the result was strangely inviting.

"Rusty?" Sophie asked as the wriggling, wrinkly puppy came bounding forward. His expression held a belligerence that appealed to Harrison on a visceral level. This dog might not be as physically intimidating as a Great Dane, but he sensed a kindred spirit. *Grump and grumpier.* "No, you don't want him. He'll be a nice emotional support dog someday, but he can't smell worth anything."

Harrison bit back his disappointment and allowed his gaze to skim over the other options. He immediately bypassed a tall white poodle that looked as if it had been recently permed and a tiny, yappy thing with eyes like raisins. A soft golden retriever with a mournful expression peeped up at him from the corner. "How about—"

Sophie coughed once more, cutting him short. When he turned to see what the problem was this time, he found her standing a few paces back, holding her hands out in front of her as if warding him off. His gaze was immediately drawn to those hands—so smooth and soft, her nails carefully polished to match her outfit. His own hands were like burned leather, cracked and calloused all over. That was what happened when you spent half of your life battling wildfires. What the elements didn't scorch, the flames did.

"What is it?" he asked, his heart sinking at the sight of those hands. They were *nice* hands, obviously, but he knew what that gesture meant. *Harrison Parks has done it again.* Ten minutes in this woman's company and she'd already seen through his sorry exterior to the even sorrier contents of his soul.

"The truth is, Mr. Parks, we only have one dog right now that matches your specific needs."

"Okay." He swallowed. "Which one is he?"

"He's a female, actually. And she's really sweet."

"Female? Sweet?" Harrison could work with that. In fact, he quite liked both of those things, despite all evidence to the contrary.

"Oh yes. You wouldn't believe the nose she's got on her. I don't think I've ever worked with a more promising puppy. We were lucky to get our hands on her. Most of our animals come from breeders, but this one was rescued from a puppy mill. She's fantastic, even if she is still a little skittish."

Skittish could have applied to several people in his life right now, including the woman standing opposite him. Ever since *the episode* last week, everyone—from his boss at the Department of Natural Resources to his doctors to his very own father—was acting as though he, like Sophie Vasquez, was one strong wind away from toppling over.

But he was *fine*. It was one small coma. He'd get a dog, and it wouldn't happen again.

"She may need some extra work because of it, but I promise she'll be worth it in the end." Sophie broke into a smile—her first since he'd walked in. It struck him forcibly that it was a good thing she'd been too wary to pull it out before now. A smile like that, so warm and real, was a transformative thing. It made him almost happy to be here.

Almost.

"The best things in life usually are, don't you think?" Without waiting for an answer, she added, "Come on. I'll introduce you. She's been eyeing you since we walked in. I think she knows you're going to become good friends."

Harrison didn't have time to fully absorb that remark before a tiny bark assailed his ears. A *very* tiny bark. One might even call it a yap.

"The great thing about this dog is that she's highly portable. You can carry her everywhere."

Portable? Carry her?

He stopped and tried to dig his feet into the concrete, suddenly seeing the oncoming disaster with perfect clarity. Unfortunately, there were some things he couldn't resist, no matter how hard he tried.

One was the power of a beautiful woman's smile.

Another was the force of a 100,000-acre forest fire devouring everything in its path.

And a third, apparently, was a pair of raisin eyes lifted to his in trusting supplication.

"You've got to be kidding me," he said as the miniature ball of fluff twirled and stuck a small pink tongue out the side of her mouth.

This couldn't be right. He was a man who spent literal *weeks* in the wilderness, fighting fatigue and flames. He walked for days with an ax over one shoulder and a team of men at his back. He needed a trusted companion, a sturdy beast he could count on to keep him alive.

Not…

"This is a joke, right? Someone put you up to it?"

"No joke, Mr. Parks," Sophie said. "Please allow me to introduce you to your new diabetic service dog, Bubbles."

It was a truth universally acknowledged that a large, gruff man in search of a puppy would always choose the largest, gruffest one he could find.

Sophie didn't know how or why it happened, but

every time a man entered the kennel, he was drawn inexorably toward the animal most like him in appearance. It was as though they walked up to each pen and, instead of seeing the puppy for its strengths and talents, they saw a mirror instead. Like getting dressed in the morning or buying a car, they wanted a puppy that exactly reflected the image they presented to the world.

Which was why she'd known, the second Harrison Parks walked in the door, that she was doomed.

"Now, I know what you're thinking," she said, watching the expression that crossed his face as his gaze shifted from Bubbles to the Great Dane and back again. *Disappointment* was a disappointingly inadequate word for it.

"No, you don't."

"And I know she's probably not what you had in mind when you signed up for this, but she's very suitable for your needs."

"No, she's not."

"Small dogs require a lot of care, which means you'll be forced to slow down a little when you're working. That's a good thing, right? To be reminded to take more breaks, to put your needs first?"

"No, that's a terrible thing."

"Plus, Pomeranians are much better suited for this type of job than you'd think. They have exceptional noses."

"No."

That was all he offered this time—just that one syllable, that one deeply rumbling sound, a death knell meant to end any and all discussion on a project that she'd thrown her whole self into prepping for. She

wasn't sure which part of it caused her to crack, but she suspected it was that last one.

Well, either that or the fact that he looked so unfairly good while he did it. From the top of his disheveled brown locks to the tips of his heavy work boots, Harrison Parks was exactly what she'd imagined when she'd heard about his case. The man was a wildland firefighter, a hero. Every year, when flames swept across the dry lands of the Pacific Northwest's interior, he headed out with his hose and his determination until every last spark was gone. He was tall and muscular, his expression weary with the devastation he'd seen.

A bit on the crusty side, Oscar had described him, *but totally harmless*.

What he hadn't said was that Harrison was also a half-buttoned flannel shirt away from being the quintessential lumbersexual—rugged and outdoorsy and built like a tank.

In other words, he was a Great Dane. A bulldog.

And he wasn't giving either Bubbles or her a fair shot.

"Listen, Mr. Parks." The sharp rap of her voice startled even herself. "I appreciate that Bubbles isn't what you had in mind, but you need to at least consider what she has to offer."

His gaze—that hard, disappointed one—snapped in her direction, and Sophie instinctively froze. Now that she'd uttered her reproach, she wasn't sure what came next. Her sister Lila would probably segue into an articulate and professional speech about the Pomeranian's finer points. Her other sister, Dawn, would try a coy smile and a low purr to get her way.

Sophie didn't have any such methods for handling recalcitrant clients. No one had let her *have* a recalcitrant client before.

"She's not nearly as bad as you think," she said, soldiering on. "In fact, I think you'll like her. You just have to take a deep breath and give her a try."

He held her stare, his eyes a stony gray that made her think of battlements and cavernous quarries, but at least he complied. Even breathing, he seemed to be exercising every muscle in his body, the swell of his massive chest like an ocean rising.

It worked though. Already, he looked much less like he wanted to storm out the door and report her to the authorities—or, worse, to her sisters.

"Okay," he said. "I'm breathing. What's next?"

Sophie blinked. Breathing had seemed like the most logical first step, but she had no idea what came after that.

Yes, she did. *Cuddles*. No one could resist puppy cuddles—it was almost as universally acknowledged as the fact that Harrison had chosen the Great Dane as his first pick. Maybe she wouldn't be so bad at this after all.

"That all depends on you," she said. "Would you rather climb into the kennel with Bubbles for your introductory session or take her outside?"

For the second time in as many minutes, his gaze sharpened as though he couldn't believe what he was hearing. He didn't blink or move, just stood there staring at her as though he were looking through a ghost. People did that quite a lot actually—looked through her as though she were nothing—but not like this.

He didn't seem dismissive of her or more interested

in the greener pastures that lay beyond. He seemed, well, scared.

"You want *me*"—he pointed at himself—"to climb in *there*? Do you have any idea how far the human body can feasibly bend?"

Sophie had to tamp down a laugh. Now that he'd pointed it out, the idea of that six-foot bear of a man climbing into a pen and snuggling with a baby Pomeranian did seem a little preposterous.

"Outside it is, then," she said. "Just scoop her on up. Don't worry—she won't be afraid of you. She likes to be carried."

He didn't, as she'd hoped, follow her orders. Instead, he glanced down at the little puppy, his brow growing heavier the longer he stood there. It was the same glower that had made him seem so fierce when he'd first walked in.

It didn't seem nearly as intimidating when he shook his head and said, "No, thank you."

She laughed again, unable to stop it from fully releasing this time. All of her tension seemed to be seeping out the more she realized this man was nowhere near as hard as his gruff expression indicated. *All bark and no bite.* "Well, at least you're being more polite about it. I promise she won't bite, and she won't pee all over you. She's a very good girl. Aren't you, Bubbles? Aren't you the most precious little ball o' fluff?"

Harrison took a wide step back from the pen and clasped his hands behind his back. If Sophie didn't know better, she'd think he was afraid of touching the puppy for fear she would infect him with her adorableness.

"No way. I'm not calling her that."

"What? Bubbles?" Laughter welled up in her throat. He was *totally* afraid of her adorableness. "Or precious little ball o' fluff?"

His only answer was a snort. Well, that and another one of those wary looks at the puppy.

"What's wrong?" Sophie asked. "She's just a honey-bunny banana muffin."

"*What?*"

"The fluffiest lady in fluffy town."

"Now see here," he commanded. "You might be able to force this animal on me, but you can't make me say any of that."

No, she couldn't. Sophie couldn't make anybody do anything. She couldn't even get rid of those pushy satellite TV salesmen who still tried door-to-door tactics. The last time someone had asked her to switch cable companies, she'd ended up serving him lemonade and buying 230 sports channels that she and her sisters never watched.

None of that seemed to matter to this man. He was a good head taller than her, outweighed her by the size of the Great Dane puppy, and wore a scowl that could have stripped paint from the walls. But as she took a step closer, he only shook his head in a frantic effort to keep her at bay. It made her feel unexpectedly powerful. Unexpectedly *good*.

"Don't say any more," he warned. "I can't be held responsible for my actions if you do."

"It's all right," she said, feeding off that sense of power, feeling herself coming alive under it. "I can take it."

And then he smiled—for real this time.

Her heart suddenly felt three sizes too big for her

chest. She'd known smiles to change a man's appearance before, but not like this. This wasn't a charming smile or a kind smile or even a dashing smile. It was *devastating*, plain and simple. All those lines and creases, the well-worn care that was etched so deeply into his skin—they disappeared only to be replaced by an expression so startlingly warm and inviting that Sophie had no choice but to fall right in.

"Sweet, soft snookums," she said somewhat breathlessly. She could have stopped there, but the urge to babble overcame her. In all honesty, it was a wonder that she was able to speak at all. "Plush princess paddywinkle. Beautiful bitty baby Bubbles."

That last one broke him. The smile vanished, but only because it lifted into a laugh.

"Oh, hell no," he said. His voice was no less gravelly than it had been before, that deep sound rumbling throughout the kennel, but Sophie detected something new—something *alive*—underscoring it. "If you think I'm going to stand here and let you make a fool out of me, you're sorely mistaken. I'm taking that goddamn Great Dane home with me, and nothing you do or say will stop me." It was said like a dare—almost as if he wanted her to try. Were they…flirting?

Unfortunately, there was no time to find out. Just as she was about to gamely rise to his bait, a voice spoke up from behind them.

"I beg your pardon?" Her sister Lila's voice, normally so polished, acted like a shock of cold water over the proceedings. Sophie turned to find her standing at the top of the steps leading from the kennel to the house they shared. "Is there a problem out here?"

Sophie did her best to put on her usual bright smile, but Lila wasn't looking at her. Her oldest sister—a tall, statuesque beauty who could command the attention of an entire room simply by walking into it—was staring at Harrison with a look that would have done their mother proud. It told Harrison that if he said one more word, goddamned or otherwise, he'd risk the full weight of her wrath.

Of course, when she spoke, her words were nothing but professional.

"I'm terribly sorry if there's been a misunderstanding," she said, and moved elegantly down the steps. Each click of her heels on the cement carried its own warning. "Perhaps I can be of assistance."

"Assistance?" Harrison echoed. All signs of laughter and friendliness had been wiped from his face, replaced once again by the hard wall that he had carried in here.

Lila inclined her head in slight acknowledgment. "Yes. Did I hear you correctly when you stated your preference for the Great Dane over Sophie's selection?"

"You mean Rock?"

Lila nodded.

"Rock. Yes. Rock." Harrison swallowed heavily, glancing back and forth between the sisters. "That's the one I want. The one that's too big to squish."

Lila smiled, but it didn't touch her eyes. She tsked softly. "You have good taste, but I'm afraid he's not available. He's already been assigned to another case. I'm sure Sophie explained that to you already."

"Actually, I—" Sophie caught Lila's eye and clamped her mouth shut. *Of course*. It hadn't even occurred to her

to try a discreet lie. When a client wanted what they couldn't have, you were supposed to redirect them, not antagonize them. *Why didn't I think of that?* "Um, no. I hadn't gotten around to it yet."

"So it would seem. Mr. Parks, why don't you come inside with me and we'll work it out? There's no need to upset the puppies with all this arguing."

"He wasn't arguing." Sophie tried to explain but was once again quelled by a look from Lila. What else could she do? Technically, he *had* been arguing—and she'd been egging him on. She'd been *loving it*.

What is wrong with me?

"This is all my boss's fault," Harrison said. His words were abrupt, his movements even more so. "I didn't even want a dog in the first place."

"It's a tricky business, matching people and puppies," Lila said, trying to soothe. "Every temperament is different—even we don't always get it right on the first try. Do we, Soph?"

Sophie knew that her sister was only trying to make up for this intrusion, including her in the conversation so she wouldn't lose *all* her professional footing in front of the client, but she couldn't help but feel miserable. What Lila really meant—and what Lila would never say—was that *Sophie* didn't always get it right on the first try.

She managed a weak smile. "No, it's not always easy."

"There. You see?" Lila extended her hand toward Harrison. "Come inside. We'll be more comfortable having this conversation in the kitchen."

"*No*." He jerked back as though Lila had shot a lightning bolt from her fingertips. "I mean, no thank you. I'm leaving. That puppy can't… There's no way I…"

He paused and took one of Sophie's deep breaths, a thing she might have appreciated if not for the look of painful reproach he shot her as he did it.

"This was a mistake," he said curtly.

And that was all. Turning on his heel, he made for the back door to the kennel.

Sophie wanted to say something to stop him—apologize maybe, or beg him to give her another chance—but he was already swinging through the door by the time she found her tongue.

"Well." Lila was the first to break the silence that followed Harrison's sudden departure. "Oscar wasn't exaggerating about him, was he?"

When Sophie didn't respond, her eyes still fixed on the gentle sway of the door as if waiting for Harrison to reappear, Lila softened her voice. "That was a pretty nasty scene I walked into. You okay, Soph?"

It was exactly like her sister to ask that question. Given the way things had turned out, Lila could have dumped any number of reproaches on Sophie's head, including the fact that she hadn't wanted Sophie to take on this case in the first place, but of course, she didn't. She never would.

Money meant nothing when compared to Sophie's happiness. Work was secondary to making sure Sophie was taken care of.

Which was why Sophie shook her head. She wasn't okay, not by a long shot. She felt humiliated and ashamed and, well, *small*—but more than that, she felt a strong compulsion to meet Harrison Parks on neutral territory once again. At first, he'd looked at her the way everyone always did, but then, when she'd pushed back,

there'd been a spark in his eyes she desperately wanted to see again.

"I'm a little rattled, to be honest," Sophie said. "He's not like anyone I've ever met before."

"No," Lila agreed. "Some men are just like that, I'm afraid."

It was on the tip of Sophie's tongue to ask what Lila meant, but she stopped herself just in time. She already knew what Lila was thinking, because it was the same thing she'd thought when Harrison Parks had first knocked on the door.

This is a man who doesn't like to be told what to do. This is a man to be wary of.

But Lila hadn't seen that smile. Lila hadn't been there when he'd quaked at the mere thought of touching such a precious, golden-haired lump as Bubbles. Lila hadn't felt the surge of exhilaration that had come from confronting him…and *winning*.

"And he wasn't necessarily wrong," Lila added. Her hand touched Sophie's shoulder. "I did warn you that Bubbles might not make a good service dog, sweetie. Not every puppy is cut out for this kind of work."

Sophie glanced down at the animal under consideration, a pang of mingled frustration and disappointment filling her gut. Okay, so Bubbles wasn't the most impressive puppy to come under their care—she was small and soft and had lingering issues from the trauma of the puppy mill—but that didn't make her *useless*.

"Don't worry about it," Lila continued softly. "There will be other cases. One unhappy customer won't make or break us. I'll call Oscar and get everything straightened out."

"No, don't." Sophie spoke sharply, using the same tone that had snapped out when Harrison had initially refused Bubbles. At her sister's raised brow, she hastily amended it with, "I'll talk to him. It's my responsibility. I'm the one who mishandled the situation."

Lila's brow didn't come down, but she accepted Sophie's decree with a nod. "Sure thing, Soph. Take the rest of the day off. Go see Oscar. He always makes you feel better."

Sophie offered her a tight smile but didn't say anything. Oscar *did* always make her feel better, but that wasn't what she meant. She didn't want a day off. She didn't want someone to hug her and placate her and tell her everything would be all right.

What she wanted—no, what she *needed*—was to get her client back.

Glancing down at the Pomeranian, who was staring at the back door as if she too expected Harrison to come waltzing back through it at any moment, Sophie decided that was exactly what she'd do too.

Even if it was only so she could feel that sudden spark of battle coming alive inside her again.

WILD ON MY MIND

Love runs wild and big-hearted animals help unlikely couples find love—from debut author Laurel Kerr

When Katie Underwood discovers a litter of newborn cougar cubs, the last person she expects to come to the rescue is her former crush—and high school nemesis—Bowie Wilson. But he doesn't seem to remember the trouble he caused her years ago…

Single father Bowie is all ears when it comes to getting his beloved but cash-strapped zoo on the map. He considers himself lucky when Katie agrees to lend her publicity skills to the zoo's rehabilitation programs…until their rivalry resurfaces. He can't figure out why the beautiful redhead hates his guts—and she's determined to protect her heart from the infuriatingly attractive zookeeper. But there's not much they can do once a lovelorn camel, a matchmaking honey badger, and a nursemaid capybara are convinced these two are meant to be…

For more info about Sourcebooks's books and authors, visit:

sourcebooks.com

TANGLED UP IN YOU

Being in the wrong place can lead to the right person in this charming romance by *New York Times* and *USA Today* bestselling author Samantha Chase

Bobby Hannigan prided himself on being in the right place at the right time...until walking in on a robbery left him with a gunshot wound that could end his career as a police officer. Being a cop is all he ever wanted, and now his world is falling apart—until he meets a woman able to see past his bad attitude to the man he's struggling to become...

"Chase just gets better and better."
—Booklist

For more info about Sourcebooks's books and authors, visit:
sourcebooks.com

RECKLESSLY
EVER AFTER

The rugged Marines of Heather Van Fleet's
Reckless Hearts series will sweep you off your feet

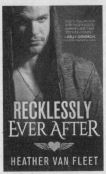

After the hell I've been through in the Marines—in life—
there's nothing I crave more than routine, stability, peace.
Until McKenna Brewer walks into my life.

She's impulsive, fiery, tempting as hell—and everything
I don't need. When our night together has unexpected
consequences, I can't help but think this might be the
perfect opportunity to show McKenna just how much I
want her…

"Emotional, heartfelt, and absolutely beautiful."
**—Jennifer Blackwood, *USA Today* bestselling
author**

For more info about Sourcebooks's
books and authors, visit:
sourcebooks.com

MEET DEBBIE BURNS

Debbie is a lifelong dog lover with two adopted shelter dogs of her own. She became passionate about the problems of free-roaming strays when she had a personal encounter as a college student with a young terrier who was in poor condition from living on the streets. Since then, the plight of abandoned and free-roaming strays has been a cause that is near and dear to her heart, and she supports the efforts of the courageous volunteers who work tirelessly to help get strays off the streets and into shelters and forever homes.

Learn more about Debbie, her dogs, and her writing at authordebbieburns.com.

The Rescue Me series by Debbie Burns
Because every heart needs a loving home

Support your local shelter.
Find it through HumaneSociety.org.

ISBN-13: 978-1-4926-7284-5

9 781492 672845

50799

S

EAN

DEBBIE BURNS

LOVE AT FIRST BARK

For Erick and Barb,

and for the mountains you move every day

66946831

Rom

Published by Sourcebooks Casablanca, an imprint of Sourcebooks
P.O. Box 4410, Naperville, Illinois 60567-4410
(630) 961-3900
sourcebooks.com

Printed and bound in Canada.
MBP 10 9 8 7 6 5 4 3 2 1

LOVE AT FIRST BARK

🐾 A RESCUE ME NOVEL 🐾

DEBBIE BURNS

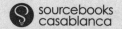

sourcebooks
casablanca

Also by Debbie Burns

RESCUE ME
A New Leash on Love
Sit, Stay, Love
My Forever Home

Chapter 5

A SECOND CHANCE

I had been escorted to a camp office on the lower level of Mr. Periwinkle's house. Now, as I waited for him, I watched the blackness outside slowly turn gray. Dawn couldn't be far off. I heard a slight nervous cough, followed by Mr. Periwinkle's voice as he entered the room and sat down behind a big wooden desk.

You'd think I'd be nervous, but there was nothing intimidating about Mr. Periwinkle. Besides, I expected to get kicked out and that's exactly what I wanted. I'd had enough of this crazy Camp Wy-Mee and all the horrible people in it. The farther away from Todd Vanderdick, the better. For the first time in my life, I actually looked forward to receiving my punishment.

"Well, Rodney, that was quite an evening you put us through," Mr. Periwinkle began.

"I didn't light the fireworks."

"Um, well, there was a good bit of evidence in your trunk that says otherwise."

"Todd put it there, and he lit it. How else would he have known to look in the trunk?"

"He claims to have seen it when you opened it to get your toothbrush, and we need to remember, Todd is a Vanderdick."

"I'll say."

"His father is a pillar of the community, and young Todd has won the Camp Wy-Mee Leadership Award the past two summers."

"Well, his plot to frame me did show outstanding initiative."

"It certainly did," he agreed. Then his face grew confused. "Oh, now, now, I think we need to dismiss the conspiracy theories. What we need—"

"Listen, Mr. Periwinkle, I don't care. Kick me out of this asylum."

He looked taken aback. He paused and stared down. His hands rested next to a paperweight and a mug full of pens and markers. "It pains me," he continued, "to hear a camper describe Camp Wy-Mee as an asylum. I think if you were to stay with us for the summer, Rodney, you would discover that this is a magical place. But, sadly, you've left me little choice. I'm going to have to call your parents to come get you." He reached for the phone.

"Per-CY!"

Mr. Periwinkle jumped, knocking over the mug of pens. "Oh dear," he stammered, looking up at the ceiling. "Coming, sweetie!"

He took off through the office door. I heard him move through the house and up the stairs. I strained my ears to hear the conversation in the room above me. It was too muffled for me to make out the words, but I could tell that whoever had called Mr. Periwinkle was a woman with a sharp, bossy voice.

After a minute I heard Mr. Periwinkle retrace his path back to the office. He looked red and more flustered than usual. He sat back down and ran his hands over his face. He exhaled and said, "Well, Rodney, it seems that Mrs. Periwinkle thinks you deserve a second chance. You've been forgiven."

"What? Why?" I stammered.

"I don't really know. In over thirty years of marriage she's never given *me* a second chance."

"So I'm not being punished?"

"Oh, I didn't say that. No, she wants you punished severely. Just not sent home."

"But I don't want to stay here. I want to speak to my parents."

"She said no phone calls."

Something seemed fishy, but I didn't care. I had no intention of sticking around to discover what these people were up to. "I'm calling home," I said, reaching over for the phone. I punched in my phone number.

"Oh dear," Mr. Periwinkle whined, biting his nails. "Oh, don't do that. You should hang up." He glanced nervously back at the ceiling.

"Hello," came my dad's sleepy voice through the receiver.

"DAD!" I yelled.

"Rodney! What is it? Why are you calling so early? Honey, Rodney's on the phone." I could hear my mom talking in the background.

"Dad, you've got to come up here and get me. Everyone here is mean. This kid framed me, said I set off some fireworks, now the camp director says I'm going to be punished severely."

"What?" my dad barked. "I didn't pay all that money to send you off somewhere to be picked on and punished. I'll have you out of there before dark! Is the camp director near?"

"Yes, he's sitting right here." Mr. Periwinkle jumped back.

"Let me talk to him."

I handed the phone over. Mr. Periwinkle held the receiver to his ear, reluctantly, as if it might bite him.

I felt great. My dad was going to get me out of here. I watched and listened as Mr. Periwinkle cleared his throat and began stammering.

"Yes . . . yes, well we did find some in his trunk and . . . well, we've decided to give him another chance. . . . There needs to be some punishment. . . . Oh, well that's too bad . . . I'm sure he'd learn to love the place. . . . What's that? . . . No, there are no refunds. . . . No, it's stated right there in the contract. . . . Yes, we have to be quite firm about the *no-refund policy*." Mr. Periwinkle listened for a moment more. "Okay, I'll give it to him." He handed me the phone.

"Rodney," my dad said, "I've given it some thought, and I've decided I didn't raise you to be a quitter."

"Dad, you just said . . ."

"Rodney. You're a Rathbone. Time to give it the old college try."

"But I'm just starting middle school!"

"Well, that's beside the point. Anyway, you need to give that camp another shot. There are no two ways about it. I know you can handle everyone there. Look what you did this past year at school. If you don't like it in a couple of weeks, call me again."

"But, Dad . . ."

"Rodney, I love you. Talk to you soon. I have to get ready for work. Have fun." *Click*. I felt my heart drop into my stomach.

Mr. Periwinkle clapped his hands together. "Well, now, that's settled. Okay, we need to get ready for breakfast . . ."

A sharp tap at the partially open window interrupted his sentence. Todd's toothy grin appeared on the other side of the screen. "I brought Rodney's things," he called into the room. I wanted to hurl the paperweight in his direction.

"Excellent, Todd," Mr. Periwinkle said.

Todd gave me one of his evil smiles. "Rodney, you're going to need to get your trunk latch fixed. Darn thing sprung open on me." I craned my neck and saw my belongings lying all over the grass.

Mr. Periwinkle spoke up. "Todd, it turns out that Rodney is going to remain with us for a while. So we'll need to get his stuff back to the cabin."

Todd frowned. "I think that's a bad idea." He paused, expecting Mr. Periwinkle to change his mind. When no reply came, he added, "Well, he's not staying in *my* cabin. My parents always say that it's important for me to associate with 'the right sort.' I don't think an arsonist is right-sort material."

"Hmmm. I guess I could change his cabin . . ."

"Put him in Loserville," Todd suggested.

"Its proper name is Cherokee," Mr. Periwinkle corrected him.

"Yeah, whatever. It would be a good way to start the healing process."

"Yes . . . so it would be. Wonderful idea!" Mr. Periwinkle turned around to face me. "Isn't Todd thoughtful?"

That wasn't exactly the word I had in mind. Todd was punching his fist into his palm and making faces at me behind Periwinkle's back.

"Now, why don't you gather your things?" suggested Mr. Periwinkle. "The cabins will be coming to line up for breakfast shortly."

Todd shouted into the office, "See you later, Mr. Periwinkle. I've got to go make my bed, wash my hands before breakfast, and see if any new kids need help finding their way around."

I wanted to puke, but Periwinkle seemed to really believe him.

"Wonderful. Thank you, Todd. You know, Rodney, you could learn a thing or two from this one. You can see why I couldn't take your framing story seriously."

I didn't answer. I may have been in a new location, but my life sure hadn't changed. I had a bully after me, no one believed what I had to say, and it looked like I might be stuck here for a long, long time.

Chapter 6

HOME, STRANGE HOME

There were about a dozen cabins in the boys' area, but I had no problem spotting Loserville. Even if I hadn't seen it during the night, you couldn't miss it by day. The cabin was sagging in the middle—but that was nothing compared to the weeds growing on the roof and the tattered canvas windows. The fact that some kid had scrawled the word "Loserville" across the front door also made it kind of easy to spot. Either way, there was no mistaking it for the Algonquin cabin.

"Catching a ray or sliding away?"

I spun around. The counselor, Woo, had walked up in back of me. He was holding a towel and probably heading back from the bathroom.

"What?" I asked.

He wore glasses with big black frames and had a black cap thing that looked like a flying saucer on his head. Later I found out he called it a beret, and the little beard on his chin was called a goatee. "Hand me that skin, daddy-o," he said, sticking out his hand. "I'm Woo, and I know what to do."

"Nice to meet you. I'm Rodney."

His head started bopping back and forth as he said, "Rod*ney*, swings from the *tree*, drinks some *tea*, gots to go *pee*." I wasn't sure if he was singing, rapping, or just having a fit. "Play sax, daddy-o?" he asked.

"Excuse me?"

"You on the stick?"

"Huh?"

"Saxophone, *man*. I need a tenor saxophone for my jazz ensemble. We play a lot of Miles Davis. I play the trumpet, the straw boss. Dig?"

I still wasn't following. "No, I don't play saxophone."

His face fell, but then brightened as he asked, "What about the bass guitar? Bum bum bum bum . . ." He stood there looking down at me making the bum-bum noise and plucking an imaginary guitar in the air.

"No," I said, "I don't play the guitar. Actually, the reason I'm here is because I was just assigned to your cabin."

A big grin spread across his face. "Well, come feel the funk and grab a bunk!"

I found myself smiling, too—for the first time since arriving at Camp Wy-Mee. This Woo guy was crazy but nice. He reached down, picked up my trunk, and announced, "Follow me, man, to Cherokee land."

And follow him I did, though I couldn't help

wondering how my new cabinmates would react to me. After all, in their eyes I was the guy who had attacked them during the night. I doubted I'd be welcomed with open arms, especially since the smell of fireworks still hung in the air.

Once inside the cabin, I noticed several kids huddled about and whispering. Others were staring off into space. Josh sat cross-legged on a top bunk, picking at his toenails. He gave me a nod. "Yo! Rodney."

"Yo," I answered back.

Still in shock—but grateful—that Josh was my new best buddy, I looked around, unsure of what to do. I figured I better claim a bunk. Sleeping bags lay on all except two of them. One of the available bunks was right below Josh, but as I approached I saw that his mattress sagged all the way down in the middle. The idea of rusty old springs an inch from my face didn't exactly excite me. The other available bunk contained a nasty-looking gray pillow. I went to move it.

Snap!

The pillow almost bit my finger off! I jumped back and watched it rise on four legs and hiss at me. It was a raccoon.

"You don't want to wake up Harry," some kid said.

"Is he like a pet?" I asked.

"No. He's far from tame. He just moved in here last summer and no one can get him out. Did you get your rabies shots?"

42

All at once those straining, rusty springs below Josh didn't seem so bad. I put my trunk next to the empty bottom mattress, sat down, and checked out my new surroundings.

There was no denying that my cabinmates were a pretty motley-looking group. Several of them still wore the smoke stains and dirt of the night before, leading me to believe that hygiene wasn't a priority in this cabin. My feeling was reinforced when I noticed another boy with sweaty armpits that had soaked through his T-shirt. He was busy picking something out of his ear. The next kid was clean, but perhaps even more disturbing. He wore a sky-blue dunce cap and matching cape. I guessed he was going for the wizard look.

Now, I've always prided myself on not being judgmental, but I was beginning to wonder if I had more in common with the raccoon than the rest of this Loserville gang. Just then the door opened and another boy stepped in. He was thin, with dark, tanned skin and brown, almost black eyes. His black hair was combed neatly back, and what was even more shocking was that he was confident and cool. Maybe he had wandered in by accident, because he sure looked out of place.

He must have been thinking the same about me. "You look halfway normal," he announced. "A relief. I'm Fernando. Who are you?"

"Rodney."

"Sure, the terrorist trainee. We know all about you."

Here we go, I started to think. Woo was on the far side of the cabin, eyes closed, tapping his foot and listening to his iPod. He wouldn't be any help. I stared back at the kid, ready for a fight—until I noticed he was grinning slightly.

"You know, Rodney, the Fourth of July isn't until next week."

"Hey, I didn't light the fire crack—"

Fernando interrupted. "Do you know that this bunch"—he motioned around the cabin—"has been whimpering for hours? Well, not that big fellow up there, he seemed to enjoy the whole show, but the explosions got Stinky sweating, and that's not fun, I assure you."

I assumed he was talking about the armpits kid. "Listen," I said, holding up my hand, "I didn't . . ."

"You didn't do it." Fernando laughed. "We know."

I thought he was being sarcastic. "I'm serious. I didn't . . ."

Fernando rubbed his temples. "You're not one of those guys that needs everything repeated five times, are you? We know you didn't do it."

"You do? How?"

"Because we know who did it. Thorin Oakenshield over here"—he thumbed back at Wizard Boy—"saw Todd Vanderdick last night."

Thorin Oak-and-something stepped forward. "I saw

44

him sneak into our cabin. I was ready to grab him, but he must have hit me with an Immobulus spell, because I couldn't move or speak."

"Yeah, that's called being too scared to move," Stinky joked.

"Scared?" Thorin snapped. "I happen to be the most important dwarf in Middle Earth!"

"Last year you were Aslan, King of Narnia, which is ridiculous since Aslan is a lion."

"Ridiculous? ROOOAARRRR!" He jumped across the cabin with his hands held out like cat claws. Stinky countered by ripping off his dingy sneaker and holding it in the air. Thorin gagged and fell away holding his nose. "Not foot odor! It's my greatest weakness!"

The two of them broke into hee-hawing laughs.

"Do you see what I have to put up with?" Fernando asked me. "Welcome to Loserville." He held out his hand. I shook it and knew right away that here was a kid I liked.

"And my name is Frank," Stinky added.

Each kid in the cabin came up and said hello to me. Even if they were a bit odd, I could see that they were genuinely nice. I relaxed and yawned. I hadn't exactly had a good night's sleep. I closed my eyes for a minute, thinking about what Todd had done to me. I sure was glad to be away from him and the other Algonquin phonies. Maybe there were no flat-screen

TVs or water beds here, but hey, my new friends seemed great, and besides, we had something you'd never find in the Algonquin cabin. I smiled as Harry the Raccoon waddled across the floor and disappeared below a bunk.

Chapter 7

LUCIFER

"Snake 'em, break 'em, and shake 'em!"

I jumped. Woo was yelling from outside the cabin. I must have fallen asleep for a minute. "What did he just say?" I asked Stinky.

"That it's time to line up for breakfast and that we're having scrambled eggs today."

"Oh." Completely confused, I followed the rest of the campers outside, where they were gathering before heading to the dining hall. By now the sun was really up and I took a few moments to take in my surroundings.

The cabins overlooked a very large lake. In the distance, beautiful green islands—some of them pretty big—dotted the surface of the deep blue water. There were canoes, rowboats, kayaks, sailboats, a dock, and swim platforms. Closer, in a clearing, were basketball courts and several poles, each with a yellowish ball hanging down from the top. Already boys were whacking the balls in opposite directions.

"What game is that?" I asked Thorin.

"Tetherball. Not exactly Dungeons and Dragons, if you ask me."

"Of course," I answered, not sure what to say.

Looking in the other direction, heading away from the lake, there was a path that eventually opened up to the large fields I had crossed during the night. I could see soccer goals and a volleyball court. I hated to admit it, but by daylight the place looked awesome. Every direction held interesting things to do. "Seems pretty nice," I mentioned to Josh.

"I guess," he answered. "Got more fireworks?"

I changed the subject. "Looks like we'll be eating soon."

"I know. Bet they'll have food."

In search of more interesting conversation, I strolled over to Fernando. "So," I began, "do you mind if I ask— how did you wind up in Loserville?"

"Same as you."

He motioned straight ahead. Todd was standing outside the Algonquin cabin talking to Magnus. He must have noticed us because he immediately pulled up his shorts as high as they'd go, stuck out his front teeth, and walked around like a nerd with mental problems. "Uh duhhh, losers!" he yelled and waved. The other Algonquins laughed, and I noticed Stinky cowering. Fernando, on the other hand, remained completely cool.

"You see," he continued, "the ladies love me, and ol' Todd over there doesn't like that, so he had me assigned here. I don't really blame him. Being as smooth and charming as Fernando is intimidating." He laughed and I joined him. "And speaking of the ladies," he turned to me, "I understand you arrived with quite a beauty last night."

I thought about the girl with the emerald-green eyes I had chased through the woods, straight to the campfire. Remembering just how good she looked, my chest pounded. I had trouble inhaling as I thought of her long brown hair. But I was supposed to be going out with Jessica. And yet . . .

"Are you okay, my friend?" Fernando asked. "We lost you for a minute."

"Oh. Um, what were we talking about?"

"Never mind for now." His gaze had returned to Todd. "I have to warn you, Rodney. If I were you, I would watch my back. That Vanderdick kid is a total—"

BLLLEEEEHHHHH, a whistle blasted.

"Line up by cabins!" Magnus yelled. "Time vee go now to da flag raising und breakfast!"

As we marched off toward a big building that I guessed was the dining hall, some other counselors started a song about sixpence, a whiskey bottle, and an unhappy wife. Many of the campers joined in. I didn't know the words but it was kind of fun striding along with Fernando, Stinky, Josh, and Thorin Oakenshield.

The sweet smell of grass filled my nostrils, and though early in the day, the summer heat was already baking the blacktop.

Despite my Todd problems—and the fact that I wanted to get back to my friends in Garrettsville as soon as possible—I could see that Camp Wy-Mee wasn't a complete disaster.

And then I saw something that made me feel even better. The girls were heading our way! There were a lot of them, and they were also singing. I strained to see one in particular. A moment later our eyes met and my knees almost gave out. In the light of day, not covered in dirt and grime, the girl I had chased to the camp-fire looked even better. I saw her returning my look. A friend of hers whispered something in her ear and she looked at me with greater intensity. I could feel my pulse quickening as we came to a stop.

Magnus hollered, "Campers, straighten out da lines and stop da talking! Vee vill now listen to Mr. Peri-vinkle, ya?"

Dressed in safari attire, Mr. Periwinkle stood on a hill to the right of the dining hall. "Okay, okay, everyone. We all need to be quiet for the flag raising. You down there"—he pointed to Thorin Oakenshield—"please remove your, er, hat. Thank you. Now for the part I know you've been waiting for all year." The crowd shifted its attention to the Periwinkle house, adjacent to the hill. The house had nice views and big old trees surrounding it. Unfortunately, my earlier visit to the camp office inside had tarnished my feelings. Mr. Periwinkle called, "Sweetie! We're ready!"

Out from behind the house appeared a large, stern woman on a horse. She sat there for a moment looking down at us, and I assumed she was the one I had heard screeching at Mr. Periwinkle last night. What came out of her mouth next sounded even more frightening.

"Oh say, can you seeeeeee . . ."

Her voice was cutting and awful and sliced right through the air. It seemed to take forever to raise the flag and I said a silent prayer of thanks when the song ended. "Is that Periwinkle's wife?" I asked Thorin.

"Yes. She rides around on that old steed as if it were Shadowfax . . ."

"Silence!" Mrs. Periwinkle shouted in our direction. Then, to her husband, she announced, "Percy, I am ready to survey the troops! I mean, campers."

She trotted down the hill on her horse, with Mr. Periwinkle running alongside. When she reached the crowd of campers, she began to ride more slowly and deliberately, looking down at each group. She wore a silver riding helmet and I felt a natural urge to stick out my chest and salute.

We were the last group to be inspected. As Mrs. Periwinkle passed by, her horse turned its head, took a step in my direction, and looked down into my eyes. It was so close I could feel the hot breath from its nostrils on my face. I didn't know what to do. Finally I said, "Hey, boy," and reached out my hand to . . .

"Neeeeigh!!" Immediately, the horse reared up and tried to bring down its front hooves on top of me. I had to dive backward and actually fell into a little ditch. As I tumbled down I heard the horse's whinnies and the shrieks of Mrs. Periwinkle, combined with a kid's voice yelling, "Whoa! Whoa!"

I came to a stop in a clump of overgrown grass. Only after I was sure the horse was subdued did I climb back up, expecting to be swarmed by concerned people. Boy, was I wrong. Mrs. Periwinkle was off the horse, helmet tilted on the side of her head. Her clothes looked disheveled. I wondered if she'd been thrown. She looked a bit like a teapot about to boil over. As Mr. Periwinkle fanned her face, she pointed a finger at me and barked, "*Who* is this ruffian?"

Mr. Periwinkle bobbed up and down several times nervously, unable to speak. It was Todd who answered. He was holding the horse by its reins and patting it like an old friend.

"That," he told Mrs. Periwinkle, "is Rodney Rathbone . . . the one who caused all the commotion last night."

She pursed her lips. "I knew it was a risk keeping this deviant about. My poor Lucifer could have been badly hurt . . . "

This was too much. "I didn't do anything to your horse," I explained.

"Silence! You are a menace. Percy!"

"Yes, dear?"

"I want this boy soundly punished for last night, and for today. Just look at my blouse."

"It looks . . . lovely," Mr. Periwinkle lied. I cringed. He continued, "How about I have Rodney here assist Gertrude and Alice with kitchen cleanup for a week?"

Mrs. Periwinkle looked at her husband. "That's a start, but I don't think it's going to be enough. First we'll suspend all his phone privileges."

"What?" I yelled. I couldn't lose my calls. I was already planning to get my dad back on the phone later that day.

Now it was Todd's turn to join the conversation. "You heard her, Rathbone." He was acting like their long-lost son, and I didn't like it. He continued, "You know, Mrs. Perwinkle, the other day, when Dad and I were standing on your schooner's poop deck . . ."

"Ha ha, he said *poop!*" Josh laughed.

Everyone glared at him, but clearly he didn't understand the meaning of eye contact and continued laughing for a bit. Mrs. Periwinkle shook her head in disgust before turning back to Todd. "You were saying?"

"Well, when Dad and I were so graciously invited on your boat, I noticed that the bottom of the schooner hadn't been cleaned in years. It's covered with zebra mussels. Have you heard of zebra mussels? They're nasty creatures with sharp shells." He looked at me with a sideways glance before continuing. "I think Rodney here should have to remove them."

"Yes," Mrs. Periwinkle replied, "that's an excellent idea, Todd. I'll have him remove them. I like that." As she pondered my punishment, she seemed momentarily calm and happy.

"Excuse me, but isn't the boat in the water?" I asked.

"Duhhhh . . . it's a boat," Todd shot back. "Of course it's in the water."

"How will I get at the bottom, then?"

Mrs. Periwinkle answered this time. "You'll swim!" Her eyes locked onto mine. Her face twisted in a sly smile, and for a dreadful second I noticed a sinister flash. A flash that, while it seemed impossible, I knew I'd seen before. I shivered.

"Enough talk!" she commanded. "Mr. Periwinkle will arrange the particulars." She took one final look at me and my cabinmates. "Now, go to breakfast, and take your greasy little friends with you!"

Chapter 8

ROUGH SAILING

The next few days consisted of basic camp orientation. We went over safety procedures and rules, and learned where everything was. It had started raining on my second night at Camp Wy-Mee and continued to pour nonstop, which gave me plenty of time to get to know my "greasy" friends. They were great and we had lots of fun playing cards in the cabin, careful to dodge the raindrops coming down from the leaky roof. Woo would play jazz trumpet in the corner, and sometimes we would all just goof around for hours at a time.

It would have been awesome, actually, except that Todd had it in for me and I was forced to spend most of my time avoiding him. Worst of all, every day I was stuck washing pots and pans in the dining hall. It got to the point where it was too much. I just wanted to go home. I liked my new friends, but I missed Rishi,

Slim, and the gang I had left behind. I missed Jessica, too. Heck, I even missed my little sister.

The worst part was that I couldn't even call my family. Mrs. Periwinkle had made sure of that when she suspended my phone privileges. I figured that some of the kids had snuck in cell phones, but everyone told me it didn't matter. Evidently, Camp Wy-Mee was the only place left on Earth without cell reception!

After each meal, with my hands stuck in hot, greasy water, I would dream of ways to escape this prison. At least the lunch ladies, Alice and Gertrude, were kind. From time to time they would wave their spatulas at me and flash toothless smiles through clouds of cigarette smoke.

It was on my last day of kitchen duty that the sun finally came out. I worked extra fast, dried off the final pots and pans, and bolted out of the hot kitchen—right into Mr. Periwinkle.

"Ah, Rodney, did you find any classes you're excited about?"

"Huh?"

"Now that the rain has stopped we can truly get going with camp."

He motioned around and I realized that tables had been arranged in the field. Campers were wandering between them, checking out the different classes being offered. I looked at Mr. Periwinkle. "Got anything on how to remove burned-on grease from soaking pans?"

"Ah, yes, that was an excellent lesson. We're all about building character at Camp Wy-Mee."

"Yeah, great. Mr. Periwinkle, can't I use the phone? It's been a week. I need to call my parents."

His face lost some of its excitement. "Rodney, if your parents wanted to talk to you, would they have sent you away to camp?"

That gave me pause. Could it be true? I shook the thought out of my head. "But . . ."

"You can write them a letter tonight. Now go out there to the field and find some nice activities . . ."

"Mr. Periwinkle, I'm not planning on staying here, so there's no need for me to pick any activities. I've had enough character building for one lifetime and I really need to call—"

"Ah, here's someone you could learn a thing or two from!"

I turned around. Josh was walking by with a big smile on his face. "Rodney, I got into riflery, archery, and rocketry. I get to shoot guns and arrows, and explode rockets! I can't wait. This place is the greatest!" He ran off with his hands raised in the air.

We watched him go. Turning back to Mr. Periwinkle, I noticed his eyes looked wet. He shook his head and said wistfully, "If I had twenty more like him, I'd have the top camp in America."

After digesting Periwinkle's drivel and realizing I wasn't going to get any further with him, I headed out into the field. I wasn't excited about looking for classes, but I figured I'd better do it. After all, it was starting to dawn on me that escape from Camp Wy-Mee might be harder than I thought. Just then I saw Fernando. "Pick any classes?" I asked.

"Not yet. It's important to know which classes they're registering for first." He seemed to be looking for someone.

"Who's registering for?" I asked.

He glanced at me with a puzzled expression, and then gazed back into the crowd. I could see his eyes darting from one girl to the next. He nodded and counted to himself as they signed up for classes. Eventually he pointed to a red-haired girl and raised his eyebrows. "That's the one for Fernando. How about you, Rodney? Whose class are you joining?"

I hadn't thought about picking classes based on which girls were in them, but at that moment Emerald Eyes walked by. She was wearing a white headband and giggling with a friend. I nodded toward her dumbly. Fernando approved. "Yes, I should have guessed. You have excellent taste."

"Yeah, well, she hates me. I've tried twice this week to talk to her and she's always walked right by. She still thinks of me as the crazy kid who chased her through the woods."

"That's wonderful news."

"Huh?"

"Don't you see?" He smiled. "The fact that she hates you will make the quest that much more interesting."

I could tell he wasn't kidding, but I also knew it didn't matter. No quests for this camper. I was dating Jessica . . . I hoped. "I have a girlfriend," I told him.

"That's nice, I have six. Now, see that one over there? I'll bet she'll love it when I speak to her in my Latin tongue."

Not quite sure what that meant or what to expect, I watched as he headed off in the direction of the red-headed girl. She turned around, looking confused, but then her eyes started to twinkle and she smiled. "Is that Spanish?" she asked. Fernando looked back at me and winked.

I laughed and started to turn away, then stopped. The girl with the green eyes had entered a building down by the lake. I noticed the sign above it: EXPERT SAILING CLASS.

Figuring I had nothing to lose, I decided to follow her in, when a little voice inside my head reminded me that I didn't know the first thing about sailing. Heck, the only boat I'd ever been on was the Staten Island Ferry!

"Who cares?" I said out loud.

Several people turned and looked at me. Woo was walking by and whispered, "Crazy like a crazy man. Cut the gas. Dig?"

I didn't dig, and I didn't care. Maybe crazy was the thing to be at this point. I walked right over to expert sailing and entered. The girl who had kept me captivated since arriving at camp was sitting alone on a bench. She looked up and my heart jumped into my throat. I wished I knew Spanish. "Hey, I'm Rodney."

"I know who you are. We kind of met already, remember?"

I couldn't believe I was finally talking to her. "Uh, yeah, about that, I wasn't trying to attack you. I was actually trying to help, but I think I, well, what I really meant to do was try and, well, if you want to know the truth, I really was planning on . . ."

She laughed. "Relax. I realize now you're not a killer. I'm Tabitha, by the way. You're signing up for this class?" She waved her hand behind her. I eyed the sails, ropes, and other widgets and gadgets that I knew nothing about. On the chalkboard was a list of unfamiliar words. Maybe I should rethink the expert sailing thing.

"Well . . ."

She interrupted. "I love sailing and sailors. I think there's nothing more amazing than an experienced sailor at the helm of a boat. The sea is so romantic. The waves and wind, it's like nothing else." Her bright eyes looked deeply into mine. "You must be quite a sailor to sign up for this class."

"You have no idea."

"I guess we'll be sailing together, then. You know, the end-of-summer sailing regatta at my father's club is probably the highlight of my year."

"Yes, same at my father's club," I lied. The only club my dad belonged to was Costco.

"I just love to be in a boat with people who really know what they're doing," she continued.

I was getting so carried away that I couldn't stop myself. "Me too. In fact, I was the New York junior yachting champ three years in a row."

Before she had a chance to answer, someone walked in carrying a box that blocked his face. "Tabitha," I heard him say, "I'm so glad you're signing up for the class. The two of us are going to have some awesome sails together this summer." I couldn't see who it was but the voice had already become nauseatingly familiar. He set the box down and noticed me. "It's you! Why don't you go slither back under whatever rock you crawled out from?"

"Nice to see you, too, Todd."

"You're an expert sailor? Look at what you're wearing. You've got to be kidding me!"

I looked down at the New York Knicks jersey I had gotten for my birthday. Then I glanced at his attire. He wore a yellow button-down shirt and baby-blue shorts with pink sailboats on them.

"I'm sorry," I told him, "I didn't know I was supposed to borrow my mother's clothes for this class."

Tabitha giggled and Todd slammed down the box he was holding. He removed his expensive-looking sunglasses and took a step in my direction. This was it.

"Ah, my expert sailors," Mr. Periwinkle greeted us. I hadn't noticed him enter the room but was sure glad to see him. "Rodney, I knew you'd find something you liked. Oh, and Todd, can I borrow you for half an hour? You other two ... no need to hang around here. I'm sure there are other classes to explore."

As Tabitha and I got up to leave, Todd whispered, "That's the last time I take an insult from you, Rathbone. Next time you won't be so lucky."

I understood all too well that his anger went beyond me. Good ol' Todd wanted Tabitha all to himself—and here I was, walking out the door with her into the beautiful sunshine.

Chapter 9

ADIOS, AMIGOS

Mr. Periwinkle found me the next afternoon as I hid—I mean, rested—under a big old beech tree overlooking the great field. I was trying to avoid Todd and the other Algonquin goons.

"Ah, Rodney, fancy meeting you here. This is a most inspiring spot. You know, I climbed this beech tree when I was a boy."

"You went to camp here?" I asked. Suddenly I pictured him at my age, climbing the beautiful tree. Its smooth branches angled everywhere. It was the best climbing tree I'd ever seen.

"Yes, Rodney. I came to Camp Wy-Mee one summer many years ago and have never really left it." The leaves rustled softly in the breeze, and I took a moment to read the various names and dates carved into the thick gray trunk over the years. "Right up there. Read that one," Mr. Periwinkle suggested.

I couldn't miss it. PERCY + HAGATHA 4 EVER.

"*Hagatha*?" I asked.

"That's Mrs. Periwinkle to you." He smiled. "I met her at age seventeen when I was a counselor here. Her family owned the camp even then." He turned and his eyes glazed over as he looked out at the fields. We could see paths heading off to the many different camp destinations. In the distance, the forest looked dense and wild. A dragonfly, buzzing like a B-17, flew right past us, breaking Periwinkle's trance.

"Rodney, there are a few things to go over. Mrs. Periwinkle hasn't forgotten about that zebra mussel punishment Todd suggested, and now that the weather is nice, I suggest you get to it. I have a paint scraper, snorkel gear, and some buckets waiting . . ."

"Wait, you want me to *collect* the mussels?"

"You bet. It'll save us a fortune." He smiled and rubbed his palms together.

"What?" I yelled.

"Never mind that. I have other news. It seems that we will be unable to offer expert sailing this summer."

Secretly relieved, I asked, "Why not?"

"Too few campers signed up for it. And besides, the insurance premiums are through the roof this year. Anyway, I've moved you, Todd, and that girl into athletics class with Mr. Cramps."

I'd heard that was a class to avoid. "Do you have any *more* good news for me?"

Missing my sarcasm, he replied, "Sadly, that's it for now, but just think—athletics class, a nice little cooling swim this afternoon . . . the world is your clam."

He turned toward his house to leave. "Jeepers!" he gasped. Panic wiped away his usual smile as his face turned pale. "Oh dear. I didn't think it would actually happen."

I spun around. Pulling up in front of the Periwinkle house was a large, black Mercedes followed by an SUV. Three men in dark suits and mirrored sunglasses climbed out of the Mercedes, and walked towards the front porch. Each carried a briefcase. We watched the front door swing open. Mrs. Periwinkle stepped outside and greeted them.

"Oh gosh golly . . . I'd better be off. Have a nice swim, Rodney."

Instead of heading home, though, he slunk into the bushes and disappeared. I looked back one last time in the direction of his house, trying to figure out what had made Mr. Periwinkle turn white and act so strange. It was then that I noticed the sign on the passenger side of the SUV. VANDERDICK ENTERPRISES.

I spent the whole afternoon in murky, slimy water, scraping the schooner clean and collecting Periwinkle's mussels. I was furious—and starving—by the time I reached the dining hall for dinner. Eventually, I exhaled in an attempt to calm down. At least I was about to eat. As I relaxed at my usual table, surrounded by my cabinmates, I became aware of an argument. Thorin Oakenshield was yelling, "Saruman is not a more powerful wizard than Voldemort . . ."

Hearing that, I almost returned to my gloomy thoughts, but Josh cut in. "You have warts?"

"No, Josh," Thorin explained. "I said Volde*mort*, not *wart*."

"I have warts, too," Josh continued. "I have a big one in my armpit. Take a look . . ."

"Do you want to see *my* armpit?" Stinky asked.

"NO!" we all answered at once.

Thankfully, he didn't gas us out. Instead he said, "Here comes Gertrude with the menu board!"

Gertrude turned the board so the mess hall could read tonight's dinner. Stinky gasped, "My favorites. Clam chowder followed by spaghetti with clam sauce."

So *that* was Mr. Periwinkle's money-saving scheme. I pictured the dirty zebra mussels and could feel myself gagging as I stormed out the door.

My horrid day fueled my pen that evening. Sitting in the cabin after dinner, I wrote a letter to my parents listing seventeen reasons why they needed to drop everything and get me out of Camp Wy-Mee. Then I started another letter. This one was to the girl I hoped was still my girlfriend.

Dear Jessica,

I've tried to find ways to call, text, or email you, but I think my parents accidentally sent me to jail instead of camp. The good news is that I'll be home real soon. I imagine my parents will be picking me up just a few hours after you read this. I can't wait to do all the things we talked about doing. I miss you.

Rodney

I sealed the envelope and tucked both letters under my pillow. Lying back in bed with my hands cradling my head, I smiled while listening to the sounds of a camp summer night. Crickets and bugs chirped and buzzed. Woo hummed jazz softly from his chair. Thorin practiced spells on Harry the Raccoon. Josh laughed at him. Fernando's comb swished back and forth through his hair as he winked at himself in the mirror. It was all music to my ears, as I knew that real soon, I'd be out of here.

The following day I dropped the letters in the mailbox outside the door of the dining hall. I whispered a little adios to Camp Wy-Mee and walked down toward the fields. It was a sunny, cool morning. The whole world seemed divided into blue and green—the big blue sky over the blue lake, surrounded by green trees and greener grass. Before moving to Garrettsville, I had grown up near New York City, and we never had mornings like this. Something hit me, and for a second I saw the world through Mr. Periwinkle's eyes. With the sun on my face and the smell of clover in the air, I felt momentarily sad about leaving.

"Amigo, get over here!"

It was Fernando calling out to me. He sat above the fields on a grassy spot between two girls. I smiled and walked up to them.

"Rodney, I want you to meet Alison and Megan. Alison and Megan, this is Rodney Rathbone." They both smiled. Megan's attention immediately went back to Fernando's hair, but Alison held my gaze for a second.

"Nice to meet you both," I said, "but I'm leaving camp."

Fernando looked surprised. "Why the rush to leave, Rodney? As you can see, there are certain advantages to camp life." His eyes darted sideways at the girls. He had a point there. He stood up and grabbed my shoulder. "Girls, pardon me for one moment. Rodney, walk with me. We must talk."

We strolled slowly along the path toward the beech tree where Periwinkle had found me the day before. "What would I do without you?" Fernando asked. "Sure, there are lots of pretty girls here, but I need a buddy to share in the excitement. Now, I admit that Josh is, shall we say, entertaining, but the conversations are limited. As for Stinky, well, normally I'd be impressed with a guy that makes girls faint, but I don't think suffocating body odor is the way to a girl's heart. Then there's Thorin. He's smarter than any of us, I suspect, but I don't speak Klingon or Na'vi, so I'm lost half the time. All I got is you, my man."

I hadn't thought about it that way. I had made a good friend, and I'd be missed when I left. "Yeah, well, I already sent the letters." I felt a little bad. "Besides, a lot of people have it in for me. Do you think it's legal to send someone under a boat to scrape off the camp's dinner? Thorin Oakenshield told me zebra mussels are full of pollutants. The Periwinkles are torturing me *and* poisoning the camp."

"I wouldn't worry. Things are looking up." Fernando's eyes were fixed over my shoulder. I turned and my heart began to beat a little faster. In a hushed voice, he observed, "Excitement seems to follow you, Rodney. I want to join you on the ride."

My attention was now on Tabitha, who had come right up to us. She stood before me, looking down at her sandal as it slowly traced an imaginary line in the grass. "Hi, Rodney. I hear we're in athletics class together."

"Uh, yeah, um, that's what Mr. Periwinkle said." My mind went blank. Fernando cleared his throat and motioned in the direction of the athletics fields. My wits returned. "We have class now, right? Maybe we could walk together?"

Before she could answer, Fernando chimed in, "Ah

yes, a summer stroll across the fields. Can't you just smell it? The air is intoxicating. Time for Fernando to be heading off."

He ducked away, leaving me nervous. I could feel my cheeks getting hot.

Tabitha had an eyebrow raised in Fernando's direction. "What's with your friend?"

Before I could answer or make some joke, she shifted her gaze back to me. Her look was intense, yet playful. Her green eyes swept me into another world.

"You know, Rodney, you and I haven't been alone together since signing up for sailing class." She took a step closer. I was about to float away or throw up, I wasn't sure which. I tried to gain control of myself. "What's the matter?" she asked. "Don't you like me?"

"Like you?" My voice cracked. "Sure I like you."

"Hey, Tabitha! Oh, I see you're busy studying the lower classes again." It was Todd, darn it! He rode up to us on some weird contraption that looked like a motorized pogo stick on wheels. "Like my Segway x2 Personal Transporter? Just had it dropped off."

"From where, Mars?" I asked.

"You know, there's something interesting about him, isn't there, Tabitha?" He talked as if I wasn't even there, or like I was some animal who couldn't understand him. "Anyway, want to ride on my Segway to athletics? It's all the way across those long fields."

I was about to tell him not to waste his time, that

Tabitha and I shared a special connection . . .

"Okay, Todd. *Awesome.*"

A knife sliced into my heart. Hurt and disgusted, I watched as she went up to him, looking slightly unsure of how to climb on.

"Just step up on the platform," Todd began. Then he smiled at me and said, "Tabitha, put your arms around me and hold on tight. That's it." With a little hidden wink in my direction, he added, "Tighter, Tabitha. I don't want you to fall off."

His smile made me sick and full of bitterness. I watched them zoom off across the fields. Yes, I knew I was soon leaving camp, and I hoped Jessica was waiting for me at home, but seeing Tabitha ride off with Big Jerk Number One made my stomach ache. I turned and walked back toward Fernando. "What were you saying about things looking up?"

He had pretty much seen the whole thing and could only manage a feeble, "The day's not over, my friend."

"That's true," I agreed. "There's still plenty of time for me to scrub some rusty ship bottoms. Maybe Mrs. Periwinkle has a whole fleet waiting for me. Maybe a tree will land on me. Better yet, maybe at archery later I'll get shot in the butt by an arrow. I'm so relieved the day's not over. Lots to look forward to."

I stomped off to athletics, alone, holding on to the only good thing I had going for me. At least the letters were in the mail.

Chapter 10

MR. CRAMPS

"Hey, Rootbone!"

It was that idiot Magnus. Over the first week, I'd done a decent job at avoiding him, but now he was approaching as I neared the athletic field. I was tired and sweaty from the long walk and in no mood to deal with him. I put my head down and just kept going—until his massive hand thumped my chest so hard I almost fell backward.

"Not zo fast, Rootbone . . ."

"It's Rathbone," I gasped.

"Dat's nice. Anyvay, thought you'd vant to know I have taken every class vis Mr. Cramps for twelve years. You could say I'm vis him always very much." Maybe his sentences came out so weird from all the raw eggs he put in his smoothies. He continued, "I told him about you and you know vat Mr. Cramps said?"

"That he's sick of you being vis him always very much?"

He rolled his neck, which crunched several times. "He told me he'd take special interest in you. Now, you go!" He gave me a hard pat on the back, laughed, and marched off.

As I approached the class I noticed a bunch of kids sitting in front of a nasty-looking older guy, who I guessed was the famous Mr. Cramps. Todd was lying on his side, poking Tabitha in the leg. She was swatting his hand, but smiling. I bit my lip in anger.

"You're late!" The crazy old guy was yelling at me. This was the last thing I needed right now. I turned around and stared at him. Like two gunfighters from a western, we took a moment to size each other up. He looked older—in his fifties or sixties—but he looked like he'd spent the last half century doing push-ups and arm wrestling. His gray hair was pulled back and his eyes burned fiercely into mine. Suddenly a breeze hit and his hair floated up from behind his head, revealing a big bald spot. I watched the hair momentarily wave in the breeze before he slapped it back down. I half expected him to start yelling at the wind. I mean, this guy looked nuts. His tight polyester gym-teacher shorts and high white socks didn't help.

And I knew right then, right before I noticed the muscle in his cheek twitch and his lips begin to part, before he uttered another word—I knew I was facing an enemy. Another enemy in a long year crammed with enemies. His words confirmed my belief. "I said, you're late! Now give me twenty!"

"I didn't bring any money with me," I replied.

Mr. Cramps smacked his forehead and pushed his fingers up through his hair. "Boy, are you thick or something?" he asked, quickly plastering his hair back down to cover his scalp. "Now do twenty push-ups!" I didn't argue. As I went up and down, Mr. Cramps counted and commented, "Don't raise your rear in the air!"

"I don't think he's going down far enough," Todd added.

"You're right, Vanderdick. All the way down, new kid!" Todd choked from laughter. Finally, Mr. Cramps called, "Twenty!" and I collapsed.

"Now, that pathetic little demonstration proves my point," Cramps instructed the crowd. "Kids today are weak and undisciplined. Fortunately for you runts, you have taken this class. Your days of video game playing, chicken nugget eating, book reading, and whining to your mommies are over! I *guarantee* . . . I will personally make men out of all of you!"

"But some of us are girls."

"That won't stop me!" Several of the girls looked at each other. "Now then, any more dopey questions?"

"Just one," I volunteered. "Did you forget to take your medication this morning?" It was out of my mouth before I knew what I was saying. My big dumb mouth. Mr. Cramps's gray eyes bored into mine and he got close to my face. I could see a vein begin to throb in his neck.

"You're that Bone kid, right?"

"Rathbone."

"Well, I sure am going to enjoy this. Yessiree. Every one of you, line up! We're going for a little jog."

Lounging on the ground, Todd called out, "Excuse me, Mr. Cramps. I sprained my ankle getting off my Segway, so I think I'll need to sit this one out." He rubbed his ankle twice and winked at Tabitha. Mr. Cramps's face tightened, and he opened his mouth, but Todd beat him to it. "You're enjoying the new baseball backstop and soccer goals my dad donated, right? I called my dad and told him to talk to Mr. Periwinkle about resurfacing the basketball court."

Mr. Cramps chewed on his plastic whistle.

Todd added, "I'm sure he'll do it, after I tell him what a wonderful instructor you are. By the way, Tabitha here is helping me keep my foot elevated." Todd placed his foot into Tabitha's lap. "It's all right if she sits out, too, right?"

Crack!! Mr. Cramps bit right through his whistle. Suddenly his hair began to blow wildly in the wind. He took a couple of deep breaths, spit a few pieces of broken whistle in the air, and grumbled, "Okay."

I thought it was worth a shot. "You know, Mr. Cramps, my *knee* seems . . ."

"MOVE IT, RAT TRAP!!!"

I took off running. The rest of the class, minus Todd and Tabitha, did too.

75

Now most gym teachers I've been around stand and give orders and watch us from afar. Well, Mr. Cramps wasn't like them. Every twenty or so yards he'd run up and shout something in my direction. "Quicker, Rathbone! My grandmother moves faster than you… and she's dead!" He was crazy, and out to get me. I figured Magnus had played a part in it all.

We were running laps around the perimeter of the large fields. Sweat dripped into my eyes and my lungs burned. The third time around the fields, Mr. Cramps decided to start running right in back of me. I could barely breathe. I eyed Todd and Tabitha as we ran past. Todd yelled out, "Looking good, Rathbone!"

"Don't listen to your friend. You look *pathetic*!" Cramps barked in my ear.

I continued running, thinking the whole time I should just run straight into the woods and keep going till I found the highway home. I couldn't take it anymore. Somehow I was moving, but my legs felt like they were about to give out.

"Don't slow down, boy!" Cramps shouted from behind. He was now two feet behind me and with every step seemed to be gaining ground. We were coming up to Todd and Tabitha again. I could see them talking and laughing, and this time I strained to hear what he was saying. I wish I hadn't.

"Tabitha, I made you this clover necklace. The

next one I give you will be made of diamonds."

It was the last straw. I stopped dead in my tracks. I don't know if I was about to ask Tabitha how she could be with such a loser, or if my legs just gave out, but I stopped short and kind of fell to the ground. And that's when it happened. Mr. Cramps ran right into my head. Immediately the air was filled with shouts of pain as he cupped his belly—well, several inches below his belly. He looked at me. His face was red as a tomato, his eyes bulged, and he stammered, "You! You, you . . ."

He stopped. Mr. Periwinkle had popped out from behind a bush.

"Oh, splendid! You two are becoming fast friends. Rodney, did you know that Mr. Cramps here has won two Ironman Triathlons? Who better to train with? What do you think, Eugene? A future marathoner here in young Rodney?"

Mr. Cramps managed a grin. "Well, Percy," he answered, "he'll either become a great runner, or he'll *die* trying."

I hoped Periwinkle could see he was crazy and save me, but he said, "Do you hear that, Rodney? Your camp experience just keeps getting better. To think, a little while ago you wanted to leave us."

He stood there beaming for a moment, then seemed to regain his purpose. "Oh yes. I know you're biting at the chomp to get back to running, but I came down here to talk to you both. Maybe Todd could join us, too.

Todd, come over here, please." We watched Todd limp exaggeratedly over to us. "Nothing serious, I hope?" Periwinkle asked him.

"Nothing a little rest won't cure."

"Oh, thank heavens. Anyway, Mrs. Periwinkle has come up with a splendid idea. Eugene, she wants you to run a softball game between the Algonquin and Cherokee cabins. Todd, Rodney, you can be captains. Won't that be fun?" Before we had a chance to answer he continued, "I'm glad you all like the idea. We'll play the game Friday after dinner. The rest of the camp can watch. Mrs. Periwinkle will be sure to be there. Maybe the excitement will get her to change her mind about . . ." He looked at us nervously for a second, then, noticing Todd's ride gleaming in the sun, changed the subject. "Todd, what is that thing you have over there?"

"Mr. Periwinkle, *that* is my new Segway Transporter."

"Ahh, well, campers aren't allowed to have motor-ized vehicles in camp, and . . ."

Todd looked pained. "Oh, that's a shame, Mr. Peri-winkle. I asked my dad to send you one, too, courtesy of Vanderdick Enterprises."

"Oh really?" A bright smile burst onto Periwinkle's face. "Why don't you show me how it works?"

The two of them walked off, leaving me alone with Cramps. I felt like I better say something. "Uh, sorry about hitting you in the, you know . . ."

He didn't answer. He seemed to be deep in thought. Then he smiled an evil grin. "A little softball game Friday night, huh? I have to hand it to Mrs. Periwinkle. Yes, something tells me it will be a real fun time."

A gleam in his eye told me it would be anything but.

Chapter 11

MIDNIGHT MADNESS

I clapped my hands twice. "More grapes." Tabitha walked over to me, bringing the green fruit. I plucked one. Then I turned to look at Jessica. She was fanning me with a large palm leaf. The breeze blew gently through my hair and I leaned back on my throne, feeling completely relaxed and happy. Someone tapped me on the head. I sighed. "Girls, girls, no more grapes right now. The prince needs his beauty rest . . ."

"Uh, it's time to go, Rodney. Everyone's asleep."

"Huh?" My eyes opened into darkness. I became aware that Fernando was leaning over me.

"You're dreaming about grapes?" he asked.

No! It was only a dream. I wanted to roll over and cry into my pillow. Maybe if I fell back to sleep, the dream would come back.

"Come on, let's go."

"You go. I was having the best dream . . ."

"Shhh, you'll wake Woo."

Every part of me wanted to stay in the bunk bed. My sleeping bag felt warm against the evening chill and I slid lower into it, hoping Fernando would go away. I had promised to go with him on a midnight mission to sneak into the girls' division. I was supposed to have stayed awake until everyone else dropped off to sleep, but I had dozed off, too.

Fernando shook my shoulder. "Come on, Rodney. Alison actually said I wasn't man enough to visit her in the night. Fernando not man enough! Can you imagine?"

"Well, you *are* only twelve," I responded groggily.

"Just the idea makes my skin crawl. Wild horses couldn't stop me now, but I need backup. And besides, I'm not going to let you mope around here for the next few days thinking about Tabitha. *Vaminos!*"

Tabitha. Hearing her name sent two emotions racing through me. One was anger. I was mad at the way she had acted on the soccer field. The other emotion, though, was anything but anger. She sure looked good walking with the grapes, and even though she was in a different cabin than Alison, maybe we'd see her tonight. I sat up and pulled my legs over the side of the bed. I was already dressed in my darkest clothes. I put on my sneakers and started to walk with Fernando out the cabin door.

"Where ya goin'?"

Fernando and I jumped. Josh was looking down at us from his bunk. "To the bathroom," I whispered. "Go back to sleep."

81

We were fully clothed in black outfits. Fernando had a bandana tied around his head. Josh's face scrunched up and his brain seemed to be struggling with something. "Uhhhhh . . ."

"Not so loud," I whispered.

"Uhhhh . . ."

Fernando spoke up. "Josh, if you must know, we're sneaking into the girls' division."

"I like girls," he announced.

Fernando's eyes flashed in the dark. "Rodney, you hear his enthusiasm? You could learn a thing or two from this one." I looked over at Josh. Apart from punching walls and setting bugs on fire, I wondered what enlightening things he could share with me. "Would you like to come with us?" Fernando asked him.

"Pretty ones going to be there?"

"I love this guy. We must be brothers. Climb down here and let's go."

And with that, the three of us headed off into the night.

Winding our way between the dark cabins, I whispered, "There's the Algonquin cabin. We can't make any noise."

While Fernando and I made our way past the cabins like two ninjas, Josh stomped like a rhino, cracked sticks, and kicked up crinkly, dry leaves. Fernando gave me a strained look.

"Hey, he's *your* brother," I reminded him.

He opened his mouth to reply, but it was Magnus who spoke next. "Iss zomebody out there?" he shouted.

For a second we froze in our tracks. Then, in a high, scratchy voice, I answered, "Just Gertrude and Alice!" A light went on in the cabin and we heard the screen door swing open. The three of us burst out laughing and broke into a run toward the woods.

"Goot back here!" Magnus demanded, but it was too late. We were now tearing along Scalped Indian Path.

"Hey, Rodney, you do a pretty good girl's voice," Fernando teased.

"You think?" I laughed. We slowed down a bit as we entered the woods. We had chosen this path earlier in the day while plotting the adventure, but at night it was a bit creepy. The trail ended at the soccer field, and from there it was just a stroll across the grass to the girls' cabins.

We moved on through the dark woods without talking. In the past, this would have been the point where my legs started shaking, but I knew the scariest thing in the woods tonight was the big goon grunting behind me. Actually, I was happy to have Josh along. The thought made me smile. Just a few weeks ago he'd have been the last guy on the planet I would have chosen to be alone with in the pitch-black woods.

Fernando interrupted my thoughts. "Listen, it's nights like this that you'll remember for the rest of your life." I smiled. Sometimes he sounded like he was twelve going on sixty. "Take a moment to soak it in. Smell the night air . . ."

I inhaled deeply through my nose. There was a strong scent of pine needles, and then a stronger scent of—"Awwwwww! Gross!"

"Like that, Rodney?" Josh grinned. "Just like my favorite song. *Beans, beans, good for the ear, the more you eat them, the more you stink. The more you stink, the more you drink, the more you drink, the more you pee, so eat all them beans!*"

"Interesting version," I commented, holding my nose. Seeing the trees thinning up ahead, I added, "There's the field."

We walked up to the edge of the forest. The soccer field looked different in the dark. One nice difference was that Mr. Cramps wasn't there yelling at us with his crazy hair flying around, but the change went beyond that. Everything was really still. The goalposts stood out in the darkness and the white lines on the grass looked like they were floating in space. On the other side of the field, a big orange moon hung just above the tops of the trees. It was a beautiful summer night and now that a fresh breeze was blowing—and Josh was safely behind me on the trail—I took a chance and breathed it all in.

As if reading my mind, Fernando said, "This place is pretty cool." Then, remembering why we were there, he added, "Just think, boys, our destiny awaits us on the other side of that field."

We walked on silently and were halfway across when a massive beam from a flashlight blazed in our direction. "Down!" I hissed.

We dropped and lay flat. I could see the beam moving across the grass. It slid over our heads. *Magnus*, I thought. I should have known the big, evil jerk would come after us. What was his problem? The light made it to the end of the field and doubled back. Lying still, we waited. The beam lit up our patch of ground, and I prayed our black clothes would blend in with the grass. I watched it reach the other side of the rectangular field and click off. After a couple of tense minutes we moved forward, crouching on the balls of our feet, ready to drop at a moment's notice.

And that's when it hit me—the real reason why I didn't want to get caught. I was afraid they would kick me out of camp! Had I suddenly gone crazy? For days, all I wanted to do was leave here, but this midnight mission had somehow changed all that. Despite Todd and Magnus, I was beginning to enjoy Camp Wy-Mee. In fact, I was having the time of my life.

As we continued on, however, a feeling of regret began to worm its way to the back of my head. If only I hadn't sent that letter to my parents . . .

Chapter 12

THE GIRL NO ONE EXPECTED

When we reached the girls' division, the cabins were eerily silent. The only sign of life was in the distance— some moths circling a lightbulb outside the girls' bathroom. But by us it was dark and every cabin looked the same. "Which one?" I whispered.

"Don't worry, when it comes to the ladies, Fernando always finds his way." He held his finger up in the breeze. "That one. Let's go."

We snuck our way from cabin shadow to rock to bush to tree and eventually arrived at the door of Alison's cabin. Fernando winked. "The journey will all have been worth it in a second." He slowly pulled the screen door open and we stepped into the lavender-scented dark. I heard the breathing of a dozen sleeping girls. As my brain digested the enormity of entering such an unfamiliar, magical place, I got a little dizzy and almost toppled to the floor. Fernando grabbed my arm. "Steady, big fella," he whispered.

A voice floated to us from a top bunk on the left. "I never thought you would actually show." Even in the dark, I could see Alison's red hair hanging down.

Fernando's white smile gleamed with satisfaction. "It is always a mistake to underestimate Fernando."

Alison whispered, "I should have known better," and quietly swung down from her bunk. "Girls, wake up. We have visitors." Shapes shifted in the dark. My pulse quickened as girls stirred and climbed from their beds. Several flashlights clicked on and one went right into my eyes and stayed there. I felt like a prisoner about to be interrogated.

"He's cute." Some girl giggled. I could live with this kind of interrogation.

"And check out the muscles on that one," another girl added. "Look at these three — our knights in shining armor."

Fernando raised a pleased eyebrow in my direction. One girl went up to Josh. "What's your name?"

"Josh."

"You look very strong."

"You want me to break something?"

"Charming, too," she said in a giggle to her friend.

Fernando pulled out a bottle of Coke he had been hiding. "Ladies, I've been saving this bottle of bubbly for an occasion like this." He turned the cap. The soda instantly foamed up and blasted out in all directions.

"How romantic." Alison smirked, wiping the drink

from her forehead. Then, to me she added, "Rodney, I'm surprised you're not poking around in Tabitha's cabin."

Now, that thought had certainly occurred to me, but I'd been around Fernando long enough to know how to play it. "Who?" I asked.

Alison rolled her eyes.

Wrrreeeeee! Suddenly the screen door creaked open. I could see Mrs. Periwinkle and a counselor or two about to enter. Fernando gave a quick bow. "Ladies, another time." He climbed across Alison's bed, lifted the window screen, and slid out into the night. Josh scrambled after him, showing some rare alertness.

I was too far from the opening and realized I wouldn't make it. I weaseled my way into a small alcove between two bunk beds just as Mrs. Periwinkle entered the room.

From my hiding spot, I could see her standing with a large flashlight. A strangely familiar sense of dread crept down my spine. "What is going on in here?" she demanded. The girls, who had jumped back into bed, pretended to wake up. It would be a miracle if she didn't spot me. I squirmed into the smallest space I could find. "I *repeat*, what is going on in here?"

Alison spoke up. "Mrs. Periwinkle, what do you mean? We were asleep."

I held my breath and watched. Mrs. Periwinkle's curly hair cast an eerie glow as she blasted the beam at Alison. "Young lady, I had a report that some boys were on the prowl. I'm checking all the cabins." She paused, then added, "I guess I was mistaken. Hold on. What is that all over the floor?" It was the Coke. She squatted down, looking just like a detective at a crime scene. She touched the soda and applied a drop to the end of her tongue. Her eyes hardened and she spat. "I taste misbe-having!" Then she slowly began moving her flashlight along the walls of the room. I knew it was only a matter of seconds before it reached my hiding spot.

"Here," Alison whispered, tossing me what looked like a dead rat. "It's a wig from last year's show."

Mrs. Periwinkle's light was almost upon me now. I stuck the thing on my head and threw a blanket over my shoulders.

"Who is that?" The flashlight was now pointed right at me. I was caught! I was doomed. "Who are you?" Mrs. Periwinkle demanded. "What are you doing over there?"

No one spoke. You could hear a pine needle drop. "Me?" I finally answered, putting on a high-pitched girl's voice. "I'm Alison's cousin." I had suddenly remembered Fernando teasing me about imitating Gertrude and Alice. I figured I had nothing to lose. "You remember me, Mrs. Periwinkle, don't you?"

She looked confused and annoyed. "What's your name again?"

"Rod . . . Rodweena."

"Rodweena what?"

"Raa . . . uhhh . . . Smith."

"Rodweena Raauhhhsmith." She seemed to ponder this. "Interesting name." Her eyes were squinting and I knew the charade was almost up. I prayed the rat-wig thing didn't fall off my head.

"Yes," I continued. "A most peculiar name. From my mother's side. Anyway, thank you for trying to capture the boys. I can't imagine anything worse than some smelly boys snooping about."

Mrs. Periwinkle seemed to soften. "Yes, I agree. And these *particular* boys I'm after are most undesirable."

"Oh, I'm sure they must be," I continued. "Anyone who would turn down a good night's rest to violate camp rules must be on a sure path to delinquency." I was on a roll now. "I sincerely hope you capture them and punish them *severely*." Maybe I had gone too far. Mrs. Periwinkle was looking at me intently and I gulped quietly.

"Well, Rodweena," she announced, "It is an absolute pleasure meeting you again. It's gratifying to see a proper young lady with a good head on her shoulders. And so pretty! I wish more of these girls had your sensibilities. Good night."

Just then the door screeched open. "Mrs. Periwinkle, we found these two snooping about." A counselor brought in Fernando and Josh.

The Periwinkle sneer was back. "So, you thought you could sneak into the girls' division? Well, as you can see, breaking the rules is not a wise thing to do. You're looking at a significant punishment. What do you have to say for yourselves?"

Before they could answer, I asked in my high voice, "Are these the two ruffians?"

Fernando and Josh noticed me for the first time and I thought Fernando's eyes were going to pop out of his head. He bit his lip to keep from laughing, but in an instant recovered his usual nonchalant cool. Josh, on the other hand, studied me closely, slowly tilting his head from side to side like a confused dog. I gulped. He was about to blow my cover. He opened his mouth and I cringed.

"Stop staring at Rodweena, you!" Mrs. Periwinkle scolded. "You're in enough hot water without upsetting this poor girl!"

Fernando strode forward and grabbed Mrs. Periwinkle's hand. "Pardon me, madame." She tried to shake off his grip, but he held tight and said, "I'm very sorry to break any rules, but ever since the first time I saw you atop your beautiful horse, I haven't been able to get you out of my mind." Now it was my turn to keep from laughing as Fernando inched closer to her. I noticed Mrs. Periwinkle had stopped shaking her arm. "Hagatha—may I call you that? Such a beautiful name deserves to be said aloud."

I expected Mrs. Periwinkle to slap him, but she was still looking almost mesmerized. Fernando went on. "I looked out at the beautiful moon and night sky tonight. It made me think of you, and it was all too much for me." He took her hand and placed her palm against his chest. "It drove me mad. Mad, I say! I knew I had to see you." It was hard to tell in the dark, but Mrs. Periwinkle looked flushed. "Punish me if you must," Fernando went on. "It was worth it. Being here with you now is worth any sacrifice."

Mrs. Periwinkle swayed on her feet and one of the counselors steadied her. Shakily she said, "Yes, well . . ."

"Fernando."

"Of course. Fernando, why don't we speak tomorrow and we'll discuss the . . . errrr . . . punishment." Something told me he wasn't going to be scraping zebra mussels off her boat.

Fernando hadn't finished. "Oh, and just so you know, the only reason Josh was out tonight was because he was trying to stop me. But stopping this feeling is like trying to stop a locomotive."

At this point the attention returned to Josh. His gaze was still fixed on me and his dopey look seemed more focused than usual. I cringed. He was going to give me away for sure. What he said next, however, was just as bad.

"Uhh . . . hi. I'm Josh." He took a step in my direction. I saw that he was blushing. "You sure are pretty. Could we, uh, get married or something?"

Chapter 13

STRIKES AND BALLS

"Hey, lay it on down, toe lappers. You got the chaws. Dig?"

No, we didn't dig. We were pretty far from digging. But Woo was our team's softball manager, so we nodded like we knew what he was talking about.

"Don't let no haze hang the cabeza. Go out there and lay it on nice and thick. You dig, Rodney?"

"Uhh . . . you're saying . . . play hard?"

"Hey now, make the bugs dance, young men with bats!" He waved for us to go out onto the field.

So, armed with the strangest pep talk in history, we ran to our positions. Josh was on first, Thorin on second, Fernando on third, Stinky ran out to play catcher, but Gabe, the head of the boys division and today's umpire, began gagging and switched Stinky to centerfield. Mr. Cramps pitched and I took my spot at shortstop. The rest of the cabin filled the outfield. Someone who made me very nervous, however, had appointed himself pitcher—for both teams.

As if sensing my unease, Mr. Cramps turned toward me and called out, "I've been looking forward to this game." He was smiling but didn't look at all happy. I could feel the wickedness pouring out of him, and my stomach twisted as I pondered what he meant.

A counselor named Gabe yelled, "Play ball!" Mr. Periwinkle stood on a hill near first base, surrounded by the whole camp. He looked like a kid on opening day. Unable to contain his excitement, he reached out and grasped his wife's shoulder. His hand was abruptly swatted as if it was a mosquito. Mrs. Periwinkle looked completely annoyed, kind of like she was inhaling the air next to Stinky. Her expression changed and her cheeks darkened, however, when Fernando passed by, smiling in her direction.

I kicked the dirt and tried to focus my thoughts. I'd had a lot of fun the other night. After the counselors took Josh and Fernando away, I said good-bye to Alison and the girls and made my way back to the cabin. When I finally got there, Josh couldn't stop talking about Rodweena. Fernando kept egging him on.

"Tell Rodney how pretty she was!" I wanted to punch him, but the whole thing was so funny that I just went along with it. In fact, Fernando had been right when he said I would never forget the evening. It cemented the belief that I liked camp and wanted to stay. And now, knowing that I wanted to be here, my main goal was to win this game and beat Todd and Magnus.

I looked at the two hundred or so kids and counselors sitting around the camp's first couple. My stomach felt uneasy and my palms began to sweat. If four hundred eyes staring at us weren't enough, I couldn't help but notice one particularly devilish pair looking my way. They were accompanied by a slight, sly grin on full lips and dark brown hair. I tried to shake it off, figuring she was probably giving similar looks to Todd.

I pounded my fist into my mitt and looked up for the first time to inspect our opponents. I gulped. *Who had invited the New York Yankees?* All right, they weren't quite the Yankees, but seeing the Algonquins stretching, taking some practice swings, and wearing gleaming pinstriped uniforms, they sure looked the part. As Magnus brought them together for a pregame conference, I realized we weren't in their league—not by a long shot. Without exception, they were big and athletic. Any swagger I possessed evaporated like a puddle in the Sahara. As the first inning got underway, I wasn't surprised to see things go quickly downhill.

Mr. Cramps began the game with a slow, soft floater to an Algonquin named Biff. Biff's bat smacked a hard grounder right at Thorin Oakenshield. My jaw dropped as he caught it. Thorin pivoted and threw the ball to first. Josh stood looking blank and made no move to catch it. The ball bounced off the side of his skull with a hollow thud. Biff was safe. Josh's expression changed from dumb to dumb and *angry*. He started to charge Thorin. I blocked his way before our dwarf-wizard second baseman was pounded into the dirt.

"Josh, you got to catch the ball, then get the runner out," I said quickly. "Catch. You get it?"

He looked from Thorin to me. "Catch ball and get runner."

"Yes. See that kid with the bat? That's who you get." Josh nodded vaguely and walked back to first base.

I turned to Thorin. "Nice play."

"I'll have you know, I'm an all-star seeker for my Quidditch team."

Well, that's comforting news, I thought to myself.

Another Algonquin, Chip, was waiting in the batter's box. He was laughing with Todd and the other guys about Josh's play. They settled down and Mr. Cramps again threw an excruciatingly slow toss that a kindergartner could have laced. Chip made contact and sent the ball bouncing toward my side of the infield. I felt the adrenaline pump through my veins as I dashed to the left. Reaching down, I was relieved to feel the ball collide with the inside of my mitt. I shifted my feet and made a perfect throw to first, all the while hoping that Tabitha was paying attention. Josh was ready this time and caught the ball. Then he yelled, "Get runner!" Next thing I knew he ran right at Chip, yanked him off the ground and body-slammed him into foul territory.

The result was pandemonium. Magnus went berserk, and after some discussion the runner was declared out, which made Magnus even crazier. He looked like an insane Viking as he screamed at Gabe and tried to grab Josh. It was nice to see him so upset, but I have to admit he had a point. In the end, he calmed down after Gabe moved Josh out to left field. Play continued.

Todd walked to the plate. He smiled and waved to the crowd. Most of them ignored him, but Mrs. Periwinkle clapped slightly. *Funny how evil sticks together*, I thought.

Mr. Cramps flipped Todd a nice, easy pitch. He didn't swing. "A little lower, if you don't mind?"

Mr. Cramps nodded and tossed a ball that was slow and sweet and right in Todd's wheelhouse. He drilled it. I watched it fly out over the infield, right to center field. Right at Stinky. I held my breath.

Stinky looked up. Seeing the ball flying his way, he covered his head and flung himself to the ground as if the softball was a grenade. The ball missed him and rolled way out toward the woods. Todd was rounding third before anyone even picked it up. I stood there watching Tabitha and the Algonquins cheer their captain as he stepped on home, making it a two-nothing game.

Somehow we started to play some defense and got the next two outs, but things didn't improve when it was our turn to bat. Thorin Oakenshield led off. I watched him pull out a wand and head to the batter's box.

"You can't use that. It's too light," I said, stopping him. "Get a bat."

"I'll have you know, Rodney, this wand is eleven inches. It's made from holly and has a phoenix feather inside. Nice and supple!" He swished it over my head. My hair tingled as it flew past. That was the end of the conversation, and he stepped into the box amid laughs and taunts from the Algonquins.

I turned to Fernando. "I thought you said he was smart."

"I figured he was because he reads a lot." He shrugged. "Evidently there's a difference."

Mr. Cramps wound up his arm and threw a very quick, hard toss towards the plate. I cursed to myself as I realized it was nothing like the lazy lollipops he'd tossed the Algonquins. Thorin Oakenshield swung his wand—which shattered the second it made contact with the ball.

"Haa haaa veery goooot!" Magnus's laugh boomed. Almost everyone else was laughing, too.

Thorin looked down at the splinters then turned back to me. "I don't understand. They say the wand picks the wizard. It spoke to me."

"What did it say? Stay away from baseball?" I led him aside. "Listen, why don't you have a conversation with one of these nice baseball bats?"

He stood there looking blank and dejected. I could hear Todd calling us idiots from the field. I looked at him in his fancy pinstripes, being nasty for no real reason, and my blood sizzled. I really wanted to beat the big jerk. That would show Todd. I grabbed Thorin's shoulder. I knew I had to speak his language. "Look at this one. It's aluminum, probably has unicorn hair in it—no, I bet it has dragon scales . . ."

He grabbed me by the shirt. "Do you really think so?" Then his eyes narrowed. "How do you know?"

"Ah, well, look at the writing . . . it's from Louisville."

"So?"

"Surely you've heard about the recent dragon sightings in Louisville? It's all over the Internet." He didn't reply. He was looking at the bat, stroking it gently.

"I think it's speaking to me," he said, eyes beginning to glaze over.

"Sure it is. It's saying to go get a hit."

He got into the box and actually ripped a line drive. It would have been a nice hit, but Cramps, looking like an Olympic gymnast, flew high into the air and made an amazing grab. He somersaulted and sprang catlike to his feet. "You're out, elf boy!" Cramps' eyes blazed at us—at me in particular. It had already dawned on me that our pitcher wasn't going to give us a fair shake, but now, seeing that nasty grin of his, I knew he was out to make sure the Algonquins won.

The rest of the inning was more of the same: fast

pitches and great plays by Cramps. Stinky struck out on three pitches. I batted third. Twice Cramps aimed for my head and I had to dive to get out of the way. I glanced back at Fernando, who was lying near the bats along with his fans, Alison, Megan, and Danielle. "I think he's trying to kill me," I called over to him.

"Perhaps, but look at the bright side."

"What bright side?"

"I'm surrounded by beautiful women! Who could ask for anything more?"

My friend was no help and the Algonquins were having a ball. "Strike him out," Todd called from first base. I would have loved to silence them, but in the end I bounced a roller to second base. Biff tossed to Todd and I was out.

Things stayed pretty much the same for most of the game. We never scored and fell further behind. As we neared the bottom of the final inning, the score was four to nothing. We were lucky to be that close. Most of the crowd was talking and goofing around, having lost interest in the pathetic, lopsided affair. The Algonquins took the field laughing, while we, the losers, were living up to our nickname. Almost immediately, we made two outs, and I sat, dejected, waiting for the game to end.

Someone else on the field was having a better time. Seeing that Josh was up, Todd laughed from first base. "This should be good. What a perfect way to end this fiasco." While brilliant at pummeling wimps, Josh hadn't done much of anything yet in the batter's box—not counting the last time up when he threw his bat into center field, almost killing the second baseman.

Some in the crowd, ready for one final bit of comic relief, focused on the at-bat. Moments later, a shocked gasp rang out as Josh topped the ball and hit a grounder toward third. But instead of running, he just stood there.

"Run to first!" I yelled at him.

"Uhh . . . duhhhh . . ."

"Run that way!" I pointed. "Step on that white thing over there!"

Lumbering hard down the base path, he headed off toward Todd, who was waiting at the base for the throw from third. Todd's usual calm, arrogant expression changed to one of shaken fear as he saw Josh heading his way. I guess no one had actually explained to Josh that you're supposed to drop the bat. Todd was so rattled by the club-swinging caveman heading his way that he forgot about the incoming ball, which sailed out to left field. Josh stopped on first, looking proud of his accomplishment.

"Run to second!" I yelled. Before he could utter another "Duh" I added, "Over there. Step on that white thing." He took off again, and neither the shortstop nor the second baseman wanted anything to do with the bat-wielding madman. "Go to third!" I hollered. "Over there!" Josh kept running. "Now, run home!"

For a moment, Josh looked more puzzled than usual, but he kept running — right off the field and into the crowd. It looked like he was heading toward the camp exit. *Huh?* Then it hit me. "Not *your* home! Run to home plate. Step on this white thing!"

He wheeled back into the field and darted toward home. With red eyes, huge muscles that swung the bat around his head, and a frothing mouth, he was a fearsome sight. I wasn't surprised when the catcher, who had received the ball from second, uttered a piercing screech and took off to cower behind Magnus. Josh, triumphant, stepped on the plate.

"You did it, Josh! A home run! We're on the board." He looked down at the plate, confused. I didn't bother to explain. Fernando, Stinky, and Thorin were all patting him on the back and cheering. The crowd loved it.

Mr. Periwinkle called, "Good show!" Then I heard him utter to Mrs. Periwinkle, "I always knew there was something special about that one."

A lot of our team's excitement died when Todd reminded us that we were still down by three runs. Then he added, "And that ape can't bat for the rest of you."

But our excitement and, more importantly, our luck, didn't die completely. Fernando, much to the delight of his screeching personal cheerleaders and Mrs. Periwinkle, hit a grounder up the middle past a diving Mr. Cramps. Then Thorin Oakenshield, while screaming, "By the power of dragons!" laced a single to right field.

Next up, Stinky somehow managed to make contact with the ball. The result was an improbable blooper over Todd's head. He scrambled for the ball, but when the dust settled, the now-attentive crowd could see that Stinky was standing safe at first.

I cheered loudly and high-fived Woo. "We're not out of it!"

"No blues in that news," he replied.

If the next batter got a hit, we could possibly win this game. I imagined the look of horror on Todd's face if we pulled it off. I smiled, pleased with the vision. As I pondered the possibilities, I looked off into the branches of a high oak tree behind first base. It was a nice moment, but then my chicken sense tingled and I knew something was off. I glanced back around. The entire camp was staring at me. I looked down at myself. Was I having that dream again where I forget to put my pants on? Seeing my shorts where they should be, I was about to exhale in relief when certain realities smacked my brain. We were still losing by three. There were two outs and the bases were loaded. And most important . . . I was up.

Woo handed me a bat and said, "All right, big daddy, get a hit and you're the cat's meow, the dog's bow wow, and the karate man's ka-pow." I nodded dumbly as my knees started to shake.

Thorin Oakenshield must have noticed. He jogged over to me from second base and whispered, "Just close your eyes and let the Force be your guide."

Before anyone else could offer me weird advice, I started for the batter's box . . . very reluctantly. This wasn't the first reluctant walk of my life. I've had to approach haunted houses and the occasional biker den, and while this was only a summer softball game, it somehow felt just as awful.

Fortunately, someone was waiting at home plate to give me some words of encouragement. Mr. Cramps leaned down and his teeth flashed as he whispered, "Striking you out, with the whole camp watching, will be the highlight of my summer. I used to be the closer for the Toledo Mud Hens. That's triple-A ball. I can still hit over ninety miles an hour on the radar gun. Have fun." He smiled to the crowd and gave me a friendly, if rather hard, pat on the back. Many clapped for the display of sportsmanship.

Previously in the game, Mr. Cramps pitched underhand, which of course is the traditional way to toss a softball. Now, he stood like a big leaguer and threw at me overhand. I barely saw the ball.

"Strike one!" yelled Gabe.

Cramps winked at me as he caught the ball thrown back by the catcher. He wound up again. As the ball flew past, I swung. I felt nothing but air as the bat twirled around me.

"Strike two."

I debated what to do. Run away?

"Ready for the heat, Rathbone?" Mr. Cramps jeered.

I noticed him give a slight nod at Mrs. Periwinkle and couldn't help but feel they were in on this together. He took a few steps toward me from the mound and said in a low, sinister voice, "I sure am going to enjoy this."

He returned to the mound and I watched his leg kick up. His arm went into its windup. I knew there was no way I would be able to hit what was coming. Unless . . .

As the ball left his fingers, I remembered Thorin's advice. I shut my eyes, put everything into it, and swung for the fences. I could hear the bat slice through the air and was fully expecting it to keep going. Only something hard stopped it. I don't know whether it was the Force or dumb luck, but the bat had actually collided with the ball. I could both feel and hear that perfect crack. I opened my eyes. Instead of sailing out past the outfielder's head, as I had hoped, the ball shot like a laser right at the unsuspecting Mr. Cramps, hammering him in the belly. Um, actually several inches below the belly.

He let out a wail and crumpled to the ground. For a moment I stood in shock, then my mind caught on and I raced down the first-base line. Fernando, Thorin Oakenshield, and Stinky were rounding second and third and on their way home. I flew past second. Mr. Cramps was still rolling back and forth, screeching. Todd tried to grab the ball but was having a difficult time getting around the writhing gym teacher. I sailed past third and headed for home. Todd finally scooped up the ball and tossed it to the catcher—a second after my sneaker stomped down on home plate. We won, five to four.

I was met by the fellas and hoisted onto their shoulders. The camp was rocking. People were laughing and pointing.

I noticed Magnus beating his fists into the ground like a spoiled two-year-old. Todd was speeding away on his Segway. Mr. Periwinkle was hugging Mrs. Periwinkle, who was doing her best to pry him off. Tabitha was looking my way, smiling. I didn't know how to react to that. It was then that I noticed Mr. Cramps. He was still on the pitcher's mound, bent over and resting on one knee.

Having been carried around on shoulders before, I cut the celebration short and decided to have some real fun. I slid into the crowd and approached the insane athletics teacher. His face looked like a beet and his eyes were wet and angry. I bent over slightly and asked, "So?"

"So . . . what?" he growled through clenched teeth.

"So, did you enjoy the game?"

Chapter 14

NEWS FROM HOME

"Make way for Orcrist," shouted Thorin, "Orcrist the Goblin Cleaver!" He was leading the way home after the ball game, the aluminum bat held out in front of him as if it were a sword. "Orcrist shall be placed on my chest when I'm buried under the mountain."

"Sure." I laughed. "Whatever you want. You and Oatmeal earned—"

"Orcrist," he corrected me.

"Yeah, you and ol' Orcrist taught the Algonquins a lesson today. We all did!"

We were straggling along in back of Thorin, the most unlikely of victorious teams. It wasn't exactly a ticker-tape parade down Broadway, but it felt that way to us. The walk back to the cabin was filled with high fives and laughs. The camp was electric. Everyone was thrilled with the Algonquins' defeat.

It sure was nice, the so-called losers being

congratulated, but some of my cabinmates were having trouble with all the attention. Stinky, for instance, panicked as the crowd swarmed around him. He ran behind Woo, who told him, "Relax, Frankie boy. No worries for the son in the sun."

I shook my head slightly, thinking Stinky needed some help, but then I noticed someone who needed it a whole lot more. My eyes popped out as I saw Josh about to punch a fan.

"What are you doing?" I yelled. I ran over and grabbed Josh, saving some little blond kid from one heck of a blow.

"They whack me on the back, I whack them in the face!"

"No, Josh. A pat on the back is a way of saying, you know, 'Good job' or whatever."

"It is?" he asked.

I could see him thinking. His face scrunched up and his big forehead was creased with lines. Fernando noticed, too, and whispered to me, "Our friends may be a bit odd, but they never cease to make life interesting."

I thought about that later on in Loserville and smiled. Yes, my new friends sure knew how to keep things interesting. I climbed into bed and let my mind play over the events of the day. Most of it was pretty funny, but then I thought about Tabitha. I tossed and turned awhile. It's very confusing when you like someone you also dislike. I rolled over and missed Jessica more than ever. Now *there* was a girl who was pretty but also nice. Of course, Alison was nice, too . . .

Eventually the sounds of night and the breathing of my cabinmates soothed my restlessness. Before I closed my eyes, the last thing I saw was Thorin, aluminum bat lying proudly by his side.

Thanks to Fernando, Tabitha was still on my mind the following morning. Eating breakfast in the dining hall, he said, "That was a lot of fun yesterday. I think Tabitha liked the game, too."

"I have no idea if she did or didn't, and I don't care," I lied.

Fernando shifted his eyes, signaling for me to look left. There she was, across the room, staring at me with her big green eyes. The runny eggs turned in my stomach. I wanted to look away, but I couldn't. She was so pretty it hurt.

"Don't fight it, Rodney. The feisty ones are the most fun." Fernando was obviously enjoying himself. Then, more seriously, he said, "Admit it. You know you don't want to leave this place."

Still caught in the trance of her gaze, I nodded dumbly. Eventually my attention shifted back to Fernando, and for the first time I told him what I already knew myself. "You're right. I don't want to leave camp."

Before I had a chance to say any more, Gabe yelled, "Mail for Rathbone!" and dropped two envelopes onto my plate. "Let's see, I have another. This one's for . . . Fernando."

A fancy pink envelope seemed to float down to the table. Even from where I sat, I could smell the perfume coming off it.

"Your letter smells nice," Stinky said. For someone who stunk like a dead fish, he sure seemed to appreciate a good scent.

"Chanel No. 5," Fernando replied, holding it to his nose.

I let the conversation fade and turned my attention to the two envelopes sitting in front of me. I eyed the first. With a sense of dread I saw it was from my parents. Would it say they were on their way to pick me up? Was this my last meal at Camp Wy-Mee? I lifted up the other letter. It was from . . . Jessica. My heart skipped a couple of beats. There's something about a handwritten letter. It's different than a text message, and I was excited to hold it. Did Jessica miss me? If she did, and I was being pulled out of here, leaving might not be so bad. All the questions and thoughts quickened my pulse and I felt short of breath. I exhaled and looked up at the ceiling. As my gaze made its way back down, Fernando asked, "Your parents?"

I nodded.

"And Jessica?"

I nodded again.

"Open them," he said.

I figured I'd read Jessica's letter when I was alone.

I stuck my finger into the corner of my parents' letter and ripped it open. I pulled out the folded stationery and noticed my mom's loopy handwriting. I gulped and began to read.

Dear Rodney,

We were so happy to receive your letter. We were even happier to read about how much you love Camp Wy-Mee.

Huh? I thought.

We are so pleased to hear that you've made so many friends, and that there are such nice counselors. It really seems like the people you mentioned, such as Mrs. Periwinkle and Magnus, have taken a special interest in you.

Was my mom losing it? I clearly said I hated them.

Knowing that there are kind, thoughtful people like them keeping an eye on you makes me very relieved. I was nervous about sending my baby away! It's also so nice that you've made a special friend in Todd.

Todd? What's going on? I never said that!

Anyway, your friend Toby has been asking about you. He said he and his older brother would be keeping an eye on you next fall in middle school. Isn't that thoughtful of him?

Aaaaarrgghhhhhh!

Well, I'd better go chase your father away from the little treat I've cooked up for you. We love you very much!

Love, Mom & Dad

P.S. I've been taking cooking classes, and the treat I mentioned was a batch of chocolate chip cookies that I hoped to bring up to you. But since you're having so much fun, we've decided to go on vacation with the Windbaggers to their house on Lake Snore. We don't want to interrupt your fun. Oh, I would have mailed the cookies, but your dad ate them. Sorry, sweetie. Anyway, I'm sure camp food is delicious!

My jaw hung open as I reread and then reread again the words my mother had written. How in the world did she come up with that load of nonsense? My letter clearly described how much I hated camp, and especially hated Mrs. Periwinkle, Todd, and Magnus. I didn't fully believe my senses. I looked around the dining hall. Magnus was singing some bizarre song and pounding his fist on the table. Mr. Cramps was adjusting a bag of ice on his lap. Seeing me glance at him, he grabbed a piece of toast and took a savage bite. Mr. Periwinkle sat looking down on all of us with his usual beaming smile. Next to him sat Mrs. Periwinkle, who I noticed with alarm was glaring right at me. What was going on?

The bizarre, screwy letter from my mom messed with my brain. I had to read Jessica's letter right away. I ripped it open. As I unfolded the page, I caught a momentary whiff of her shampoo. It may not have been Chanel No. 5, but it sent a shiver down my spine. What I read almost sent my eggs back up my throat.

Dear Rodney,

I was very upset by your letter. I thought you really liked me. I can't believe you're breaking up with me! I almost cried when I read it but Toby reminded me that there are lots of other boys

113

around. So you have fun at your camp and have a
nice life.

Jess

It was the hammer blow. The page fell from my hand
and my face landed with a thud on my plate.

"Wow, Rodney, you must be real hungry," Josh said.
"Let me try eating like that." I heard what sounded like
a pig eating from a trough, followed by, "Mmmmm."

Shakily, I lifted my head from the plate. Some egg
fell from my cheek and landed in my lap. I was too upset
to care.

"Let Fernando see," Fernando said. He picked up
my letters and read both. When he was finished he set
them down and looked at me.

"Well?" I asked.

"You're screwed."

"What?" I blurted.

"Someone is intercepting your mail. Devious move,
too. Let's think about this. Do you have any enemies?"

The whole table cracked up laughing.

"Yes, silly question. Rodney here seems rather gifted
at getting people to dislike him. Let's make a list."

"Mrs. Periwinkle hates him," Stinky said.

"Yes, good. That's one," Fernando replied.

"Magnus can't stand him," Thorin added.

"Yes, that's true." Fernando nodded.

"Todd, and Chip and Biff and Skip and . . ."

"Yes, very good, all the Algonquins hate him. I get it. Who else?"

Stinky thought and said, "Mr. Cramps was trying to kill him with the softball."

"Excellent point, Frank."

"Don't forget Mrs. Periwinkle's horse, Lucifer!" Thorin added excitedly.

"Very good, although I think we can cross him off the letter plot. Okay, I'm sure Rodney has at least a dozen more enemies we don't know about . . ."

"Hey!" I interrupted. They all looked at me. "My girlfriend just broke up with me. Listening to how many people hate me isn't helping."

"Well, *we* like you. Right, boys?"

"Yeah!" they replied in unison.

Fernando went on. "We'll do whatever it takes to solve this mystery. Right, boys?"

"Yeah!" they said again.

"Even if it puts us at great personal risk. Right, boys?"

The usually loud table went silent. Everyone seemed to be studying their forks and spoons with great interest. Fernando leaned across the table. "I'll run any risk. And I've already identified our first opportunity to investigate."

"What opportunity?" I asked.

"Feast your eyes on this." He handed me his perfumed letter.

Dear Fernando,

You're invited to my home to discuss your punishment over lunch Friday at 12 p.m. I hope lobster is fine with you. I look forward to seeing you then.

All the best,

Hagatha Periwinkle

"Sounds like you're in for a rough time," I observed. "I scrape mussels and you eat lobster."

Fernando smiled. "We all have our roles in life. But don't you see? This is just the chance we need."

"How's that?" I asked. The rest of the table moved in closer to hear him.

"I'm invited to Mrs. Periwinkle's house. She's the most likely culprit. Even if those other people hate you, they probably don't have access to outgoing camp mail."

"That's true," Stinky added excitedly. "Good thinking." Everyone at the table, including me, was beginning to like Fernando's plan. That is, except for Fernando. A look of disappointment came on his face.

"What's wrong?" I asked.

"I just realized that I have no idea what I would search for. She's probably destroyed your original letters by now."

Almost in unison, my cabinmates and I sat back dejectedly.

"Not necessarily!" Thorin shouted. We sprang forward again and leaned in closer to hear what he had to say. After all, the kid was pretty smart.

Thorin rose up and his eyes glazed over. "Think of Muad'Dib's poor father, done in by a traitor!"

The whole table sat back slowly. Smart, yes, but nuts.

"No," he continued. "Don't you see? Spies! And in this case, our spy would need samples of your handwriting. When Baron Vladimir Harkonnen infiltrated House Atreides with the Suk doctor Wellington Yueh—"

Fernando coughed and interrupted. "All right. Enough gibberish for a moment. I'm trying to focus . . ."

"Wait, he's making sense," I said.

"You're scaring me, Rathbone. You mean you understand all the Baron Whookahaka stuff?"

"Not that. The letters. If she's forging my handwriting to fool my parents and Jessica, she's probably held on to my letters to keep copying my handwriting. Brilliant, Thorin!" Thorin took an elaborate bow. "Of course, it won't be easy for you to go snooping around."

"True. A lady's attention rarely strays from Fernando. It will probably be impossible for me to slip away. We'll need another way in, and sadly, campers are rarely invited into the Periwinkle house. However, Alison did mention that she was invited next week to something they have every year called the Girls' Cotillion Dinner."

"So was Tabitha," I added. "She told me like it was some big deal—that only the most popular girls get invited."

Fernando continued. "Alison said there'd be ten or eleven girls going. The perfect number for someone to slip away and snoop and not get caught. Too bad none of us are girls, though."

"Hello, boys." A silky voice interrupted us. I spun around. Alison's red hair blew in my direction. Her hand held a fancy pink envelope similar to Fernando's. She looked at me teasingly and I noticed her eyes sparkle. "I think this belongs to you." She smiled, handing me the envelope.

A little confused, I took it and removed the letter.

"Read it out loud," Thorin pleaded.

I cleared my throat and began:

Dear Rodweena,

It was truly a pleasure meeting you the other night. I think you are just the kind of young lady to invite to the annual Girls' Cotillion Dinner next Friday evening at 7 p.m. I look forward to seeing you there.

Sincerely,

Mrs. Periwinkle

"Excellent. That's it!" Fernando said with a beaming smile. "Problem solved."

As the meaning of his words became clear to me, my face fell forward into my plate for the second time that morning.

Fernando patted me on the shoulder. "Come, my friend, it is time to leave. And think on the bright side."

"What's that?" I muttered into my eggs.

"At least you're one of the popular girls!"

Chapter 15

HIGH HEELS AND DEER GUTS

A couple of days later, I met Alison out in the woods, past the archery range. We had arranged to go over a few details before my big change into Rodweena. Stinky came along too and sat on a stump, itching himself.

"What is that stuff?" I asked Alison.

"It's called blush," she answered, rubbing some on the top of my hand.

"What does it do?"

"Rodney, it makes your cheeks look red, like you're blushing. Boys like it when girls blush."

"They do? I mean, we do?"

"Yes, you do." She examined my hand. "I guess this color will work. Now, the night of Mrs. Periwinkle's party, you're really going to have to clean your finger-nails. Look at those cuticles!"

"What's a cuticle?"

She rolled her eyes and pulled out a bottle of perfume.

"Don't tell me I have to wear that, too," I groaned.

"No, this is for him." She turned and sprayed Stinky a few times.

"Hey!" he whined.

She ignored his protests and continued talking to me. "This plan of Fernando's has a long way to go."

"You're the one who volunteered to help me," I reminded her.

She continued like she hadn't heard me. "Listen, the night of the party I'll meet you here, where no one will see us, and I'll help you get dressed. I still have the wig and I borrowed some pretty high heels."

This whole plan was sounding more and more impossible—and way more embarrassing if I got caught. Nevertheless, I was committed now. Plus there was something reassuring about Alison. I watched as she arranged everything, like she had done this a hundred times before. I liked the way she didn't make a fuss about things.

The summer leaves rustled in the afternoon breeze. In the distance you could hear kids shouting down by the lake. It felt fun to be meeting secretly like this in the woods. Alison had picked the spot—the old stone chimney. It was a chimney left standing in the middle of a small clearing. I guess a cabin had once surrounded the chimney, but it was long gone.

"Some farmer and his family probably lived here in the olden days," Alison said.

"I bet *he* didn't have to wear high heels," I joked.

She gave me a big smile and our eyes met. A second later her cheeks turned bright red.

"Is that blush you're wearing?" I asked.

"No, Rodney." She sighed, looking down.

I realized I really liked her. I was in the middle of admiring her long red hair and tan skin when she glanced up. Her deep brown eyes looked into mine. I gazed into them, starting to feel . . .

"Buuuurrrrrppp!" Stinky exploded.

Spell broken, Alison said, "Okay, I'm going to be late for windsurfing. Rodney, practice walking on your toes, with your hand on your hip. That will help you get ready for the high heels."

"Uh, all right. Thanks, I guess."

"Bye, Rodney. Bye, Frank."

"Bye, Alison," Stinky called.

I watched her walk down the path toward the lake. She rounded a bend in the trail and was gone. I stood for a second breathing in the warm, woodsy air. For the first time in a couple of days, my stomach wasn't in a knot over the sadness with Jessica.

Stinky and I turned and walked off in the other direction. I had athletics with Mr. Cramps. In no rush to do my usual assortment of push-ups, crunches, squat thrusts, and mile run, we took the longcut along a trail that followed a small creek. After a while I decided to practice walking on my tippy-toes. "Does it look like I'm walking like a girl?" I laughed.

Stinky answered, "I'm not sure. You *do* look pretty weird."

I tried a few more times. Then I put my hand on my hip, like Alison said. "How about now?"

"Get a load of this guy!"

It wasn't Stinky's voice. I spun around. Now, I've faced some pretty bad situations in my life, so I can't say I was completely surprised to see Todd and his usual pack of Algonquins. They were sitting on a log off the trail.

"Nice walk, Rathbone," Todd shouted, getting up. The Algonquins laughed and all rose off the log, starting to walk in our direction. Todd was actually wearing white pants and a white shirt. His hair shimmered in the sun.

"Nice outfit," I said. "I'll take a snow cone."

He wasn't amused. "So this is what you losers do for fun? Walk around like girls? Let me try." With that, he began to walk crazily down the path. "Look at *meee*. I'm Rod-*neee*! Whoop-*eee*!" The other Algonquins were laughing. Todd kept going, "La la—*ow*!" He stopped short and rubbed his forehead. "That hurt! What was that?" He reached down and picked up an acorn. "Did you throw this at me, Rathbone?"

I hadn't thrown anything. "Maybe the sky is falling."

"You're dead."

"Relax," I said, "we didn't do anything. Right, Frank?" There was no reply. I glanced over at him. "Right?"

Stinky shrugged. "Seemed like the thing to do at the time."

I couldn't believe it! Here, in the middle of the woods, Stinky suddenly decided to act brave. While I understood his logic, I also knew what would come next.

"Open fire!" Todd shouted. Within seconds, acorns whizzed through the air. I felt sharp stings on my shoulder and back. I scrambled behind a tree and looked for ammunition. Stinky was already launching acorns as fast as he could and I heard a couple of yelps from the Algonquins.

We put up a good fight that day, but as the battle wore on it was obvious we were outnumbered. My body stung in a dozen places where the acorns hit their marks. Todd threw an enormous acorn that zipped past my head and bounced off the tree with a loud whack. I knew I couldn't stay trapped behind the tree forever. I ran a few feet, jumped over the small, muddy creek, and turned and nailed Skip in the neck. As Stinky jumped over the stream to join me he let out a yell. A rock had left Todd's hand and hit him on the elbow. Stinky grabbed it and grimaced in pain. Todd wasn't playing by the rules.

"Hey, no rocks!" I yelled angrily.

Todd laughed. "Or else what? You going to tell your mommy?"

The last thing I wanted was a fight, but I was sick

of Todd thinking he could bully me. I looked around. "Come over here and I'll show you what I'll do!"

Todd smiled. "This ought to be interesting."

He took a few steps closer and was just on the other side of the stream when I made my move. "Hey, your shoelace is untied."

"Is that all you've got, Rathbone?" he laughed, turning to smile at his fellow Algonquins.

"Yeah . . . and THIS!"

In front of me were some large rocks. With two hands I grabbed one that weighed about forty pounds and heaved it into the creek. By the time Todd realized what I was doing it was too late. My boulder landed and sent up a wall of mud that covered him from head to foot, white pants and all. I locked eyes with Stinky. "Run!"

We spun around and took off, not on the path but straight into the woods. "You're dead!" Todd screamed, bounding after me like a madman. Small branches scraped and scratched my face but I kept running. Stinky got blocked by some thick underbrush and ran off in another direction. Unfortunately, there was no shaking Todd. As he closed in on me, I realized that maybe the mud thing hadn't been such a bright idea.

I ran a few more steps, suddenly finding myself on a rock ledge with nowhere to go. I think Todd tried to stop but it was too late. He smashed into me and we both flew through the air before dropping hard to the ground. My ankle twisted awkwardly when I landed. I tried to stand and balance on one foot, bracing for the punch that was surely coming my way. I could hear the other Algonquins, and hopefully Stinky, scrambling down the ledge. Todd said, "Now you're dea—"

He didn't finish. Something shut him up. I followed his gaze. A deer's head was hanging from a tree. Todd jumped and actually grabbed my shoulder. I followed his gaze. Several ratlike animals were nailed to another tree. We both gulped and looked further into the woods. Standing with the sun behind him, so that we could only see his dark outline, was a large man dressed for a horror movie audition moving closer.

I turned, trying to run, but pain shot from my ankle and I stumbled to the ground. Not surprisingly, Todd didn't pause to help me up. He was too busy tearing off at full speed, following everyone else. I watched, helpless, as he walked toward me. This was really it. Less than a half hour ago I was worried about high heels. Now I was about to die like some character in a bad horror movie.

"Yo Rodney," the guy greeted me. "You finally came out to my shack for that arrow shooting lesson. Good timing, too. I just cut out some deer kidneys. I'm frying them up right now for a snack."

It was Survival Steve, and I wasn't dead. In fact, he helped me up and almost lifted me over to his shack. He went in and came back out, handing me a tin plate. "Dig in!"

To be polite, I gagged some down. They were still kind of raw and disgusting, but at that moment I was so relieved not to be up in the tree with the deer head that I'd have eaten dog doo.

"Guess you could use a drink, too," he said as I sat on a stool, wiping deer blood from my chin. "Let's see, I got some two day old coffee, some goat pee, some . . ."

"I'm fine, thanks. The kidneys hit the spot."

"Yeah, they do, don't they? Now let's go shoot some arrows." I stood to follow him and winced. He looked down at my ankle.

"Well now, that's something, ain't it? No matter, got just the thing." In no time he had pulled out some sticks and rawhide rope and was weaving me a splint. He talked while he worked. "I was attacked by a moose up in Alaska one spring. Almost broke my legs in two. I fashioned myself some leg braces and walked two hundred miles to Anchorage . . ."

"Sounds like a nice vacation," I quipped.

"The best," he agreed. "Now, stand up."

It was amazing. Somehow the splint thing took almost all the pressure off my ankle. I walked around. "I can't believe you figured this out using just your survival instincts."

"Yeah, that and a degree in orthopedics from Johns Hopkins." I glanced up at him. He continued, "Hey, are we going to shoot arrows or what?"

Steve lived up to his promise and for the next couple

of hours we shot arrows at a big old stump. He showed me how to hold a bow and how to control my arm's motion. I couldn't believe it, but I was pretty good. I hit the target again and again. After I hit the same small spot fourteen times in a row, Steve howled enthusiastically, "You're a natural, Rodney!"

"This is a lot of fun," I answered.

"You bet, but it'll be dinnertime back at camp soon. Your counselor will be wondering where you are."

I pictured Woo, head bopping, lost in his own jazz world. I doubted he would miss me. I was having a good time out at the shack. I said, "All right, but not before I shoot this arrow into that birch trunk down there."

"Way down yonder?" Steve asked.

"Yeah, down yonder." I smiled to myself, realizing I sounded like a hillbilly.

"That'd be some throw, I doubt—"

I didn't wait for his reply. I stepped in and let the arrow fly. It sailed straight and sweet and landed with a *thunk* right where I said it would go.

"Whooooeeeeeeee! Come back next week and I'll teach you how to wrestle a bear. All right, let's go. I'll help you back. Oh, here."

"What's this?" I looked down at something wrapped in wax paper.

"It's another deer kidney. I know how you like 'em."

"Mmm, dessert," I said, holding it up.

We walked back through the woods. Along the way Steve pointed out different streams, climbing trees, caves, and even the entrance to an old mine.

"Where does that go?"

"Well, if you stay to the right in the mine, you'll wind up down by the lake, near the boys' cabins. Dangerous place, though. Stay out of it."

Eventually, we neared camp. I could see the dining hall through the trees. "Guess you can manage from here," Steve said.

I smiled, said thanks and good-bye, and walked up the hill to the dining hall. Everyone was lined up waiting to go in, and I thought I heard my name mentioned a few times. Mr. Periwinkle was busy questioning Woo, who was staring off singing, "Nothing's gonna bring him back." Seeing me emerge from the woods, my cabinmates let out a shout and came running.

"Glad you made it!" Stinky yelled.

"Piece of cake," I said, smiling.

"I didn't know what to do," Stinky continued. "I tried to get help, but when I got out of the woods, Magnus told me to be quiet and sent me back to the cabin."

Todd and the Algonquins had also walked my way. "I thought you were dead," Todd said. I noticed he had changed into clean clothes.

"Sorry to disappoint you. Oh, here's a souvenir. I kind of tore it out of that guy while we were fighting."

I tossed him the now-unwrapped deer kidney. He caught it, looked down, and screamed, "Whoooaaahhh!"

I laughed. And then, along with my friends, I headed into the dining hall, where over a fine dinner of dry meatloaf, lumpy mashed potatoes, smelly green beans, and a cup of red bug juice, I related my adventures.

Chapter 16

RODWEENA'S NIGHT OUT

Alison and Fernando helped me stumble out from the woods where I had climbed into my Rodweena outfit.

"My, my, Rodney, you look . . ."

"Zip it, Fernando. I'll give this crazy plan of yours a shot, but I don't have to like it." Both of their eyes were sparkling, and I could tell they were really enjoying seeing me grumble about being dressed like a girl. "Do you think this is going to work?" I asked.

Fernando and Alison looked at me closer. Fernando said, "You'd better stay out of the kitchen."

"Why, does this outfit make me look fat?"

"No, the bright lights will give you away. Keep to the shadows. I don't know how long it will take, but someone will probably realize you're not a girl. And if that happens, I'm glad Fernando won't be there to see what Mrs. Periwinkle does to you."

I tried to block that frightening thought as I

concentrated on the task at hand. My time would be limited. I had to act fast and get out before getting caught. Get in, get out.

"Remember, the office is down the hall to the right," Fernando continued. "If she has your letters, that's where you'll probably find them." I nodded. Fernando had done some preliminary scouting during his punishment luncheon of chilled lobster and chocolate-covered strawberries. "All right, good luck, girls!" he called with a laugh as he turned and headed off.

Alison and I walked up the steep hill leading to the Periwinkles' house. It was a nice night, with fireflies flashing everywhere and a million stars overhead. I took a second to sneak a glance at her. At least one of us was looking good tonight. Funny, I hadn't really paid much attention to Alison when I first got to camp, but now . . .

Arriving at the house, she fixed the wig on my head and said, "Remember, tonight you're a girl. Act like one." Before I had a chance to run, she knocked.

A moment later the door opened and I could see Mrs. Periwinkle standing behind the screen. Her eyes lingered on me for a few torturous seconds. Was I caught already? Then she smiled. "Oh, Rodweena, so nice to see you. You look very . . . uh . . . pretty. What an interesting hairstyle you're wearing. Hello, Alison. That's a very nice dress." This was definitely a different Mrs. Periwinkle than the one who cursed me under her breath every time she saw me. "Come in, come in," she continued. "The girls are all out back. Just make your way straight through the house."

I was feeling nervous as I passed her so I kept my head down and speed-walked my way through the living and dining rooms.

"Rodney," Alison whispered from over my shoulder, "you're stomping around like a soldier. Remember, you're a girl."

"Oh, yeah. I'll remember. Thanks." I felt like I was going to get caught any minute. Mrs. Periwinkle was right behind us in the hallway. I don't know if it was my nerves or all the bug juice I drank at lunch, but suddenly I had to go to the bathroom real bad. "Mrs. Periwinkle," I asked in my highest voice, "may I use the restroom?"

"It's just through the kitchen," she replied.

The kitchen! I braved the bright lights and crossed to the bathroom door. Once inside, I turned the lock, exhaled, and stood there taking care of my business. When finished, I actually felt a little better. "Remember, act like a girl," I said to myself in the mirror. "And remember to get in and get out. No small talk with anyone. Don't even stay for dinner." I opened the door and walked smack into Mrs. Periwinkle. "Oh, excuse me."

"Careful, Rodweena." She stepped past me and headed into the bathroom. "I'll be just a minute."

The lock clicked and so did my brain. Get in, get out! I could go to the office right now, find the letters, and be out into the night. I glanced back and forth. Which way?

"AAAAAAAAEEEEEEEEEAAAAAAAAHHH-HHH!" A howl exploded from behind the closed door. What happened? I heard more grunts, angry snorts, and banging. I had just decided to run for it when the door swung open. Mrs. Periwinkle's dress was wet and twisted and she looked even crazier than usual. In a loud, clipped breath she said, "Rodweena, why on earth did you *PUT THE SEAT UP?*"

Oh no! I was pretending to be a girl and I did the one thing no girl would ever do. My mom always yelled at me for that.

"Well, I, uh . . ."

"I was momentarily stuck!" she howled. "I could have drowned! And look what you did to my beautiful evening gown."

Mrs. Periwinkle adjusted her outfit. The pause allowed my brain to kick into gear. Remembering something my great aunt Evelyn usually said, I offered, "But Mrs. Periwinkle, I didn't use the toilet. I was just powdering my nose."

Her sneer lost its ferocity. I tried to look sincere and she softened more. "Well, I guess that makes sense. It is always smart for a young lady to check herself before entering a social gathering. Well done, Rodweena. But if *you* didn't put the seat up . . ." Her face looked thoughtful and then suddenly furious. "PERCY!"

From somewhere above I heard a startled jump, and then silence. Mrs. Periwinkle gazed at the ceiling, her eyes blazing once again. After a minute of huffing, she looked back down and said, "I'll deal with him later. Let's go enjoy the night."

After our rather eventful trip to the john, we walked outside. Before me I saw three tables covered with white linen. Fireflies flew between pink and yellow Chinese lanterns suspended from several old oak trees that surrounded the back patio. Soft music played. I had to admit, it was very nice.

Alison was already sitting at a table under the largest of the oak trees. I headed in her direction, but Mrs. Periwinkle stopped me. "Rodweena, I feel positively awful about what just happened. Come sit at my table."

"But . . ."

"There are no buts about it. I insist. You shall be the guest of honor. You know, I was very impressed with you the other night and I want to talk further."

"Sounds wonderful, Mrs. Periwinkle," I lied. The last thing I wanted was to be stuck with her. I'd be found out for sure, and any chance of slipping away would be very small.

She motioned to the table that had the best view overlooking the camp fields. As I stood there awkwardly, stalling so I didn't have to sit, I realized that the whole plan was dumb. I wanted to get out of there. It was pointless anyway. The chance of finding the letters was slim, and if I ran off before getting caught nothing bad would happen. No one knew who I *really* was, anyway.

I was just turning to leave when I noticed who was seated at Mrs. Periwinkle's table.

Tabitha was wearing a light-green dress that matched her eyes. They glowed more wonderfully than any of the fireflies or lanterns. I stumbled as I ran to take the seat next to her, banging my knee into the table leg. *Get in, get out* was suddenly replaced by. *Be cool, act cool.* I placed the napkin in my lap and gave her a wink.

She made a weird face and I remembered who I was—or, perhaps more appropriately, who I wasn't. "Oh, a mosquito flew into my eye," I said, rubbing it. Tabitha seemed to accept this. I looked around at the other girls. I recognized some but didn't really know them. So far Alison was the only girl there who knew my real identity. I noticed that she was looking at me from the other table—and she didn't look happy. Was it because I was sitting next to Tabitha?

Mrs. Periwinkle stood behind her seat, cleared her throat, and announced, "Young ladies, I'm delighted you could all join me tonight for the annual Girls' Cotillion Dinner." She beamed at us. "Cotillions are traditionally gatherings where young people learn the manners of polite society. It's important to have a few moments like this, away from the dining hall with its often loud and raucous behavior. Tonight we can engage in refined conversation, practice proper etiquette, and talk about subjects young ladies find interesting." Boy, was this boring. I wished I was in the *dining* hall. "Also, I have made sure that we have an excellent menu tonight . . ."

What's that? It was then that I noticed some waiters and a catering van parked below us in the driveway. *Let's hear it for cotillions!* I thought.

"Tonight we'll be partaking of shrimp cocktail, Caesar salad, lobster bisque, and filet mignon. Nothing is too fine or expensive for you young ladies. After all, I'll soon be coming into quite a bit of . . ."

She seemed to think better of continuing, but we all knew she was about to say "money." I didn't really care. I was too busy drooling and trying to quiet my growling stomach. After weeks of Gertrude and Alice's cooking, McDonald's would have seemed like gourmet dining. My thoughts of making a quick escape faded as I contemplated a mouthwatering steak. Mrs. Periwinkle concluded, "I hope you enjoy."

She sat down and smiled at the table. "All right, girls, I've really been looking forward to tonight. Sometimes one needs to spend time with just the girls. Don't you agree, Rodweena?"

"Oh, I agree, Mrs. Periwinkle. A night away from boys is like an oasis in the desert." I could tell she liked that one. Her face beamed with warmth. It went cold, however, following a loud crash from inside the house.

"Who's in there?" she snapped loudly.

Mr. Periwinkle's face slowly rose into view through the kitchen window.

"What are you doing?" she growled.

"I was just making a sandwich. I dropped the mayo . . ."

"*Get back to your room!*" There was another bang as we heard him scurry away. Mrs. Periwinkle exhaled slowly. "Yes, Rodweena, an oasis."

A waiter placed a tall glass with three large shrimp in front of me. I almost elbowed Tabitha out of excitement. I licked my lips, grabbed a shrimp, dipped it in the cocktail sauce and opened my mouth to take a bite.

"So, Rodweena, the other night you made so much sense and had such strong convictions. What would you like to talk about tonight?" Everyone turned to me expectantly.

I lowered the shrimp. "Well, I wonder who's going to win the AFC East this fall. I like the Jets, and I can't stand the Patriots, but with their quarterback . . ." The collection of female faces looked surprised—and disgusted. I came close to smacking my forehead. I gathered myself and gave a big laugh. "Baseball! Hah! Can you believe boys waste their time talking about such nonsense? I'd love to talk about jewelry. That's a nice necklace thing, Mrs. Periwinkle." Their faces relaxed.

Mrs. Periwinkle smiled and I went to bite the shrimp.

"Rodweena," she continued. I lowered the shrimp. "I thought we might want to talk about the many fine young gentlemen around camp." A couple of girls giggled. *Okay*, I thought to myself. *You talk about whatever. I'm going to finally eat this shrimp.*

It was halfway to my mouth when Mrs. Periwinkle said my name again. "Rodweena, I bet you and young Todd Vanderdick would make a darling couple . . ."

"What?" I shouted, forgetting to disguise my voice.

Mrs. Perwinkle seemed to study me a bit closer. Was I caught? I put the shrimp back down and added, in a more girl-like voice, "Why, whatever gave you that idea?"

"Oh, *everyone* likes Todd. Isn't that true, Tabitha?" Tabitha stirred in her seat and smiled slyly. Mrs. Periwinkle sure seemed to be enjoying herself.

I could feel my mouth getting tingly, and I said, "Tabitha, I thought you liked Rodney Rathbone?"

Mrs. Periwinkle recoiled. "Rodweena, just *hearing* that name gives me indigestion. Let's not spoil a lovely evening. Surely Tabitha has more taste than to give that horrible boy any thought. Am I right, Tabitha?"

"Absolutely, Mrs. Periwinkle."

I felt a little anger smoldering, but I did my best to hide it and decided to finally eat my shrimp. Just as I reached for one, the waiter whisked the three juicy beauties away and replaced them with the salad. I almost cried. With a growling stomach I took a bite and discovered that it was actually good. It had a tasty dressing and big, crunchy croutons.

Not everyone agreed with me. "Where are the

anchovies?" We all looked up at Mrs. Periwinkle, who was rooting around her salad with her fork. "I distinctly requested anchovies in the Caesar." I looked down fearfully, afraid that I might find slimy bits of fish hiding between my lettuce leaves. "Unacceptable!" Mrs. Periwinkle dropped her napkin on the table and stomped off in a huff after one of the waiters.

Tabitha leaned in to me and asked, "Rodweena, who told you that I like Rodney? I've never even seen you before." I was stuck, but before I could make up an answer she added, "And why are you bringing him up around Mrs. Periwinkle? She can't stand him."

"Oh, sorry. Anyway, I just assumed you liked him. I didn't know you didn't."

"Who says I don't?"

"Well, you just did . . ."

Tabitha smiled and said in a quiet breath, "Don't be silly, Rodweena. I do like Rodney. I think he's a bad boy. He's exciting."

I never thought of myself as an exciting bad boy before. Feeling pretty good, I asked, "So you don't like Todd, then?"

"No, I like him, too. He's got lots of money. Do you know his dad has a yacht?"

My good feelings died, but I asked, "So which are you going to . . . you know, date?"

"Both," she said, taking a bite of lettuce like it was nothing.

"Both? What if one of them finds out?"

"Rodweena, they're boys. *Clueless!* There's absolutely no chance either will find out."

"The odds might be higher than you think," I added. Tabitha laughed and shook her head at me like I was crazy, and then shifted her eyes upward to tell me Mrs. Periwinkle had returned.

The two of them were making me lose my appetite and I suddenly focused again on the reason for being here. I had to complete the mission.

"Excuse me, Mrs. Periwinkle. I need to use the bathroom."

"Well, you know where it is," she responded, followed by, "and make sure the seat is down."

I pretended to laugh at her little joke and rose from the table. As I passed Alison I gave her a subtle nod and continued into the house. It was now or never. *Get in, get out.*

Chapter 17

THE PLOT THICKENS

Instead of heading through the kitchen toward the bathroom, I turned left down a dimly lit hallway. I could see a faint green light shining under the door. If Fernando's description was accurate, my letters home would be in the private den.

I grasped the cold glass knob. My heart started to beat hard and fast. This was it. I could barely stand to watch detectives on TV when they might get caught, and now I was sneaking into an office. It felt strange, almost like I was watching someone else's hand twisting and pulling the knob. I entered and quickly closed the door behind me.

Knowing I had limited time, I dove right into the papers on the desk, looking for the letters. It was easy to see because someone had left on an old-fashioned desk lamp that gave off a weird green glow. The papers were only about some boring legal stuff, something about wetland development and parking lot design. I pushed them aside and looked through several folders. Again, nothing. I stole a glance and noticed one last folder with a red tab that read PSYCHOLOGICAL PROFILE— DANGEROUS CAMPER. That caught my attention. Was there some dangerous person lurking around Camp Wy-Mee? It'd be a good idea to know who I should avoid.

I looked for a name, but all that I could see was *Camper RR*. The next page had all the basic information, such as age, height, eye color, hair color. Other basic characteristics were listed. It could be anyone. Heck, it could be *me*. I read on:

> Hagatha, please remember that Camper RR must
> be watched at all times. On the surface he appears
> normal enough, but don't let that fool you. His
> mind is constantly working out dangerous, evil
> plots. Making him even more of a threat is his
> knack for emboldening the usually quieter children.
> Some thick-headed adults are also captivated by his
> sickening charm . . .

Who wrote this thing? Who was Camper RR? My hand bumped against the mouse and the computer screen came to life. An icon on the screen flashed: "Urgent email." My curiosity got the better of me and I opened it. It read:

Hagatha, I'm disappointed you haven't taken care of our little problem by now. Must I handle everything? I'll be seeing you real soon. Love, Big Sis.

What was that about? Could it be about Camper RR? About me? And who was Mrs. Periwinkle's big sister? I turned my attention back to the matter at hand. I had been snooping around the office for two minutes and would soon be missed. It was then that I noticed the corner of two white envelopes sticking out from under a book. My heart started to beat even faster. The envelopes looked just like the ones my mom had given me before camp so I could write home. This was it. I reached out and started to lift the book. Then I saw the phone and another idea jumped into my brain.

While everyone else had been allowed to use the camp phone once a week after dinner, my privileges had been suspended. And now there it was, a phone just waiting for me. Before I had time to think, I reached into my wallet, took out a piece of paper with a number scribbled on it, and called Jessica.

"Hello."

It was her voice. My heart beat hard. "Hi, Jessica. It's Rodney."

"Rodney? I didn't think I'd hear from you after that terrible letter you sent..."

"Jessica, I didn't write that letter. I know it sounds crazy, but someone's been intercepting my mail—"

"You're right, it does sound crazy. Now I need to go."

"Don't hang up, Jessica. Why would I break up with you? I spent the entire year trying to get you to like me. You're the coolest, prettiest, best girl in Ohio . . ."

"Do you really think so?"

"Absolutely! I would never write horrible things to you."

"It really hurt my feelings."

"Jessica, I'm sorry that happened to you. I want you to know that I would never do anything mean or rude or—"

I smacked down the receiver. The doorknob was beginning to turn. There was a closet on the other side of the room. I wouldn't make it in time. Instead, I jumped behind the curtains as the door opened and closed.

From my hiding spot I couldn't see who had entered the room, but I was sure that whoever it was could see me shaking like a leaf behind the curtain.

"Hello, Bill. It's Percy." Mr. Periwinkle must have come into the office to use the phone. He was whispering and talking very fast. "Hagatha is having a girls' dinner here so I can only talk a second. I wanted you to know that I got your message and I think it's great. Endangered salamanders might be our last chance to save this place. If that doesn't work, Hagatha and her battle-ax sister will have their way for sure. I know their plan will make us all rich, but these woods are worth far more to me. Of course, I only have a slight say in the matter . . ." His voice seemed to trail off. "Thank you for trying, Bill. We'll talk more tomorrow."

After a moment I heard the door close. Peeking out from behind the curtain, I checked that the coast was clear and ran over to the desk. I could still hear Periwinkle walking about and I knew time was running short. I pulled the two envelopes out from under the book—and stood looking down at my own handwriting. Mrs. Periwinkle really had intercepted my mail!

For a moment I debated whether to take the letters, but in the end I left both. I wanted to talk to Fernando before I did anything. I needed to figure it all out. What kind of person kept secret files on campers? What kind of person forged a kid's letter to his parents? And why was Mr. Perwinkle talking about salamanders?

It was time for me to get out of here. I slid open the window facing the woods, lowered myself down, and ran off to the dining hall, where I ditched my Rodweena costume under the steps. It felt good to be dressed like myself again. It wasn't until I was back in my bunk that I remembered the worst part about the night. I had hung up on Jessica and didn't even call her back! Imagining her reaction to my bonehead move was harder to digest than Mrs. Periwinkle's nonexistent anchovies.

Chapter 18

MY SPECIAL VISITOR

I was shaken awake early. Thorin, Josh, Fernando, and Stinky were all standing over me. "Well?" they asked.

I sat up and told them the details of what I had read and heard in the Periwinkles' office. Everyone listened carefully—even Josh. When I finished, Fernando let out a slow, quiet whistle and Thorin said, "It reminds me of the plots of Morgan le Fay."

As usual, Thorin was met with a round of blank stares. And as usual, he didn't notice. "Perhaps, Rodney," he continued, "she sees you as Arthur Pendragon."

"And perhaps you could join us on Earth," Fernando suggested. "Now, we need to figure some things out. We know Mrs. Periwinkle intercepted the mail, but we don't know why. We know she and this big sister of hers are plotting something against the camp. But we don't know what. Gentlemen, there are questions that need answers. We must go out there focused"—he pointed to the door—"and keep our eyes open."

"And our ears," Stinky added.

"Yes, Frank, and our ears."

"And our elbows," Josh added.

"Uh, okay, right."

BLLLLLAAAAAAAAAAAAAAAAAAAAAAHH-HHHHHHHH! A siren wailed so loudly that it actually shook the cabin's frame. It sounded like it was blaring all over camp.

Stinky screamed, "It's Mrs. Periwinkle! She's bombing us!" and went scurrying under his bunk bed. Thorin grabbed Orcrist and held it ready to strike any goblin that should appear. Josh lifted his trunk high over his head and stood there grinning, caught up in the excitement.

"No time for da nerves, everyone," Woo announced as the siren slowly came to an end. "It's Secret Special Visitors Day. Let's go play. Whaddaya say?"

Josh looked disappointed as he lowered his trunk, but the rest of us were relieved. After he climbed out from under his bunk, Stinky remembered what the whistle meant. It seemed that Secret Special Visitors Day was a yearly event. The campers never knew when it was coming and enjoyed being surprised by their family members. I was a little skeptical.

"*Everyone* has a visitor?" I asked. "I mean, what if someone can't make it?"

"No," Stinky explained. "They almost always have one hundred percent attendance. It's written into the

Camp Wy-Mee application or something. It's manda-tory. Mr. Periwinkle thinks it's a big deal and insists on it. Anyway, the day's great. There are fun activities and there'll be a big barbecue tonight!"

"So when do we see our visitors?" I was starting to get excited. "I can't wait!"

Woo said, "Don't be impatient, don't you whine, your visitors will be there, now get in line." He strutted toward the door.

Josh was the first to follow him. Woo turned back to him, smiling. "Come on, Joshy. I know you got the gift. You're the Knick with the knack, so rap, rap, rap. Give me a rhyme while there's still some time."

Josh was lost. If his jaw hung any lower, it would have dragged on the floor.

"Just say a word, Josh." Woo smiled. "Any word."

Josh, who was about to step outside, looked down and managed to utter, "Stair."

"Yeah, man! No sittin' in the *chair*. Keep breathing the *air*. Why should you *care*? Drag that comb through your . . ." Woo pointed at Josh.

Miraculously, Josh uttered, "Hair."

"SNAP!" Woo clapped his hands together. "My car has a *spare*. My favorite fruit is a *pear*. I like to watch the Fresh Prince of *Bel-Air*. When I drum I use a *snare*. In the woods I tracked a . . ."

"Wolf!" Josh exclaimed proudly. He held up his hand to high-five Woo.

For once, Woo was at a loss for words. He dumbly tapped Josh's hand.

I pushed past them with Fernando and wandered over to the line. Since last night, my head had been consumed with evil plots and conspiracies. Now, with the knowledge that in ten minutes I'd be seeing a family member, my worries faded. Who was it? My brain ran through the possibilities. According to the letter I had received, my parents were away on vacation. And then it came to me . . . the one relative who'd be more than willing to head off to camp for a day of fun. Aunt Evelyn! I was all smiles as we walked the familiar path to the dining hall.

As we approached, I watched the girls walking from the other direction and I could hear a steady hum of conversation pouring out from the dining hall windows. Who was in there waiting for me?

We still had to line up and do the usual flag-raising and singing ceremonies. During "America the Beautiful" I made eye contact with Alison. I could see that she was itching to find out about the rest of my night. I, too, wanted to hear what commotion Rodweena's disappearance had caused.

The singing ended and Mr. Periwinkle climbed on top of the announcement boulder, waiting for us to quiet down. I noticed he wore his special-occasion pith helmet.

"May I have your attention? I realize you're excited,

but a few words first. Right now your visitors are seated in the dining hall. After you have brunch with them, there are numerous activities arranged for you to enjoy together. It should be a splendid afternoon. Tonight we will finish the day with the annual camp barbecue—and *I'll* be manning the grill. Oh yes, one more thing." Suddenly Mr. Periwinkle looked right at me. "Rodney and Todd, may I see you for a moment? Everyone else, off you go."

The crowd stampeded toward the dining hall like a herd of hungry cattle. I wandered over to Mr. Periwinkle. What did he want to talk to me about? Was he going to tell me that I didn't have a visitor? Had he found out about Rodweena and that I went through his desk? If so, why was Todd there? Maybe he was going to ask Todd to beat me up. I didn't like this one bit.

Todd and I reached him at about the same moment. Todd's eyes gave me a nasty squint, and we turned to Periwinkle. Up close, despite his fancy helmet, I could see that Mr. Periwinkle looked jumpy and nervous. "Okay then," he began. "I asked to talk to you two because your special visitors are not in the dining hall." My heart dropped into my gut. I *knew* no one was going to visit me. "They are up at my house." My heart leaped back up into my chest. "We'll be dining there this morning."

Todd smirked, "Did Dad bring me anything?"

"I'm sure he did."

"Who's *my* special visitor?" I asked.

"Well, Rodney, I can't tell you that. She insisted that it remain a surprise." Looking back on it, I remember his voice sounded strained as he said this, but at that moment my brain was focusing on "she." It *had* to be my great-aunt Evelyn! She could charm a person in seconds and Mrs. Periwinkle must have asked her up to the house. Aunt Evelyn would know what to do about all the problems and how to save the camp. The rest of the summer was going to be a breeze! I was so happy I called out, "Come on, Todd, old buddy! I'll race you to the top of the hill." He just looked disgusted and trudged along behind me with Mr. Periwinkle.

I was way ahead of them as I weaved through the old oak trees from last night and crossed the patio. I knocked on the same screen door where Mrs. Periwinkle had greeted Alison and me—I mean Rodweena—just hours earlier. Mrs. Periwinkle's voice called out, "Come in, Rodney."

As I turned in to the living room I saw Mrs. Periwinkle, who was in a chair facing me. She lifted her head and smiled. She was talking to someone across from her. The person's face was blocked by the chair's high back. I yelled, "Aunt Evelyn!" and ran around to the front of the chair.

It wasn't Aunt Evelyn.

It was someone I knew real well, though. If spending the day with my aunt was going to be a dream, the dream had instantly become something so terrible that the word *nightmare* wasn't even strong enough. For sitting there, with an evil smile playing around her gray, ugly lips, was my greatest enemy—an enemy who made Todd, Magnus, and Mr. Cramps look like a group of Care Bears. It was Mrs. Lutzkraut, my former teacher.

I thought I'd escaped her evil plots when the school year ended, but seeing her sitting there smiling her wicked grin I knew I was in trouble. She was the nastiest person I knew, my greatest adversary, and I was a long way from home.

Chapter 19

THE MILLION-
DOLLAR BET

"Did you miss me, Rodney?"

I felt dizzy. My heart was still beating fast from the run up the hill—and now this. I couldn't answer. I couldn't even think.

Mrs. Lutzkraut lifted a teacup and took a noisy sip. "Come now, Rodney. I'm disappointed. That famous mouth of yours has nothing to say?"

"Uhhhh . . ." I thought I was going to be sick. "What? Who? Uhh . . ." Nonsense poured out from my mouth.

"I see that intelligent conversation is still light-years beyond you. I was hoping the camp air might have done you some good. Tell me, Rodney, are you enjoying your summer?" That famous wicked smile wouldn't leave her face and I could tell she was now enjoying *her* summer to the fullest. My brain began to piece things together.

"You're Mrs. Periwinkle's older sister?"

Mrs. Lutzkraut almost spit out her tea. "We prefer

'big sister'," she corrected me. "Anyway, that's a fine deduction. Apparently my efforts teaching you this past year weren't a complete waste." She reached into a bowl of chocolates on the coffee table. As I watched her pick at the silver foil surrounding each candy my brain began to kick into gear. Of course! *She* was probably the one who had told Mrs. Periwinkle to steal my mail.

"So tell me," she continued, picking some chocolate from her teeth with a finger nail, "How has Josh Dumbrowski been treating you?" Her smile gained a little ferocity. No doubt, she thought he was giving me a hard time.

"Good," I answered. "We're great pals now. Thank you for getting us together."

The side of her face twitched for a second. "It looks like you're having yourself a very nice little summer." I thought I caught a swift, nasty glance aimed at her sister. "*Too* nice a summer."

Mrs. Periwinkle added defensively, "Helga, I did everything you asked of me. I even—"

"Silence!"

We both jumped. Mrs. Lutzkraut regained her composure before continuing. "Rodney, I saw your friend Jessica in Garrettsville. She looked very happy. She was walking with some tall, handsome lad. I think he's a quarterback."

That one hurt. Mrs. Lutzkraut saw it on my face and her eyes twinkled. She stood up and walked over to the window. After a minute she motioned for me to join her. I glanced around nervously, but decided to do what she wanted.

"Rodney, look out there and tell me what you see."

I gazed out the large bay window. The fields and woods stretched out before us. The trees seemed to go on for miles. "Woods," I answered.

"That's right, Rodney. Woods. Deep, dark woods. Woods that can be a very perilous place for an unsuspecting young person . . ."

Still nuttier than a fruitcake, I thought to myself, remembering one of my dad's favorite expressions.

"There are no parents in the woods," she continued, "and no *Mr. Feebletops*." Her voice shook at the mention of my former principal, who had always been kind to me. "I want you to rest easy, though, Rodney. I want you to know that for the remainder of the summer, *I'll* be spending lots of time at Camp Wy-Mee. Do you know why?"

"Because they ran you out of Garrettsville?"

"No, smarty-pants. Because I own this camp with my sister and I want to make sure my former star student receives all the extra attention he deserves."

She gave me a gentle pat on the shoulder. Despite it being early August and close to 90 degrees, her touch turned my body to ice.

I was rather used to Mrs. Lutzkraut's veiled, evil threats, but this one made my heart miss a beat or two.

In the past, when I was a student in her class, I would return each afternoon to my nice, safe house. The fact that I was now in camp—a camp she apparently owned—made it a whole different ball game. Easily disguised disasters could befall me in a variety of ways, and with no parents for hundreds of miles, I was in deep . . .

EEEErrrrrrrrrrr!! I jumped as the screen door creaked open. Todd and Mr. Periwinkle walked in. "Where's my special visitor?" Todd demanded.

Mrs. Lutzkraut's whole look changed. A genuine smile replaced her snakelike expression, and she replied lightly, "Oh, your father is just out back. Hagatha, go tell Mr. Vanderdick that his son is here."

Mrs. Periwinkle went out the back door and Mr. Periwinkle began to follow. "Not so fast, Percy!" Mrs. Lutzkraut snapped. I looked over. Mr. Periwinkle had one foot out the door. "Now that I have you and Vanderdick in one place, we're going to finish this thing once and for all."

She seemed to have momentarily forgotten about Todd and me. I slid back into the shadows of the dining room, wondering what "this thing" was.

I didn't have to wait long. Mrs. Periwinkle returned, trailed by a man in a lime-green shirt, a blue belt with sailboats on it, and fancy-looking tan pants. I noticed that he was wearing leather shoes and pink socks. This had to be Mr. Vanderdick. He flashed a perfect smile as he engulfed Todd in a hug, his white teeth contrasting sharply with his dark, tan skin. Vanderdick released his son, peeled off his sunglasses, and turned to face the women in the room. "Helga, Hagatha, how are my two favorite sisters?"

Helga? It was the second time I'd heard Mrs. Lutz-kraut's first name, but now, slightly removed from immediate harm, I had time to think about it. The first syllable sure made sense to me.

Mr. Vanderdick continued, "Are we ready to become even richer?"

Mrs. Lutzkraut, smiling, answered, "We most certainly are."

Snap! Vanderdick's fingers made a crisp, sharp sound. The back door creaked open and three guys in dark suits walked in carrying brown briefcases. Was this part of "the thing" Mrs. Lutzkraut had mentioned? My curiosity was aroused. I slid behind a chair, figuring she'd kick me out of the house if she saw me.

"I brought all the final paperwork," Vanderdick announced proudly. "Three signatures and Camp Wy-Mee becomes Wy-Mee Estates. Over a hundred townhouses surrounding the lake, four hundred time-share units where the cabins now stand, an eighteen-hole golf course and clubhouse, and, of course, the Wy-Mee Mega Mall. It will be the flagship property of Vander-dick Global Enterprises."

"What about the Applebee's, Dad?"

"Yes, Todd, we will build an Applebee's."

So *that's* what Mrs. Lutzkraut had meant! Vanderdick was a developer, of course. The camp was going to be bull-dozed over for a mall and some dumb houses. I thought of all the spots I had come to love—the woods, Steve's shack, the campfire pit, the lakefront. I realized it would all be chopped up, carved up, and messed up. A feeling of disgust rippled along my skin as I looked around at the faces of the people prepared to do this thing. Mr. Vanderdick and Mrs. Lutzkraut were beaming. The lawyers looked serious and blank. Todd gazed at his dad as if he were some conquering hero. Mrs. Periwinkle smiled, but seemed nervous. I followed her glance.

Mr. Periwinkle's whole body seemed to be sagging to the floor. He hugged his pith helmet tight to his chest and his eyes held the look of someone learning about the death of a loved one. And as I thought about it, he was.

Mr. Vanderdick spread the papers on the coffee table and pulled a gold pen from his chest pocket. He said, "Your lawyers have gone over all the particulars. Here are the three places to sign. As fifty percent owner of Camp Wy-Mee, Helga, you sign here." He handed her the pen and she signed without even reading a word. "Now," Vanderdick continued, "Hagatha and Percy, since you jointly own the other fifty percent, I will need both of your signatures to make this complete."

Mrs. Lutzkraut stared at Mr. Periwinkle. "Percy, come over here and sign the paper."

"I can't do it," he whimpered.

"*Percy . . .*," Mrs. Lutzkraut growled in an icy tone. "We've gone over this a hundred times."

"I know, but I can't. I won't . . ."

Now it was Vanderdick's turn. "Listen, Percy, you know you're never going to get another offer like this. I bought up all the land surrounding the camp and I swear that I'll ruin the area for any other developer. Does the word *strip-mining* mean anything to you?"

Mrs. Lutzkraut took a step closer to her cowering brother-in-law and exploded. "You blithering idiot! Don't you realize how much money we could make? Millions and millions of dollars! And you're going to throw it all away over some trees and a frog or two? Why my sister married you I'll never know, and why my moron of a father gave you authority to block this deal I cannot imagine, but I will not have you ruin it!"

Mr. Periwinkle looked like he wanted to slide behind the chair with me, but he said again, "I won't sign the paper."

"AAAAAAAArrrrgghhhhhhhh!" Mrs. Lutzkraut was ready to rush at him. Then she turned to Vanderdick. "Isn't there some way we can still make this deal without him? I'll sell you my half right now."

"Helga, you know we can't. After your sister married Percy, your father specifically wrote it into the will that the camp could not be split up or sold without *everyone's* signatures. If you were to remarry, we would need *your* husband's signature as well."

I took a good look at Mrs. Lutzkraut and doubted they would ever need a fourth signature. Smoke seemed to shoot from her ears and nostrils. Then she screamed at her sister, "Why did you marry him? WHY?"

Mrs. Periwinkle looked confused and kind of sad. Her eyes went from her sister to Mr. Periwinkle. Before she had a chance to answer, Vanderdick motioned to the three guys in suits to leave. They immediately marched out the door in single file. In an instant, the fake smile vanished from Vanderdick's face and he turned toward Mr. Perwinkle. "Percy, when we went to Camp Wy-Mee together, I beat you in every competition. I beat you then and I'll beat you now. Some things never change, just like I know that Todd will be having his name carved in the totem pole as this year's canoe-race champion!"

"Well maybe this year the Cherokees will win!" Periwinkle snapped.

"Right. And maybe you'll grow a full head of hair!"

"That's it!" shouted Mr. Periwinkle, jamming the helmet onto his head and taking a step closer to Vanderdick. "You bullied me around all those years ago at camp, but I won't have you bully me in my own house. You want me to sign the papers? Fine, I'll sign them . . ."

A smile spread across Mrs. Lutzkraut's face.

"I will sign them," continued Mr. Periwinkle, "but under one condition . . ."

The room went silent. All eyes were on the man who, for the first time that day, was standing tall and proud. I almost shouted out, "What's the condition?" but I managed to keep my mouth shut.

"I will sign the agreement if, and only if, the Cherokees lose the end-of-summer canoe race."

I almost cheered this, but then I wondered what the canoe race was all about.

Mrs. Lutzkraut's smile snapped back to its usual sneer. "What's this nonsense you're mumbling about? Canoe race? We're talking about millions of dollars here and you're playing games."

Mr. Periwinkle turned and looked right at me. Mrs. Lutzkraut followed his gaze. Seeing me, she waved her hand at me in frustration. "I forgot you were here," she shouted. "It figures that this harebrained notion has something to do with you. What have you two cooked up?" I was curious, too. I had no idea how I had stumbled into the latest plot.

Mr. Periwinkle stepped forward. "Young Rodney here, and his Cherokee cabinmates, are my entrants in the canoe race. It's the oldest Camp Wy-Mee tradition. It dates back—"

"I know what it is, you nincompoop!" screamed Mrs. Lutzkraut. "My family's owned the camp for eighty years. I'm not basing millions on some camp competit—"

"If you want me to sign the agreement, you'll listen,

you . . . you . . ." He seemed to think better of finishing the sentence. He turned back to Vanderdick. "Rodney and his cabinmates will beat the Algonquin cabin. If Rodney's cabin wins, I don't have to sign the agreement and Camp Wy-Mee is left untouched—*and* you have to set up a land trust promising you won't develop any of the land adjoining Camp Wy-Mee you own. However, if the Algonquins win, I'll sign the papers. What do you say?"

I think you're crazy, I thought.

"I think you're crazy!" Lutzkraut yelled, actually scaring me, since it was the first time I had ever agreed with her. She continued, "You think I'm going to let Rodney Rathbone decide my fate? He cheats. He's a scoundrel. He's . . ."

"A loser," Todd interrupted.

"What?" Mrs. Lutzkraut asked, whirling around to face him.

"Look at him, the way he dresses, the way he acts, the kids he hangs out with. He's a born loser. The canoe race is a grueling two-day event. We'll have a blizzard in August before that kids beats me."

Mrs. Lutzkraut rubbed her chin. "Hmmmmmm."

"I am the camp's best canoer," Todd continued. "With Skip beside me, we'll win by ten miles. Mrs. Lutzkraut, Mrs. Periwinkle, Dad—the money is in the bag!"

Mr. Vanderdick puffed out his chest. The sisters looked thoughtful. I felt sick. Todd was right. There was no way I was going to win a canoe race.

"I won the canoe race three times when I was an Algonquin." Mr. Vanderdick laughed. "Remember, Percy? You were always so mad at us. How many years have the Algonquins won in a row?"

"Um, about twenty-two," Mr. Periwinkle said.

Todd looked up at his dad. "Soon to be twenty-three. No way we lose. We're going to pound that bunch of losers!"

"That's my boy," Vanderdick said, tousling his son's head. Then he pointed at me. "By the way, what cabin are you again?"

"Cherokee," I answered.

"Loserville?" Vanderdick laughed. I wanted to kick him in the shin. He looked over at Mr. Periwinkle. "No wonder you've got a soft spot for this kid. I seem to remember you were a permanent resident of Loserville. How many times, exactly, has that cabin won the canoe race?"

"Zero," Mr. Periwinkle said flatly.

The more I listened, the nuttier the whole thing sounded. Why was Periwinkle doing this?

Mr. Vanderdick looked down at his son and smiled. Then he said to Mrs. Periwinkle, "You know, this bet idea isn't so crazy. I don't see how we can lose. No way that runty kid beats my son. I'll have the lawyers put together a new agreement. You'll be counting your millions in no time."

"*Millions,*" she repeated dreamily.

"And now," Vanderdick announced, "it's time Todd and I got out there and enjoyed Secret Special Visitors Day!"

"Wait!" Mrs. Lutzkraut exclaimed. "You haven't tried my famous egg salad sandwiches yet."

As much as I hated Todd and his father, I almost screamed, "Run!" I remembered those putrid sandwiches from all the times I had to sit in her classroom during recess.

Vanderdick excused himself with a "Next time" and headed toward the door. Then he stopped dead in his tracks and put his hand to his ear. "Wait. What's that?"

I listened, but all I heard was the sound of kids in the distance shouting and having fun.

"What is it?" Mr. Periwinkle asked.

Vanderdick faced him with a big grin. "I thought I could already hear the bulldozers knocking down your forest!" With that, he and Todd burst out laughing and walked away under the midday sun.

"Why did you come up with that bet?" I asked Mr. Periwinkle as we headed down the hill to join the other campers. He had volunteered to be my Special Visitor after the mean trick played on me by Mrs. Lutzkraut.

"Well, Rodney, that's tough to answer, but maybe you'll understand when you're a bit older. You see, Todd's father and I go back a long way, and he has always thought himself much better than me. I guess I just got

165

sick of it back at the house and decided to challenge him. If you and the other Cherokees can win the race, it would be the greatest day in the history of Camp Wy-Mee."

"Yeah, and if we lose it will be the *last* day of Camp Wy-Mee."

We walked along in silence for a while and soon found ourselves by the old beech tree. "What he said was true, you know," Mr. Periwinkle continued. "I, too, was in the Cherokee cabin. I was your age, and they called us losers even then. Every year we would come up short, but this year we won't. This year, we have a secret weapon. This year, we have Rodney Rathbone— New York junior yachting champ! I know you never wanted to boast about it, but I overhead you earlier this summer . . . when you told that Tabitha girl at sign-up for expert sailing class."

Not knowing how to respond, I stared out at the pines and oaks and wondered what kind of desserts the new Applebee's would serve.

Chapter 20

MY LIPS ARE SEALED

The next morning after breakfast Mr. Periwinkle met my cabinmates and me down by the dock.

"Okay, boys," he began, "I suppose by now Rodney has filled you in on the canoe race and what's at stake." Everyone nodded. "Good. Now let me explain the race. Each boys' cabin has to put one canoe team into the event. That means twelve cabins will have a canoe in the race. Each year we have a winning team, but this year, even if we don't come in first, we have to finish ahead of the Algonquins."

"Who won last year?" Stinky asked.

"The Algonquins, but—"

"How about the year before that?" Thorin asked.

"The Algonquins. Now if—"

"How about the—"

"Look! They've won for the last twenty years or more. Let's not dwell on minor details, okay? Back to the race. It takes two days. You will canoe all day Saturday on the Drownalott River, camp out at Skull Rock, and finish the race on Sunday. The team that finishes first on Saturday will have a head start Sunday morning. If you finish ten minutes off the pace Saturday, you have to wait ten minutes Sunday morning. Make sense? Any questions so far?"

Josh raised his hand.

"Yes, Josh?"

"What's a canoe?"

No one answered. What could we say? I finally pointed to a canoe floating next to the dock. Josh walked over and examined it.

"That's a boat." He smiled proudly.

"A canoe *is* a boat," I explained.

Mr. Periwinkle shook his head from side to side. Eventually his gaze returned to the rest of us. "Where was I? Oh yes, the canoe always has two paddlers and a person sitting in the middle. I've given some thought to who should be on our team. Rodney, you're a no-brainer. We already know what kind of boatman you are. I assume a sailing champion can handle one of these?" My stomach tightened. Mr. Periwinkle scanned the lot of us. "Who else? Thorin, what do you know about being out on the water?"

Thorin stepped forward. "I know the Lady of the Lake rose from the waters and gave King Arthur"—he lifted both arms in the air for effect—"Excalibur!"

Mr. Periwinkle's smile lingered strangely for a

moment. "That's wonderful. Now, why don't you go stand over there?" He pointed inland, away from the dock. "Fernando, do you think you're up to the race?"

Fernando smiled and nodded. "Mr. Periwinkle, Fernando has many talents. Tell me, how many women will be at this . . . Skull Rock?"

Mr. Periwinkle gave a nervous giggle. "Maybe you could keep Thorin company." He looked at Stinky, who wasn't listening. His attention seemed occupied by whatever lay deep within his nose. Mr. Periwinkle flinched.

Josh was still staring at the canoe. Mr. Periwinkle walked over next to him and looked down. "Handling a canoe can be tough, my boy. Do you have any experience?"

Josh punched his fist into his palm. "I can handle anything tough."

"Can you paddle?"

Josh turned to him and practically yelled, "I can paddle, punch, bash, maul, crunch, punch, bash, punch, uhh, punch!"

"I think we've found our man." Mr. Periwinkle turned back to the rest of us. "This year, there's been a change of rule. You see, in order for Camp Wy-Mee to avoid a Title Nine lawsuit"—at the mention of the word *lawsuit* he gave a little shiver—"there must be a third person in the canoe. And that person must be one of the girls from camp."

Fernando left Thorin and hovered near Mr. Periwinkle with renewed attention.

Periwinkle continued, "I believe this is a distinct advantage for us. You see, I've noticed that one of you is quite gifted when it comes to courting young ladies . . ."

"Some call it a gift, some fools say it's a curse. I don't know why things are the way they are, but ever since Fernando was a little niño, I've—"

Mr. Periwinkle interrupted, "I'm sorry, Fernando, this is a busy week and the speeches will have to wait. As I was saying, young Rodney here holds the interest of a girl who knows boats and the water. You know who I'm referring to, right, Rodney?"

I knew, but after her comments at the cotillion dinner, I wasn't so sure I could count on Tabitha to join our team. I didn't say anything. Periwinkle added, "We need Tabitha and her boating skills, Rodney. With her on board, we'll have an excellent shot at winning. In fact, it's probably our best chance. Now, everyone, off to your next activity!"

The pressure was on—and it wasn't even nine thirty in the morning. This was going to be some day.

News of the race and the bet had traveled throughout the camp. Most people no longer saw us as the "losers." We, and especially yours truly, were the saviors of the forest, the defenders of the lake, and the knights of all things good. If I had wanted, I could have been carried around that week in an Adirondack chair or even a canoe. You'd think I would have enjoyed all the attention, but to be honest, there's nothing comforting about everyone depending on you when you know the truth—that you're only going to let them down.

Right after my meeting with Mr. Periwinkle, on my way to arts and crafts, was when I first noticed the attention. Countless people patted me on the back and wished me good luck. As I walked along, even the birds seemed to sing more and the insects bite less. I shrugged this off as some weird natural occurrence, but when the bushes bordering the soccer field said, "Beat those jerks, Rodney," my throat ran dry and I strongly considered a visit to the camp infirmary for a psych evaluation. Before I went, I remembered what my aunt had once told me: *Madness is no excuse for bad manners.* I answered, "Thank you, errr . . . Mr. Bush."

Survival Steve's head popped out from between the branches. "Mr. Bush? What are you going on about? Rodney, do you know that Vanderdick is planning to turn my shack into a Starbucks?"

I pictured a cappuccino machine with antlers.

"Are you listening, Rodney?"

"Sure."

"Well, I know quite a bit about canoes. Built one myself once."

"Did you make it out of moose skin and bear bones?"

"Nope, I used an advanced fiberglass polymer. I've

taken that canoe down the Snake River, the Mohawk River, the Rio Grande, and the Colorado. You bring your team down to the canoe beach tomorrow night and we'll work on your skills." His head dropped back into the bush.

After what seemed like a few hundred pats on the back and high-fives, I finally arrived at arts and crafts. I had just started the class the week before. Alison told me to sign up for it. While I loved going to art museums back in New York City with Aunt Evelyn and my parents, I wasn't the most skilled at putting together the little crafts projects Sunshine, the art counselor, had waiting for me. This didn't matter much, since Sunshine spent most of the time weaving flowers in her hair and smiling.

I sat down next to Alison, feeling stressed out. I definitely wasn't in the mood to be creative with so much riding on me. Alison looked like she wanted to talk. She was just opening her mouth when Sunshine stepped out of the shed—only it wasn't Sunshine.

"I don't believe it," I managed to utter.

"Believe it, mister," Mrs. Lutzkraut said. "I'm keeping a close eye on you and your inevitable mischief." She leaned down above me as she said it, and we held each other's gaze until the prolonged sight of her awful face made me queasy. I looked down and she announced, "Good morning, boys and girls. I'm afraid Sunshine has taken ill. My name is Mrs. Lutzkraut. I thought I'd fill in, as I have been a teacher for some years. Now, today you may make either a clay sculpture, or an architectural design out of Popsicle sticks. Rodney, after looking at last week's attempt at creating a mosaic, let me suggest you stick to clay."

Alison turned to me. "I heard all about the canoe race. I also heard you had to pick a girl to join you. So who are you picking?"

Alison, who was usually so calm and cool, looked unusually eager. I could see a problem looming. I began, "*Well . . .*"

"I just want you to understand that I know how important winning the race is, and I want you to know I'm ready."

"Um, are you a good canoer?" I asked, squeezing some clay.

"My grandpa has one in his garage."

"Have you ever been in it?"

"The garage?"

"No, the canoe!"

"Not really."

"How about another canoe?"

"No."

"A kayak?"

"No."

"A rowboat?"

"No."

"Have you ever been in a boat?"

"Of course, Rodney. My family took a Disney cruise last winter."

"You realize a cruise ship is a little bigger than a canoe, right?"

"Duh, Rodney. What's that got to do with anything?"

Why couldn't the girl I found myself liking more and more be the boating expert? I doubted asking Tabitha would help my relationship with Alison. In thinking of girl problems, I cringed as I remembered hanging up on Jessica the other night at the Periwinkles'. Nothing was going right.

"Can you swim at least?" I asked.

"Of course I can swim, Rodney. I even won a race at swimming last week."

Finally, some good news! Having a fast swimmer in the boat could be important. I felt more hopeful as I pictured her freestyling across the water. "What stroke did you use?"

"Doggy paddle."

"Uh, yeah. I missed that stroke in the last Olympics." My brief feeling of optimism left me like air rushing from a deflating balloon. "How about I talk it over with Josh and let you know later?"

She seemed to accept that. Happy to avoid continuing the conversation, I worked on my sculpture of a cobra and thought about all the mounting pressures facing me.

A little later Mrs. Lutzkraut strolled by. "Let's see what you've managed for us today, Rodney." I had rolled coils of clay together into a spiral to look like a snake getting ready to strike. "And what is that?" she asked.

"A snake."

"A snake? It looks like something my neighbor's dog

leaves on the lawn. For that revolting little creation you can clean up today's mess. Everyone else, off you go to your next activity."

The group dispersed. Alison lingered to help me but Mrs. Lutzkraut shooed her away. Under my old teacher's amused, evil eye, I scrambled to pick everything up. I jammed the Popsicle sticks and glue sticks into boxes to carry to the shed. One glue stick rolled off the table. As I bent down to get it, Mrs. Lutzkraut announced, "You know, Rodney, when we start building here we're going to make an exclusive private school for the Dry Lake Condo Community." She was sitting in a chair fanning herself. I stuck the glue stick in my pocket and turned to face her.

"What makes you think you're going to start building? This camp is staying just the way it is."

She ignored my comment and asked, "Do you think I should make myself principal of the new school? What would you think of that?"

"I've always thought you'd make an excellent warden," I answered, stuffing a pair of scissors back into their holster.

"That's right. Keep those fresh comments coming. I'm going to take enormous satisfaction the rest of my years knowing that my life's greatest victory—and most profitable moment—came with your defeat. This weekend will be such fun. I can hardly wait." She glanced at her watch. "I need to go meet with the architects. Off you go. Run along!"

She didn't need to tell me twice. Normally, I wouldn't be in a rush to get to my second activity with Cramps, but I knew Tabitha would be walking there too, and I needed to speak with her. I realized that this might mean an end with Alison, but I also knew Periwinkle was right. She was the most talented boater in camp. I scrambled along quickly, trying not to attract attention from my new fans.

I spotted her walking on the other side of the softball field in the direction of the volleyball courts, where Mr. Cramps awaited. I whistled. Her head turned and she started to make her way across the field toward me. Her long brown hair blew in the hot summer wind, and I felt a strong need to make a good impression. I pushed my hair down, smelled my breath, and felt around in my pocket for the lip balm stick my mom had packed. I pulled it out and rubbed it across my lips as Tabitha gave me a little wave.

It took a couple of minutes for us to meet in centerfield. She was the first to speak. "I thought I'd be hearing from you today," she said. "Did you know that Todd was waiting for me outside my cabin this morning? He asked me to join his canoe team."

I didn't like where this was going. I was worried. Was I already too late? I also began to worry about an odd tingling sensation on my lips.

She kept talking. "I told him I'd think about it, but the truth is, I'm not sure yet. So why'd you whistle? Do you have something to ask me?" Her smile told me I had a chance.

Well, she couldn't have made that any easier, I thought to myself. I went to open my mouth to invite her on the team, but I just couldn't do it. It wasn't that I had lost my nerve. My lips were actually sealed shut! "MMMM-MMmmmmmmmm!" was all I could utter.

"Mmmmmm? You're eating something tasty?" She looked confused.

"MMMMMMMM!" This time I waved my hands in the air and started jumping up and down.

Her face went from confused to angry. "How rude! I turned Todd down because I figured I would be on your team, and now you stand there acting like an ape."

"MMMmmmmMMMM." I pointed to my mouth. Then I grabbed my lips with my hands and pulled. They wouldn't budge.

Tabitha didn't wait while I struggled. She made a look of disgust and shouted, "You're a weirdo! What did I see in you? I'm joining Todd's team!"

My lips finally ripped open. The pain was immense. "Aaarrghhh!" I yelled. My eyes welled up with tears, making it difficult to see. The one thing I noticed was Tabitha moving away rapidly. That was bad enough, but I apparently had even worse things to deal with. What was wrong with me? Did I have lockjaw? I remembered the lip balm. What had my mom given me? I yanked it out of my pocket and read the label: OLD HORSE SUPER STRONG GLUE STICK.

I had grabbed it while cleaning up for Lutzkraut! There was no way she could have known—or could she? Either way, the outcome was the same. My team's odds of beating the Algonquins had now dropped from bad to impossible.

By the time dinner rolled around, I was feeling almost numb, like a prisoner resigned to his fate. The weekend's race would be a disaster, and I was on the way to my last meal. Two people waited for me by the dining hall entrance. Periwinkle spoke first. "Did you get her? Did you get Tabitha?" He looked eager, but at the mention of Tabitha's name, the other person frowned.

I looked over at Alison. Her beautiful eyes looked into mine and I suddenly felt happy. "I was lucky enough to get someone better," I explained.

"Really? Who?" Mr. Periwinkle asked.

"Mr. Periwinkle, this is Alison. She's completing the dream team."

Alison tried hard to conceal her smile, but you could tell it was just the news she was waiting for. "Thanks, captain," she whispered.

"Well, now, Alison," Mr. Periwinkle asked as he turned to enter the dining hall. "Tell me about your paddling experience."

"Actually," she answered proudly, "I just won a paddle race last week."

"Really?" Mr. Periwinkle clapped his hands together and beamed at me. "Well done, Rodney. I knew you'd come through!"

Chapter 21

A RAT ON THE
SHORE

Twelve aluminum canoes lined a sandy stretch along the bank of the Drownalott River. Each team, along with the Periwinkles, Mrs. Lutzkraut, Survival Steve, Mr. Cramps, a host of other camp personnel, and a few random campers, had made the long van trek to the starting point of the big race. The day was hot, which added to the tension that hung over the gathering.

Mr. Periwinkle adjusted his pith helmet. "We're all set to start the race. You know the rules. Today you will paddle for ten miles to Skull Rock. You'll spend the night there. Along the way, Mrs. Periwinkle and I will watch you from various checkpoints, which are accessible by Jeep. Mr. Cramps will be in the Zodiac motor boat and Steve will be in his own canoe . . . in case you need assistance out on the water."

I didn't like the sound of that and wondered what kind of assistance we might need. I didn't like any of this.

A couple of months ago I had never even heard of Camp Wy-Mee. Now its fate rested on my shoulders, all because Mrs. Lutzkraut was prepared to stop at nothing to get rich. She stood behind Mr. Periwinkle, looking in my direction. I couldn't tell if she was frowning or smiling. All I knew was that she was up to something. But what?

Mr. Periwinkle continued. "At Skull Rock we will record your time and start you accordingly tomorrow morning for the final leg of the race . . . "

He went on blabbing about the rules and I found myself zoning out, like I did in school. I looked off into the woods. I wasn't the only one not paying attention. Woo appeared to be singing with several frogs. He saw me and shouted, "They're doing bebop!" As usual I didn't know what he was saying and just smiled. He turned back to the frogs and yelled, "Go, man, go!"

"Rodney, please pay attention," Mr. Periwinkle scolded. "As you might imagine, this is all very impor- tant. Now, tonight we will have a cookout, and then we'll split into two groups. The boys will be sleeping in an area with me, Mr. Cramps, and Steve, and Mrs. Lutzkraut and Mrs. Periwinkle will be camping with the girls. Your sleeping gear and tents have already been delivered to the site. The food will be dropped off later."

Under other circumstances, the race actually sounded like a great time. Too bad there was so much riding on it.

"Okay, does anyone have any questions?"

Antsy to get started, I prayed no one did. Unfortunately,

Skip raised his hand. He was standing next to his big jerk canoe partner, Todd. "Mr. Periwinkle?" he began.

"Yes, Skip?"

"I, um, I . . ." Suddenly he grabbed his stomach and fell to the floor.

"Oh no, what's the matter?" Mrs. Lutzkraut yelled, rushing over to the Algonquin canoe. "What is it, son?"

Son? I had never heard her speak nicely to anyone. Something was up. Skip rolled around on the ground holding his stomach. Todd leaned over him. "It's his stomach, Mr. Periwinkle. There is no way he can race. We'll need a substitute canoer."

"How dreadful," Mrs. Lutzkraut said, but a look on her face—combined with some pretty poor acting by Skip and Todd—told me this was all fake. "Todd," she asked, "do you have anyone in mind to replace Skip?"

"Well, now that you mention it, what about . . . hmmm . . . Magnus?"

Mr. Periwinkle jumped in. "Hold on a minute, this is a camper race. Magnus is a counselor. He's twice your size. He's not allowed to participate."

"Percy," Mrs. Lutzkraut observed, "I see you haven't consulted the rules. They clearly state counselors are allowed to race."

"Helga, the rules don't say that. They—"

Mrs. Lutzkraut yanked a book from her purse and thrust it at Mr. Periwinkle. "It says so right here on page forty-three."

Mr. Periwinkle looked. "This is nothing. The rules have been crossed out and someone wrote new ones in pencil. They've been changed . . ."

"Changed by me, as camp director!" she snapped. "I am majority owner, and I feel it's much safer to have some counselors out on the water. If you're worried about fairness, you may certainly replace Joshua or Rodney with Woo."

Everyone turned to look at Woo. He was still hunched over the frogs, singing. Mr. Periwinkle bit his lip.

Magnus spoke up next. "Goot ting I just happen to have my paddle." He pulled out a cello case from the back of a van. Was he going to join Woo in a duet? He set the case on the ground and I leaned forward to watch. He clicked open the clasps and lifted the lid. A shiny, dark, wooden paddle lay surrounded by purple velvet. "Dis beauty helped me win the Scandinavian Rafting Championship on the Sjoa River three years in a row."

Mrs. Lutzkraut acted surprised. "A rafting champion? Who would have guessed? My, Percy, you've really recruited a talented staff this year."

Mr. Periwinkle didn't respond. Instead, he gathered Alison, Josh, and me to the side. His face looked very tense, and I understood why. Todd and Tabitha were already heavy favorites. Adding a Scandinavian rafting champ made them unbeatable.

He swallowed hard and cleared his throat. I could tell a big speech was coming. "Okay, this is it," he began.

"It's time. Remember, they're bigger than you. They're faster and more experienced. They've canoed longer and they fight dirtier . . ."

If he's trying to build our confidence, he's going about it in a weird way, I thought.

". . . Not one Cherokee team has ever won, and the Algonquins almost never lose. Right now, Vegas has you listed as a thousand-to-one underdog . . ."

Now that Magnus was in their canoe, that didn't seem high enough.

". . . Furthermore, if you don't win, everything will be destroyed. All these trees you see in every direction will be cut down. All the animals will die. The world will be one step closer to global warming and ruin. Simply put, this is the most important canoe race in the history of mankind." His eyes looked wet and his skin was changing color, but then he exhaled and seemed to gather himself a little. "Anyway, the important thing is to have fun!" He gave us each a pat on the back and walked off into the woods, where he hugged a tree and collapsed.

"Well, that certainly made me feel a lot better," I said to Alison.

"Yeah, real inspiring."

"Okay, racers, into your boats!" Mrs. Lutzkraut called. She was holding a cap gun and was ready to start the race.

If canoes had names, ours should have been the

S.S. Impossible! Josh, Alison, and I climbed in. We were about to embark on the most important canoe race in the history of mankind . . . or something like that.

Satisfied that she had everyone's attention, Mrs. Lutzkraut shouted, "Get on your mark. Get set. Go!" She fired her cap gun. Maybe it was just my imagination, but I think it was pointed right at me.

We pushed the canoe out into the water. The sand made a grating noise as it scraped the bottom of the aluminum. We banged into other canoes and paddles as we jostled to get out into the river.

Josh sat in the front, swinging his paddle wildly. I couldn't be sure if he was trying to whack a turtle or clobber Todd, but either way Tabitha was getting splashed and screaming at him from the Algonquin boat. This had Alison laughing, and I would have joined her but Mr. Periwinkle's encouraging words, "Everything will die," echoed in my ears. I yelled, "Josh, start paddling!"

He looked back at me with a vague expression.

"Remember what Steve showed you?" As I said this I mimicked the basic pull with my paddle and Josh slowly began to nod. I nodded, too, as encouragement. Josh's paddle dipped into the water and off we went.

Once he got the hang of it, it didn't take long for us to find a rhythm. Alison sat in the middle of the canoe on the floor. The middle person doesn't paddle but can usually switch when one of the two paddlers gets tired. The rear of the canoe, where I sat, is reserved for the person who does the steering. And while I may never become a sailor, I took to canoeing fairly quickly. True to his promise, Survival Steve had spent the past few days working with us on a variety of paddle strokes and techniques. Josh, on the other hand, learned only one. He could paddle the basic front pull stroke—but that was enough. His tremendous strength made this one basic paddle stroke long and swift.

I felt him pull us along. I dug deep in the water, also pulling hard, and I kept us going straight down the middle of the river.

It wasn't long before ten canoes fell back behind us, which was encouraging but not good enough. It was the eleventh canoe that mattered. I glanced over at it. Todd was in the front, pulling long, even strokes. While he wasn't able to rival Josh's power, it was obvious he knew what he was doing. And then there was Magnus. It was easy to believe he had won those championships. Being a big, full-grown counselor, he had every bit of Josh's strength. As I watched his fancy paddle caress the surface of the water, I realized that he also possessed all of Steve's expertise. Tabitha sat in the middle and occasionally gave me a nasty look.

For over an hour we battled hard, grunting from the strain. I couldn't help notice that Todd and Magnus seemed to be struggling, too. Catching my eye, Todd yelled, "Give it up, Rathbone!" I ignored him but he continued. "Guess what? With the profits from the construction, my dad's getting me a Ferrari."

Tabitha almost fell out of the canoe. "Really, Toddy? Your own Ferrari? Will it be red?"

"Sure," he answered, smirking back at me. I wished I had some snappy reply but my mouth was dry from breathing hard, and as much as it disgusted me, I knew Tabitha would look good in the front seat of a Ferrari. Besides, what could I offer her? A ride in my father's old Honda?

We were beginning to fall back. My shoulders and back burned and I fought off annoying thoughts of Todd and Tabitha zooming by in a red sports car. I eyed the back of Alison's head. Why couldn't she be some big Scandinavian canoe girl who could give me a few minutes rest? All Alison ever managed to do when we practiced was drop the paddle overboard and scream. Really, other than making the canoe heavier, she wasn't doing anything. She was, as Survival Steve had put it, dead weight.

Then she turned back to me. Her red hair spun out over the water as she turned. I could see her brown eyes through her sunglasses, and I thought, *That's the prettiest dead weight I've ever seen. . . .* She smiled and said, "Keep going, you're doing great. Did I ever tell you that you look cute canoeing?"

"Thanks," Josh grunted.

Alison and I both laughed. I shrugged off my previous feelings. I felt happy she was with us, and the Ferrari thoughts didn't bother me much after that.

What bothered me was the fact that, try as we might, we couldn't keep pace with Todd and Magnus.

And then we came around a bend and caught our first break.

Several yellow ropes were tied across the river. A big red sign stated: DANGER. WATERFALL. PORTAGE TO RIGHT. A portage meant we had to paddle to the side and carry our canoe on land for a while. If you ignored the sign and somehow pushed under the ropes, a twenty-foot drop and probable death awaited you. I figured if we couldn't beat them on the water, maybe we could pass them on land.

Todd reached the bank first. We were about ten yards behind. The three of us jumped out, pulled the canoe high up on the bank, rolled it over, and hoisted it over our heads.

They say aluminum is a wonder metal because it is strong and light. It wasn't long, however, before the wonderful lightness faded and my arms and shoulders began to burn from the strain of constant lifting without a break. Alison, to her credit, held up the middle of the canoe and grunted right along with us. To carry a canoe any distance, you have to put it over your head and hold it shoulder-height as you walk along. Our heads would occasionally crack against the inside of the canoe. Having your head stuck within a canoe makes vision difficult, and right away we were stumbling and going off course.

But that wasn't the worst part. Unfortunately, half the

mosquitoes in Ohio suddenly decided to pay us a visit.

They announced their assault with their famous, high-pitched, "Eeeeeeeeeeee" noise. One of them circled my head and bounced off my forehead and neck. Then it landed on the tip of my nose. It sat there for a second, looking me in the eye. I went cross-eyed returning the stare. I'm sure it was my imagination, but it seemed to be smiling, and then . . . *chomp*. I felt the little sting, and even worse, I saw all of the little vampire's friends zooming in under the canoe's metal edge to join the fun.

The attack was on—and it was a one-sided battle. If I used my hand to whack them, I'd drop the canoe on my skull. It wasn't long before all three of us were cursing and whining. The mosquitoes, realizing their victims were helpless, charged with greater ferocity. I tried shaking my head, or blowing hard puffs of air at them, but nothing worked. I was close to going insane.

In the end, it was Alison who saved us. "Boys, I'm going to let go. The load will get heavier but I'll squash the mosquitoes!" She let go and started slapping us.

"Slap harder!" I yelled. "Get the one on my neck!"

"And my legs," Josh called out.

After about two minutes of Alison waving her arms and slapping us silly, the bites slowed and my sanity returned.

Not everyone, however, had found relief. From up ahead we heard Magnus shout, "Deese bugs drive me crazy!" followed by a large BOOM. We paused and lifted the canoe higher to see. The Algonquin canoe had fallen, rolled down a hill, and gotten wedged between two boulders. Magnus was jumping around and scratching at his face.

"The canoe!" Todd shouted. "We have to get it!"

"Deese bugs! No bugs like deese in da fjords!" Magnus tore off toward the river.

With Alison managing our bug problem, this was our chance to pull ahead. We hurried past our Algonquin enemies and I caught a glimpse of Magnus plunging his head underwater. Tabitha was whining about a broken fingernail and Todd was busy trying to remove a mud stain from his shirt. They definitely appeared to be a defeated team.

We reached the riverbank below the waterfall and resumed the race. Once underway, I looked back. Their canoe was stuck in an awkward spot and Tabitha and Todd were struggling to get Magnus out of the river.

The lead was now ours. Alison turned to me from her spot in the middle and yelled, "It would take a miracle for them to catch up to us today!" You could see she was happy and proud. I smiled back, but it was only for her benefit. She had never spent an entire school year in Mrs. Lutzkraut's class. I knew it was only a matter of time before our luck changed.

We were still paddling hard, but slower and more consistently. It had been an hour since we left the Alqonguins.

The Drownalott River had lots of twists and turns. There was no way of knowing how far ahead we were or how much time the Algonquins had lost trying to free their canoe. Alison, who was proving her worth again and again, spotted Mr. and Mrs. Periwinkle on the side of the river.

Mr. Periwinkle was running and jumping along the bank. "You have the lead! Way to go! Only two miles left to Skull Rock. Wa-hoo!" Josh and Alison waved at him and cheered back.

I didn't join them. I was watching the opposite bank. Mrs. Lutzkraut had emerged from behind a boulder. She had her hands on a walkie-talkie and I could see her mouth moving a mile a minute. I noticed a large bag of some kind by her side. She caught my gaze. I had hoped to see panic in her eyes, but they held an evil confidence that shook me.

"Paddle faster!" I hollered.

The canoe wobbled as Josh's thrusts increased. I knew something was about to happen. I could just feel it. I looked around. The river was calm. Bugs danced on the surface of the water. Maybe I was wrong. Maybe nothing bad was coming.

And then I heard it.

Vrrooooom! It was a motor and it was gaining on us. I looked back at a bend in the river just in time to see a rubber motorboat zooming our way. Cramps! I knew he'd be making an appearance. His comb-over flapped in the wind like a weird pirate flag as he bore down on us. Would he actually ram us? I didn't think he would go that far, but I also knew who we were up against. Lutzkraut and her henchmen were determined to win at any cost.

Josh turned back and smiled. "Cool!"

"No, Josh," I shouted. "Definitely not cool."

Cramps was about to smash us but veered to the right at the last second, sending a huge wake over the bow of the canoe and knocking Josh back onto Alison. The canoe rocked violently. I had to lean in and balance to keep it from going over.

"Did I get you kids wet?" Cramps yelled with an evil smile. "Gee, that's too bad. Don't tell your mommies." He gave a little laugh and zoomed away up the river.

Alison was sitting in six inches of water. "Forget about him," she suggested. "Let's keep going. You two paddle and I'll bail out the water."

We resumed paddling, but with the added water the boat was heavier and harder to move. Fortunately, like some big plow horse, Josh didn't seem to notice and never tired. He kept pulling us along.

Was that the best Lutzkraut could do? I wondered. It would take more than a little wave to stop me from saving Camp Wy-Mee. I could feel confidence filling my chest. I was beginning to wonder whether Todd, Magnus, and Tabitha had even gotten their canoe free from the boulders.

"Look!" Alison screamed. She was pointing in back of me. My confidence turned to indigestion as I whirled around, half expecting to see Lutzkraut bearing down on us in a gunboat.

The reality was almost as bad. Coming around the bend was Todd's pink shirt and perfect hair. Seeing me look back, he and Tabitha gave little waves.

Alison bailed faster, and Josh and I dug in for more frantic pulling. Already I could feel blisters forming on my hands. My back and shoulders and arms and, well, everywhere ached. We still led by more than a hundred yards, but despite all our effort, the lead had dwindled. I couldn't believe how fast they were gaining—and yet they hardly seemed to be paddling.

"There's Skull Rock!" Alison yelled, pointing ahead. She was right, and I immediately saw why they called it that. An ancient rock the size of a house stuck out from a cliff above the river. It looked just like a human skull. Below it, tents dotted the shore. My stomach did a nervous flip as I realized that this is where we would be spending the night.

"Eat our wake, losers!" Todd yelled. I jumped and nearly tipped the canoe. How could they be right next to us already? Magnus and Tabitha weren't even paddling! They were busy lifting something into a duffel bag.

"What's in the bag?" I called over to Tabitha, trying to regain my calm. I wanted to act like I was unconcerned that they had overtaken us.

"Suddenly you remember how to talk?" she sneered, zipping the bag shut. It was then that I realized I had seen the bag before. I was sure it was the one I had seen Mrs. Lutzkraut carrying earlier.

I was about to ask, when Magnus gripped his paddle and swung it over his head like a deranged Viking. "Yaaa!" he roared, smashing it onto the water's surface. A great splash shot our way and hit me in my open mouth. I spit out the river water.

As they pulled away, Todd yelled back, "Hey, Rathbone, you really did eat our wake. What a loser!"

I could only gape, dumbfounded. The three of them didn't even look tired. For a few seconds, Josh, Alison, and I stared blankly. This was nothing new for Josh, of course, but Alison and I were coming to the same conclusion. We had somehow lost the day's competition.

"Come on, let's get to camp," she said sadly.

Exhausted, we continued the rest of the way in silence, finally paddling up to Skull Rock a full four minutes behind the Algonquin canoe. With our big lead lost, it was doubtful we could catch them tomorrow. In fact, it was looking doubtful that anyone but construction workers would be visiting Camp Wy-Mee next summer.

Chapter 22

SKULL ROCK

I climbed from the canoe with Skull Rock staring down at me through the darkening sky. Just seconds before, out on the water, I had been upset about losing the lead to Todd and Magnus. Now, as I looked around at the clearing of dirt between the river and the creepy woods, a different fear gripped me. I would be spending the night in a tent in the middle of nowhere surrounded by some of my worst enemies. If the bears didn't get me, Todd would.

"Hey, Josh, great paddling back there," I said, making sure to stay close by his side.

"Uhhh, thanks," he answered. "Look." He was gazing proudly at a beetle he had just squished on a rock.

Alison shook her head. "Gross. Come on, guys, let's join the others."

The three of us wandered toward the clearing. I was happy to see Survival Steve's white van parked back in the bushes next to an overgrown dirt road. Mr. Periwinkle met me. "What happened out there? You had the lead."

I shrugged. My mind still couldn't make sense of how the other canoe passed us so quickly.

Periwinkle looked glum. All he said was, "Your gear is leaning against the van. Set up your tent and start gathering firewood. You don't want to be out here in the dark without a tent or a fire." His tone suggested that he really meant it, and I didn't wait around to be told again.

For the next hour I sat on the ground, trying to figure out the tent instructions. After finally assembling what looked like a sagging hot air balloon with poles sticking out, I headed into the woods to gather twigs and branches. I made sure not to go too far. The last thing I needed was to get lost again, like on the way up to Camp Wy-Mee.

I made several trips, and each time I returned to camp I noticed that another canoe team had arrived. It felt better with more people there, but it was still pretty scary, and getting dark real fast. The large stones and boulders at the bottom of Skull Rock formed a sinister smile that seemed to grin right at me. This was going to be a long night.

I decided to head back into the forest for one final haul of firewood. This time, I had to walk further in to find any. It was almost night now and I began to feel that maybe I had wandered off too far. When a wild animal started shrieking across the river, I spun around to head back to Josh and Alison. I hadn't gotten very far when

I bumped into two people, but not the two I wanted.

"Woot have we here?" Magnus asked.

"Is that you, Rathbone?" Todd demanded, peering at me through the dark. "You shouldn't be out this far all alone. Legend has it Skull Rock is cursed." I wasn't going to argue with him on that one. I tried to walk past but he stopped me with a shove to the shoulder. "What's the rush?" He leaned in closer. This wasn't good. Todd was pumped up, toughness no doubt coming easier with Magnus standing behind him. "Upset you're going to lose the race?"

"Like he ever hood a chance," Magnus gloated.

Todd laughed. "Come out here to cry, Rathbone?"

They couldn't see my face in the dark, and it was a good thing, too. I actually *did* feel a little teary. I was wishing I was back home in my bed instead of standing in these scary woods with two idiots. My home, and even Camp Wy-Mee, seemed like a world away.

Fortunately, my focus shifted from fright-inspired homesickness to the matter at hand. Knowing something awful was about to happen, and knowing my shaking chicken knees were going to give me away, I came up with a brilliant escape plan.

"Your shoes are untied." I pointed to their feet. I knew such an old and obvious trick didn't stand a chance, but I was desperate.

CLUNK!

I was so shocked to see their two heads bang together

that I almost didn't run. As the echo began to fade, my feet kicked into gear and I slipped through several bushes and dodged in and out of the trees.

Magnus boomed after me, "Nice try, but you can't trick ooos."

Under other circumstances I might have stopped and pointed out that I *had* just tricked them, but I kept moving.

"We'll get you later, Rathbone!" Todd yelled. "Better not leave the fire and your buddy Josh."

I ran straight through the woods until I emerged in the clearing. Steve was crouching over the fire ring, a few small flames dancing on the kindling. Everyone was crowded around him. No doubt the creepy surroundings were affecting them, too. I joined Mr. Periwinkle, Alison, and Josh.

"Look at you, Rodney," Alison said. "You look like you've just seen a ghost."

"He probably did," Steve replied, cracking a branch over his knee. "Plenty of ghosts out here by Skull Rock. There was a massacre here during the French and Indian War."

Mr. Periwinkle shivered more than me. "Remind me," he asked Steve, "why we have to camp here every year?"

Steve smiled. "What could be better than skulls and ghosts? Now *that's* camping. Besides, it's accessible by dirt road, has a nice clearing to set up tents and build a fire, is halfway between the starting point and camp, has a gentle, sloping bank for the canoes . . ."

"Okay, we get it," Mr. Periwinkle muttered impatiently. "Just hurry with that fire."

"I reckon it's going now. Anyway, Perce, when's dinner?"

"I'm not sure. Helga was taking care of the food."

For the first time I noticed Mrs. Lutzkraut. She was standing beneath a dead pine tree. Seeing her face hovering in the dim light was worse than staring at Skull Rock. From her spot, she snipped, "I'll have all of you know that Mr. Vanderdick personally offered to bring in the best steaks money can buy."

Mr. Periwinkle rubbed his hands together. "I can't wait."

"Well, keep waiting," Lutzkraut ordered her brother-in-law. "You and most of this mob are getting franks 'n' beans. The steaks are for today's first-place finishers."

I watched Magnus and Todd emerge from the woods and high-five each other. "Awesome." Todd beamed. Then he walked right over to me and whispered, "We'll get you later."

I pretended I didn't hear him and tried to keep my mind on the food situation. To be honest, I didn't share Periwinkle's disappointment. At that point, after a hard day on the water, I was real hungry and franks 'n' beans didn't sound bad at all. Spending the night in a tent with Josh after he ate several bowls of beans—well, that would be another matter.

Half an hour later the fire had grown large and strong and I was glad I had gathered so much wood. My fellow campers and I had to slide back from the heat. It was a good campfire, but everyone was beginning to grumble. Vanderdick hadn't shown up yet.

Thirty minutes became forty. Then an hour passed, and I could hear stomachs growling in tune with the loud August bugs. *He's not coming*, I thought. *We're out here in the middle of nowhere.* Somehow, hunger made the whole place more dismal and frightening. I looked off into the trees. What was lurking in there? I peered into the blackness where the river should be. Was someone or something out there watching us? Ready to attack us as soon as the fire died down? I kept telling myself that as long as Steve was around, we'd be fine.

"I'm starving!" Tabitha moaned.

Mr. Periwinkle turned back to Mrs. Lutzkraut. "Well, where is he? He should have been here ages ago."

Taken by surprise, Mrs. Lutzkraut appeared to shove into her mouth something that looked a lot like a chocolate bar.

"Are you eating?" Mr. Periwinkle asked.

"Mmm, no, mm, I just had a tickle in my throat. It's the night air." She wiped her mouth on her sleeve. "I tried calling, but there's no cell service. I'm sure he'll be here soon."

"I doubt it," Steve said. "Only a crazy person would

try driving that road at night. Looks like dinner's on me."

He walked over to the van, reached in the back, and pulled out what looked like a bow and arrow. Josh's eyes almost popped out of his head. "Can I come with you?"

Steve seemed to think it over for a moment before answering, "Sure. Just keep real quiet."

The two of them were heading toward the woods below Skull Rock when Mr. Periwinkle whimpered, "Steeeve. We can make it one night without food. You two better not go out there." Clearly he shared my feelings about Steve—and even Josh—sticking around.

Steve laughed. "No worries, Perce. These here woods are a virtual supermarket. We'll have dinner in a jiff." And in a jiff, they disappeared into the dark.

Once they were gone the woods seemed to close in on us. The night noises grew louder and we huddled closer together. I had to pee, but there was no way I was leaving the fire. Not yet, at least.

The various small conversations that were already thin and forced died. Even Tabitha stopped complaining to Todd about his father. For the past hour she had been making nasty little comments, like, "Your dad's probably still at the country club," or "Don't those fancy cars he drives have navigation devices?" Evidently, you didn't want to be around Tabitha when she was hungry.

While we humans had fallen silent, the night was far from quiet. There were the usual insect sounds, but there were also strange and chilling hooting noises.

From across the river I could still hear that animal screeching, like it was being murdered. Sometimes I thought I heard voices, and laughter, and crying . . . all shifting around in the dark. I was so hungry and tired from canoeing that I was beginning to hallucinate. I closed my eyes and imagined I heard a roaring sound like a waterfall. It was quiet at first, but it grew and grew, till soon its roar was drowning out all other sounds.

I opened my eyes and was shocked to see that every face around the fire was on the verge of panic. Something terrible really *was* out there. It sounded like a hundred motors approaching. Was it a pack of maniacs with chainsaws?

Lights burst down from the skull's eye sockets. Everyone screamed. Several campers ran off. I was frozen in fear.

The lights grew brighter and I could tell they were reflections from the road. At once I knew what was coming. Bikers! Steve had said only crazy people would drive out here at night. What kind of crazies were coming on motorcycles?

Out of a dark dust cloud the motorcycles rumbled past the van and into the clearing. I counted six grizzly-looking guys on Harleys. As I got a better look at their horned helmets and bushy beards, any glimmer of hope that they were trucking in Vanderdick's dinner for a bunch of scared and hungry campers vanished.

They rode around in a circle, herding us closer to

the fire. The revving engines roared like savage demons, and I could barely hear the people screaming around me. One thought eclipsed all others in my mind: *I should have peed when I had a chance.*

To her credit, the only person trying to combat the bikers was Mrs. Lutzkraut. She swatted at them with her purse and howled, "Scat, you ruffians!"

After several minutes of chaos and terror, they parked their bikes and turned off the engines. The cloud settled and they walked toward us. One of them stepped out before the others. He was big and frightening, with a bushy orange mustache that hung down way below his chin. He frowned, rolled his head from side to side, and shouted, "What d'you think you're doing? You're on our family's land! I'm givin' you two minutes to pack your crap and get out of here!" The other five bikers approached us with nasty smiles and dark, red eyes.

"We'll do no such thing!" Mrs. Lutzkraut yelled. "You boys are in big trouble! I'll have each of you arrested! Isn't that right, Percy?"

A bush by the edge of the woods answered, "Let's not be rash, Helga."

Ignoring the bush, one of the bikers approached Mrs. Lutzkraut. "I like my women old and feisty!" He had bad teeth and an enormous belly. He gave her a wink.

Mrs. Lutzkraut snapped, "How *dare* you? In the

public schools I've dealt with much worse than you, and I will not have—"

The leader with the long orange mustache snapped his finger in front of her face. "You ain't never dealt with the Ratfields, lady. Your chatter is givin' me a headache. One more word out of you and I'm going to toss you in the river."

While the thought of her flying into the river was oddly appealing, I was concentrating on something the biker had said. I got closer to get a better view of his face.

By now the other bikers were cracking open beer cans and yelling and laughing and scaring everyone. One of them was acting like a dog and barking at the crowd. All the while I angled over toward the leader, who stood watching his friends with his hands on his hips and a smile curled over his teeth. Suddenly one of the bikers grabbed a burning stick from the fire and started waving it around at the terrified campers.

"Todd, can't you do something?" Tabitha whispered.

Todd, who was crouching behind a shaking Magnus, had his eyes shut tight and didn't even answer.

I stepped forward and in my loudest voice declared, "*I'll* take care of this."

"Oh, thank goodness!" blurted the bush.

"Rodney, what could you possibly do?" Alison asked.

"Be careful," Tabitha added.

I didn't answer. I swung around, came up beside the

leader, and bumped his elbow. He looked down at me. I watched his smile turn to a sneer. If my plan worked, I wouldn't have to worry about Todd and Magnus or anything else. If it failed, I was about to take my last breath on this planet.

Before the biker could say anything, I stuck my right thumb up my nose and wiggled the rest of my fingers while waving my elbow up and down.

"He's gone nuts!" Mrs. Lutzkraut exclaimed.

The biker leader squinted his eyes and stared down at me. "What the . . . ? How do you know . . . ?"

"Don't you remember?" I whispered. "T-Bone, you taught it to me."

His eyes focused and they seemed to soften as he recognized me. "Ratbone? Holy smokes. I gotta tell the boys that the kid who took out the McThuggs is right here."

Even though I doubted the other campers could hear us over the crackling fire, I whispered, "Wait, T-Bone. I need a favor first. Can you just go along with whatever I say?"

He looked a bit suspicious and glanced at Lutzkraut. "You ain't gonna make me kiss the old witch, are you?"

"No, nothing that bad. Just make it like you're scared of me when I start yelling."

"Okay."

I took a step away from him and shouted, "*What* did you say? What did you call me? Do you know who you're dealing with?"

"Uh, sorry, kid. I didn't mean any disrespect."

I couldn't tell who was more shocked—the biker gang or my fellow campers.

"Sorry won't cut it!" I continued while crunching my puny knuckles. "You're coming with me. And tell your little friends to stay put and behave!"

"You're pushing it," he whispered. Then, turning to his gang, he yelled, "Hang back. Give us five."

We walked off about twenty feet into the dark and came out in a spot next to the river. "Thanks, T-Bone. Guess I got a bit carried away."

He laughed. "Ratbone, we take care of our own. By the way, what you did to the McThuggs was the talk of this year's Sturgis Motorcycle Rally—and I haven't heard a peep from J.D. and his boys in almost a year."

Back in Garrettsville, where I live, I had kind of accidentally attacked a rival biker family with a bee-hive. It's a long story, but T-Bone had tracked me down once to thank me and made me an honorary member of his family, the Ratfields. That's when he showed me the secret handshake where you stick your thumb up your nose.

"So what you wanna talk about?"

"Well, I'm in this canoe race . . ."

"That sounds cool."

"It isn't." I explained all about the race and Lutz-kraut and Vanderdick's plans for the property.

He listened and when I finished he asked, "They're going to cut down all my woods?"

I nodded.

"And build a Starbucks?"

"Yes."

"Those *are* bad people."

I nodded again.

"Well, you better win that race."

"We're already losing by over four minutes." I told him how Todd and Magnus had passed us on the river.

"They went right by you?"

"Yeah."

"What did they have in the boat with them?"

"Nothing. Just this girl Tabitha and a red duffel bag."

"What's in the bag?"

"I don't know, but I wanted to talk to you, because maybe if you ruined the race, then they wouldn't win."

He looked at me. "How would we do that? No, we can't ruin the race. If we did anything that crazy lady down there really would have us arrested." I must have looked disappointed. "But maybe I *could* help you win it."

"Really? How?" I asked.

"My family's been in these parts for years. Most people don't know about the Moonshine Canal. My great-grandpappy Rat Ratfield dug it out with his boys back in the twenties. It's a shortcut. You see, downriver, the Drownalott winds all over the place for a spell.

Moonshine Canal cuts straight through the backwoods and joins up with the river after a mile. You'll save lots of time . . . although no one really goes back in there anymore. Trust me, you don't want to meet up with any of the locals."

"Huh?"

"Never mind that. I'll tell you how to get in there. It's hidden." We talked for another couple of minutes and he told me how to find it. Then he said, "Best be getting back to the others. So, we good?"

"Uh, yeah, but could you do me one final favor?"

A minute later the kids and counselors around the fire saw the head of the biker gang come charging up from the river. "Boys, get on your bikes and ride!" he shouted frantically. "Rodney Rathbone is madder than a drunk mule and coming this way!"

They looked at him slightly confused.

"Move it or lose it!" He jumped on his motorcycle. The other bikers—seeing the biggest and baddest Ratfield take off like that—must have figured something awful was approaching, for they soon dropped what they were doing, jumped on their bikes, and rumbled off.

I ran out of the bushes with fists clenched yelling, "Where are they?"

Periwinkle emerged from his hiding spot. "You scared them off? I mean, you scared them off! Good old Rodney."

I ignored him. Instead I yelled, "I'm fired up! If I can't get my hands on those bikers, where's Todd and Magnus?" I spotted them. Making my eyes go crazy, I walked toward them. "Ready to continue our conversation?" They shook their heads and slid behind Mrs. Lutzkraut.

It took a few minutes for everyone to calm down. The group around the campfire was happy I had chased off the Ratfields, but they were confused and wanted to know what happened in the woods. I just shrugged and let their imaginations go to work.

After a while Todd said, "Too bad they ran away. I was about to show them . . ."

"Oh shut up, you wimp," Tabitha scolded. "Rodney is the only brave one around here."

"Yeah," Alison added, suddenly touching my arm. "And that's why we're going to win the canoe race tomorrow."

Just then Survival Steve, followed by Josh, burst into the firelight. "I got two possums and some wild mushrooms," he said proudly. "I'll have it all roasting in minutes. Who wants the tail? Nothing beats fresh possum tail. Did I miss anything while we were gone?"

Everyone was too shocked, and disgusted, to answer. We just stood there watching the hair crackle off the skin of the possum as Steve fussed with the fire. We were even more shocked when he cut the ratlike tail off the thing and sucked it into his mouth like a strand of spaghetti. My appetite instantly disappeared. Steve motioned to the one remaining piece of firewood. "Hey, Josh, throw that on the fire for me, will you?"

"Sure," Josh answered, not looking up from the possum he was busy examining. He walked toward the wood but came back with the red duffel bag. Before anyone could stop him, he tossed it with a thud right into the middle of the flames.

Todd, Magnus, and Lutzkraut all yelled, "Hey!"

Todd screamed at Josh, "What did you do?"

"Uh, Steve told me to throw it on the fire."

"What's that?" Mr. Periwinkle interrupted. The nylon bag had burned off and we all saw a small outboard motor lying amid the red-hot embers. Engine oil spluttered out from the metal and shot bright yellow flames into the air. Mr. Periwinkle turned towards Todd. "Why do you have an engine?"

"What? That's not mine."

"Yes, it is," I said. The mystery of their great speed on the river had been solved.

"It wasn't theirs," Mrs. Lutzkraut said. "I brought it in the van, just in case." While I knew she was lying, the evidence had burned up in front of me. In any event, Josh had taken care of one problem—and I hoped T-Bone's plan would take care of the rest.

Mr. Periwinkle stood up. "All right, everyone. We've had enough excitement for one night, and we have another big day ahead of us tomorrow. I'm sure we'll be able to get some breakfast brought out in the morning. Right now, though, time for bed."

Mr. Periwinkle was right. It had been some exciting night, but before I got into the tent there was one unfinished piece of business that needed attention. I walked to the far side of camp—away from the glow of the fire and out into the dark. I was no longer afraid of the night. In a weird way, I felt like I had conquered it. I walked a bit further down a dead-end path that came to a stop directly below Skull Rock.

As I finally took that long-overdue pee, the skull seemed to be smiling right along with me. "Good try," I said, looking up at its hollow eyes, "but it takes more than a few shrieking owls and some bikers to scare off Rodney Rathbone."

I thought I heard something move by my foot and bolted back to the tent.

Chapter 23

A FIGHT TO THE FINISH

Maybe it was just the way the sun hit it. In the morning light, Skull Rock barely looked like a skull. In fact, there was nothing scary about it at all, and the surrounding woods actually looked green and inviting. As I took down the tent, I noticed some dragonflies circling over the river. You could still smell last night's fire in the cool morning air, and I even managed a brief smile thinking about T-Bone and how everyone had thanked me afterward for running the bikers out of camp.

Yes, it should have been a great morning—the best ever—but it wasn't. It was, after all, the day that would decide the fate of Camp Wy-Mee. If we won the race, it was a day that all future generations of campers would look back on like the Fourth of July. They'd probably sing songs about me . . . maybe even put up a statue! But if we lost, well, I'd be letting down my new friends, Mr.

Periwinkle, and every tree, animal, and fish for about ten miles around.

Nothing like a little pressure to start the day.

"Okay, down to the river, everyone," Mr. Periwinkle called out. "Take your spots."

Despite Josh having tossed the Algonquin's motor in the fire, they were still beginning the race four minutes ahead of us. Sitting there and watching them paddle off was painful. Each second that clicked away on Periwinkle's stopwatch was like a teensy dagger to my gut.

I shifted anxiously on my canoe bench, waiting for our turn and looking at Alison. Earlier that morning, I had quietly explained the Moonshine Canal plan to her. Now, as I watched Todd and his crew disappear around a bend in the river, I wondered if the new plan would be enough.

"Three seconds!" Mr. Periwinkle called, looking at us briefly. "Now!"

This was it. We pushed our canoe off from the shore, jumped in, and . . .

"We're sinking!" Alison screamed. On the bank, I hadn't noticed anything strange. But she was right. The canoe instantly filled with water. "There are little holes everywhere!" she yelled as cold water came up to our necks. "Someone drilled holes in the bottom."

We had to scramble out and wade to shore, where Mrs. Lutzkraut greeted us with, "My, that was scary. It looks like your canoe is damaged and you're out of the race." Then she clutched at her heart and added, "But you're safe and that's what counts."

Survival Steve strode up carrying his canoe. "Like heck they're out of the race! Climb aboard, kids!"

"Not so fast, mister!" Mrs. Lutzkraut blocked our way. "This canoe isn't the same as the others. I'm afraid it's not regulation."

Mr. Periwinkle, who seemed unusually calm, remarked, "Well, that may have been true in the past, Helga, but I believe things have changed. After I bumped into you last night *by the water*, I took a closer look at the rules and had a talk with Steve here." He pulled Mrs. Lutztkraut's rulebook out from his back pocket. "I've particularly studied the rule rewrites you've made."

Hearing this, Mrs. Lutzkraut opened her purse and fished around for the book. Not finding it, she snarled and attempted to snatch it from Periwinkle, who flinched and ducked behind Steve. Her face began the familiar twitch that I had always assumed was caused only by me. In addition to the twitch, she bit down savagely on her lip and clenched her fingers into fists.

Mr. Periwinkle continued. "Good. Now that you seem nice and calm, I just want to point out a few interesting little tidbits. You've stated on page forty-nine that campers may use personal equipment, and that they may alter or change their crafts. Also, by allowing the use of a counselor with his own paddle, you've in fact created a case of past precedence, which in turn could be argued that modifications made in the hull material and the internal structure—"

"Silence!" Lutzkraut snapped. "I can't stand listening to your drivel." Then, looking at me, she barked, "Take the canoe! You're already more than eight minutes back. You'll never catch up. I'm heading down the river. And later, at camp, I'll be watching Todd, Magnus, and What's-her-face cross first. The camp will be mine to do with as I see fit. Maybe I'll have the bulldozers get started early . . ."

The thought seemed to lift her spirits and she walked off to join Vanderdick, who was sitting in his Hummer with the motor running, watching us. He had finally arrived with food just after sunrise—greeted by a mixed chorus of boos and cheers.

Steve and Mr. Periwinkle rushed over to help us get situated. Steve said, "You're far behind, but you really do have a chance. This is the finest canoe there is. I made it myself. In just a few strokes, you'll feel the difference."

Mr. Periwinkle added, "And remember what I told you. Be careful when you see the grove of white pine trees on the left bank."

Alison and I looked at each other. "You didn't tell us anything," I informed him. "And what are white pine trees?"

"Well, they're just called that. Eastern white pines, to be exact. Actually they're green." I was getting a headache and was about to ask how we were supposed to tell these trees from all the others in the forest, but he continued talking. "The trees are right before where the river empties into Lake Wy-Mee and the finish line. Stay to the left side when you see the white, I mean green, pines. The river temporarily forks and the right side is named Broke-Neck Rapids for a reason."

"Wait, hold on there." I was suddenly faced with yet another concern. "What's this about breaking my neck?"

Mr. Periwinkle wiggled his hands impatiently. "Nothing to worry about. The river's calm this year . . . except for that unfortunate incident last month with those twelve rafters."

I could feel the blood leaving my face. "But Mr. Periwinkle . . ."

He ignored me and kept talking. "They are, after all, the only Class Six rapids in America—or something like that. Anyway, you're not going down them, and there's a big warning sign. Just stay to the left at the white pine trees, which are actually—"

"Enough!" Steve shouted. "The Algonquins are probably at the camp already. Now git goin'."

He gave us a hard shove off the bank and into the river's current. This time we stayed afloat. Knowing that we'd have to break every canoe-race record, we paddled like demons. I was also aware that Steve hadn't been lying when he said we'd notice a difference. The canoe was super light. It floated higher in the water and glided much more gracefully than the aluminum one. If we'd had it yesterday, we'd have zipped right by the Algonquin boat.

For a little while we toiled along the winding Drownalott River. The day was already getting hot and a bead of sweat dripped down into my eyes. I rubbed it away with my shoulder and kept studying the shoreline. T-Bone had told me to look for an old boathouse on the right. After about twenty minutes, Alison spied it.

"Josh, paddle up to that shack on the water," I said. The boathouse was crumbling into the river. A section of the roof had fallen and was partially submerged, but the walls still stood on the solid rock footing. We were able to paddle right inside of it.

"Is this the finish?" Josh asked. "Did we win?"

"No, this is the shortcut. The back wall of the boathouse should open if we push on it." I paddled the canoe till it bumped quietly against the old rotten wood.

"This place is creepy," Alison said.

I certainly agreed, but I braced the canoe against the fallen roof for leverage and said, "Push!" As the three of us applied muscle, the back wall slid up on rusty hinges, opening just enough for us to paddle under. Even so, we had to bend down in the canoe to squeeze through. Slimy drops of water fell on our hair as we passed under the wall.

"There's the canal, I think," Alison said.

I understood her hesitation. The surface of the water

was completely covered by a green scum, making it look more like a path than a stream. I took my paddle and ladled some of the murk aside. What lay below was brown and smelly, but it was liquid and we could paddle into it. The canal was shallow—I could touch the bottom with my paddle — and only about five feet across. It was pretty straight and led into the overgrown woods.

"Do you think it still connects with the river?" I asked Alison.

"Only one way to find out."

My instincts were naturally screaming to turn around, but Alison seemed up for the adventure. Having her on board was proving to be valuable, especially when she suggested that we could make better time if she helped us push along the bottom and sides of the canal. "I just need to find a big stick."

We made our way to the side of the canal and held the canoe steady while Alison jumped out and looked around on the forest floor. "Hmm. This should work."

She climbed back in with a long, rusty pole that was attached to some rotting wood. We shoved off. It was tough to maneuver at first, since the canal was so narrow, but somehow Steve's canoe seemed to flex through the tight spots and slide easily over submerged logs. I wondered what the canoe was made of.

Leaves and branches hung low above us and we had to push our way through the growth. At times creepy little critters fell onto us. I knocked one large, black bug from the top of Alison's hair before she noticed, and I prayed nothing like it was crawling down my shirt. The thought gave me the heebie-jeebies, and I almost yelled, "Hallelujah!" when I noticed the passage widening up ahead.

Escaping the branches and creepy-crawlies did little to make me feel better when I saw an old collapsing bridge above the canal. On the bridge a boy stared down at us. His skin was very pale, which contrasted drastically with eyes so dark and black that they didn't seem to have pupils. He flashed an unnerving smile of greenish teeth, held up a banjo, and began to play.

The notes sounded sinister on the deserted canal, and we paddled harder. After we passed underneath I looked back. He was still playing and still smiling, but suddenly he shook his head back and forth.

I shivered. Something didn't feel right. T-Bone had warned me about avoiding the locals, but I wondered how you could avoid anyone along this route. It only went one way, and we were like sitting ducks in the canoe. I also realized that nobody in the world had any idea where we were, and traveling down this dark, lonely stretch of water, shortcut or no, was a real bad idea.

"Hi," Josh said. Startled, I looked at the left bank. An old man stood there, his arms hanging straight down at his sides. His clothes hadn't seen laundry detergent in years. Neither smiling nor frowning, he just stared down at us. The blankness of his face was oddly terrifying.

I nodded at him and tried to look pleasant, but through clenched teeth I hissed at Josh, *"Keep paddling."*

"Hi," Josh said again. More people were walking up. Josh was smiling at them. *Of all the times for him to work on his social skills.*

The new arrivals also held blank expressions and wore scraggly, dirty clothes.

"Keep paddling."

Another guy appeared, leading what looked like a mountain lion by a chain.

"Nice kitty," Josh said and held out his hand.

This time it was Alison's turn. *"Keep paddling, Josh."* I could hear the strain in her voice.

Mountain Lion Man growled, "You wanna come over for lunch?"

That made me cringe. What could they possible be serving? *Could it be us?*

"I'm hungry," Josh said.

"No, you're not." Then louder, so that our host could hear, I said, "You know, we'd love to, but we're actually in a race and we have to keep going."

The man's face darkened. He spat some thick brown liquid down on a rock. Alison looked nervously back at me. I could think of only one thing to do.

"Your shoe's untied," I said, looking down and pointing at his feet. His *bare* feet! Not good.

He turned to the growing crowd. "Let's show these folk how we treat uninvited guests." With that, everyone started walking toward us. We were goners. In a flash I thought of my family and friends back home. They were probably playing volleyball at some picnic, while I was about to get eaten by backwoods zombies.

"I'd stop right there if I were you!" The voice was loud and clear—and belonged to Alison. She was standing in the center of the canoe holding up the long metal rod she had used as a paddle. With the piece of wood attached, it was a dead ringer for a hunting rifle—if you were blind. "Let us be on our way and no one gets hurt."

"Sit down, Indiana Jones," I whispered. "And Josh, move it!" I pulled as hard as I could on the paddle and we lurched ahead.

Expecting to see some maniac or mountain lion in hot pursuit, I was afraid to look back, but Alison's bluff seemed to be working. All three of us were now paddling and pushing as fast as we could, and Steve's canoe had taken on a life of its own. Alison looked back and slowly blew out a large breath. Maybe we had escaped after all, but it wasn't until we broke out into the sun and the fresh swirling water of the Drownalott River that I breathed my own sigh of relief.

Being clear of the murky canal, the dense plants, and weird threatening people brought on a wave of joy. I laughed. "Alison, what the heck was that back there? Are you nuts?"

"Hey, you inspired me, the way you scared off those bikers last night. But anyway, I should smack you with your paddle for taking us in there in the first place. That had to be the worst idea ever, Rodney!" She was also laughing now.

I listened, but something held my gaze. "Worst idea ever, huh?"

"Yeah, worst idea ever!"

"Look up there and tell me how bad it was." She spun around and I heard her gasp in disbelief. Todd, Tabitha, and Magnus were within sight. It was clear they hadn't noticed us. They were taking their time. I could see Todd pointing at something in the trees.

"Keep quiet, so we can sneak up to them," I whispered.

"HUH?" Josh yelled.

I cringed and watched helplessly as Magnus turned around. We were just close enough to see his eyes bug out in surprise. I heard him yell, "Goot moovin'!" Their paddles began to hit the water with a renewed fury.

Just like that, it was back to the frantic sprint of the day before. They held the lead and weren't worn out from trying to avoid a hillbilly luncheon, but we had Steve's almost supernatural canoe, and it was clear that we were keeping up with them. Unfortunately, we weren't really gaining ground.

For the next hour or so, we put everything we had into it. Steve's special canoe almost seemed as if it was paddling, too. I could sense the Algonquin team's growing frustration that they couldn't shake us, and I began to think a win was possible. That idea was just the motivation I needed, for the paddling had become the most grueling thing I'd ever experienced. Every part of my body ached and I gasped for each breath. My head swirled from the extreme exertion and I felt an almost dreamlike state come over me. Until Alison broke the silence.

"Look up ahead! I think that's the grove of pine trees Mr. Periwinkle told us about. That's where the river splits."

I did see some pine trees in the distance, but we had passed lots of pine trees. Hoping Alison was right, though, I called to Josh, "Come on. Paddle faster! The finish line should be coming up soon."

While my body struggled with the rigors of the race, my foggy senses soaked in views of the mountains and the sharp, rocky ledges surrounding us on both sides of the river. The shadowy boulders and wildflowers were very cool, and through my exhaustion I remembered once again why it was so important to win. None of this would be left if Vanderdick and Lutzkraut got their way. I even spotted a deer at one point, and a little later a hawk swooped down above us. Rounding out the wild-life visits, a trout jumped out of the water and hit Josh in the side of the head.

"Hey, fishy likes me," he said, turning around. He was smiling, but his head looked kind of slimy.

"That's great. How 'bout paddling now?"

He resumed, and I felt reenergized by our animal cheerleaders. That good feeling lasted until we got closer to the pine trees and I sighted one more creature on the shore. This one was horrible. It looked hideous, with its strangely colored orange hair, evil eyes, and angry mouth. It saw me and clawed savagely at the air.

"Hey, look, there's Mrs. Lutzkraut!" Alison yelled.

She was standing next to a big sign with a red arrow pointing to the right. Under the arrow, wet-looking letters declared: DANGER—KEEP TO RIGHT.

"Didn't Mr. Periwinkle say the rapids were on the right side of the pine trees?" Alison asked.

So much had happened since his early-morning talk, and I had been so confused about the color of the trees, that I couldn't remember for certain. "All I know," I told Alison, "is that I definitely don't trust Mrs. Lutzkraut."

Mr. Cramps had now joined her and the two of them were pointing at us and laughing. For the first time I became aware that the river was starting to move a lot faster. I looked up ahead to see which way Todd and Magnus had gone and with a rush of panic realized that they were nowhere in sight. I had been too busy looking at Cramps and Lutzkraut on the shoreline to notice which course the Algonquins had chosen.

"Nice try, Rodney," Mr. Cramps yelled into a megaphone, "but the best team is about to win!"

He handed the megaphone over to Mrs. Lutzkraut. "You've come mighty close," she shrieked, her voice mixing with a terrifying sound from up ahead—the rapids. We were getting close now, but which way to navigate? Mrs. Lutzkraut continued. "As you can see, you're passing the pine trees and that means Camp Wy-Mee and the finish line are under a mile away. You'll never catch them!"

We were out in the middle of the river. The thunderous roar of the rapids was getting louder by the second. I noticed a subtle current starting to pull us in their direction—to the right. Frantically, I yelled, "Paddle!" I dug my paddle in deep on the right side to push us away. I could see the calm river to the left and couldn't understand why we weren't making any progress reaching it—until I noticed Josh. He was busy paddling on his left, which pushed us ever closer to disaster. "Paddle on the right, Josh!" I yelled. "Right!"

"Yes!" he called back and kept paddling on the left.

"Right!" I shouted. I wasn't sure if he couldn't hear me because of the rapids or if he'd gone completely stupid on us.

"I know. Thanks!" he answered.

Alison got in on the act. "No, Josh. Not right like correct. Right like right!" Seeing that her words only confused him further, she shouted, "Switch sides!"

"Okay!" Josh turned around in his seat so that he faced Alison and me and began paddling backward. I smacked my forehead. By now the canoe was spinning around in circles. I couldn't help but notice Lutzkraut and Cramps on the shoreline hooting with laughter.

Alison screamed, "We're heading into the rapids! I can't swim!"

"I thought you were Miss Doggy-Paddle?" I said, trying one last time to steer us away from certain death. It was no good.

"Rodney, *do* something!"

The canoe slammed into a boulder, and we spun viciously into the fast-moving current. We were done for. I was too scared to do anything other than hang on. It felt like we were on a roller coaster designed by some deranged lunatic who had skipped every safety class at engineering school. We bounced off rocks and crashed down waterfalls. Several times we almost flipped into the churning white water. As I gripped the side, I realized that if we had been in an aluminum canoe, we'd have been crushed like a soda can.

The rushing water was so loud that I couldn't hear Alison's screams or my own. I had been in so many tight spots and experienced so many horribly dangerous moments that I should have been used to it by now. *But no*, I whimpered to myself, *this is the most terrifying of them all.*

That is, except for what happened next.

So much water had splashed into my eyes that I could barely see. I was choking on the spray. I could feel the canoe being pulled ever faster along the surface of the water. I temporarily let go with my right hand and wiped my face. I spotted one last waterfall. It was over ten feet high and I knew we were finished. I tried to yell, "Help!" but a vicious wave blasted into my open mouth.

As I gagged up the water we shot off the ledge, heading—no doubt—for some jagged rocks below. Instead of falling straight down, though, the canoe caught the air and we launched forward, momentarily sailing parallel to the river. We came down seconds later, like a snowboarder nailing a jump. Instead of fine white powder, however, a spray of foam encircled us . . . and to my extreme relief, we came out into the calm of Lake Wy-Mee.

"We're alive!" Alison cheered. "Great paddling, Rodney. You saved us!"

I quickly picked up my paddle off the floor of the canoe. "Er, thanks."

"I can't believe we made it in one piece!" she continued.

"Not only that." I smiled, having spotted something rather spectacular off to my left. "We're winning!" Josh and Alison turned to port and saw that we were at least twenty feet ahead of Todd's shocked face.

"This has been a day of shortcuts." Alison laughed. "And Steve's canoe was amazing the way it floated in the air back there. I wonder what it's made of?"

"Moose guts," Josh said. "He told me about it last night."

Alison and I jumped up and wiped our pants—but only for a second. Something had caught her eye. "It's just ahead!" she shouted. "The finish line. Let's get going."

We clearly had the momentum. Todd and Magnus tried frantically to catch up but were no match for the Moose Mobile. Josh and I were able to easily hold them off. Soaked to the bone, as in a dream, we paddled under the big banner that read FINISH.

The whole camp erupted into cheers. Everyone was jumping up and down on the floating docks calling out our names. Well, almost everyone. Surrounded by six beautiful girls, Fernando was resting in a lounge chair overlooking the lake. Hearing the commotion, he turned in our direction and raised a glass.

Before leaving the canoe, I hugged Alison and called over to Josh, "Hey, buddy, we did it!"

"Did what?" he asked.

"We won, Josh." I laughed.

"Won what?"

"Never mind. High five!"

The following smack nearly broke my hand, but the intense pain didn't dampen my spirits at all. We had won. We had saved Camp Wy-Mee.

Chapter 24

GROUNDBREAKING NEWS

I was soaked, shivering, and completely exhausted as I climbed from the canoe, but it didn't dampen the excitement I felt as a horde of campers and counselors charged onto the dock to greet us. I quickly learned how a college basketball team feels when the student body rushes the court after a championship game. Alison and I had to duck in behind Josh to keep from being crushed or knocked into the water. Kids I hadn't noticed all summer were slapping us on the back, and they all seemed to be shouting at once:

"Way to go!"

"You saved the camp!"

"Amazing!"

"Someone finally beat the Algonquins!"

Perhaps the biggest kid of all pushed his way through the crowd. "Well done, Rodney!" Mr. Periwinkle beamed. "I knew you could do it."

"Really?"

"No, but let's go celebrate."

The pandemonium lasted for at least another hour. Throughout it all I was cheered, tugged, hugged, congratulated, and forced to recount our adventure. It was almost as tiring as the canoe race! Most of it blurs in my mind, with the exception of one mental snapshot.

For a brief second, the crowd parted and I noticed a sour-looking group off to the side. Mr. Vanderdick, Mrs. Lutzkraut, and their henchmen leaned against a table, not speaking. They appeared to be in total shock. Their faces wore an expression of disbelief. Above them, gold and black balloons spelled out VANDERDICK MALL GROUNDBREAKING.

I gave a little wave.

That sure broke their trance. Vanderdick snapped the handle of a gold-plated shovel over his knee and stormed off. Three guys in black suits disappeared among the kids. Lutzkraut, on the other hand, remained motionless. Her eyes—staring deep into mine—flashed a look of horror and hatred.

I didn't dwell on her feelings. Right behind her, I could see that the table was piled high with fancy sandwiches, two big hams, at least five different desserts—you name it. Vanderdick must have had the groundbreaking ceremony catered. I hadn't eaten a real meal in forty-eight hours and my stomach rumbled. As Lutzkraut lifted a glass of champagne to her lips, I turned to my hundred new friends and yelled, "Let's get some food!"

The crowd loved the idea, but not Mrs. Lutzkraut. She dropped the champagne glass and ran screaming from the approaching mob. We surrounded the table and attacked it like a pack of wolves devouring a deer. As I gnawed on some shrimp and a lobster tail, I figured the spread hadn't been meant for us, but I didn't care. It was celebration time and I had earned it.

And the celebration didn't end with a full belly. As the sun lowered in the sky, Mr. Periwinkle announced we'd have a special campfire in honor of the momentous day.

Not too long after that, Josh, Alison, and I found ourselves sitting on the Log of Honor, closest to the crackling fire. It had a great view, but my eyes burned from all the smoke that kept blowing in my face. Directly behind us sat Fernando, Stinky, Thorin, and a group of Alison's friends, who were now packed rather tightly around Fernando. I was pleased to notice that the Algonquins had decided to boycott the campfire and that Lutzkraut and her crew were nowhere in sight.

For entertainment, the counselors performed skits. Woo played the trumpet, and Gertrude and Alice did an interesting, if not a little weird, musical number by banging on a bunch of pots and pans. When they finished, Mr. Periwinkle stepped up to speak.

"As you know, camp ends in two days. Two more days to enjoy everything that Mother Nature has to offer us in this magnificent setting. Of course, we will have many more summers now, thanks to Rodney Rathbone and his canoemates." He pointed our way and there was a round of cheers. Periwinkle waited for the crowd to quiet down. "I want to remind everyone of the last-day-of camp awards ceremony. It's in two days. After your parents have settled in, we will hand out the many summer awards, all leading up to the most important honor—the honor that *you* will decide by camp vote tomorrow. I am referring to none other than the annual naming of King and Queen Wy-Mee."

He paused for a moment, his face becoming more serious. "Yes, it's no ordinary award. As many of you know, the king and queen, under Camp Wy-Mee by-laws, have the power to change one camp rule or influence one camp decision."

Make a camp decision? What was this? They let kids decide policy? I smelled potential disaster and raised my hand.

Periwinkle looked down at me and smiled. "I know what you're thinking, Rodney. It's one of those brilliant rules that distinguishes Camp Wy-Mee from other camps. When we say the opinion of the camper matters, we mean it!" Some people clapped. I began to sweat. Periwinkle continued, "For example, has anyone had to eat Gertrude's salmon loaf this summer?"

"No!" cheered my fellow campers.

Gertrude looked taken aback. Alice pretended to threaten Periwinkle with a wooden spoon and everyone laughed. "Precisely!" he continued. "It's an example of a policy change made by a former camp king and queen ... after spending an unfortunate night in the infirmary."

I couldn't take it anymore and had to ask the question that was making *me* sick. "Could the king and queen decide to tear down the trees and develop the camp?" I blurted.

Mr. Periwinkle frowned. "I'd have to ask the lawyers, but why on earth would you want to do that?"

"Well, I wouldn't, but what if someone whose father stood to make millions of dollars happened to win?"

Mr. Periwinkle laughed. "Rodney, it's like a big popularity contest. Everyone's going to vote for you." He laughed some more, nervously this time, and turned to the crowd. "Aren't I right?"

"Yeaaahhhhhh!" the crowd screamed before breaking into chants of "ROD-NEY! ROD-NEY! ROD-NEY!"

You would assume hearing the cheers would make me feel pretty good, but as I sat there before the fire I couldn't shake the thought: *What if I don't win?*

When the chants finally died down, Mr. Periwinkle announced, "All right, it's getting late. There's only one more thing to do this summer to complete the ultimate camp experience. It's time for the greatest of all camp traditions ..."

I noticed Mrs. Periwinkle walking toward us. My mind raced with unlikely camp traditions. Was she about to walk barefoot on burning coals? Reenact someone getting burned at the stake? This was getting interesting . . . until I noticed her take a seat in front of her husband. Mr. Periwinkle gave her a big smile and turned to the rest of us. "Campers, it's time for that great Camp Wy-Mee tradition—a fireside ghost story. Steve . . . ?"

A scary story? This was one camp experience I could do without.

Survival Steve appeared out of the smoke. "I'm going to tell you a story. It's a darn scary one, and it's true, so if you don't think you can take it, you best leave now." I began to rise, but then Steve added, "It's called the Legend of . . . *Greeny*!"

My fellow campers snickered. Someone called, "Oooooooh, Greeny! I'd better cover my ears." Even Stinky, who was scared of just about everything, had a smile on his face. Greeny? How scary could this be? I looked over at Alison and we both smiled. I settled back onto the Log of Honor and decided to enjoy the story. Maybe it would get my mind off of this King Wy-Mee stuff.

Steve's face remained dark as he looked around at each of us. Flames from the fire reflected in his eyes. His voice dropped to a deep, unsettling level. "We'll see how many of you are laughing when the fire dies low, you're alone, and thoughts of Greeeeeny come back to haunt you."

Again there was laughter, although it sounded a bit uneasy.

"The tale starts twenty years ago. A boy, not much older than most of you sitting before me, was arrested. The crime was so gruesome and horrible that I could never live with myself if I described it to you now, but I can tell you that the judge and half the jury that listened to the case went . . . crazy."

He paused. One nervous giggle. I felt my chest begin to tighten. I also felt Alison nestling closer to me. I liked that, although it reminded me of a rather unpleasant memory involving Jessica, a scary movie, and a Coke. At least this time there was no soda for me to spill on Alison.

"The boy," Steve continued, "was sent to Skruloose Asylum for Violent Offenders. The same Skruloose Asylum that isn't too far from Camp Wy-Mee. The boy was so savage and dangerous that they stuck him in the thickest padded cell in the deepest basement. But it wasn't enough. In less than a year he managed to escape."

I glanced behind me. So many girls now clung to Fernando that he looked like a human magnet.

"The manhunt lasted for a whole year. Hundreds of police, bloodhounds, helicopters, and even a psychic failed to find him. He had disappeared into the woods. *These* woods," Steve exclaimed, motioning all around us.

Alison's hand gripped my bicep. Stinky chewed his sweatshirt sleeve. Josh sat with a dopey grin.

"Every now and then people thought they saw him, a boy gradually becoming a man and turning green from living alone, like an animal in the woods. *These* woods. Every now and then a hiker, or a boater, or a *camper* would disappear. Some foolish people said these people just ran away or moved, but deep down everyone knew what had really happened. Greeny got them."

I looked over and realized I was now gripping *Alison's* bicep. *Good thing I'm not holding a Coke*, I thought.

"And then the sightings ended. People stopped going missing and the citizens in the towns around Camp Wy-Mee forgot about Greeny."

That was good, I thought. I took a deep breath.

Survival Steve raised his pointer finger in the smoky air and paused momentarily. "However, the people should have been more careful. They should not have forgotten about Greeny. They should have remembered that he was still out there somewhere, hiding in the woods. Parents should have thought twice about sending their little loved ones off to camp."

My heart was in my throat. Steve leaned down over the fire and took on an orange glow of his own. "Yes, *your* parents should never have sent you here. And you shouldn't be here right now, sitting around this fire. Do you know why?"

No one could answer.

"Because *I'M* Greeny!!" he shouted, leaping right in front of us.

"AHHHHHHHHHHHHHHHHHHHHHHHH!" Everyone, except maybe Josh, screamed. Mr. Periwinkle bolted off into the woods. Alison and I flipped backward, falling off the log. She landed on me with a thud.

For a second I was in a fear-induced coma, but as I came out of it I realized that someone was actually laughing. I strained my eyes to look up, and there was Steve, tears streaming down his face. "Ha-ha-ha-ha-ha! Boy, that was fun. Nothing like a good ol' ghost story 'round the campfire."

Alison, who was taking her time getting off my chest, said, "Your friend has a weird sense of humor."

"That's one way to describe it," I muttered.

"And look at you, lying there. What about protecting me from Greeny?"

"At least I broke your fall."

She smiled at that. "My hero." Then her eyes looked more closely into mine and I felt my heart begin to hammer in my chest. "It's kind of sad," she continued. "The end of camp is in two days. After that we go home."

"Uh," I managed to reply.

She kept looking at me expectantly, slowly twirling strands of her red hair. Did she want me to kiss her? Looking at her in the firelight, I wanted to, but another part of me wrestled with the same Jessica questions I had battled all summer. My heart beat faster. My mind grew hazy. Jessica was miles away. I knew I had to . . .

"Would someone please find my husband?" Mrs. Periwinkle demanded. "He's heard that stupid story for nineteen years and runs every time." She noticed us on the ground and asked, "What are you two doing down there? Get up!" Focusing her gaze squarely on Alison, she scolded, "I can tell you one thing, young lady. You'd never catch a nice girl like Rodweena rolling around in the pine needles."

"I wouldn't be so sure of that," Alison said.

Mrs. Periwinkle had broken the mood and saved me from an awkward situation. As she walked off with her friends, Alison gave me a little wave. I waved back. The campfire was over and there was a lot to digest. Needing time to think, I cut away from the crowd of boys heading back to the cabin. I realized that I would soon have to face the decision I'd been avoiding for much of the summer. In two days I'd finally be seeing Jessica. Was she still my girlfriend? There was still a slight chance she was, but Alison . . . I couldn't deny how I felt about her.

My mind was wrestling with the girl dilemma when I rounded out from behind a row of thick pine trees and onto the soccer field. Something caught my eye and stopped me dead in my tracks.

Up on the Periwinkles' balcony, Mrs. Lutzkraut sat rocking slowly in a chair. I could see a smile etched on her face in the moonlight. I stood there watching her rock back and forth. Why was she smiling? Considering that she had just lost her chance to sell the camp, she should have been packed and gone by now. And definitely not smiling—unless, of course, she was planning . . .

Without warning, her head swiveled sharply in my direction. I panicked and dove into the trees, not sure if she saw me. Fear coursed through my entire body. Within the past twenty-four hours I had confronted bikers, slept out on Skull Rock, been chased by zombie hillbillies, barely survived Broke-Neck Rapids, and been scared out of my wits by a ghost story. How much could one coward take?

I didn't stick around to find out. Before Mrs. Lutz-kraut or Greeny or Todd could catch me alone in the woods, I took off at full speed for the one place I felt safe. Loserville.

Chapter 25

UNDER THE OLD BEECH TREE

Awakening from a horrendous nightmare, I flung myself out of bed—still wrapped in my sleeping bag—and tumbled to the cabin floor like some loser in a potato-sack race. Luckily my face broke the fall. When the pain eventually subsided to excruciating, I eyed the room and noticed that everyone seemed to be up and gone already. At least no one had witnessed my nosedive. What had made me jump out of bed like that?

I unzipped the steamy sleeping bag. As the cool morning air rushed in, I lay there trying to remember the nightmare. Staring up at the beams, I noticed a spider watching me from the corner of its web. It was hairy and creepy and reminded me of . . . Mrs. Lutzkraut! That's it! I remembered the dream. Mrs. Lutzkraut had been smiling evilly at me in the moonlight, rocking back and forth in her chair. It was all too horrifying. I exhaled and said aloud, "Thank goodness it was only a . . . crap!"

"Did you have an accident, Rodney?" Stinky asked from the doorway.

"What? No! Wait a second, where is everyone?"

"They're all coming back from breakfast. We decided to let you sleep. You were tossing and turning all night. And hey, don't worry about the accident. I have them all the time. Just the other day, I . . ."

"Frank, did you see Periwinkle? I have to talk to him!"

"I saw him walking to his tree, but I don't think you have to tell him. Just take a shower and change."

"I'll see you later, Frank. Uh, good talk. Remind me never to borrow your shorts . . ."

I left Stinky standing there looking perplexed. My dream was no dream. Lutzkraut had been smiling up on the porch. If there's one thing I'd learned this past year, it's that a happy Lutzkraut is a dangerous Lutzkraut. She had a plan, all right, and I needed to stop it. Warning Periwinkle was the first and most important step.

I dodged most of the campers who tried to congratulate me on the race, but one was a bit more aggressive. Practically tackling me, Tabitha asked, "Rodney, where are you going so fast?"

"I have to take care of something," I panted, trying to step around her.

She blocked my course. "Are you up to one of your adventures?"

I smiled weakly.

240

"You know," she continued, "that canoe race was amazing. I was in the other canoe and all, but I was rooting for you." She smiled and leaned closer. "I can't believe you went down Broke-Neck Rapids. That's very exciting."

"Yeah, it was. Now I really need—"

She grabbed my hand. "Rodney, I was just on my way to vote for the Camp Wy-Mee king and queen. I'll vote for you, if you vote for me. Wouldn't we make an awesome royal couple?"

"Um, sure. Bet we would. Now I really need to go."

She looked puzzled as I took off around her. A few seconds later she yelled, "Hey!" but I kept moving across the soccer field. The beech tree was in my sights.

As I sprinted up the final steps to the tree, I could see Mr. Periwinkle sitting in a plaid folding chair enjoying his favorite view. I bent over to catch my breath before sputtering, "Mr. Periwinkle"—*gasp*—"Mrs. Lutzkraut"—*gasp, gasp*—"she's up to something . . ."

"Of course she's up to something. She's helping to arrange the end-of-summer awards ceremony. Isn't that right, Helga?"

I was still bent over. *Helga*? I raised my eyes.

Just to Periwinkle's left sat his wife and sister-in-law. Mrs. Periwinkle was looking at me with a serious expression, but Lutzkraut wore a devious smirk. She said, "That's right, Percy. I'm helping to make sure that the camp grand finale goes off without a hitch."

Red flags smacked me in the face with each word, but Periwinkle just kept on beaming. "Isn't that wonderful, Rodney? There's a lesson here. Mrs. Lutzkraut suffered a disappointment, but instead of dwelling on it, she's accepted it, embraced our vision for the camp, and offered to help. Truly a noble gesture, wouldn't you agree?"

"No!" I shouted. This was no time for tact. "Mr. Periwinkle, you can't possibly trust her."

"Rodney, that's rather rude. Mrs. Lutzkraut is sitting right here. She was just telling me how she'd been mistaken all along. The money blinded her, and now she sees what's really important. Isn't that true, Helga?"

"That's right, Rodney," she answered, not looking at me but staring straight ahead. "Look out at that view. To think, I almost uprooted acres of poison ivy and killed thousands of innocent mosquitoes, and for what? Millions and millions of dollars? What could I have been thinking?"

Mr. Periwinkle nodded. "Everyone deserves a second chance."

Mrs. Periwinkle kept her mouth shut and tried to look calm, but her eyes told a different story. She was staring at me so intently that she seemed to be trying to see right through me. It was kind of freaky, so I looked back at Mr. Periwinkle. He picked up a glass of lemonade from where it was balanced between two roots, took a long sip, and placed it back on the ground. "I'm just so thrilled you've seen the light, Helga." He smiled.

"Me too, Percy. I can rest easy now knowing that dirty little campers will be scurrying over these grounds for generations to come." Turning to me, she suddenly asked, "Did you vote yet for king and queen? I hear you're the favorite. Just imagine, one of my former students, King Wy-Mee! You have no idea how that makes me feel."

The sarcasm and wickedness dripped off each syllable. My throat was dry. So this was how she intended to destroy the camp. She was going to rig the king and queen elections.

Mr. Periwinkle beamed. "Oh, Helga, this is going to be a glorious end to the summer."

"Glorious will be an understatement," she said, still smiling at me. "It will be the happiest day of my life."

I had to try one last time. "Mr. Periwinkle, there's too much at stake for second chances. Don't you see? She's going to—"

"Now, now, Rodney. Don't be so suspicious. It's bad for the digestion. Helga, reassure poor Rodney that you no longer care about developing Camp Wy-Mee."

"Why, Percy, I'm hurt that you would even suggest such a thing." Her bottom lip began to quiver. "A deal's a deal, and I intend to honor my end of the bargain."

"You see, Rodney? She's the picture of sincerity."

As Mr. Periwinkle leaned over to pick up his lemonade, Miss Sincerity gave me a nasty wink and held up two crossed fingers.

"What?" Mr. Periwinkle barked.

Oh good! He had spotted her. *Now* he'd listen to reason.

"There's an ant in my glass! Little guy is trying to drink my lemonade."

Of course he hadn't seen her. Mrs. Lutzkraut was too good at this.

"I don't blame the little creature," he continued. "Mrs. Periwinkle makes the best lemonade in all Ohio. Don't you, Hagatha?"

I looked at Mrs. Periwinkle. She didn't react to the compliment. Her eyes were still drilling into me.

Mr. Periwinkle gently dropped the ant to the grass. "Next time we'll have to bring a whole pitcher just for the bugs."

Mrs. Periwinkle ignored her husband and asked me, "Who was that you were speaking to down on the field?"

I didn't see the harm in telling the truth. "Tabitha."

The name wiped the smirk right off Lutzkraut's face. She blurted, "Tabitha? Isn't that the one you recommended, Hagatha? If Rodney's got his hooks into her . . ." She caught herself. Although she tried to regain her easy-going, relaxed act, the eye twitch I'd come to know so well had returned. She half mumbled, "We'll talk later." Then, a little more loudly, she spat, "Rodney, I think it's time for you to go."

Still smiling, Mr. Periwinkle said, "Yes, go vote, Rodney, and get some rest tonight. Big day tomorrow."

Well, at least he was right about one thing. Tomorrow would be a big day.

I wandered out onto the fields and did my best to sort things out. I tried all afternoon. Later, though, while brushing my teeth in the bathroom before bed, I realized I hadn't gotten anywhere. Sure, I had an idea of what Lutzkraut was up to, but I didn't know how to stop her. My friends had been no help at all. They just laughed. Woo's advice was to "chill," and he played me some new jazz music. It sounded like a bunch of geese getting run over, so I went looking for Alison, only every time I tried to talk to her there were other kids around. Nope, this time I was definitely on my own. It seemed no one could grasp the obvious—Lutzkraut was prepared to stop at nothing to get her way!

I finished in the bathroom and walked out into the darkening evening. Most campers were already in bed. I was alone on the trail that cut through the pines back to Loserville. I came around one particularly large tree and stopped short. There was something odd about the shadows coming from behind the tree. I snuck off the path and came around the tree from the rear. Todd and Magnus lurked.

"I'm gootin' tired of waitin'," Magnus whispered.

"Just a bit longer," Todd whispered back. "He's gotta come this way soon. It's our last chance to give him a little going-away present."

My instincts had saved me again. I slid back quietly into the dark. Their last chance was blown. I was safe. I relaxed and was just starting to sneak off when an icy hand gripped my shoulder.

"Say nothing. Just listen."

The mystery killer in the dark didn't have to worry. I was too terrified to even gasp. The hand spun me around so I could see my end. A faint light from the moon revealed Mrs. Periwinkle's face. It brought little relief. She growled quietly, "I've been looking all over for you. We need to talk."

My heart pounded in my chest but I managed, "You could have waited until breakfast."

"No, I couldn't," she hissed. "We can't be seen together, and we haven't much time."

This was almost as scary as her icy hand. I squeaked, "Why? What's going on?"

"Your suspicions earlier today were justified. My sister's going to change the election results so that you lose. We have only one chance to save the camp, and you're that chance."

Something wasn't making sense. "Mrs. Periwinkle," I asked, "I thought you didn't want the camp saved? I thought you wanted all that money."

"Oh, that doesn't matter anymore. I was wrong. What matters is that I'm desperate. I need to know if I can depend on you. I need to know: Can I count on your help . . . *Rodweena*?"

Chapter 26

THE TRUTH REVEALED

As I rolled up my sleeping bag for the last time, I knew it would be a day of good-byes. A sour kind of sadness squeezed my gut. I'd miss this place. I'd miss my friends. I'd miss the lake and the trails—even Harry the Racoon.

I looked around at my friends. We'd be going to the awards ceremony soon, but this would be the last time we'd be together in the cabin. Without saying anything, we realized it was time for good byes.

Fernando handed Stinky his best bottle of cologne. "Here, you need this more than me."

"Thanks, Fernando!"

Thorin came up to me and gave me a book. "It's *The Hobbit*, by J.R.R. Tolkien . . . my favorite."

"Thanks," I said. "I'll be sure to read it."

"It will change you. Might make you more like me."

I said, "One can only hope."

Thorin turned to Josh. "This one's for you." It was *Green Eggs and Ham*.

Josh opened it up and began to read the first page. "I am Sam. Sam I am." Suddenly he stopped. "This book is broken. I am Josh, not Sam!" He threw it down and put Thorin in a thank-you headlock. I watched the two of them wrestle for a moment.

Fernando walked over. Looking at them, he said, "You can't go wrong with the classics." Then he turned to me. "And so it ends. We had a pretty good run. The ladies, they loved us. You must have some Latin blood in you."

I thought of Aunt Evelyn and how she loved to mambo. "It's possible."

"Rodney, it was an honor and a privilege being your friend. If you're ever in Canton, give me a call." He gave me a slight bow.

"Yeah, I will. I'm not sure I would have made it this summer without you," I said, shaking his hand.

He smiled. "We'll have to do it again next year."

I smiled back, but his words cooled the warm moment. There was a very good chance there wouldn't be a next year.

I went to the wall and began pulling off pictures that I'd hung. I tried to get excited that my parents were on their way to Camp Wy-Mee to pick me up. Then I tried to feel happy that I might even be seeing Jessica when I got home tonight.

Then I stopped pretending. This was no good. Try as I might, I couldn't fight it off any longer. All morning, one emotion had reigned above the others. It was even stronger than the sadness about leaving my friends.

It was fear.

It was the last day, and somewhere out there, while I packed my dirty underwear into my trunk, an evil mastermind was plotting. Somehow once again it had fallen onto my narrow shoulders to stop her. Last night in the woods, Mrs. Periwinkle had outlined perhaps the most ludicrous plan I'd ever heard. Before I could argue and tell her it wouldn't work, she disappeared into the dark like a chubby ninja.

My thoughts were interrupted as a group of counselors marched into the cabin, grabbed our trunks, and loaded them onto a cart. Fernando's trunk seemed to be giving them the most trouble. You could see it was heavy. Suddenly it fell with a crash.

"Hey, easy with the products!" he yelled. "I have to look good for the girls back home."

I sure was going to miss him.

We stepped out of the cabin to walk down to the soccer field for the last time. Woo called, "You've been a group of cool cats this warm verano. Time to drift on out." He put his trumpet up to his lips and played a slow, sweet song. We could hear the notes wafting gently through the hot end-of-August air as we met up with the other boys' cabins and headed off to the ceremony.

When we got to the soccer field I couldn't believe how great it looked. The place was loaded with parents, who cheered and waved as we approached. On the other side of them, I could see the girls approaching. There was a big farewell banner over an awards platform set up on the hill leading up to the Periwinkles' house. Both Periwinkles and Mrs. Lutzkraut were already stationed on it. My stomach tightened at the sight of them. I was never going to be able to pull off Mrs. Periwinkle's plan.

The parents were sitting on the field and a space was reserved for the campers. Mrs. Periwinkle's voice boomed over the loudspeaker. "I know many of you want to see your loved ones, but we're rather behind schedule. The hellos and hugs will need to wait until after the awards cere—"

She stopped speaking. One parent was ignoring her. He ran through the crowd yelling, "Rodney, where are you?"

"Over here, Dad!" He ran up to me and gave me a hug. Seeing this, many of the other parents ran out to hug their children, and it was some time before the ceremony could begin. My mom joined us and also gave me a big hug. She said, "Rodney, we've missed you so much. We can't wait to hear all about it." Then, to my dad, she scolded, "We've been asked to sit down. Come on, Donald."

"Is Penny here?" I asked.

"Your sister had to go to the bathroom." With a smile, my mom added, "Someone took her who I know you'll be excited to see."

"Is it Au—"

"*We're* not telling," my dad cut me off. "We know how you love surprises. I was just reminding your mother how stunned and excited you were two months ago when we told you about coming here. Don't you—"

"Donald, we have to take our seats! See you soon, sweetie."

I went and found where my cabinmates were already sitting on the grass. It felt great seeing my parents, but they weren't going to surprise me. *This time* I was sure Aunt Evelyn had made the trip.

I looked up at the platform. Mrs. Periwinkle still held the microphone. "Thank you for your considerate cooperation." She glanced my way for a moment before handing the microphone to Mr. Periwinkle.

He wore his favorite pith helmet and his smile was wider than ever. "It is a glorious morning. A glorious end to a glorious summer. And what could be more glorious than a final awards ceremony, where we award the glorious achievement of your—"

"Yes! *Glorious*. We get it!" snapped Mrs. Lutzkraut over his shoulder into the microphone. "Many people have long drives ahead of them this afternoon, so let's get a move on with this glorious event."

"Of course, of course." Mr. Periwinkle motioned

toward Lutzkraut and spoke to the parents seated before him. "I'm sure you all know our codirector and my lovely sister-in-law, Helga Lutzkraut." Several suppressed coughs and a couple of lethargic claps rose from the audience.

For the next fifteen minutes, Periwinkle announced the award winners. The awards ranged from the standards, like best swimmer and best artist, to the more bizarre, like loudest whistler and most enthusiastic vegetable eater.

The only time I really focused was when Josh won for best camp spirit. He walked across the platform to receive his medal and Periwinkle asked, "Being our most enthusiastic camper, do you have anything you want to say about Camp Wy-Mee?"

"This camp is, uhh, good."

Mr. Periwinkle clapped and turned to the crowd. "Did you hear that everyone? A modern-day Longfellow. Josh, may we use that in next year's brochure?"

Josh took his medal off. "You want to use this in your brochure?"

"Ha-ha, I love your wit! Okay, go have a seat now." We all clapped and Josh eventually found his way back to us.

"Now for the moment we've all been waiting for," Mr. Periwinkle suddenly announced. My heart began beating faster. "Here at Camp Wy-Mee, we continually strive to make this the best camp experience in the nation. One way we try to achieve greatness is with the crowning of King and Queen Wy-Mee. You see, the king and queen get to create, or alter, one camp policy. The only rule is that the two of them must agree on the decision. No other camp does this. Not Camp Hiawatha, not Camp Granada, not Camp Walden, not Camp North Star, and not Camp Crystal Lake!"

"There's a good reason they don't," I growled, unable to help myself.

Someone in back of me said, "Shhhh!"

After smiling for another minute, Periwinkle added, "This year, Mrs. Lutzkraut was kind enough to run the voting." A bead of sweat ran down my back.

Mrs. Lutzkraut smiled and took the mic. Another bead of sweat ran down. I knew what was coming—I just didn't know if I was brave enough to do what Mrs. Periwinkle expected of me.

"I want to let you know," Mrs. Lutzkraut droned on, "that Mr. Cramps and our gifted, handsome counselor Magnus personally triple-checked the ballots. They then sealed the results in two envelopes. I'm as ignorant as you as to the winners." I doubted that. "Please bring them out."

Magnus walked out and handed the letters to her. By now my shorts were getting soggy from the waterfall pouring down my back.

"I'll announce the king first . . ."

"ROD-NEY!—ROD-NEY! ROD-NEY!" All around

me, campers began to chant. I looked up at my parents. My father was smiling proudly.

Mrs. Lutzkraut scowled and eventually the "Rodneys" faded. "As I was trying to say, the Camp Wy-Mee king *should* be a young gentleman who epitomizes proper behavior, possesses exemplary leadership skills, and will no doubt go on to great things. This year's winner is . . ." She tore open the envelope and made a fake look of surprise. "Todd Vanderdick!" The crowd groaned and gasped, and one parent booed until his wife elbowed him.

Unlike everyone else, I had expected the moment, but it was still hard to take. Mrs. Lutzkraut's plan was moving along. Now there was no doubt. If Camp Wy-Mee was going to be preserved for future generations, it was up to me to save it, and I knew I had to act in the next minute. Suddenly both my legs began shaking. I doubted I would even be able to stand.

Todd, however, had no problem standing up. He jumped to his feet and clasped both hands over his head in victory. There was a smattering of applause from Mr. Vanderdick, his lawyers, and some polite parents who didn't understand that Mr. Creepy was our new king.

Todd made it a point to walk past me on the way up. "You better behave, Rathbone, or I might have your head lopped off." The thought clearly pleased him, but then his face turned harder and more sinister. "You know what? Keep your head. I'm going to use my power

254

in *other* ways. And I'm sure that whoever the queen is, she'll agree." He winked over at Tabitha. She smiled and adjusted an imaginary crown on her head. "You see? My queen is all set." He gave me a stinging pat on the back and walked up to the platform.

Stinky said, "That's weird. I thought you were going to win, Rodney."

I didn't respond. I watched Mrs. Lutzkraut take the second envelope from Magnus. She shot a quick look at her sister. Mrs. Periwinkle's attention was fixed on me.

Mrs. Lutzkraut continued. "Now, for the Camp Wy-Mee queen." Mrs. Periwinkle's eyes looked like they were going to pop out of her head. She mouthed the words, "Now! Go!" I looked away and pretended not to notice.

Mrs. Lutzkraut opened the envelope and smiled. "I have heard a lot about this young lady this summer. I know you made a wise and excellent choice in her." Tabitha stood up and straightened out her summer dress. "The winning young lady is . . . Rodweena Raauhhh-smith. Rodweena, please come up here."

Tabitha stomped her foot and sat down. Alison looked at me, shocked. Fernando, for the first time all summer, lost his cool. He blurted, "Did she just say Rodweena? That can't be possible."

My heart was pounding so hard that I was surprised the microphone on the stage didn't pick it up. It was now or never. If I went through with the crazy plan, I'd be embarrassed in front of hundreds of parents and my fellow campers, face a lifetime of jokes that I could never live down, and possibly be arrested for impersonating a nonexistent person.

Well, I guess no one ever said being a hero was easy! I got up and bolted out of the crowd and around the side of the dining hall. I heard Todd call, "That's it, Rathbone. Run away, you sore loser."

Mrs. Lutzkraut blurted, "Typical." And if she said more, I didn't hear her. I was now around the side of the dining hall, out of sight from the crowd, searching frantically under the stairs. I crawled about and eventually stumbled onto what I'd been looking for. As my fingers clenched the soft material and something hairy, I smiled to myself. Superman sure had it easy compared to me.

"Rodweena!" I could hear Mrs. Lutzkraut shouting into the microphone. "Rodweena, if you don't step up to the stage, we'll have to select another queen."

"Good idea! Don't wait!" yelled a certain brunette.

Mrs. Lutzkraut ignored her and called one more time. "Rodweena!"

"I'm sorry, Mrs. Lutzkraut. I had stepped out for some shade," I called in my high-pitched voice as I made my way back through the crowd.

"Oh, there you are. Wonderful! Come on up." Mrs. Lutzkraut looked relieved. Tabitha stuck her tongue out as I climbed the steps onto the platform. Todd glanced at me, winked, and gave me a sickening smile. Lutzkraut moved away from the microphone and came over to me. "I was beginning to worry . . . Rodweena. Oh my. What happened to your hair . . . and your *dress*?" I looked down. The dress was covered with dirt. A month spent under the steps wasn't exactly a visit to the drycleaner.

I thought fast. "Mrs. Lutzkraut, I'm sorry. I was walking back when I heard my name called and this *awful* boy came tearing around the side of the dining hall and knocked me to the ground!"

"Are you all right?"

"I think so." I held my chest and continued, "It was very traumatic."

"I'm sure it was, and I think we know which boy did that to you." As she said this, her face scrunched up as if she'd just sucked a whole lemon. "Well, never mind that now. Even in a dirty dress you are still the finest young lady in the camp." She walked back to the microphone. "Rodweena has made it!"

There were some muffled cheers. I looked down at my friends and gave them a little wave. They were all in shock, except for Josh, who was blushing and fixing his hair.

Mrs. Lutzkraut said, "I want you to stop for a moment and gaze up here at this fine young gentleman and proper young lady. These are exactly the types of people we are looking for at this camp."

While she talked, Todd whispered in my ear, "I'm surprised we haven't met before. Better late than never."

He gave me a sly smile and said, "Did you know my dad has a yacht?" He nodded as if to answer his own question. I noticed his arm reaching to take mine.

"What kind of girl do you *take* me for?" I gasped, swatting his hand away.

Mrs. Lutzkraut turned back to us and announced, "Once I place these crowns on your heads you will be the official Camp Wy-Mee king and queen." There was some applause again from the Vanderdicks—and now my friends, who knew something was up.

Lutzkraut placed the crown on Todd's head. Todd wasted no time. "With my power as king, I say we demolish the camp and build the biggest megamall this side of the Mississippi!"

"Noo!" gasped Mr. Periwinkle.

"Oh yessss!" hissed Mrs. Lutzkraut, careful to step away from the microphone so no one could hear. "You thought you could defeat me? Your little friend Rodney has already run off. As soon as I place this crown on Rodweena's head and she gives the go-ahead, that bulldozer over there"—she pointed to a tarp that some of Vanderdick's men were removing to reveal a gleaming yellow dozer—"is leveling this place! Come here, Rodweena."

We moved to the edge of the platform in front of the microphone. She carefully placed the crown on my tangled, muddy wig. I looked around for a moment, actually enjoying my coronation. After all, it's not everyday you get crowned queen. Then I said into the microphone,

"With my power as Queen Wy-Mee, I say . . . *I say* . . ."

"Yes? What do you say?" Lutzkraut burst out.

"I say, we give Gertrude's salmon loaf one more try!" Gertrude yelled, "Hurray!"

"What?" Someone else didn't seem to like my plan. "You're supposed to develop the camp," Mrs. Lutzkraut hissed so that no one could hear. "I was assured you would play ball. Enough joking around. Tell everyone that you want to develop the camp."

"Nope, I don't think I will." I approached the microphone. "Salmon loaf for everyone!"

"What?" Lutzkraut rounded on her sister. "You said she was the perfect choice!"

In the commotion she didn't notice me drag the microphone to where she was yelling. What came out next boomed so loud that you could hear it echo off the faraway hills: "THERE'S NO WAY VANDERDICK AND I WENT TO ALL THE TROUBLE OF RIGGING THIS ELECTION FOR SOME CRUMMY SALMON LOAF!"

Her deafening roar was followed by deafening silence. Half the parents were holding their hands up to their ears. Vanderdick's attorneys could be seen scattering in all directions. Slowly, Lutzkraut turned away from her sister, looked out at the audience, realized what had just happened, and turned her gaze to me. She was crazed. I smiled, knowing that her public admission of the rigged election meant that the camp was finally, truly saved.

Seeing me standing there with a grin did little to help her calm down. "Recount!" she screamed. "Recount! Give me back that crown!"

I didn't have time to react. She swung toward me and gripped the crown, yanking it off my head. She got more than she bargained for. Strands of the wig were tangled in the crown, and it came right off in her hand.

The crowd let out a gasp. Mr. Periwinkle fainted. I didn't have time to look about and soak in the various reactions. Mrs. Lutzkraut's face had turned bright red and looked ready to explode. "YOU? RATHBONE?!!!!" It was the craziest I'd ever seen her and I prepared to defend myself from an attack, but all she could do at this point was shake up and down and tear the Rodweena wig to tatters. She turned on her sister. "He can't do this! He doesn't have the power."

"Actually, he does," Mrs. Periwinkle said. I noticed her husband open one eye. Mrs. Periwinkle held up the rulebook and waved it slowly in the air. For the first time, I saw that Survival Steve was standing to the side of the stage. He gave her a big thumbs up.

"It's good to be the queen," I said to no one in particular.

Lutzkraut looked back and forth from me to her sister. Mrs. Periwinkle tried to calm her. "I'm sorry, Helga, but Percy was right all along. I see that now. This place *is* special."

"Special my—"

The microphone erupted in feedback. Mrs. Lutzkraut kept on screaming. "This place is insane! I knew when you married him"—she looked at Periwinkle pretending to sleep on the stage—"that I inherited all the intelligence in the family, but now, now . . . ARRRRRgghhhhhh-hhhh!" She howled, jumped off the platform, and with surprising agility stormed off into the woods.

By now the assembled crowd was beginning to understand what had just happened. There was some cheering, followed by the "Rodney" chants. I started to walk over to Periwinkle to tell him it was safe to get up but was met by a hard shoulder. Todd stood before me, with Magnus just behind him. He growled, "I hate you!"

"Does this mean I'm not invited on the yacht?" I asked. That only got him madder. His fingers tightened into a fist.

"You wouldn't hit a girl, would you?" He looked mad enough that he probably would, and I knew I was in trouble, but before he could do anything a booming rumble sounded from behind the Periwinkles' house. It was so deafening that Mr. Periwinkle sat up and turned to see.

It was an alarming sight. The Vanderdick bulldozer was moving toward us. Mrs. Lutzkraut was at the controls, laughing wildly. Seeing us she screamed loudly over the engine noise, "You think you can ruin all my plans? Well, now I'm going to ruin something of yours. This camp needs more parking! Say good-bye to your precious beech tree!"

"Noooooooo!" Mr. Periwinkle wailed. "We have to stop her!"

How do you stop a bulldozer? I wondered. The great tree looked doomed.

The bulldozer rumbled right by the platform. Mrs. Lutzkraut leered down at us and with a cackling laugh screeched, "Full speed ahead!"

I watched her push down on a control stick. Instead of gaining speed, the dozer turned sharply to the right. Trying to turn it back, Lutzkraut pulled hard on another lever. Hundreds of campers and parents were running in every direction. With a cloud of black smoke blasting into the sky from the exhaust, the yellow monster shot forth at an amazing rate.

Now it was Todd's turn to yell, "Nooooooo!" I doubted he cared much about the beech tree and I craned my neck to see what lay in the dozer's new path.

"I can't control it!" Mrs. Lutzkraut called out. "Help!"

The next thing I heard was a loud smash, followed by the sound of breaking wood. The bulldozer had finally come to a stop—in the middle of the Algonquin cabin.

Unfortunately, no one was hurt. Just in case, an ambulance was called for Mrs. Lutzkraut, but she eventually climbed down from the dozer by herself. The EMTs tried to put her on a stretcher as she ranted and raved. After finally getting her into the ambulance, I heard one of the drivers call to the other, "We'd better head straight to Skruloose with this one."

"Don't worry, Rodney," Mr. Periwinkle assured me. "She just needs a little rest and relaxation, and she'll get plenty of it where she's going."

I didn't have time to reflect on that. My friends were climbing on the stage and talking all at once. I quickly tore off the Rodweena dress—it felt good to be back in just my shorts and T-shirt—and for a few minutes I got caught up in the usual exciting euphoria of having just defeated the enemy. I had won again! Camp was over and so was the greatest summer of my life. Full of confidence, I smiled. Nothing could bring me down now.

I turned to rejoin the fun, but my attention was immediately seized by something wonderful. Three gorgeous beauties were running rapidly toward me with arms outstretched. For a moment I truly believed I was in heaven, but then my eyes recognized their faces and a stark realization hit me. I was in big trouble. Three girls? What was Jessica doing here?

The girls were so completely focused on me that they didn't see each other until *clunk!* Their heads banged and all three fell to the platform directly in front of where I stood. Rubbing their bumps, they focused on each other. "What are you doing here?" they yelled. "What are *you* doing here?" I was startled, shocked—and a bit thrilled—to hear the same reply from each: "I'm Rodney's girlfriend!"

As their collective words soaked in, Tabitha, Alison, *and Jessica* stared up at me. Jessica and Alison looked horror-stricken, while Tabitha's face formed a slight smirk.

"Uhh-uhh." I let out a nervous laugh, sounding a lot like Mr. Periwinkle. My brain was swimming. I couldn't think of what to do next. What could I possibly say to clear this up? Who should I help up first? I stood frozen, realizing my *glorious* summer couldn't have ended any worse.

"Look at him, honey," I heard my dad say as he made his way through the commotion. I turned my head groggily. My mom was just behind him. My dad continued, "Didn't I tell you how he loves surprises? Rodney, wasn't it great to see Jessica? I knew bringing her here with us was a fantastic idea."

"Uhhhh . . ."

He laughed. "And I know that you'll be equally excited about the other big surprise we have for you."

My mother beamed. "Rodney, we've been dying to tell you! Your father got a new job while you were away. Allow me to introduce you to the new Vice President of Development at Vanderdick Enterprises!"

I could barely hear her voice as I collapsed and fell from the platform.

"You see, sweetie?" my dad added. "I *told* you he loves surprises."